The KINS

Undying is full of humour, passion and the kind of multi-layered portrayal of the British Muslim community that you don't often find in fiction. It shouldn't be possible to pull off such ambitious political scope alongside laugh-out-loud comedy.
Viv Groskop

This is a gloriously readable novel, in which rich magical elements intertwine with an intimate portrayal of the inner lives of sisters, skilfully walking the line between realism and fantasy. A gripping theatre plot demonstrates the subversive nature of collective performance and its power to give shape and voice to alternative realities… startlingly relevant.
Jamie Lloyd

The narrators are two sisters alternating between chapters, changing perspectives, winning and losing the sympathies of the reader. The books shift between the real and spectral worlds, lived realities and imagined scenarios. You end up wanting more.
Yasmin Alibhai-Brown

Undying is huge fun. Sibling rivalry, evolutionary science, theatre, film and even magic all have a part to play in an exuberant tale of a romantic triangle that also touches on questions of belonging and identity.
Boyd Tonkin

Undying is a visceral, darkly comedic whirlwind of a novel that is part Bronte sisters, part *Four Lions*. Seamlessly interweaving insights from evolutionary biology into a story of sibling rivalry, it examines the politics of identity, kinship and history, whether in families, communities or nations. A playful tone and plot belie the fact that this is, above all, a book of ideas.

Wayne McGregor

Entirely original, by turns hilarious and beguiling, and always thought-provoking. I loved *Undying*, and couldn't put it down until I had reached the last page.

Stef Penney

The KINSHIP *of* DJINNS

BOOK ONE
of
UNDYING

A Novel in Two Parts

AMBREEN HAMEED
& UZMA HAMEED

FIRED
UMBER
BOOKS

Published by Fired Umber Books

ISBN: 9781838341602

Cover by Nell Wood
Typeset by Clio Mitchell

British Library Cataloguing in Publication Data
A catalogue record for this book is available from the British Library.

www.undying.co.uk

For our parents
Nusrat and Ajmal

Who gave us so much
And who are not the parents in this story

'I'm no good at being noble, but it doesn't take much to see that the problems of three little people don't amount to a hill of beans in this crazy world'

\- Casablanca

Prologue

IT WAS THE WORST OF times, the worst of times, that day when Doubt disappeared and certainties as heavy as jumbo jets rose into the air, casting huge shadows across the earth. On that day, the usual certainties stood tall and unsuspecting, comfortable in the belief that theirs were the longest shadows on the world. They weren't expecting the winged certainties, loaded with deaths.

The sky went black. Tiny people leapt wingless into open space. There was no one to catch them. As we watched, we tried not to believe, but it wasn't a day for non-believers. Where was Doubt when you needed Him most?

When this story happened, it was still some years before the worst of times. But, if we had looked closely even then, we would have seen that the certainties were already putting on their clothes of metal and concrete. In fact, they had put on all sorts of clothes and were coming and going quite freely among ordinary people. And on that day when my sister and I met our childhood sweetheart again, that day when reality seemed to each of us to be a delicate dream, the concrete and metal certainties were closer to us than we knew.

Saturday 11 July 1998

Sufya

I MUST ADMIT THAT I was curious about seeing H again. But I almost decided to stay at home that day after Mum told me on the phone that she'd been indulging in some kind of ritual involving quranic verses and photographs of me with H. It was the kind of nonsense which Dad affectionately called 'your mother's *janter manter*', refusing to assimilate the (to him) inexplicable fact that Mum's superstitious practices had snowballed over the years into something of a covert career as sorceress to 'the community' – or at least to those in it who fervently believed that the spirit world was willing to assist in pursuit of divine gifts such as Mercedes Benz S-Class and bigger breasts.

'Mum! *Why* do you have to do this type of thing?' I found myself yelling down the phone – yes, *yelling*, because before I knew it, the lid was somehow off the bottle and all those long-buried feelings were gurgling up inside me, freshly poisonous with their ancient, bitter flavours: her Expectations, my failure, her disappointment, my Loss.

'Sufya, I am just asking for blessings for you and blessings for your Heathrow *bhai*. If we don't ask, how will we get? Life is what you make it, *hai na, beti*?'

Yes, I thought to myself, but now that I'm thirty bloody something, why is it still my life and you making it?

In the old days I wouldn't have let her get away with it, and we'd have screamed at each other, and I certainly wouldn't have come to dinner. But – partly because we had been in détente for a while, so I was caught slightly off-guard – and partly because there remained that part of me that wanted to see H again, I wrestled the old-time feelings back into their bottle, told her I'd appreciate it if she left me out of any further hocus-pocus, and went to dinner anyway.

After all, it's not every day that your girlhood crush (and unofficial ex-betrothed) is back in town after a thirteen-year absence – thirteen years during which your only contact with him has been what you've read in the papers.

It so happened, too, that H's return from his travels fell in a week when I was extracting myself from the most recent of a string of inappropriate entanglements, the relentless pattern of my unwise twenties. And though the past was still snapping at my heels in the form of recriminatory messages from my latest ex, and while I was certainly not in the mood for moving straight on to another dysfunctional liaison, the sudden entrance of H onto the stage carried with it an odd feeling of possibility, of the future – even (though I, as a scientist, did not believe in the generally understood version of it), of *destiny*. Unscientific as it was, hadn't everyone always said that H and I were meant for each other?

I reasoned that, as he would be coming with his unfeasibly

Punjabi father, Uncle Bogie, H was guaranteed to be late, and, anxious as I was to avoid the stresses of unnecessary pre-dinner exposure to my family, I decided to delay my own arrival, pulling up outside our childhood home in Balham well after the hour at which Mum had ordered my attendance.

The front door swung open to reveal Zarina – her mass of hair swelling like a storm around her small-boned face, her long eyes shadowy with resentment. Instantly, I deduced the cause. Booming from the living room beyond came the unmistakable tones of Uncle Bogie holding forth on one of his favourite topics – Islam And Its Benefits For Woman – his resonant monologue punctuated by the copious tinkling of cousin Ayesha's Karachi-socialite laughter. (Only Ayesha could respond to Bogie's religious rants as though they were witty dinner-party banter.)

And if our perfect cousin was here, I realised with sinking heart, so must be her creepy husband Habib (disgustingly styled 'Bibbles' by Ayesha, who loved to flag-wave her domestic bliss in Zarina's and my unmarried faces.) The trio of Bogie, Bibbles and Ayesha would test anyone's patience. But with the addition of Mum – who, in anticipation of the evening's matchmaking must by now be in a superstitious frenzy – as well as Dad, whose helplessness was usually directly proportional to Mum's zeal, the combination was enough to try far more placid temperaments than that of my high-strung sibling.

There it was, then, the familiar twist of guilt that I always felt when I saw my little sister. Once again, I'd left her to face our relatives alone, and the list of my crimes against her had just got longer.

'Couldn't you have come a bit earlier?'

'Stuck at work. Sorry.'

I struggled out of my jacket, as Zarina hovered accusingly. Given that Bogie was very much in evidence, it was strange that I could not detect H's voice among the babble from the living room. Stranger still, and somewhat irritating, that I was experiencing an irrational increase in pulse rate.

'He's not here yet,' said Zarina.

'Oh yeah?' I feigned a shrug.

'And you won't believe who our delightful cousin has brought with her, supposedly as an attempt to find me a husband…'

'Who?'

'Only *hairy Asif*! And worse still, he's been on a jaunt to Pakistan and come back as a fundie with a hideous jutting beard!'

I cringed inwardly. What were the chances, after all, of Ayesha digging up – as some kind of consolation prize for Zarina – the same shambolic character my sister had gone out with two years ago, only to discover he'd been two-timing her with an older woman, (whose key attraction, which detail the creep had for some reason seen fit to disclose to Zarina when she dumped him, was a predilection for pouring red wine onto Asif's unthinkable private parts).

Coincidences happen to most people, but something so branded with the mocking grin of fate could only happen to Zarina. For her, such events were unsurprising, only serving to confirm the ill-fortune that she considered to be her portion of the sibling cake. And, of course, it *would* have to happen on the day when I, her sister, always the lucky one, was to be reunited with the romantic icon of my teenage years, now a famous and eligible film-maker.

'For God's sake. Why didn't you just refuse to let him in?'

'Of course! What better way of telling everyone I went out with him? So he's in there now all puffed up with the beard. I mean, as if he wasn't off-putting enough already…' muttered Zarina, her diminutive frame quivering with the ferocity of her indignation. 'And, of course, Bogie and beardy have teamed up with Habib and spent the last hour going on about Islamic values. It's been *so shit*, Sufya!' Despite her characteristic vitriol, I knew she was on the edge of tears, and the old, unspoken question clawed at my heart: Zarina was always so close to some edge or other – was I the one who put her there?

'We're just going to have to see it as another comedy chapter, Zee – more material for your writing. I mean, what are the chances…' I said lamely, hoping that Zarina's trademark black humour could get us both out of this.

'That's easy for you to say, when you don't live here any more. I have to put up with this all the time!'

I swallowed my irritation and headed for the living room. 'By God, Ahmed *yaar*,' Uncle Bogie was declaring hotly to Dad as I arrived unnoticed in the doorway, 'if this Monica had obeyed the Quran and dressed modestly, we wouldn't be all shaking in our damn bloody shoes now! This is why Islam gives woman instructions on behaviour, because when man commits this kind of *paap*, the whole damn bloody society suffers!'

This was the story which had been running all year, the alleged misdemeanours of the leader of the free world with a White House aide. It had been the subject of much serious discourse, but, of course, it was left to Uncle Bogie to link it – as he could do with most troubles in the world – to the failure of modern woman to act with appropriate decorum.

Dad, who enjoyed Bogie's rhetoric more for its style than its explanatory content, nodded neutrally, but, seated beside Habib and Ayesha on Mum's favourite red velvet chaise longue, hairy Asif was vigorously bobbing his newly acquired 'jutting' beard in earnest agreement. I noted that, though it had been some years since I had met him during his and Zarina's brief relationship, he was still sporting the waist-length ponytail – the one which, he had confided in Zarina, 'all the white girls love'. Clearly his vanity had not been affected by his new-found religiosity. 'I agree, Uncle!' he drawled. 'People don't realise that these aren't just rules about sexual relations, they're the whole basis of a decent society!'

'I mean, damn bloody cigars, for God's sake!' Bogie shook his lion-like head, as Ayesha tittered melodiously. '*Astaghfirullah*! I tell you, *yaar*, somebody somewhere is going to get a damn bloody flying slipper from Billy Clinton to make sure we all forget about those cigars!'

I had just read a study of male baboons in the wild which showed that 'displacement aggression' – the tendency of a humiliated animal to beat up a smaller individual – is a highly effective character-trait for a baboon male. Individuals who regularly vent their frustrations in this way are significantly more stress-free, as measured by levels of glucocorticoid in their blood. Among chimps, a high-ranking male who has been put in his place by one of his 'superiors' will actively seek out a weak low-ranker, and will exhort others of high rank to band together and hunt him down – sometimes resulting in the brutal execution of the target. Perhaps it's a social safety valve – the letting off of steam for high-rankers who might otherwise destabilise the hierarchy – or it may be a means of reasserting one's position in the pecking order after a beating, but, whatever its function, such behaviour is so common among primate males that human nature is highly unlikely to be free of the tendency. (Indeed, a similar behaviour in our own species is known as 'scapegoating'.) Thus, I secretly considered that Bogie might have a point: finding a common target around which to rally his critics *was* likely to have been a tried and tested method for Bill Clinton's alpha ape ancestors. However, there was no way on earth that I would have given Bogie any further ammunition – not that he believed in evolution anyway.

I cast a swift eye-roll at Zarina, standing beside me in the hallway. The two of us were, as always, on the threshold – neither in nor out. 'Has he been going on like this all evening?' I whispered.

'You should have heard him holding forth on how Brazil is going to lose the World Cup tomorrow because of too much extramarital copulation,' she returned, grimly. I couldn't restrain a snort of laughter and a smile flashed across Zarina's lips.

How, I wondered, would H have responded had he been here, the third point of our once immutable triangle? Of course his indomitable father had not discovered religion till H had long since gone off into the big, wide world. But from the very moment he had first turned up in our lives, when I was five and Zarina only three, Uncle Bogie with his booming laughter, his six-foot-two stature, his Italian suits and over-applied French aftershave, not to mention his wild gesticulations and ludicrous opinions, had inspired in us a mixture of amazement, embarrassment and horror. In those days, he was newly returned from a minor acting career in spaghetti westerns with Hollywood Brahmins like Sergio Leone, from which glamorous exploit he had earned the glorious – if genre-confused – nickname of 'Bogie' among his old Lahori friends. (Once we children had discovered *Casablanca*, we understood the connection – our 'uncle' did indeed have something of the untamed edge of Bogart about his defiant jaw and glittering eyes.) His Mediterranean colouring meant he could just as easily play Mexican bandit leader, Indian (the 'red' variety) chief, or sunburned cowboy, and he had spent years filming on location across the world, boasting first-name chums such as 'Greg' (Peck) and 'Jimmy' (Stewart).

But just as a first-class, post-colonial, Pakistani education had had little impact on refining his sensibilities, neither had exposure to the Hollywood set. Though he brandished black and white photos of himself in elegant tuxedo with Sophia Loren and Claudia Cardinale, Uncle Bogie retained somehow the unabridged manners and perspectives of an astonished Punjabi peasant boy. 'By God, Ahmed *yaar*, damn bloody Italians! They know how to make a damn bloody shoe!' he would boom in wide-eyed reverence to our bemused father, gesturing at his huge, gleaming Armanis, as someone else might have marvelled at the Taj Mahal.

Even as little girls, Zarina and I had been mystified as to how Bogie could be the parent of the gentle dark-haired boy who was our best friend. It was not until we were old enough to understand the story of H's adoption that it made sense. H with his thoughtful nature and subtle responses was nothing like his explosive and ridiculous father. And though he, too, was now in the film industry, his reputation for making courageous drama-documentary about the world's dispossessed could not have been more opposed to Bogie's superficial swashbuckle.

Yet the mode of our trio, I remembered, as I watched Dad and his old college friend communicate at time-honoured cross-purpose, had never been an explicit rallying against our parents. Yes, we found them foreign and uncomprehending, but we felt the same about many of our Brownie-going, football-obsessed contemporaries – from those who thought 'curry' was 'pongy', to those who chuckled when teachers mispronounced our names, and those who employed the word 'Paki' as straightforward descriptive terminology. And when we were together none of these alien beings seemed to matter: we inhabited a world in which they, not we, were out of place.

'Have you ever noticed,' H had once said, (perhaps he was nine years old at the time), 'that when there's one of us, or when there's two of us it's not as great as when there's three of us?' He was lying on his back on the discoloured asphalt of our garden-shed roof, his hands cupped under his head, his legs crossed, and a wide smile on his lips. 'It's like one plus one plus one equals *more than three.*'

It was a bright summer afternoon and the shed roof was one of our favourite hideouts, screened as it was from the house by a voluminous pear tree. The leaf-shadows flickered on H's skin and dark wisps of hair had fallen across the wire frames of his beloved new, Lennon-style glasses, but I could make out the ebony clusters of lashes on his cheek and knew his eyes were closed. Lying beside him with Zarina, I was struck by how unusually still he was, as though pinned by the sharpness of the realisation that was coming to him.

After a moment, he spoke again, articulating slowly. 'The thing is, when I'm with you two, I feel like I'm more than just me. I mean: I feel like I could do *anything.*'

'I feel the same!' I murmured, half-closing my eyes to watch a small white cloud sailing high above us in the blue.

'*We're a magic spell!*' yelled Zarina, who, at the age of six, rarely spoke without shouting when the three of us were alone, though she could barely be persuaded to whisper if anyone else was present.

Then, with his characteristic switch of mode, H sprang to his feet, grasped my hand and Zarina's and pulled us up. 'That's it!' he said, fiercely. 'It's not ordinary magic, like your mum does, but when we're together it's like we have extra powers, isn't it? We *are* like the ingredients of a magic spell!' His face had changed completely, his eyes blazing as he searched first my face and then Zarina's for the understanding he knew would come. At that moment, coming from the centre of the circle formed by our joined hands, I suddenly felt the pull of a strange gravity, as though everything outside us had become thin and weightless. Without looking at Zarina, I knew that she could feel it too: one of those moments of wild, world-spinning possibility which only happened when it was just the three of us.

Suddenly I experienced H's absence more keenly than I had done for years. Would the man he had become still have something of the treasure of the boy he once was – the wholeness of the children we once were? How could I have forgotten what he had meant to me?

I needed to compose myself and seeing that everyone was too engrossed in, or deafened by, Bogie's pontifications to have noticed my arrival, I was just thinking of sneaking upstairs to hide out in the old playroom until H arrived, when I was spotted by Ayesha. 'My God, Sufya! At last you've come! But *what* are you wearing?' She smiled languidly from the chaise longue, dripping with jet-set glamour in diamonds and cashmere as always, and speaking loudly to make sure Mum – hard at work in the kitchen – could hear her. I looked down at my jeans and dark vest combination, which had somehow looked less bland when, as a last-minute nod to expectations, I'd made a vague attempt to dress it up by adding a favourite leather jacket and a pair of Jade's chic sixties earrings; but, now – without the jacket – I had to admit that it was hard to tell that I'd made any effort at all. 'Today of all days,' laughed my cousin, 'you turn up looking like a *jharu wali*.'

'I came straight from work…' I muttered ineffectually, but it was too late: the hue and cry was up and the hounds were baying. Emerging on cue from the kitchen, Mum was reproaching me, with Dad on her heels wearing a plaintive look so that I wouldn't react. '*Hai Allah*, Sufya!' wailed Mum, fanning her face with a pretty *dupatta* end, to remind me of her blood pressure. 'Ayesha is right! What man will be interested in you if you go around like this? Why are my girls so stubborn? No wonder nobody wants them! *Hai Allah*, Ayesha, Zarina, tell her!'

I was ordered upstairs to apply some of Zarina's make-up. 'If she wasn't so tall, she could wear something pretty of her sister's!' Mum moaned, perhaps for the hundredth time in my adult life. '*Beta*, don't worry!' boomed Uncle Bogie, now also in the hallway to provide the divine wisdom which in his opinion was sure to resolve any all-too-human uncertainty. 'In Islam it's OK to dress up nicely, as long as the ornaments are covered!' (Did he imagine I had dressed down in order to be a better Muslim?)

I was not inclined to beautify myself for the purposes of Mum's matchmaking – not that H would have cared how I looked anyway – but being allowed to escape upstairs had self-evident advantages. As I retreated from the berating procession of parents, I caught a glimpse of Bibbles and Asif in the background. Our fine representatives of watered-down British-Asian manhood were exchanging simpers at the carrying-on of my comedy family. Irony being their chief joy in life, what satisfaction they received as the thin veil of my, and Zarina's, fine Western education was lifted to reveal our mother's Pakistani village roots. How post-modern, they smirked to each other.

Zarina

WHAT A DAY, what a day!

A day of resurrection!

The lover has once again broken free from his chains.

The words of his favourite poet were tumbling over each other in my mind, like roses scattered across the homecoming path. The last time I saw him, he had kissed me and promised not to forget. That summer there had been nothing in the world but the two of us. Now he was coming back. And, despite the fact that thirteen years of punishing silence had passed in between, all I could think was: at last! At last, he was coming to finish what he had started.

Of course, I had reckoned without the interference of my family which, following this brief moment of euphoria, began to manifest itself in a series of increasing outrages. First of all, on my return from the gym, I found Mum on the phone to Sufya who, it transpired, had known about Heathrow's impending reappearance at least a week before – not, as in my case, on the morning of – the event. Even pumped up with endorphins from my extended session on the treadmill, I was far from impervious to the sting of that particular barb.

'Why was it so important to tell her, and not me?'

Mum, of course, acted astonished that I should be upset and returned to her frying with a forceful slamming of utensils, and mutterings about her spoilt daughters who, even though they were *middle-aged*, still acted like children. Dad tried to cover it up: 'But *beta*, your mummy had to tell Sufya first because she doesn't live here.' An excuse which just added insult to injury – after all, wasn't I the one who had heroically held the fort ever since *she* freaked out and left us?

Next, Ayesha turned up with Asif who, I should have guessed from the law of proliferating fungus, was great friends with Habib, and who, by the look of it, had been born again as a satyr. '*Assalam-u-alaikum!*' he grinned, as I opened the door and froze. The three of them exchanged excited, conspiratorial looks: clearly Asif had told Ayesha and Habib *everything*, and they were all now confidently expecting his newborn mullah-dom to be the answer to my prayers – and the means by which I would be catered for and therefore out of the way.

Ironically, just as the outlook for my happy-ever-after was turning gloomier by the minute, a ray of hope was provided by Sufya herself. She had turned up with that defensive look she always wore to family functions, and had hardly set foot in the house before she was hounded upstairs by Mum to put on some make-up. I followed her into the bathroom where she shrugged at herself in the mirror.

'I don't know what all the fuss is about,' she said. 'I think I look fine.'

She did, as always: like a fine, nervous giraffe, all lanky limbs and large, Ava Gardner eyes, her closely cropped head balanced elegantly on top of her long neck. (She had inherited Dad's height, whereas I had only got his flat chest and Mum's tiny stature.) And whilst I had dressed carefully as usual – opting for arty-chic in a pale blue lace top with a black trouser-skirt – Sufya somehow looked effortlessly funky in her lady-builder outfit.

'Mascara?' I suggested, passing her the wand. 'You realise they've practically got the wedding planned down there.'

'Very funny, Zee,' she snapped. 'I would have thought it was bloody obvious by now that I'm not interested in arranged marriages.'

'But this isn't your typical candidate – we are talking about Heathrow here,' I probed further. 'So what's wrong with it?'

'Everything!' she said with her characteristic iron logic and a glare that ruled out further discussion. I wondered if she would change her mind once she actually saw him. After all, from what we heard, it sounded as though the adult Heathrow had more than fulfilled his early promise. Then again, changing her mind wasn't Sufya's style. Besides, wasn't she a master of moving on? It was unlikely that she had even given Heathrow a passing thought in the last thirteen years. He had probably long since been jettisoned along with the rest of our shared past.

And so, when we went downstairs together, I was in a reasonably optimistic frame of mind – which was just as well considering that another more serious setback awaited: Heathrow did not appear. Not in the next hour – not even in the next *two* hours.

Eventually Mum decided to serve dinner without him and, although this was a further blow, we all knew from experience that low blood sugar at family gatherings could easily turn a volatile peace into out-and-out warfare. So, with murmured agreement that the guest of honour would surely be joining us shortly, everyone clustered round the table. Habib was shooed away from the chair next to Sufya, which was obviously reserved for Heathrow, but nobody seemed to mind when Asif plonked himself beside me.

Without further ado, Uncle Bogie bellowed an emphatic '*Bismillah*!' and ripped off a piece of chapatti whilst everyone hastened to pass the various dishes in his direction first. 'Ah, Ayesha *beta*, this must be the *bhindi* your auntie was telling me you cooked! Very good, *beta*, well done!'

As he dolloped out a generous portion, I had to repress a little shudder, recalling Sufya's theory that our uncle, on discovering religion, had replaced fornication with food; which, considering that his appetite was indiscriminate, insatiable and noisy, didn't really bear thinking about.

'I like to cook, Uncle,' Ayesha took back the half-empty dish, 'which is lucky because Habib likes my food so much that he refuses to eat out any more! *Bhindi*, Bibbles?' She held out a spoonful to her husband who stared at her lewdly as he replied, 'I believe the English name is ladies' fingers,' and put one straight into his mouth.

Ayesha giggled, Sufya frowned, and I considered showing Habib the actual finger. Given that their marriage had been arranged right in front of us, why did they always pretend to be so lovey-dovey? And what, for that matter, could she possibly see in him? She was like an Eastern princess with a degree in medicine, whilst he, on the other hand was a British-Asian sad case who thought wearing a dodgy brown *kurta* over jeans was some kind of cool cultural statement. ('I think the attraction was the British passport, dear,' my friend Ravi had explained at the time, 'not the terrible shirt.')

Mum, of course, was taken in. 'So nice to see a happily married young couple,' she said, and sighed in the direction of her single daughters.

'I agree, Auntie!' Asif lost no time in boosting his parental ratings. 'One man, one woman. I play guitar for an Islamic rap group, and one of our songs is about how the Western dating scene is demeaning for both men and women.'

Only for anyone unfortunate enough to go out with you. But all I said was, 'Islamic rap group? I thought music was *haraam* to your lot.'

'Depends on the message, sister!' Asif said smugly. 'The music is only the means to the end. All's fair in love and war, as they say.'

'And which one are you advocating?' Sufya asked.

Habib decided to back up his friend. 'You're right about Islamic marriages, man,' he agreed. '*Some* people have airy-fairy notions of romance but, speaking from experience, what could be more romantic than husband and wife coming together in dignity and pureness?'

Oh, please! Had they rehearsed all this outside? I could just imagine Ayesha – *They need to hear it from someone their own age, Khalajaan!* I looked at Sufya who crossed her eyes imperceptibly as she passed me the rice, and said, 'Actually, I was under the impression that arranged marriages were based on economic considerations.'

'Were you?' Ayesha replied, sweetly. 'Well I'll ask you again later, when a certain someone arrives!'

'But our girls are busy with their careers,' Dad intervened hastily, glancing at his indignant eldest. 'Sufya's science writing is going very well, and Zarina…well, Zarina is interested in theatre right now but she will find a good job, she's a very clever girl,' he finished with damning encouragement.

'*Haan*,' Uncle Bogie allowed, sucking food from his teeth with a resounding *cheeeeeep!* 'They are brilliant girls: Oxford and Cambridge, by God! But marriage is important! A woman is not complete without a husband and children.' He looked at Sufya and added, 'And my boy too – he needs someone to pull his bloody ear and make him settle down!'

Yes, we were back there again: *Heathrow-and-Sufya-were-destined-for-each-other-in-the-cradle-blah-blah-blah*. My family must have had their collective memory erased during some alien encounter, for the scale and unanimity of their forgetting was truly spectacular. They had forgotten how, the summer before he left, it was Heathrow and *Zarina* who had unexpectedly become the subject of their speculation. They had forgotten (despite their huge dismay at the time) how Sufya had abruptly informed us she intended to stay in Oxford over the holidays. And how Heathrow and I, thrown together like two loose pieces of a puzzle, had found that we fitted.

They had also, as my sister had correctly suspected, cheerfully forgotten her views on being married off, despite the bloody and turbulent history of the subject, and despite the well-known fact that she had, at the last count, been going out with adoring Stan, a graphic designer on her magazine who, judging by the periodic bleeps from her mobile phone, was still very much on the scene.

Sufya herself seemed to be playing it cool for now. She had turned her back on everyone, and started talking to Dad about strategic alliances amongst male baboons, a gesture of defiance which was lost on Uncle Bogie, who was busy tossing pieces of cucumber off his plate, but not on Mum who had specifically vetoed any 'monkey-talk' at the table. My sister did not even appear to be aware of the empty chair beside her, let alone perturbed by the growing possibility that its intended occupant might not show up at all.

I, on the other hand, was having a hard time slapping down the fear which seemed to leap at my throat with every break in the conversation. *Surely, if he really wasn't coming, he would have called and said so? It has to be a good sign that we haven't heard anything, doesn't it?*

Meanwhile, Asif's unwelcome presence was all too visible. 'Mmm, you smell nice!' he murmured in my ear as, simultaneously, I realised I was beginning to sweat. 'It's so great to see you again, Zee. I missed you.'

'I didn't invite you!' I returned, without looking at him, the sheer humiliation of it all breaking over me again. How dare he inveigle himself into my home? How dare he sit there breathing down my neck?

Mum, failing in her attempts to break up the monkey-talk, and vexed that this unofficial betrothal dinner was not turning out as planned, now vented her frustration on Uncle Bogie: '*Bhai sahib*, where is Heathrow? *Yeh koi baat hai?* So late?'

But he, unfazed by her aggression, simply threw up his hands and bellowed mid-mouthful, 'Damned if I know, *Bhabijaan*! Bloody disciple of an owl said he had an errand to run!'

Ever the air of mystery, still the unanswered questions. At least, I thought, in this Heathrow was unchanged. It had been that way since the day Bogie discovered him, a dirty, abandoned little urchin, wandering the concourse at Terminal 3. In response to questions about whom he belonged to or where he came from, 'the little gipsy', as our uncle described him, simply repeated some unintelligible gibberish. And, when enquiries by the relevant authorities confirmed that he was indeed all alone in the world, Bogie, unwilling to see him consigned to an orphanage, adopted him as his four-year-old son, assigned him the same birthday as John Wayne, and, believing that everyone should have a sense of their origins, named him Heathrow after the place where he had been found.

'What do you expect from Airport Boy, by God?' Bogie was in his stride. 'He's got to live up to his name! Bloody timetable mix-up! Arrival delay!'

It was an old joke but Sufya and I did not join in the laughter. Even as children it had seemed beyond the pale. For a start, Heathrow had had a harrowing phobia of airports for years, and, although he had later conquered it through a determined study of self-hypnosis, we would never forget the sight of him, head lowered, gripping onto a chair in the departure lounge whilst Miss Riddlesdown rang Uncle Bogie and we were hurried away to the plane to join the rest of the school choir.

'Is it true he hasn't been back at all, Uncle? Hasn't he been to see you in all these years?' Ayesha was now asking, as she offered Bogie another chapatti.

'He's kept in touch,' said Bogie. 'And if I had asked him to come, he would have. But Airport Boy goes his own way. I was the same as a young man.'

I speared peas carefully onto my fork. *Don't contact me*, he had said. *It's just for a while. I need… I need space*. It still hurt. I knew he hadn't said it to any of the others (although, apart from the odd note to his father, he hadn't been in touch with them either). But if, just say, he didn't come tonight, would it be because of me?

'Your Uncle left home to work in the films,' Dad said, 'and so did Heathrow. In fact, these three children used to make films together when they were little. What was the name, *beta*?'

'The Magical Movie Company,' I mumbled into my plate, loath to have the treasures of our childhood raked over for the amusement of Ayesha and co.

'Well, I'm looking forward to running a couple of ideas past him – about breaking stereotypes of Asian culture,' Habib pronounced. He was doubtless referring to his *Secret Muslim Sex Lives* TV idea, with which he habitually boosted what he considered to be his avant-garde image to anyone who would listen.

'I doubt he'll be interested,' I responded before I could stop myself and then – to cover it up – added, '… his style's a bit more experimental.'

'Like that bit at the end of *My Uncle's Son*?' Asif asked, referring, of course, to the much-commented-on credit sequence during which seemingly dead teenagers from both sides of the Middle East conflict rose from the dust and processed in a disturbing, disjointed dance along the roadside (*chilling and sublime*, the critics had said, *where documentary becomes prophecy*). 'Yeah, I was wondering how he did that.'

Heathrow (as anyone more astute than Asif could have worked out) had asked the actors to walk backwards and then reversed the film – but I wasn't about to let on.

'It's an old Magical Movie trick,' Sufya said. Then, as everyone turned expectantly towards her, she helped herself to salad and starting eating it. Was it possible that she too still felt a trace of the old allegiance?

'Zarina, *beta*!' Dad attempted to divert attention from my sister's loud lettuce-crunching. 'Tell us about the play you are writing. Uncle Bogie is very interested. You should ask for his advice about films and plays.' (In our parents' minds the two things were eternally the same, and you got nowhere trying to argue.) 'He will help you.'

'Err…' I considered how I could best scupper any such likelihood without incurring accusations of disrespect from Mum, but Bogie was one step ahead.

'*Haan!*' He took up Dad's cue. 'Your papa tells me you are writing about the Mughals! Very good, *beta*, you youngsters need to tell people about your own culture and the Muslim civilisation. *Wah!*'

'It's more like an examination of the love story behind the Taj Mahal,' I said, in a pointless attempt to keep things on track, 'with a modern perspective.'

Only when talking to Pakistani elders did I sound, even to myself, so flat, constrained, and *English*. Confident and professional was what I was aiming for, but faced with that first-generation integrity – and its absolute, bulldozing conviction – I only ever came across as an amateur.

'A beautiful story,' Mum (probably thinking the same) embellished for me. 'An emperor labours twelve years to build for his beloved wife a tomb – a tomb so splendid that it can never be equalled.'

'*Wah!* I have brought you an old book of mine, *beta*,' Bogie continued, reaching behind him and producing a hardback from his Gucci bag. 'It is written by a Pakistani. It is very important for you to read what our own scholars have got to say about our history!'

Mughals: Zenith of Culture and Civilisation in Indo-Pak Subcontinent. Somehow I doubted this offering would be helpful, but I took it with muttered thanks.

'Well, at least you'll get more funding for writing about

something Indian this time,' said Habib, seeking revenge for before, 'instead of all that arty European theatre you usually do. Just don't get too intellectual.'

'It's true, Zee,' Asif said. 'People want gritty reality from the community!'

Perhaps I should have come up with a withering response, or at least been more articulate about my play, but most of my energies were focused on listening for the doorbell. My heart hammered against my ribs as I imagined opening it to Heathrow any second now, and I quickly swallowed some water to steady myself.

Sufya

Over dinner, I had been on the defensive on more than one front – firstly against the matchmaking campaign (Ayesha's arch prodding and Mum's tight-lipped mutterings), and, secondly, against a panoply of obnoxious pronouncements from Bogie, Asif and Habib (each bolstered in his ill-founded interpretations of piety by the presence of the other two, resulting in an unholy trio even more confident than the sum of its smug parts). Thirdly, of course, there was the simmering accusation that was Zarina, intermittently inflamed by Asif's continuing and shameless advances.

But alongside the distinct itch to cut my losses and run, there remained the question of H. With dinner over and still no show from the guest of honour, Bogie, under pressure from Mum, had tried his son's mobile a couple of times, but had apparently encountered only voicemail. We had all decamped to the living room, and were trying to loll away the effects of overeating, the evening's anticipation having mutated into a subtle sense of betrayal. I was wondering about the meaning of such lateness without explanation or apology. What could it imply other than that our family – our childhood bond – held very little interest for H now that his travels and his fame had made him part of some much bigger world?

'That was a wonderful film – *My Uncle's Son*. Didn't he win an Oscar for that?' Ayesha was asking, draped again across Mum's chaise longue.

'It was the Palme d'Or,' Zarina informed her. 'He was nominated for the Oscar but didn't win.'

Habib, cross-legged on the Persian carpet next to his bearded buddy, shook his head. 'Political, of course! A film about Palestine by a Muslim film-maker is never going to win an Oscar, is it? I mean, Uncle – you worked in Hollywood – you know what it's like...'

'H's religious background had nothing to do with it!' I interjected, hoping to torpedo Bogie's inevitable polemic about the Jewish bias in Hollywood. 'It was raved about by Jewish reviewers – even in Israel – as well as the rest of the world, because it portrayed the viewpoint of *children*, not Muslims!'

It was true. H's film about two ten-year-old cousins – one Muslim, one Jewish – had, according to one critic, 'captured the clear-eyed vision of children and freed us from the trap of our tired categories.' And that was it – H's trademark: the revelation of the world as seen through the eyes of children; a world not fixed and unfixable, but one which was liquid with possibility.

'That's not how *they* look at it though, is it, sister?' said Asif. He glanced at Zarina, no doubt hoping she might approve his political astuteness, but received only her fine and resolutely stony profile. 'Anyway,' he continued, 'I don't think making films about his own community is anything to be ashamed of. I mean, we're under attack all over the world, and we need to speak up for ourselves!'

'What are you *talking* about? Who is "*we*" anyway?' demanded Zarina, suddenly turning on him. I noticed Mum and Dad stiffen. We all knew that soundless crackle in her voice.

'Where have you been, sister? The Muslim *ummah*, of course!' replied Asif, with what was probably intended as a winning smile. 'All I'm saying is: the *kafirs* are making films for themselves, we need to do the same!'

There was a moment of uncomfortable silence – it was not a word that my parents or Bogie would ever have used for non-Muslims. A shadow flickered across my sister's brow. Had Asif really thought this militant posturing would impress her?

'*Haan, haan,* Asif *beta,* you're right!' boomed Bogie. Even if he was disconcerted by Asif's language, he was a sucker for anyone who cited the cause of the Muslim nation. 'It's good to see our young people know who they are, *hai na,* Ahmed?'

Dad looked shifty. 'I think a rational approach is best,' he ventured, avoiding the glare that he knew this response would elicit from Mum, who, though she probably cared very little about Asif's extremism, nurtured a decades-old rage about Dad's refusal to step up with appropriately 'manly' behaviour.

I could not help thinking of the recent writings of primatologist Karen Strier, and her theory that the muriqui monkeys of Eastern Brazil might be the most peaceful primate males on the planet. Even around a sexually attractive female, males do not enter into aggressive competition, but are content to patiently wait their turn, empowering the females to act just as they please. 'I have often seen a female avoid a [genital] inspection by one male only to present herself with suggestive grins and twitters to another,' Strier observes, memorably.

What would Mum have made of the hypothesis that the reason for the muriquis' pacifism lies partly in their disproportionately large testicles? If a male can produce enough sperm to win the race for fertilisation, Strier suggests, he no longer needs to keep other males away from his mate. The battle is now between individual sperm, rather than individual animals.

When I had come across her work in the course of research for my book, I had been struck by the implications: in the animal kingdom 'increased maleness' (as in species where the male is much larger than the female) tends to go hand in hand with more aggressive male behaviours. Yet in this case, the suggestion was that the muriquis' oversized gonads may have resulted in a more peaceable society. I had entertained myself with unscientific extrapolations: what might the muriqui case tell us about the root cause of violence in human societies – that the male of the species was *too* male, or that he was *not male enough*? To put it crudely: if men had bigger testicles would they behave worse, or better?

Mum muttered something under her breath, clearly directed at Dad, and marched out of the room to make more tea. My frustration increased. What was the point in staying? He was obviously not coming. But the flutter of expectation had not left me, and, if anything, had become more intense.

I was amazed at myself. I had become so used to reflex-kicking away all my parents' suggestions on my love-life that it was nothing less than self-betrayal to consider – even in a detached way – a man whom my parents once considered an ideal husband for me. And yet I was actually finding it difficult to breathe at the thought that he might at any moment walk into the room.

'You young people should be thinking about having children

now you are married!' Bogie was announcing to Ayesha and Bibbles. 'It's the first duty of Muslims, by God!'

Habib pretended to be engrossed with the biscuits, but Ayesha smiled and laid a creamy paw on Bogie's arm. 'You must be hoping for your own grandchildren soon, *hai na*, Uncle?'

'Yes, of course! I told that good-for-nothing film-wallah pup! I said to him, damn bloody Airport Boy, what do you think? *All* bloody children are found on the concourse at Terminal 3?'

Everyone laughed, and suddenly all their eyes were on me, expectations grasping like tentacles. I felt myself shrivelling back through time into my resentful teenage skin, the one inside which, years ago, I had successfully brazened out so many such assaults.

'*Cho chorry*, darling!' Ayesha pouted, extending cool manicured fingertips to my annoyingly hot cheek. 'Don't feel bad! You know we just want you to be happy, isn't it, Suf?'

'No, it's fine!' I muttered. 'Actually, I'm just worried because I have a date tonight, and at this rate, I'm going to have to leave before H gets here.'

My adolescent self noted with satisfaction the heartbeat of shocked silence around the room. Even Zarina looked up from her studied avoidance of Asif's efforts to make intimate eye contact.

'You will have to cancel it!' said Mum, sharply.

'Sorry, can't!'

'But your mother has gone to so much trouble...' said Dad, gently.

'She does not care about that!' shrilled Mum. 'She doesn't care about anyone but herself, she never has!'

The same spiteful mantras, the same ugly alchemy, the same mutual spiral of overreaction. The ancient-bitter flavours were in my mouth again, and I found myself rising to my feet, ready as ever to deliver my part in the overplayed family scene. To my surprise, I noticed that Zarina was rising to her feet too – was it possible that she was abandoning the scripted alliances, and would for once take my side?

Of course, in retrospect, it was not strange that he chose that moment to return. A moment when I was feeling once more like the terrified, trapped girl that I was in the days when he had calmly disappeared out of our lives. Now, just as calmly, he walked back into the room – taller, straighter-shouldered, the once wispy, wild hair cropped thick and dark, the boyish vagueness replaced with a distinct air of purpose.

In slow motion, I turned to face him with a surge of panic – this wasn't right, I didn't want him to see me still acting like a teenager. Then my eyes met his and, though it is of course a phenomenon unheard of in any biological text, it was as distinct, or more distinct, than anything I had ever felt: a bolt of silver lightning blazed through me, lighting up my innermost structure like an x-ray on a light-box.

H smiled, and opened his mouth to speak. The air in the room hummed with expectation. What would be his first words after more than a decade of unbroken silence?

'Did I miss anything?' he said.

Zarina

JUST WHEN I HAD given him up, there he was.

'Not too late, am I?' he said, sweeping me into a hard hug. (Head down to accomplish a swift exit from the whole farce, I had almost collided with him in the doorway.)

'Depends what for!' I just about managed to retort, through adrenalin whiteout.

And for a moment, we were holding hands and laughing, my soulmate and I, while everyone else just gawped. He was the same, but different too. The glasses had gone, the face was stronger, more defined, but most of all, the offbeat charm had intensified into an electric energy that seemed to radiate off him.

I was not the only one who felt it. Within a second, apparently forgiving his lateness, they were all glued to him, and jostling him into the room like the celebrity that he was. And he, in turn, responded as though he were used to being mobbed every day, somehow managing to reply to the barrage of simultaneous questions and to give just the right amount of attention to everyone. He warmly returned Dad's speechless handshake and lingered gently in Mum's tearful embrace, apologising for his lateness – held up in a meeting at Channel 4, apparently. He distributed gifts from his travels – an intricately engraved Persian astrolabe for me – managed to appear genuinely interested in Ayesha and Habib, and was even friendly towards Asif, though I detected a little look of curiosity when the latter was introduced as 'a friend of Zarina's'.

Then he said, 'God, it's good to be home!' and sat down.

Home? In fact, he looked almost comically out of place, his six-foot frame folded into Mum's powder blue armchair with the lacy antimacassar on the back – but the comment was lost on no one. Airport Boy was ready to settle down, Uncle Bogie trumpeted – told you so. Mum handed Heathrow a plate piled with food and agreed: it was fun to travel and all, but everybody had to come home in the end, *hai na, beta*?

Witnessing this instant assault, I rolled my eyes at Heathrow, and Sufya too threw him a sympathetic look, but he didn't seem to need any help. He just laughed and said, 'Who could stay away from *shaami* kebabs like these? Isn't anyone joining me, by the way?' At which everybody, embarrassed to admit they had already stuffed themselves, murmured yes, yes, and rushed towards the kitchen en masse to refill their plates.

Naturally I hung back till they had all gone, then sat down on the sofa opposite Heathrow, who was now tucking in to his dinner. In all my imaginings of What He Would Do When He Arrived, *eating* had simply not occurred to me and, although this was a totally reasonable and predictable event, it also qualified as a huge anticlimax for our first moment alone.

Still, it was an opportunity to get a good look at him. The eyebrows that arched together over the thin nose had given him a Persian look in his youth. But now that his once delicately oval face had developed distinctly chiselled contours, he was more difficult to place. His eyes seemed fractionally deeper set, like those of a habitual observer, and the full, squarish lips which had only ever given an impression of innocence, had a new resoluteness about them. A white half-sleeved shirt with a soft collar, dark grey linen trousers and heavy leather sandals completed the picture, the feet inside tanned and with perfectly trimmed toenails. Somewhere in the last thirteen years, the young student I remembered had morphed into a successful man who knew how to present himself. There was something both attractive and slightly intimidating about that.

Heathrow looked up with a grin. 'You look great,' he said. 'Exactly the same as before.'

'Thanks… Not much changes around here.'

'That's not what the papers say – I saw your Edinburgh reviews. "Malik skilfully blends film and dance to create theatre which is hypnotic and magical." Which made me smile, because it reminded me of our movies – you always were the one with the original ideas! Actually, I was invited to speak at the film festival last year and I was hoping to come to the show, but in the end I couldn't make it.'

'Oh.'

I was temporarily floored. To me the distance had seemed so wide, the silence so dense. Yet here he was, casually chit-chatting as if he had been a stone's throw away, and on the point of picking up the phone all along. True, I had been told enough times that I could be 'oversensitive' when the other (male) party was being 'reasonable'. But no, I had taken it seriously when he told me not to contact him and if that ban had expired at some point down the line, it would have been nice of him to let me know. My tongue locked painfully and I stared at the astrolabe which I held on my lap. It was shaped like a crescent moon, the heavy brass tapering to exquisitely pointed tips.

'Nomadic Muslims carried them on their travels.' I looked up to find his eyes fixed on me. 'So they could always tell the hour of prayer, even when they were far from home.' He smiled tentatively. 'Sorry if I gabbled a bit. I must be nervous. What do you say after thirteen years?'

'It's OK.' I quickly blinked away the tears. 'It's just... I missed you.'

'Yes,' he said, 'me too,' and reached out his hand.

But before I had time to take it, they were all stampeding back.

'Heathrow *bhai*, I can't tell you how much I loved *My Uncle's Son*!' Ayesha said, slipping onto the sofa next to me. 'It was beautiful, you must be very proud.'

'Thanks, but it was all because of Ayub and David, really. I just stuck a camera up and, luckily, they were relaxed enough to be themselves!' Recalling his little protagonists, Heathrow's eyes showed the infatuated goofiness with which he used to regard any annoying kid who nearly knocked our heads off with a football. 'Actually, it looks as though I'm going to be working with them again. Channel 4 are commissioning a follow-up for next year. It'll be an hour-long documentary about both boys as they turn fifteen.'

'So that is why you are in town? To meet the Channel 4 people? That sounds like a really worthwhile project,' Dad said.

Dad was genuinely interested. He certainly hadn't meant the question to come across as an accusation, but it was as though Heathrow had been looking for an opportunity. He put his plate aside deliberately, and then he was on his feet, looking around at us.

'Uncle,' he said, 'Auntie... You are so kind, welcoming me back into your home after all this time. I definitely don't deserve it after disappearing without trace—'

At this Mum and Dad tried to demur, but Uncle Bogie said let him bloody well apologise to his elders, and Heathrow said, 'That's right. I want to apologise to all of you. And to thank you for treating me exactly the same as if I had only just gone away. At the time, I thought it would be two, three years at most, but I was trying to get established, one thing kept leading to another and somehow it was never a good time to step off.'

As he spoke, the old intensity was still visible, but it was now harnessed – in the measured, thoughtful delivery of someone who was used to leading from the front. 'I hope you'll believe me when I say that I'm not just here because of Channel 4. It was my decision.'

He paused and ran his fingers through his hair in the familiar gesture. 'Erm... not to make a big deal of it but I had malaria recently when I was on a recce in the Zagros mountains— No, I'm fine, don't worry, it was my own fault really, I didn't think there was a risk that time of year. The point is: for a while it was pretty bad, and when I was lying in my tent, thinking my number was very possibly up, I started to imagine coming home. I imagined what each of you would be doing – all the details, what you might be wearing, what you would be saying to one another. When my body wasn't holding it together, I made a place in my head where I could be with you. And I promised myself that if I got through it, I'd come home for real.'

Heathrow had been close to death. He had tried to play it down but that just made it worse. For a split second, nobody reacted. Then, as one, our parents clustered around him, Bogie holding his son in a silent bear hug, Mum uttering prayers of thanks for his deliverance, while Dad gently reproached him for not asking someone to get a message to us, and Heathrow himself started apologising all over again.

If only I could hurl myself at him and cling on like a limpet so he could never take another breath without me. But for now, there was no getting near him. As everyone sat down again, and Dad brought in green tea with cardamom, the celebration of Heathrow's return finally got going. The family who loved him found any hint of awkwardness that they might have felt earlier forgotten in the aftermath of his frank and open speech, which likewise had made those who had only just met him (and up till now had been merely impressed) well and truly besotted.

How was it, working in Israel? Asif now piped up. As a Muslim film-maker? There were also many Jewish Israelis who were committed to fighting the system, Heathrow told him, including on his own team. For him, the camera was a way of seeing without categories, of revealing the individuals who were hidden by them. If he allowed himself to get carried away by the 'us and them' story, he wouldn't be able to listen properly. To see Asif beaming and nodding agreement, you would never guess that scarcely half an hour earlier he had been branding the entire non-Muslim world as '*kafir*'.

Did that mean he was less a traditional director and more a *facilitator*? (Habib, self-importantly.) Probably, Heathrow grinned, he always felt he didn't get to order people around enough! But yes: he had found that both Palestinians and Israelis would leap at the chance to tell their stories, they were so tired of being misrepresented in other people's narratives. For him that was the whole point. 'And when you listen to those stories, you can't help feeling humbled. What you absolutely don't want to do is to make their lives harder still.'

Mum, of course, kept trying to facilitate conversation between Heathrow and Sufya, with only sporadic success, so eventually she pressed her hands to her cheeks, said *hai hai* we forgot about the sweet dish, and sent them into the kitchen together to get it. 'Beautiful couple, *hain*?' Ayesha hissed, playfully shoulder-butting me as they left the room.

Meanwhile, Mum swiftly reorganised our seating positions and, when Sufya and Heathrow returned saying, '*Khir*, anyone?' she grabbed the fragrant, pistachio-topped bowl ('*firni*, Sufya, not *khir* – *khir* is just rice pudding!'), practically pushed the two of them onto the now vacated sofa, and placed Ayesha and Habib's wedding album on Heathrow's lap.

'*Yeh dekh, beta*! My niece's marriage. Beautiful, *hain*?'

Heathrow, apparently registering neither the ambush, nor Sufya's furious embarrassment next to him, opened the book and turned the pages slowly. Ayesha had juxtaposed the official bride and groom shots with wonky behind-the-scenes Polaroids, captioned in gold rollerball. *Last morning as a single! Hairspray! Habib gets flower-power!* And so on.

Heathrow smiled at a picture of me and Sufya, sitting on the steps of Wandsworth Town Hall, mugs in hand: *Tea ladies*!

'I wish I'd been there.'

'*Koi baat nahin*, Heathrow *bhai*.' Ayesha waved her dessert spoon nonchalantly. 'No worries. You get married, and we'll all come to your wedding! *Hai na*?'

He was still looking down, so we couldn't see his expression as he carefully turned another page and said, 'Actually, I was married.'

Everything went black, as though I had crashed through a frozen lake. Then, I heard my own voice: '*No!*'

'WHAT THE BLOODY HELL?' Bogie drowned me out.

'*Arre, beta!*' Mum's hands flew to her mouth. '*Yeh kaise?*'

As my eyes began to focus again, I saw Heathrow facing the general shock and disappointment, and noticed, for the first time, that he looked tired. There were shadows around his eyes, showing up like bruises against the pale skin. As everyone waited for him to say more, I folded my arms around my ribcage and steeled myself.

Heathrow, when he spoke, was calm. 'It was a mistake,' he said. 'It was a few years ago now. I'm sorry, Papa. She wanted to keep it a secret. And then it ended. So there wasn't anything to tell.'

'Sounds rough,' Sufya said, obviously deciding to be the sympathetic one.

Heathrow smiled faintly. 'I had some romantic notions about her being Iranian. Something about finding my place, I suppose.'

'Because you always thought you might have come from there? It's understandable.'

No it wasn't! So every now and then someone would rush up to Heathrow in the street and start talking in Farsi. How could that be a reason to disappear off to Tehran and marry the first woman he came across? What about true love? What about him and me?

'Thanks. But she clearly didn't feel the same way because she left me after a year. All in all, not my finest hour.' He glanced at me. 'OK, I was an idiot.'

'*Bas?*' Bogie growled. 'That's all? No other bloody bombshells you want to drop?'

'Nope, that pretty much covers everything. I was going to fill you in tomorrow, Papa, but since it came up, I thought, I'm among family, you're all going to find out anyway, so you might as well hear it from me.'

He said goodnight soon afterwards. Telephone meeting with his American agent.

The family, after the initial clucking and commotion, decided Heathrow's marriage had been just 'a foolish mistake', and 'actually a plus', because he had clearly learnt his lesson and was now looking for 'the right girl'. And when my sister huffed and left, presumably for her date, Mum stood up and put us on notice that our mission henceforth was to get Sufya and Heathrow together – and all extraneous claims on Heathrow's attention were to be immediately dropped. (This last was directed at me.) As she bustled into the kitchen with Ayesha, the men turned on the TV and I escaped upstairs to my room, closing the door behind me.

So he had been married. Me, he had missed, but clearly not enough to prevent him falling for someone else. My head ached. How was I supposed to make sense of it, let alone forgive him?

I placed the astrolabe on my dressing table beneath the glowing mosaic mirror Ravi had brought me from the Alhambra. *Nomadic Muslims carried them on their travels so they could always tell the hour of prayer...even when they were far from home.* What had he meant? Was I the one he carried with him and, even after the false homecoming of a foolish marriage, the one who could bring him back to himself?

In the mirror, my face wore an almost comedic expression of shock. But my body still vibrated from the force of his embrace.

Tuesday 21 July 1998

Zarina

'"1631. ACCOMPANYING her husband on a military campaign, Mumtaz Mahal, beloved wife of the Emperor Shahjehan, dies while giving birth to their fourteenth child. Grief-stricken, Shahjehan returns to Agra and commissions the Sufi craftsman, Suleman, to design a magnificent mausoleum for the body of the Empress, little suspecting that Suleman has also loved Mumtaz, and he too mourns her death."' Ravi shook his head at the notes. 'You think you know someone, eh? But let me read on – I sense a tragedy unfolding!'

I smiled, helped myself to a sip of his cappuccino and leafed through his library book, which was lying on the table: *Ghosts of Sodom: The early writings of Lord Byron*. If Ravi was looking for advice on how to come out to his mum, I thought, he wasn't likely to find any in there. Around us the café at Battersea Arts Centre buzzed with artistic conversation: the earnest tones of the nice theatre-in-education girls, the pretentious guffaws of the young-director-of-the-year types.

'"The ghost of Mumtaz yearns for freedom but she is impaled upon the anguish of the two men who cannot let her go. She visits each in turn, begging them to release her. Shahjehan is overjoyed to see the ghost, believing Mumtaz has returned to him. But when he discovers that Suleman too has been visited by his wife's spirit, he flies into a jealous rage, and cuts off the architect's hands..." Nice: bit of blood and gore always brings the punters in! How much of this is true, by the way?'

I explained how I had come across the hand-cutting legend in my research – the purpose being that the architect should never again create something as splendid – but decided it would be more interesting if it could be presented as the revenge of a wounded husband.

'Actually, there's no evidence that the designer of the Taj was anyone other than Shahjehan himself. I made up the character of Suleman because—'

'—three's more fun than two, I get it,' Ravi finished. 'Not that I speak from experience. How do we cast these guys then?'

'Shahjehans here, Sulemans here, Not-Sures in the middle, Nos in the folder.' I laid out submissions on the table. 'These are the ones I've already done.'

Ravi looked at the piles. 'We seem to have a lot more Shahjehans than Sulemans.'

'An emperor's more straightforward to cast. The architect, on the other hand, shouldn't be just a classic leading man, which is what most of these are. He's a Sufi mystic – he needs to be somehow spiritual.'

'What about him?' Ravi waved a photo at me. 'He looks like the sensitive type.'

'Not sure if he's handsome enough… Stick him in the folder.'

Ravi looked at me ironically. 'So he's got to be this amazing architect who designs the Taj Mahal, *and* is poetic and soulful, *plus* unbelievably gorgeous. Hmmm, who could play a part like that?… Oh my God, I know: Heathrow!'

He burst into loud laughter, but seeing that I was not amused, stopped at once and put his elegant hand over mine. 'How's all that going, sweetheart?'

I relayed the latest on Heathrow's ex, gleaned from Mum who had got it via Bogie. Leili, as she was called, wrote short stories, and he had met her in Tehran while he was making a piece on women writers under the revolution. They had got married secretly because her family wouldn't have approved. But while he was away in Israel filming *My Uncle's Son*, he had got a letter from her saying it was over, and exercising her Islamic right of divorce. The whole thing had lasted less than a year.

'Anyway, nobody seems to care, as long as he marries Sufya next.'

Ravi tutted. 'Families are such a nightmare! Honestly, as if it isn't hard enough finding the right guy without them putting spanners in the works! I've only managed to throw mine off the scent because they all think I'm going out with you… Which of course I would be, if only I were straight.' He groaned. 'It's the tragedy of my life that I can't throw you across this table and make passionate love to you right now!'

What would I do without my wonderful best friend? Inconceivably loving, loyal to a fault and irretrievably gay. We had met six years ago at the cultural show Auntie Mehbooba had organised at Wandsworth Town Hall. On the programme was *Ravi Banerjee & dancers: Kathak dance of northern India*. I wasn't expecting anything special – I had only gone along because Mum needed a lift. But as Ravi performed the intricate footwork, endlessly dividing the rhythm, spiralling away into complex improvisations, only to return effortlessly to the *sum*, the cathartic first beat of the time cycle, I sat transfixed. Suddenly, I found myself resonating with an aesthetic that seemed distinctively Islamic (in a good way): that sense of divinity within the abstract, that reaching for the sublime through the intricacies of form, that longing for completion which I recognised from the Rumi poems that Heathrow loved, and which the Spanish, influenced by the Arabs, call *duende*.

Ravi, it turned out, was the British-born prodigy of a well-known Calcutta dance family. 'I teach a class on Saturdays,' he said when I went to meet him after the show. 'Why don't you come along? What else are you going to do on a weekend?'

So Ravi taught me to dance. And although I obviously never attained his speed or strength, I was successful enough at the acting side to occasionally partner him in the 'dance-dramas' of star-crossed lovers – *Sohni Mahiwal, Heer Ranjha, Laila Majnun* – beloved of Asian arts programmers.

It was Ravi who always picked up the pieces when my half-hearted attempts at a love-life without Heathrow ended in tears. 'Darling, I know you just want a nice boyfriend,' he would soothe, 'but maybe it's not *them*, it's *you*. Deep down you're comparing them all to your true love and, trust me, they're twigging that they don't match up!'

And Ravi was the one who encouraged me when I told him I was thinking of starting my own theatre company: 'Thank God. No more playing Lord Krishna for me!' He was my confidant and partner in everything.

Which was why I now carefully placed the scrap of yellow paper on the table between us. 'There might be a way to get what I want, despite my family.'

Ravi peered intently at the curious little grid filled with Arabic numbers. 'Is this what I think it is? A *spell*?'

'A *wazifa*,' I corrected him, 'but basically, yes. It fell out of a textbook Uncle Bogie gave me. I don't think he knew it was there.'

In fact, the torn edge suggested that the paper had been hurriedly ripped out of a book of some sort, but it was brittle and old. Perhaps, long ago, some desperate individual harbouring a forbidden secret had stolen it and hidden it in a volume of Mughal history for safekeeping. Had they had the chance to use it? Had it worked?

'What's it for?' Ravi licked his lips in anticipation.

'This is in Urdu.' I pointed out the writing underneath the grid. 'I went through it with the dictionary and I think it says' – I took out my notebook – '"To attain your beloved, bury this diagram with a likeness of him and a lock of your hair. Be assured, he will come to you."'

A shiver ran down my spine. Was it me, or did it suddenly feel colder in the BAC café? People sitting at the other tables didn't appear to have noticed anything, but as I looked back at Ravi, I could see he had sensed something too. His eyes were wide and his black hair seemed slightly spikier than before.

'Amazing!' Ravi breathed. 'Are you going to do it? Tell me you are!'

'I don't know… You don't think it's *dabbling*?'

'Of course not!' Ravi scoffed. 'It's harmless old wives' stuff. It's not as if you're sending anyone a flying *haandi*!'

'A *what*?'

'A small earthenware pot, used in cooking and—'

'I know what a *haandi* is, Ravi!'

'Oh, yes, sorry. Well, a flying *haandi*,' Ravi's eyes sparkled, 'is legendary Bengali black magic! According to my grandmother, if someone got their nose put out of joint by another person in the village, they could send them a flying *haandi*, bearing a curse. The *haandi* would shatter in the victim's courtyard, and without fail, within a few days, that person would be dead!'

'Are you serious?'

'Oh yes. *Dadi* said it was commonplace to see them whizzing over your head when you were sitting outside shelling peas. Unfortunately, she didn't tell me how they did it,' Ravi said regretfully. 'I could have sent one to number seventeen when those skinheads set their dog on me... Anyway, this spell – sorry, *wazifa* – is nothing evil like that: it's more like giving fate a helping hand. We already know Heathrow likes you, he just hasn't had an opportunity to let it develop – and if your family have their way, he won't get one. Your Mum's probably got life-size voodoo bride dolls of him and Sufya hidden in the pantry! I think you should level the playing field – if this actually works, that is.'

'Well, Mum swears by *wazifas*,' I said. 'They seem to work for her.'

Only last night, Auntie Tahira had been in tears of gratitude on the doorstep after her errant son had dropped his druggie mates and gone back to his accountancy studies. ('I burned the neem leaves, as you said, Apa,' Tahira had sobbed, 'and I whispered into his right ear when he was sleeping. It was exactly as you said, Apa! Forty nights and my son came back to me!')

Of course, Mum had, for years, been trying to make me employ 'spiritual remedies' to secure a husband, grumbling that the only members of the community not to have reaped the benefit of her wisdom were her own thankless daughters. Once, she had even suggested I recite *bismillah* a thousand times over the rice pudding we were going to serve to a bunch of Habib's university friends.

'Up until now, I haven't wanted to go there,' I told Ravi. 'It's not that I don't believe it could work – I'm more worried that it might. I mean, I don't want it to be the only way I can get Heathrow – it's so…*desperate*!'

'Darling, we *are* desperate.' Ravi rolled his eyes. 'A few years ago, we were both blushing virgins who believed in fairy tales. And what have we got to show for it? A string of exes who could run the four-minute mile, and faces to turn the milk sour!'

I quickly corrected the frown I was midway through making, but I had to admit my friend had a point. If these were desperate times, didn't they call for desperate measures?

'There's no such thing as coincidence,' Ravi was saying. 'This spell came to you the same day Heathrow walked back into your life. You found it for a reason. Come on, Zee, take control! Think Madonna!'

Monday 27 July 1998

Sufya

IT IS UNPALATABLE to think that the murder of babies is a 'natural' practice but, in fact, competitive infanticide, as it is known, is a pervasive feature of the natural world, and is a trait that comes perilously close to our own species in the family tree of the animal kingdom.

Take, for instance, the Hanuman langurs of northern India. As with most monkeys, langur troops are organised around a core group of female relatives and their young, with some males attached to the group, but observing a strict hierarchy. (When they sleep, this hierarchy applies quite literally, with the alpha male sleeping highest in the tree, while lesser males, usually adolescents, are condemned to lower branches, where they are vulnerable to leopards.) Adolescent males are eventually kicked out altogether – an adaptation to avoid the risk of inbreeding – and will join or form roaming gangs of young, bachelor males.

Periodically, these roving adolescents will invade more established groups and challenge the dominant male to a confrontation. If the invaders succeed in driving him away, the gang leader will first assert himself by chasing off his own former comrades. He will then snatch from its mother any monkey under six months old, and will – quite systematically – sink his teeth into each infant's skull.

Since the 60s, competitive infanticide has been documented in many species, including almost all primates. Its existence corroborates the prediction of gene-based evolutionary theory that one's own biological interests (the survival of one's own young) override loyalty to the interests of the species (the survival of the maximum number of young).

Until recently this grim blueprint was thought to be the genetic inheritance of all primates to some degree or another. But now, studies of bonobos by the eminent Dutch primatologist, Frans de Waal, suggest the possibility of starkly contrasting ape behaviour. De Waal reports that among bonobos, there is no recorded incident of competitive infanticide, and he theorises that this result – unique among primates – is linked to the famed sexual promiscuity of the females.

On any given day, a bonobo female will have sex with other females, in groups and with any number of males. Next to her, other primates seem buttoned up and prudish. She will often use sex to solve social problems – for instance, intervening in disputes between males by inviting both combatants to have sex instead. The 'slack morals' of the female bonobo, posits de Waal, could well be a winning gene strategy. The genes which dictate her sluttish behaviour would have the effect of making it impossible for males to tell whose offspring are whose. In this case, the genetic incentive for infanticide would be removed, and males, instead of murdering one another's offspring, could maximise their chances of gene replication by having as much sex as possible with as many partners as possible. The pay-off for bonobo females? – nobody is out to kill their offspring. As de Waal puts it with his characteristic wit: 'That's why the lady is a tramp.'

If the sexual codes of bonobos are to some extent the product of competition between males and females for gene replication, then could this be the case for human 'sexual morality', too? And if so, are there winners and losers in this battle? Aren't bonobo females winning when they achieve safety for their offspring by providing sex on tap for males? Aren't chimp males winning when they murder another's young, thereby wasting all the resources already invested in them by their mothers? So, who is winning among humans – men or women – and how?

'You're right!' said Richard, with a trace of vengeance, as he looked up from reading my proposal. 'You haven't got far with this, have you?'

We were having sangria and cigarettes in a bar on Broad Street, a place I couldn't recall, despite Richard's insistence that 'we used to come here together all the time'. He had been waiting on the platform at Oxford, his narrow face in the crowd somehow drawing my gaze in a way that was both reassuring and disconcerting. Like the city itself, the clear-water eyes and the fine build of his jaw struck me as considerably altered by intervening years, and yet a little too familiar. I suppose I had expected – hoped for – more distance.

I must have flinched, because he quickly qualified his remark.

'But these things are always most tricky at the beginning, in my experience!' Despite the fact that he was one of the youngest biology professors in the country, Richard had always been an unwilling alpha male when it came to being strict with students – even those, it seemed, who had previously broken his heart. I detected from the quiver of a certain muscle under his cheekbone that he was regretting his ignoble undertone.

'You don't think there's something in the different infanticide rates of the bonobos versus the langurs?'

'I think it's a dramatic starting point, yes, but I'm afraid you told me most of this six months ago, when you first said you were going to write this book.'

I was sorry – as I had been all week – that I had allowed Richard to overrule me when I had tried to postpone our meeting. After all, when I had made the appointment all those months ago, it had been in the hope that I would by now have a first draft, or at least something close; and it had been far enough away for the prospect of seeing my former PhD supervisor, (and possibly still-embittered ex-lover), to seem an unthreatening unreality. Indeed, I had only asked him to be a consultant out of a sense that I needed to impose some deadline, some journalism-style discipline, onto my research. But now, unsurprisingly, given Richard's razor intellect, here I was being uncomfortably reminded that I had already squandered nearly half my sabbatical from *European Scientist* in rather directionless reading.

'Sufya,' Richard was now saying, more gently. 'This… *preoccupation*…with infanticide…?'

'I guess you've come across that new study about how a human male provides his embryo with a gene that fuels the growth of the placenta at the expense of the mother's body?'

Richard nodded slowly. We both knew I had cut him off. One of the reasons I had decided to terminate our relationship all those years ago had been because of this very habit of placing a precise needle of scrutiny on the sorest points of my psyche. The other reason had been that, as my PhD ended and I prepared to move back to London to take my first post as a science journalist, he had announced he was ready to leave his wife of ten years. Despite our compatibility, and despite my not inconsiderable feelings for him, this news threatened violation of the half-conscious rule which had dictated all my relationships with men ever since Steve: I was unavailable for commitment.

My most recent affair with Stan, a graphics editor on the magazine, had ended when he stormed out over my refusal to introduce him to my family. 'Thank you for wasting my time,' he muttered in bitter tones as he left. And I had to agree that on the charge of time-wasting I was probably guilty. So I had ignored his subsequent calls for us to 'try again', and had promised myself that I would stay away from men until – if ever – I could imagine doing without the deep and bridgeless moat that I had dug between my family and my personal life.

'One of the advantages of being away from the family – much as we love them all,' H had said on the night of his return, as the two of us, pointedly despatched to the kitchen to warm up the dessert, stood slightly awkwardly beside the steaming *khir* pan, 'is that eventually – after years and years – you can just about begin to forget that they officially own you for all eternity, and that it's their absolute right to scrutinise all your behaviour for evermore, and to tell you what to do until you die.' We both laughed, and I felt a flood of relief. Without sneering or condemning, he had let me know that he understood the effects of all those expectations.

Then, in the pause that followed, H said quietly, 'Can't have been easy, Suf.'

'Fucking right!' I said, rather loudly, to break up the sudden constriction in my throat. What did H know, what had he been told, about what had really happened? And suddenly, as we stood side by side sprinkling crushed cardamom seeds and pistachios over the pudding, I was surprised to find myself wishing we didn't have to go back into the living room.

But, in the two weeks that had followed, I had begun to distrust my memory of that moment. After all, wasn't it likely that my psyche had *generated*, rather than *detected*, the closeness between us? Wasn't my post-Stan state ripe for such self-trickery? And might not years of alienation from my family finally have taken their toll, causing me to conjure a convenient fantasy solution?

'There's something in it, Richard, I'm sure of it. And, if Karen Strier is right, muriquis are less aggressive because of the male–female dynamics, too. I'm beginning to wonder if it might be true that human females in some sense have evolved different moral systems to males…'

'Sufya, you're sounding like someone writing for *Spare Rib*, rather than a first-class biologist!' Richard snapped. 'You can't get away with these kinds of generalisations and you know it. What exactly is going on with you, anyway?'

I made a lengthy and incoherent attempt at convincing Richard that I truly felt I was onto something, but I could see from the way he was looking at me that I had not satisfied him on the question of what was 'going on' with me.

Of course, it's widely suspected that the biological origins of what we call 'love' – of nurturance and kindness towards fellow creatures – must lie in motherhood. Female nurturing of young is so widespread and powerful a drive across so many species that it almost has the status of a biological rule. Nature will favour the inheritance of 'nurturing genes', just as it favours the inheritance of 'genes for aggression'. And so, in somewhat simple terms (although not simplistic), it could be said that we emerge into the world as genetic mixtures of our mothers' love and our fathers' aggression – destined forever to be torn apart by our own conflicting nature.

Were there any other species, then, where mothers themselves ordered unborn babies to be torn from their gestating bodies, as I had once done? And was it possible, as I had once convinced myself, that such an act might be carried out not for the benefit of the individual, but for the benefit of some wider group, whose moral code required it? Had this act then been a manifestation of a natural propensity to operate as a social animal, or had it been in fact some deviant outrage – a treachery against nature?

It was questions such as these that had opened up and darkly swallowed my work on the book. Perhaps Richard had guessed something, given what little I had told him about my history before I knew him, but he could not know about the nightmares which were once again becoming more frequent, nor the extent to which I had begun to be troubled with the notion that these terrors might be generated by the screaming of genes whose true purpose had been murdered.

Wednesday 29 July 1998

Zarina

'BUT I STILL THINK it's a cop-out,' I said, as we left the NFT bar. Although it was late, the South Bank was crowded with people enjoying the warm summer night. 'I mean, the boy lies, steals and ditches his best friend for a bus ticket, but we never find out if he gets to see the football match in the end or not!'

Heathrow grinned. 'Well, knowing that kid, he probably did. But the long shot of him alone on the bus said it all for me. It can't be a safe Hollywood tale about a boy who tries and succeeds – he lives in Iran, after all.'

We had been to see *The Traveller*, which was on as part of a season of Abbas Kiarostami's work. Secretly, I had wanted *Out of Africa*, but Heathrow had been going on about Kiarostami for months, and was studying the work of the Iranian director for his final year dissertation at film school. So even though it was a treat for my eighteenth birthday, I had pretended to be equally enthusiastic, and chosen the movie for his sake.

'OK, but I'm going to believe he *did* succeed – unappealing brat though he was.'

'That's the genius of it – he's so real, you want him to win. It's only his passion that makes him unscrupulous... Actually, he was a bit like you, don't you think?'

'Hey!'

I felt my knees give way, and sat down hard on the ground. Nobody seemed to notice – the stream of revellers simply continuing around me.

'Zarina, are you OK?' Heathrow's voice, shaking with laughter, was at my ear. 'Here... up you get. How many vodkas did you have?'

'I don't remember... there were quite a few glasses on the table.'

'I'm sorry. I should have kept track.' He walked me towards the railing. 'I didn't realise we'd gone on that long.'

'It's OK,' I said thickly. 'I'll be a student soon. I need to practise.'

It was quieter by the river. And despite the hustle and bustle a few feet away, the water had something impersonal about it, something that didn't belong to the city or to now.

'How are you feeling?'

'Pleasantly dizzy, thank you.'

'Well, don't tell Auntie – she'll say I corrupted you!'

The lamps cast shimmering orbs onto the silently flowing water: golden on the surface, turning purple and finally black as they dropped deeper.

'I'd never tell on you, Heathrow.'

He ruffled my hair as I leaned against him. 'I know. Me neither.'

⁂

In my research for *Taj*, I had read the diaries of the Mughal emperors, and I admired how great rulers of the past had embraced arts as diverse as statesmanship, divination and alchemy. There was, I believed, humility in accepting that not everything in the universe was visible to man, and wisdom in cultivating alliances with those forces which human understanding could not fathom. This was no mere matter of gabbling a prayer over a pot of rice pudding, mind. This magic was an elegant and complex practice, harnessing the power of symbol and ritual. As a theatre practitioner, it excited and intrigued me. I felt I would be equal to it.

The ritual I was contemplating, however, did contain one slightly unnerving detail, which I had thus far brushed aside, namely: interment of the magical components *in a burial ground*. Also, despite what I had implied to Ravi, the mysterious paper bore scant resemblance to the *wazifas* to be found in Mum's collection of books which contained only quranic texts and were blessed by holy men. This diagram contained strange words which, as far as I could make out, were neither Arabic, Persian nor Urdu, and nowhere was the all-important qualifier, *Insha'allah*: with the Grace of God. I had wanted Ravi to talk me into taking action, but would he have been quite so obliging if he had thought I might be messing with dark magic?

I soon quelled my misgivings on that front. After all, Ravi's argument still stood: I was intending no evil, nor wishing harm to anyone. And it was only superstition that deemed burial grounds to be sinister. More importantly, they were places where the world made manifest met the realm of the spirits – the realm which I was summoning to my aid.

Did Islam allow such interventions? I had to ask the question because, unlike Sufya who had long since declared God null and void, and despite my non-adherence to almost all religious tenets, I still considered myself, on some level, to be a Muslim. I was aware that the Quran warned against sorcerers. On the other hand, it also, time and time again, advised the faithful not to slavishly follow rules but to use their God-given wit – in other words, Allah helps those who help themselves.

Help existed, that much I knew from experience. A glimpse of it had come to me unexpectedly in the days following Sufya's harrowing exit from the family home. Not a time I cared to recall much: my sister gone, Heathrow gone, Dad a ghost, Mum in and out of hospital, trying to die – it was as if a giant wrecking ball had demolished our house in one blow, leaving us dazed among the rubble. I would switch off the lights in my room and sit on the floor, slowly giving up to the weight of the surrounding darkness, almost willing it to break through the barrier of my skin and merge with the equal darkness inside.

One night, almost without realising it, I began to pray – just words at first, then slowly, carefully assuming the positions. *Bismillah al Rahman al Rahim, Al Hamdu lillahi Rabbil Alamin*… How long I repeated the words taught to us in childhood, I did not know, but I remembered feeling, quite suddenly, that someone or something was kneeling next to me: something strong that was effortlessly peeling the clinging darkness off me and lifting me up. Released, I breathed in, and a jasmine-scented peace poured in through my nostrils and seeped into every corner of my body, which was now being borne smoothly to my bed. I peered into the gloom to see who or what was there, but all I could make out was a soft, sand-coloured glow, like the light shed by a candle, before my eyelids gave up and shivered shut.

What was the source of the succour I had received? I seriously doubted that the Almighty had singled me out for rescue, given my general disregard of Him. It seemed more likely that the power of prayer, as I had experienced it, was generated by something else – some mysterious property, belonging to the words themselves in specific combination, which had concentrated some kind of spiritual energy into a potent manifestation of support. From that day on, whenever I needed to source extra strength, physical or mental, I had only to spread out the prayer mat, and focus my mind on the *salaat*.

But prayer alone, however powerful, was not going to get me Heathrow – not with Mum lining up all the aunties to deploy her invisible arsenal. I needed something stronger. And so, to be honest, the possibility that the origins of my *wazifa* might be occult rather than quranic, made it more attractive, not less.

Thus decided, I gathered together the requisite ingredients for the spell: a picture of Heathrow, snipped from a group photograph of the three of us at his graduation from the National Film School. Next, some of my hair: the spell called for five filaments, which I retrieved from my hairbrush after attempts to tweeze them from my head brought about a violent fit of sneezing.

It was easy to pick a burial ground. West Norwood Cemetery was one of the densest in Europe, making it less easy for anyone to spot me from the road. With its tall, wrought-iron gates, lush greenery and tumbling gravestones it was also oddly romantic, as I recalled from an afternoon with Heathrow many years ago, when we had taken refuge there from the fierce summer sun.

Everything was ready – but again I hesitated. Did I really *need* to do it? I thought of Heathrow holding out his hand on the night of his return, eyes dark and full of regret. Shouldn't I, before magically summoning my beloved, at least give a go to more conventional methods? Shouldn't I, for example, even though it went against the edict issued by Mum, just ring him up?

'He's out house-hunting,' Uncle Bogie said. 'Wants somewhere quiet to work. As if an old man like me is making a bloody din in his sensitive ears! I'll give you his mobile number, *beta* – he's a big shot film-wallah now.'

I dialled the number and waited with a racing heart. Why did this feel even more desperate than doing a spell? It was ridiculous, we used to ring each other all the time, there was nothing untoward—

Hello? H-Heathrow? Zarina hey where have you been we've hardly spoken, Where have I been where have you been? Sorry it's been crazy I was away again and I've been looking for a flat, So Bogieman says you don't want to live with him, Well what I actually said was Papa if you continue to wake me up for prayers twice a night, I'll have to give up work and we won't be able to afford Sky TV for you to watch the cricket on any more, So have you seen anywhere nice? As a matter of fact I've just come from a place in Camberwell it's a six-month let I'll probably take it you have to come over when I've moved in so we can talk properly, As long as you don't invite the rest of the family, They do seem to have been dogging my every step don't they never mind they'll get bored with me soon, Heathrow are you back for good? I hope so Zarina if it all works out it's been such a long time since we—

But that was the point at which Mum, whom I had thought safely occupied at her sewing machine, snatched the phone and started painstakingly giving him the address of Sufya's lab. 'Have you written it down, *beta*? Sufya told me I *must* give it to you!' (Of course my sister had said no such thing.)

Such a long time since we what? What had Heathrow been about to say? I gestured furiously at Mum to give back the handset, but she waved me away like an annoying fly. '*Haan*, so try to make it, *beta*, she will be so happy! What about next week?' I couldn't believe my ears: she was using my phone call to fix a date between Heathrow and Sufya!

She really meant to keep him from me. And after everything I had done for her in the aftermath of Sufyagate – even going along with her plans to arrange a marriage for me! Whilst all my university friends were off beginning their lives and embarking on exciting careers, I had been at home, wheeling in the tea-trolley, grinning at the potential dragons-in-law and tolerating their comments on my complexion! I had done it all without complaint. In fact, if Mum herself had not baulked at the 'quality of boys these days', I might even have given up waiting for Heathrow, and meekly conjoined myself to the pampered offspring of some loudmouth *masala*-millionaire. Didn't she owe me?

Of course, I couldn't say any of this to her. Since the crash and burn of those days, you never knew when an argument might lead to actual health issues. As I watched my mother chattering away on the phone, I realised that, while Sufya's apostasy seemed to have lessened with time, my subjugation had somehow become permanent. It had been years since I had stood up to Mum over anything.

What if I tried to pursue Heathrow in secret? No, sooner or later – probably sooner – I would be discovered, and the same bloody conflict would ensue. Only the supernatural option offered a neat, under-the-radar solution – Heathrow and I would be a done deal before anyone found out, and then they would just have to be happy for me. There was also, potentially, the added satisfaction of beating Mum at her own game. Ravi was right: that spell had come to me for a reason.

And so, driving home the following day from a seminar at the Arts Council, (aptly entitled *Empowering the Practitioner*), I switched direction and headed for Norwood Road. The traffic was heavy and the sun was getting lower as I pulled up outside the cemetery, grabbed my bag and jumped out of the car. I hovered casually outside for a moment and, when I saw that the coast was clear, slipped through the gates.

Immediately, the noise from the road was silenced. It was as though I had stepped into another world – one which bore no resemblance to my picturesque memories of that last visit with Heathrow. In the gathering darkness, the cemetery was rapidly losing its pleasant, welcoming aspect. It regarded me coldly as I trespassed on its twilight transformation. Visiting hours were over, there were no relatives laying beautiful flowers for their dear departed, there was no sign of life other than my own.

'Take control! *Think Madonna!*' I muttered sarcastically, plunging in. As if the Queen of Pop would be scrambling ignominiously over people's bones in her Jimmy Choos. Think Van Helsing racing to reach Castle Dracula before sundown, more like. The sooner I did the deed and got out, the better.

Deep inside the cemetery, I found a good spot where a huge old gravestone, adorned with a protective angel, caught my eye. Glancing swiftly around me again, I produced Dad's garden trowel from my bag, dropped to my knees and started to dig. The earth was unyielding…as though it were gorged with corpses, I thought involuntarily. Six inches would have to do: I didn't relish the thought of what I might find if I dug much deeper. Besides, my hands were trembling. Without ceremony, I flung in the photo, the hair and the magical paper, and raked earth and leaves over them with my fingers as quickly as I could. But barely had I finished than darkness fell completely and – there was no mistaking it – a cold wind started to blow. I leapt up hurriedly only to come face to face with an ugly black crow, eyeing me from the top of the angel's head. It opened its beak and let out a harshly echoing *Kraa-aark!*

Running helter-skelter for the exit, it occurred to me that in my panic I had abandoned Dad's trowel. But there was no way I was going back to get it: I would have to stop at B&Q on the way home and pick up another one. As it turned out, it was just as well that I wasn't carrying it, because when I burst out onto the pavement, Dad was standing right there, looking at me accusingly.

I came to a halt as casually as possible, fighting the impulse to leap into his arms. 'Dad! Hi!' I said, my voice sounding weirdly shrill. *Act normal!* 'Erm…what brings you here?' I batted my arm vaguely above my head in case the crow had followed me.

'I was coming back from the superbugs conference. I saw your car.' Dad gestured at the lonely, red Micra parked incriminatingly by the entrance. 'What are you doing, *beta*?'

Going for a walk? Doing stone-rubbings? Picking blackberries? 'Research,' I said, without missing a beat. 'For the play. You know – death, the tomb, remembering versus commemoration. We're planning to have some projections of gravestones.'

This appeared to work: Mum or Uncle Bogie would have been more difficult to satisfy with regard to Good Reasons for Going into a Graveyard at Twilight. Dad, however, was a rationalist by nature as well as by virtue of his scientific training: he only believed what the evidence of his eyes and the power of his reason could confirm. 'OK,' he shrugged, 'let's go home. It's going to rain. I'll follow you.' He waited while I got in, then hurried back to his Audi.

I had done it! And deflected Dad into the bargain! Revving the engine, my fear gave way to exultation. Now it was my turn to crow. Think Madonna? Think Bonnie Parker! As I swung away from the kerb, thunder rent the heavens and the rain that had been threatening for the last few minutes descended in a torrential downpour. I could barely see the road ahead of me.

Sufya

It was late July but the evening sky had darkened so suddenly that I had to get up and put on the laboratory lights in order to carry on with my reading. As I returned to my seat, I noticed Darwin pretending that his elbow was stuck between the bars of his enclosure. He did this very often when I was alone in the lab with him, and his intention, I knew, was to get me to open the cage door at which point he would sweep me into his hairy arms and try to kiss me.

By now I was unfazed by this behaviour, having known Darwin since the early days of my PhD, when he had briefly and memorably come to live in Richard's home in Oxford. Richard had saved the young chimp's life during a research project at Arnhem after Darwin's mother had inexplicably attacked him, biting him almost to death. Richard and the other Arnhem scientists had bandaged Darwin up and fed him back to health, but all their attempts at reintegrating him into the colony failed. Although Darwin's mother seemed to want her baby back, it was the infant that now rejected her. Indeed, it seemed Darwin had rejected not only his mother, but his entire species, and now saw himself as human. (And, judging by his refusal to take off Richard's spare lab coat, he may even have perceived himself to be a research biologist.) It was as if the brutality of his welcome into the world, coupled with the kindness offered to him by Richard, had awakened in the young chimp a determination to transcend his origins and forge a new destiny.

When I was living in London again, I had visited Darwin at University College where he had by then been adopted as lab pet by an old friend of Richard's who headed up the behavioural science department. I had been touched by Darwin's instant recognition and had agreed to help babysit him on days when there was nobody in the lab. It was not flattering to be an object of amorous attention from a chimpanzee, even one with high aspirations, but as time went on I became impressed by Darwin's loyalty and tenacity. It was characteristic of his refusal to be true to his roots that he had responded to two years of rejection from me without any show of aggression, not even a little tantrum. Instead, he was endlessly inventive in his attempts at seduction, and good-humoured about his relentless failure.

I took the make-up mirror from my bag and approaching Darwin's enclosure, slipped it into the flailing hand of the arm that was supposedly stuck between the bars. Instantly the arm was unstuck, and Darwin was clacking his teeth with delight while studying his rear end in the mirror.

Chimpanzees, baboons and orangutans are the only species apart from humans who know that what they see in a mirror is themselves. (Other animals react as though they are looking at another creature, and respond with aggression, flight or even sexual interest.) There is much heated debate as to what extent the reaction of a chimpanzee to a mirror indicates a *sense of self*. Certainly, watching Darwin, it *seemed* like he had a sense of himself, indeed had something approaching *self-esteem*, as he took pleasure in seeing aspects of himself that he could not ordinarily enjoy.

Fond as I was of Darwin, I could not resist a slight shudder as I watched him, his passion for me forgotten, twirling and posing with the mirror. After all, if chimpanzees were our closest evolutionary relatives, what might such behaviour suggest about our own species? Despite myself, I thought of H and wondered whether he too had the equivalent of his rear end in the mirror – that thing that would make him forget even the woman that he loved?

'Who's the fairest of them all?' said a voice behind me.

I turned to see H standing there in a weather-beaten tan leather jacket, his black hair coiled into small wet curls. My heart, unmistakably, missed a beat.

'Well it *was* me…until he got hold of that mirror. How did you find me?'

'Oh, you know, my contacts in the CIA, your mum, my dad. For some reason they tell me all your movements. Mondays and Tuesdays in the British Library, the rest of the week working at home, and every other Wednesday and Saturday you're at UCH apparently, to look after a "damn bloody gorilla". Anyway, I was passing and I wanted to see you. And it was raining. I hope you don't mind?'

'I don't mind. I wasn't getting much work done anyway,' I gabbled.

H looked at me carefully and seemed about to say something.

Then his expression changed to one of slight alarm. 'I think your friend minds,' he said.

There was a sudden deafening screech and I felt my head jerk back and impact violently with the bars of Darwin's enclosure. Keeping his grasp on my hair with one hand, Darwin slid his other hand through the bars to grip my throat, all the time letting out blood-curdling shrieks of warning. I felt myself choking.

For a moment H did not move. Then, quite suddenly, he bent his knees and lowered his head, and began to edge towards the cage speaking in a low voice. 'Don't worry, my friend,' he was saying. 'I get you, she's all yours…' The squeeze on my throat increased slightly, and I gaped for air, but H kept inching forward, talking softly all the time. Just when my chest felt like it would explode, H reached the cage and suddenly moved his head towards me and Darwin. With my back to the bars I could not see it, but I certainly heard it. Right by my ear H whispered, 'For the record, a kiss is just a kiss,' before he kissed Darwin loudly on the lips.

The pressure on my throat released, and I managed to step away from the cage before I fell to my knees spluttering and taking great gulps of air. It was a few seconds before I could turn to look at Darwin, by which time he had already picked up the discarded make-up mirror and was innocently re-examining his posterior.

'How did you know what to do?' I asked H half an hour later, as we walked down Gower Street together under a newly purchased umbrella.

'I did some reading on primates when I was studying conflict resolution before going out to Gaza.'

'You studied primates for *My Uncle's Son*!'

'Just a bit of reading, really. Inspired by you, in fact. Which doesn't sound right, does it? What I mean is, I remembered you quoting me something Darwin said – let me get this right – to understand metaphysics, study baboon – you remember?'

I nodded, feeling a certain childish pride at my influence.

'I wanted to have some tools for handling situations that came up when we were out there and I thought it might be useful to find out how our animal relatives get themselves out of conflict – I figured that when push comes to shove, it's more likely to work if you appeal to the animal in someone, rather than the human. I always liked the idea that the supreme gesture of reconciliation for chimpanzees is a kiss on the lips. If only Yasser Arafat could sort out Netanyahu as easily.'

'I'm afraid the chimpanzees are ahead of us on that one.'

'I'm not sure even chimpanzees would kiss Netanyahu though, no matter what the pay-off,' mused H.

My throat still hurt from Darwin's grasp, and I shivered as I recalled his clear malign intent. 'You know, it's very strange – Darwin's never attacked anyone before.'

'Perhaps he doesn't like other males.'

'But there are males in the lab all the time, and he never seems bothered. He's always been so un-chimpanzee about our relationship.'

'Maybe the chimpanzee in him has had enough of pretending. He's realised that denying your instincts is a big mistake.'

'He's always struck me as reaching for something higher.'

'But we're all struggling with our complicated natures. One bit of us wants to help our fellow man or woman, the other wants to bite off our fellow man's head and run off with his woman. Chimps probably have the same dilemmas, don't they?'

'That's what my book is about!' I told H. '…The evidence that animals have the seeds of moral systems, and how they can help us understand our own morality.'

'Well of course I'm not a biologist,' began H, thoughtfully, 'but I suppose there's quite a lot of evidence that animals are capable of love—'

'Attachment,' I corrected him.

'Attachment, if you prefer,' said H, with a smile. 'So I guess once you've got the love, a moral system must follow.'

'Might I suggest that you're reverting to that hippie phase you went through when you were seventeen and did all that Zen meditation…'

'Meditation is still one of the most useful strategies I ever learned, Dr Malik, and your own damn bloody scientists, as my dad calls them, will nowadays officially tell you the same. But what? Are you telling me love is *not* all you need?'

I explained to H that, according to current ideas, it was not so much 'love' that was the prerequisite for a moral system to evolve in a species, but rather a strict social hierarchy, run by dominance and submission, through which 'rules' could be enforced. H seemed fascinated by the idea.

'You mean to say,' he said, 'that we only have a moral system because some of us want to dominate others?'

'Well, the interesting question is *what else* in us leads us to a moral system, but it certainly seems like hierarchy is a necessary precondition. If you think about wolves, for instance, the strict pack rules of hunting together, sharing the food and so on are all only possible because the top dogs always make sure – using dominance and fear – that the rules are passed from generation to generation. That's the reason you can teach a dog to obey you, but not a cat – the cat doesn't come from a hierarchical pack society, so it can't learn rules…'

As we talked, we wandered down to the British Museum and stopped for tea in the café. When we were in our teens, H had always been easy with new ideas, and was familiar with offbeat texts about obscure subjects. Now that we were together again, I noticed, it seemed as though our childhood dialogue had never been interrupted.

'It's strange,' I found myself blurting suddenly, 'it's like you never went away.' What was the matter with me? Why did I find it possible to be so unnervingly open with this man I had not seen for over a decade?

H was sitting next to me on the long bench, facing away from the table, his upright back resting lightly against the edge of the table top. At my words, a shadow flicked over his face. Then he turned his head, quite deliberately, to meet my eyes, with the fierce, direct look that had always wrenched my guard away.

'It's quite a connection.'

I nodded, unable to speak. Perhaps we both withdrew our gaze at the same moment.

Later, as we left the museum, H said, 'Maybe your chimpanzee friend wasn't upset by having another male around. Maybe it was something else…'

'Like what?'

'Maybe it was *your* reaction to the other male.'

In her astringent vernacular my friend Jade loved to point out what she called the thin line between being a hero and being a prat.

'You know, if anybody else had said that, it would have been completely unacceptable.'

Again, a shadow crossed his face. 'So. Was it all right for *me* to say it, then?'

'Yes. It was…very all right.'

There was a deafening clap of thunder and the rain, which had hitherto been just a drizzle, began to come down in torrents. And as the storm raged around us, the small circle of our umbrella became a warm, melting space where I suddenly felt the unfamiliar sensation that no harm could ever come to me.

And so I had to admit to myself that, even though he had recently done the same to a chimpanzee, I was not unhappy when H stopped walking and, tenderly, kissed me on the lips.

Zarina

As we passed Tandoori Junction, I slowed and glanced into my mirror, awaiting Dad's signal. On cue, he flashed his lights: 'Stop for pakoras!'

Inside we were greeted by the aroma of whole roasting tandoori chicken, and the TV tuned to the Hindi movie channel. For as long as I could remember, Tandoori Junction had been our local takeaway and a hub of community life. Auntie Khan, the elderly owner, presided like a diminutive angel over all important Muslim rites of passage – catering for weddings, teaching the Quran to generations of children, and preparing the dead for burial.

Flushed with the daring of my cemetery escapade, I drooled at the fragrant dishes arrayed behind Auntie Khan's gleaming glass counter. Dad was pretty flushed too – about the conference he had just attended on intriguing bacterial mutations, the so-called 'superbugs'. Superbugs were Dad's passion – a modest passion, of course – which, thanks to his position as Senior Food Scientist for BestCo Supermarkets, he had frequent opportunities to indulge. While Auntie Khan's gigantic son wrapped our potato pakoras, chicken biryani and fresh chapattis, Dad regaled him with the latest discoveries in food hygiene.

'You wouldn't dream of not cleaning your surfaces with an antibacterial detergent at the end of the day, would you, Afzal? No, it's a matter of public health. But when we wage war on germs, they respond by changing their shape and becoming stronger. Whatever we exterminate them with, they will come back!'

Auntie Khan's son shrugged good-naturedly. 'Maybe, Uncle, but I'll be in trouble with Ummi if I don't clean. Six fifty, please.'

'Don't worry, *beta*, you carry on!' said Dad, handing over the cash. 'Some people think we should stop using chemicals, and go back to cleaning with lemon and vinegar! But I believe in progress! We can't go backwards. If science has created a problem, science will solve it! *Chalo*, Zarina!' And he flung open the door.

Good old Dad: as far as he was concerned, science could solve any riddle in the universe (though the metamorphosis of humble bacteria into brilliantly inventive super-villains ought to have at least flagged up that not everything in said universe was willing to act in accordance with scientific 'laws'). 'Think methodically!' he used to advise us as children, regardless of whether the problem was knotted shoelaces or a fight over the TV. 'Use logic, not emotion – you are intelligent girls!'

His views on magic were dismissive: 'Strictly for the birds and your mother, *beta*!' But, as I could have told him, the ancient practices, too, had a rigorous discipline: for each conundrum a specific procedure, and each procedure part of an integrated system – a vision to bring order out of chaos.

However, I did wholeheartedly agree with his pragmatic, problem-solving attitude. 'Where there's a will, there's a way!' I rejoined, and followed him out of the shop.

When we arrived home, we found Mum and Uncle Bogie perched on either end of the chaise longue, watching an old Indian movie, recognisable immediately as *Chaudhvin Ka Chand* (Full Moon, or more romantically in Urdu, moon of the fourteenth). Set in the courtly era of old Muslim Lucknow, with its princely poets and veiled beauties, this film was a long-standing favourite in our household, even tolerated patiently by Dad although he did not understand how Mum could watch it quite so often and cry every time. This evening, although brimming over with superbugs, he registered Mum's absent-minded greeting, deduced that a climax was approaching, and concluded that the wise move would be to sit down quietly. This he accordingly did, between Mum and Bogie, and opened *The Times* with as little kerfuffle as possible. I arranged the food on plates, listening to the film's familiar dialogue.

Pyare Miyan, a young nawab of Lucknow, has been called to the bedside of his beloved, now dying, mother. It is her ardent wish to fulfil the Islamic duty of Hajj but she has been deemed too ill to travel. As sanctioned in such cases, the family's *maulvi* has agreed to perform the pilgrimage on her behalf, but says he cannot risk the long and perilous expedition until his only daughter is safely settled in marriage. Pyare Miyan's mother has decided it is rightfully her son who should marry the young woman, and now begs him to organise it post-haste, so that the *maulvi* can depart at once to save her soul. From filial devotion, Pyare Miyan cannot express his own wish – which is to marry a beautiful maiden whose momentarily unveiled face he has glimpsed in the bazaar, and whose identity he has secretly been striving to discover.

In desperation, the nawab goes to his best friend, Aslam, and laments that this arranged marriage to the *maulvi*'s daughter spells the end of his hopes and the death of any chance of happiness. Seeing the anguish of his friend, Aslam heroically agrees to marry the young woman himself. Loyal and true, he declares the requested sacrifice to be a trifle, and trusts that, God willing, he will be rewarded with a lovely bride – so lovely, he jokes, that Pyare Miyan will envy him if ever he should have the good fortune to glimpse her face.

Alas, Pyare Miyan does not know that Aslam's laughing words are a deadly prophecy because, as ill fate would have it, the *maulvi*'s daughter is, in fact, the very same beauty from the bazaar. Nor can he foresee that his best friend will fall deeply in love with his new bride, only to later discover the mix-up – at which point he will be driven to plan suicide in order to leave his beautiful widow to Pyare Miyan.

Aslam is supposed to be the tragic hero of the film, torn between love for his wife and devotion to his friend. But tonight, I was feeling more sympathy for the nawab. To overlook the right girl for the wrong reasons – that was the real tragedy. Heathrow had done that already, and I wasn't about to let him do it again. Once more, I felt a surge of elation at having done the *wazifa*. Ravi was right: it felt good to take control. I sat down in front of the TV with a large plate of food, to watch the rest of the movie.

In the iconic scene, Guru Dutt as Aslam was lifting his wife's veil on their wedding night and gazing in wonder upon Waheeda Rehman's lovely face, as the intro to the romantic title-song, 'You Are The Full Moon' began—

'Oh, nine o'clock!' interrupted Dad, and suddenly Bill Clinton's face was all over the silver screen, blaring yet again, 'I did not have sexual relations with that woman!'

'What is this you have done?' shrieked Mum.

'Put it back, Dad!' I yelled, through a mouthful of rice.

'Oh *yaar*, you've ruined the whole mood, by God!' bellowed Bogie, throwing up his hands in disgust.

'Just a minute, just a minute!' Dad responded, holding the remote control out of reach. 'You can finish it afterwards, this is important!'

So, instead of the tragic climax – in which Pyare Miyan discovers the truth and swallows poison – we found ourselves watching the latest in the Clinton and Lewinsky scandal.

President Bill Clinton has agreed to provide testimony for Independent Counsel Ken Starr's grand jury, as it continues its probe of the sex-and-perjury allegations against the president. The president's lawyer, David Kendall, announced today that Mr Clinton will submit to questioning at the White House on 17th August.

'Shameless son of an owl!' Mum sniffed. 'I am not interested in his dirty habits!' And she went to put the kettle on.

Why was Clinton letting them drag him into court over it? It was becoming pretty clear that all the smoke had been caused by a fire of some description. Why didn't he just come out and admit it? Surely the electorate would forgive someone like him – an all-American hero with those sincere blue eyes, and that great voice? He was everything that won the west.

'Dirty behaviour, dirty politics!' snorted Bogie. 'This chap has no morals! Look at what he is doing in Iraq: half a million children dead from the effect of his sanctions.'

'It does not hurt Saddam to starve the people,' Dad agreed. 'It only makes him stronger.'

'Hurt Saddam, *kya, yaar*? They are quite happy for him to rule over a crippled country, as long as they keep control of the oil. Self-interest, *bas!* Bloody Americans – worse than the damn British in India!'

I stared at Uncle Bogie, who was now fiercely glued to the news, *Chaudhvin Ka Chand* forgotten. *Worse than the damn British in India?* Of course there was no point in challenging him on this position. He would definitely have told me I was young and foolish, but it just seemed hard to believe that all Americans, and Clinton in particular, were that bad.

And hadn't it always? I saw myself about seven years old again, standing bemused on the stairs. Sufya was in the hall below, our furious altercation on whether Starsky or Hutch was better-looking having been silenced by Mum who burst out of the kitchen, snapping, 'Be quiet! What Starsky and Hutch? You girls are not allowed to marry Englishmen anyway!'

Well, that wasn't too bad: I didn't know any Englishmen I wanted to marry. Weren't they all like that horrific Benny Hill? But foreboding was beginning to dawn. I looked from Mum to Sufya.

'What about Americans?' I asked.

My sister rolled her eyes and Mum looked at me for a moment as if she thought I was joking. I wasn't. I waited for an answer, the urgency of my question radiating through every seven-year-old pore. Surely, the Six Million Dollar Man couldn't be included in Mum's prohibition? Or Steve McGarrett-Five-O? Surely not the good guys?

Mum decided she had to spell it out. 'Yes, Zarina: English, American, it's the same thing!' and she went back into the kitchen, shaking her head at my obtuseness, while I stood in shock, trying to re-process everything I had understood about the world thus far. Judging by her reaction, Sufya had been unsurprised by Mum's revelation. How had she, as usual, known? And what now? Were we supposed to grow up and marry *Pakistanis*?

That was the first time I discovered it. *Us and them.* I recalled it clearly – my shock, Sufya's half-exasperation-half-concern, the kitchen door swinging behind Mum. *Us and them*, Bogie was repeating now. Americans, British (and other white Westerners) had their own team. We (and the Iraqi children) weren't on it.

Aged seven, perhaps even more disconcerting than the possibility that I might not be part of 'them' was the sneaking feeling that I might not be part of 'us'; that I didn't really fit in with *our* team. Later on, of course, I had embraced that difference, refusing to be limited by outdated definitions. And, over the years, while the older generation ground their habitual axe at those they identified with the former colonial masters of their homeland, I had kept my counsel. So, as Bogie and Dad now withdrew the benefit of the half-hearted doubt they had granted President Clinton upon his election, I decided that I would stand by him.

Wednesday 5 August 1998

Sufya

'BETRAYAL,' SAID H, bleakly. 'There's no other word for it. Betrayal.'

The three of us were slumped in the darkened living room, in the silence left by the whizzing of Uncle Bogie's projector. Our parents could be heard laughing and chatting in the kitchen, clattering teacups and munching on snacks, for all the world as though nothing had happened.

Suddenly H leapt up, heading for the door. Zarina and I scrambled to our feet and rushed after him, as he burst in on Mum, Dad and Bogie. '*Is that it?*' he accosted his father who was in the process of lifting a hefty kebab roll to his wide-open mouth. 'Does she just *disappear off* with Victor then?'

'*Haan,*' replied Bogie, astonished. 'She goes with her husband where she bloody well belongs! What did you expect? She would go with that loafer number one?'

'He's not a loafer number one!' piped up seven-year-old Zarina, adding coyly, 'He's the *hero*!'

'*Achha, baba,*' Bogie patted her head. 'I didn't make the damn film. That's the way it is. That is life!'

'Well, it's *stupid*!' I said.

'What is this?' Bogie boomed, a glint of amusement in his eyes. 'Mutiny on the Bounty?'

'*Yeh, koi Bounty Shounty nahin hai, Bogie bhai,* only *badtameezi!*' snapped Mum. 'Disrespect! These girls do not know how to speak to their elders.'

'They are too young for these films, Firdaus!' murmured Dad. 'It's not their fault.'

'*Chalo,* in future, no more films for them, until they learn how to behave!'

'We don't care!' yelled Zarina and I, as Mum began to harry us up to bed while Bogie guffawed. 'We don't like your stupid films, anyway!'

And we meant it. *Casablanca* had been the third and last of Bogie's prized 16mm prints, the other two being *Chaudhvin Ka Chand* and *Mughal-e-Azam* – both, if we had been old enough to analyse them, alike in their tragic theme of love versus duty – and its bittersweet conclusion had for all three of us been some kind of last straw. We had no intention of congregating for after-dinner family film evenings in our living room any more, enthralled by flickering images overlaying the flock wallpaper only to be left at the end feeling cheated.

I glanced back from the stairs to see H being gently batted down the unlit hallway by the giant paw of his still chuckling father. 'Time for bed, director *sahib*!'

But as Bogie opened the front door to usher him out, H turned and stood defiant on the threshold, glaring at all three of our parents. The murky orange streetlight glowed on his cheekbones and upturned chin, while beneath his glasses, his black eyes seemed to me like craters.

'One day,' he announced, and I noticed the fist glued to his side as though he was holding himself together with sheer effort of will, '*one day, I'm going to change all the bad endings!*'

With that, he shot away into the night and disappeared. It was the small hours of the morning before he was returned to his distraught father by two policemen. 'By God, *yaar,*' we heard Bogie tell Dad in hushed tones later, 'that little owl was *bilkul besharam* even after a night on the streets and a telling-off from the police! Shameless! If it was me, I would have been crying like a puppy by then!'

It was two days after this event that I was awoken at dawn by the arrival of H in our bedroom, a parka thrown over his pyjamas, and carrying a huge black holdall. 'Don't worry – I borrowed Dad's spare keys. Good job you told me how to shut down the burglar alarm,' he grinned to my wordless gape. Then he ran over to Zarina's bed. 'Wake up!' he said. 'I have seriously important news!'

'What *is* it?' whispered Zarina, wide-eyed, as H carefully lifted a large, heavily-shrouded object from the bag. He laid it on the bed and we gathered round in the dark as he unwound the towels with which he had carefully wrapped it.

We gawped when it lay unveiled on the bed.

'*Where* did you get it?'

'It's my dad's. From Hollywood. He keeps it locked in the basement. Turns out I'm quite good at breaking and entering.'

'D'you know how to use it?'

H reached into the holdall and pulled out a hardback library book, shoving it into my hand. In the dim light from the streetlamps outside I read out loud: *'Make Your Own 16mm Films by Keith Meredith.'*

'You mean…?' gasped Zee.

'Yes!' H's eyes met hers with a smile. 'This is how we're going to do it. We're going to make our own movies – without the bad endings!'

For months, all three of us spent every moment of spare time poring over Keith Meredith's dense text. In Bogie's basement, H informed us, there were piles of unused film-stock. (His father had once had aspirations as a film-maker, H said, having been given the equipment by an ex-colleague who had left the industry. However, it seemed to us that, as Bogie had abandoned these treasures in the basement, destiny had always intended that they should fall into *our* hands.) We discovered to our amazement that we could edit film using nothing more advanced than scissors and Sellotape. No sooner had we leapt around the room in joy at this, however, than we were plunged into despair over the revelation that we would need to pay for film to be developed in a laboratory before editing. Some days later, after an adrenalin-pumping afternoon when H put on his deepest voice and called three film processors in the Yellow Pages, we compared our post office accounts and discovered that from all our combined birthday and Eid presents over the years, we had enough to process around six rolls of film – a whole hour of footage!

For our first movie, we emptied a can of baked beans onto H's head (having taken the precaution of sitting him in the bath before we did it) and – without moving the camera – we filmed the slow progress of beans and sauce down his face, neck and chest. When, as planned, we reversed the film in the edit, we were delighted to see the beans creeping eerily – and somehow *deliberately* – upwards from his body, and finally converging in a weird, hillock-like congregation on the top of his head. The very best bit, as Zarina put it, was the moment at which H had put his tongue out to catch a bean that was in the process of dropping from the tip of his nose. This bean, long since digested, was to be resurrected in the edit to emerge from H's mouth on the tip of his tongue. From there it made a jaw-dropping hop to nose-tip, to join its fellows in their upward crawl.

We were jubilant. And we were even more delighted when we came up with the name for this first venture: *Hill of Beans*.

We experimented with other manipulations of reality – I was filmed running into the garden, violently kicking off my shoes and then flailing my arms and legs to remove – as fast as possible – as many items of clothing as I could, taking care to project them far into the distance. Then I had to drop to the ground as though lifeless. Once this film had been reversed, the action would show me being hoisted up like a marionette, and then clothes would shoot onto my body from all parts of the garden! (This fantastic project, however, had to be abandoned when Uncle Bogie came charging out into the garden during filming with a bath towel and flung it over me, yelling at H that this was disgraceful and what did he think he was bloody doing?) On another occasion, we filmed me drinking a milkshake through a straw, and then reversed the action to make Zarina wriggle with delighted horror.

Our production meetings were heated and joyous, and often left us unable to sleep at night. It was H that put into words the heady feeling that we were experiencing: 'It's like there's more reality when you look at it through the camera than there is in the real world,' he said.

'One plus one plus one is more than three!' shouted Zarina.

But dizzying though its achievements were in our eyes, the Magical Movie Company was not destined to manifest its full delicious potential until it generated something *with a proper story*, and that landmark creation was to be H's famous solo film, *Maulvi Madness*.

The eponymous Maulvi – whom we never dignified with any more elaborate title or proper name – was a shifty, little cleric with a sheep-like odour, who had been dug out from the local mosque by Uncle Bogie, at Mum's behest, to enable the three of us to 'finish Quran' at home. When an exuberant Bogie introduced him to our surly trio, Maulvi made no sound or gesture apart from flicking a small lizard-like tongue over his lips. A few minutes later, when Mum closed the door behind her and we were alone with him in the living room, he chose to open our learning with a contemptuous grunt, stabbing his forefinger abruptly in the direction of Dad's Persian rug. It was an early attempt to assert authority, and it was a severe tactical error.

H threw me a brief look of incredulity, and then quite deliberately plonked himself down on the sofa. Z immediately followed suit, making a little jump so that her legs were curled under her. All that was left was for me to sit down beside them and the tenor of our relationship with our new teacher was set. That first day, it took him twenty minutes to get us to sit on the floor, only to discover our Qurans were not to hand so we had to get up again to fetch them.

Maulvi must have thought us the most ruinously anglicised children in the entire *ummah*. It was a mark of his reciprocal stubbornness, or perhaps his very thick skin, that he did not refuse to teach us, but to our disappointment returned week after week, inching our unwilling triumvirate through a religious 'education'. (This consisted of us – painfully slowly, in Arabic and without understanding a word – reading aloud from the Quran while the cross-legged Maulvi rocked to and fro over his musty socks yapping 'No! No! No!' at our errors.)

Neither Zarina nor I knew at what stage H had started secretly filming Maulvi. But when he showed us the genius that was *Maulvi Madness* it was clear that he must have rigged the camera in the living room, probably between cushions on the sofa, during our classes. What amazed us especially was how neither of us had noticed when H must have escaped from Quran class long enough – perhaps on a toilet break? – to grab Maulvi's strange little rubbery black shoes from the hallway and film the close-up shots of running feet on Dad's treadmill. He must have had the camera set up in Dad's study in advance for the shots, somehow without arousing Dad's suspicion, and would have had to remember to hide the camera and return the shoes – all within the few minutes when he was out of class. He must have planned the whole operation to the second.

Maulvi Madness was a silent movie, had a very simple plot and only lasted for around one minute, but what an inspired minute it was! The star of the film was seen initially from the waist up, rocking to and fro and – though there was no sound – unmistakably mouthing the words 'No! No! No!' – these same words then appearing dramatically handwritten in chalk on a blackboard from our playroom. The camera then cut away to reveal running feet (presumably H's feet in Maulvi's shoes) on a treadmill. The next shot showed the rising needle of the speedometer on the treadmill, quickly followed by another shot of Maulvi's rocking upper body – now sped up a little – with more shouts of 'No!' (Another blackboard shot with a huge 'NO!' scrawled over it by H.) Zarina and I watched open-mouthed as, moment by moment, the running machine's speedometer reading increased, while the lip-licking Maulvi sped up against his will, culminating in a terrifying burst of flames and cut to black. The final shot revealed Maulvi's shoes lying empty and dishevelled on the carpet.

It was the beginning of the Easter holidays when H revealed the film to us. Zarina and I were beside ourselves with the thrill of seeing Maulvi so helplessly manipulated. The sheer *potential* was mind-blowing to us and, from that day on, it was official: the Magical Movie Company was in the business of serious alterations to 'reality'.

That holiday, the three of us were hard at work again. First, we discussed what aspects of our lives might be improved by magical editing. What scores did we have to settle? After Maulvi, number one on our hit list was Jason Hyland's dad.

Jason Hyland was a surly boy who was in the year above H at our school, and who lived round the block from H's house in a road known to us as Skinhead Street because of the crowd that frequented the pub on its corner. Last year, our basketball had gone over H's back fence and into Jason Hyland's garden, and when H and I had gone to ask for it back, Jason's dad had answered the door in a dirty, too-short T-shirt which revealed a protruding overhang of pale hairy belly, and grubby shorts. While I stared at the baggy folds of skin around his knees, he snarlingly told us our ball wasn't in his garden and that if he found it there, we would be sorry. The next morning, Uncle Bogie had opened his front door to find the ball on the doorstep. It had a large gash in the side of it, and was completely useless.

Dad refused to believe what Jason Hyland's dad had said to us, arguing that the ball must have got damaged on a tree branch. But the more closely we examined the ball, the more we became convinced that Jason Hyland's dad had stabbed it with a knife. We could not think of any reason why he would have done such a thing, as we had never had anything to do with him before. As for Jason himself, we had never spoken to him either, as he was usually skulking alone at school, and ignored us whenever we passed him in the street.

The Magical Movie Company decided that the best approach to making a film about Jason Hyland's dad would be to follow him and get as much secret footage as we could. We reasoned that once we had a range of shots, we would be able to assemble a suitably humiliating storyboard, and shoot any supporting 'cut-aways' that we might need for the plot.

Hanging around outside Jason Hyland's house was fraught with threat – as we were all rather afraid of his dad – but H and Zarina, as usual, poured scorn on my worries about what would happen if any of us were caught. I, too, was soon swept along by the mission, and it quickly became a matter of honour for each of us to spend long, heart-pounding hours running for cover between the neighbours' hedges, crouching behind parked cars and ducking out of sight of the local skinheads. We broke our days into shifts, with one of us on filming duty an hour at a stretch, after which he or she would return to base to report on adventures and on footage obtained, before the next person took over. It was the job of whoever was at home to log footage and recharge batteries. With this system, two of us were always indoors to create an impression of innocent pottering for the benefit of our parents.

However, despite the exhilarating sense of danger, purpose and system, after a week of thrilling activity we only had a few uninteresting shots of Jason Hyland's dad, getting in and out of his battered brown Vauxhall Cavalier. We decided that to achieve a variety of shots we would have to step up the risk and follow our target wherever he went. For this to work, it would be necessary to conceal not just the camera operator and equipment while filming, but also a bike, so that we could try to follow Jason's dad's car. This was too much to manage for the person who was filming, as it was often necessary to shift vantage point during shooting, because of irate neighbours or traffic issues, so two of us would need to go on each shoot, one as an assistant.

It fell to H and Zarina to take the first such shift and to my alarm they did not return for nearly two hours. I had been craning out of the front room window for what seemed like for ever, when Zarina arrived, breathless and red-cheeked.

'Smelly JHD went to the skinhead pub, and he was in there for ages, and when he came out he *vomited all over the street* and *nearly fell over*!' she yelled, brandishing the camera. 'H says this footage is *gold dust*! He's still following him on his bike, and he's going to call us *from a phone box* to let us know where to bring the camera when the battery's charged! Can I go out again, Suf? *Please*, can I?'

'No way! It's your turn to stay home!' I said irritably, plugging the battery into the charger. I wished I could have been there when this major incident had been captured magnificently on film. I knew H and Zee would go on about it for days, and I would have to listen to the story over and over, pretending not to be jealous. I just hoped that I could get something as good when my turn came.

Only a few minutes later, H called, and Zarina and I grappled with one another in the hall to answer the phone. Mum appeared briefly in the kitchen doorway and told us off for fighting before disappearing again.

'I lost him,' reported H, glumly, at the other end of the line. 'I'm going back to his house to wait for him. Meet me there?'

I was out of the house like a shot, with Zarina still grabbing at my sleeve and begging to have another turn. I raced straight to Skinhead Street and scanned the usual hedgerow vantage points. When I spotted H, my heart leapt. He was *inside Jason Hyland's front garden*, crouching under the bay window of the front room. He beckoned to me to bring the camera over. I checked the coast was clear, crouched low and scooted through the front gate to land breathless beside him.

'*You're mad!*' I breathed, admiringly, wishing it had been my idea to go this close.

'We need to see what happens next,' he replied. Unlike Zarina and me, who were usually on the verge of giggles, H was always serious when filming. 'Can you get the camera up to the window?'

'OK, but we can't stay here long,' I whispered, as I lifted the camera above our heads and over the window sill. 'What if someone walks by?'

'I'll keep watch. You just film!'

I raised my nose above the window sill and peered through the viewfinder into the murky interior of Jason Hyland's front room. The curtains were drawn across most of the window, but I had fortuitously stationed myself by a six-inch gap which allowed me a line of sight into the room. What I saw inside made me gasp.

'What is it?' said H.

I nodded to him to look. He leaned up to the viewfinder and his face turned white. Neither of us knew that much about sex, and we had certainly never seen any, but we were old enough to know what was happening in that front room – what Jason Hyland's fat dad was doing to Jason.

'Shall I stop filming?' I stammered, suddenly feeling a crushing sense of shame for Jason.

'No!' replied H, fiercely. He reached over and took the camera from my hands to make sure.

I turned away from the window, crouched down and silently retched. H continued to film. We must have been there only another minute or two, but it seemed an eternity. Across the street, a girl in a pink dress came out of a house and set off down the road without seeing us, her blithe skip seeming unreal as a backdrop to what I knew was occurring a few feet away.

Finally, H lowered the camera. 'Let's go!' he said grimly, *and stood up*.

I tried to grab him back out of sight, but a moment later I realised that he had done it on purpose, and I found myself standing up too. For a brief moment, we were side by side in full view of whoever might be looking out of Jason's front room window. Jason's dad, zipping up his trousers, gaped at us, realisation convulsing his flabby jowls and widening his eyes. His son's face was still hidden in the sofa – I was grateful he at least had not seen us. Then H cupped his hands to his mouth and put his face to the glass. '*Evil fat bastard!*' he shouted, and we ran.

When we got home, H showed the film to our horrified dad, who called the police. Shortly after that, Jason stopped coming to our school, and rumour had it that his dad was in prison. For years afterwards I would feel sick when I recalled what we had seen through that window, but H and I refused to tell Zarina any details, and we never showed her the film, despite her furious tears.

After that, we didn't make any more Magical Movies. But the three of us had learned something: film really could alter reality. None of us realised then that the unplanned liberation of Jason Hyland would be the inspiration for H's future career.

⁂

'Why are all these women attracted to this creep?' exclaimed Jade, looking up from *The Guardian* when I came down to breakfast. 'I can't wait till Monica testifies tomorrow – I've spent so much time reading about her sex life this year that she owes me a proper explanation!'

'Probably the age-old alpha male thing,' I muttered, fumbling to find the coffee jar in our cupboard where it had somehow become buried underneath boxes of Jade's herbal teas. 'You can't get more alpha than President of the United States of America.'

'Well, *I'm* not attracted to him. Are *you*?' Jade pushed her voluminous red locks away from her face with both hands and narrowed her green eyes to get a better look at the latest photo of Bill, pictured beating a grim-faced retreat from reporters. Her mystification was genuine, and I could not resist a smile, having seen enough of her chain of flaky-musician boyfriends to know that her own rationale for finding partners was quite explicable on the basis of the alpha male theory, whether she would admit it or not. Jade and I had been at Oxford together, where she had studied anthropology for a year before dropping out and disappearing off on far-flung travels. But when she returned to London to teach yoga and share my flat in Brixton, I quickly learned that her horizons had not widened when it came to her taste in men.

'We probably *would* be attracted to Clinton if we had to work with him,' I replied. 'That kind of thing's pretty much hard-wired into our genetic make-up. We're really only here because our great-great-great grandmothers had a thing for powerful males.'

'So Monica couldn't help it?' snorted Jade. 'That's a bit unfair on the woman. Maybe she made a poor choice, but surely she *had* a choice?'

I shrugged a smile, wishing we could drop the subject so I could be left alone with my thoughts. Since that twilight kiss in the pouring rain, I had spoken to H every day on the phone, but he was busy with research for a new film, and I too was under self-imposed pressure since my crushing meeting with Richard, so we had not seen each other for over a week. Now, suddenly, an entire day and night had passed without a call from him, and I found myself uncharacteristically shaken.

'Of course, if females are naturally attracted to the big, powerful ones,' continued Jade, thoughtfully munching her muesli, 'the males don't have to be big and powerful in order to get us, they just need to *give the impression* of being big and powerful …'

'Exactly. Which in turn means it's in the interests of females to have developed genetic lie detectors…'

'…which *I* clearly have, because *I* don't fancy him!' finished Jade, triumphantly, prodding the newspaper. 'Whereas Monica's genetic lie detector must be totally up the spout! Talking of which, what's up with you, anyway? You've checked your phone about ten times in the last three minutes.'

'Oh, nothing. I think there might be something wrong with it, that's all,' I lied. I might have known I would be caught out by Jade's observational powers.

Jade sat back from the table where she had spread her newspaper and surveyed me. 'Of course, this is on page one of the Bloke Handbook,' she said solemnly, 'and you *mustn't* call him. Also on page one.'

According to Jade's fictitious but authoritative 'Bloke Handbook', men were simple, and our downfall as women was that we had fallen for the story that they were complicated and interesting. Feminist ideas of getting men to behave like human beings were as misguided, said Jade, as pre-feminist ideas of depending on them to protect and provide for us. 'You're the biologist, Dr Malik,' she would tell me. 'Didn't they teach you this at Oxford? Maleness overrides species boundaries. They are males first, *Homo sapiens* later. If female chimpanzees could speak to us about their love lives, we'd know exactly what they were talking about.'

'The thing is,' I found myself confessing, 'it's different with me and H. There hasn't been any game-playing. He's rung me every day, sometimes two or three times, and it *did* seem like he just wanted to talk to me.'

Jade remained cynical. 'I don't doubt that the *Homo sapiens* in him did want to, but only because the maleness in him has a deeper strategy. Now that *Homo sapiens* has got you hooked, he's been switched off, and you're dealing directly with the guy holding the remote – the maleness, the head honcho, the Top Monkey.'

'OK, OK,' I laughed, wishing I had not told Jade quite so much about primate studies. 'And just remind me, what's in it for Top Monkey to stop calling me?'

'Fear, my dear.'

'Fear of commitment, right?'

'Not at all. Top Monkey hasn't even heard of Johnny-come-lately notions like commitment. No, Top Monkey is afraid of something far more primal than that. He's afraid that if he lets *Homo sapiens* run the show for too long, *Homo sapiens* might shift the balance of power, turn the tables, get hold of the remote control: *Homo sapiens* might even learn how to switch off Top Monkey.'

Zarina

THE DAMN THING OBVIOUSLY had not worked, which, as I complained to Ravi over the phone, meant that I had gone into that spooky cemetery for nothing! A week had gone by and Heathrow had definitely not appeared with declarations of undying love. In fact, he had not appeared at all. When Bogie turned up that evening brandishing a letter to Bill Clinton, in which he urged the US President to pray for humility, I was so desperate that I feigned interest in order to glean something, anything, from him.

'Of course I'll add my signature, Uncle. It's wonderful that you're trying to...help him. Erm, has Heathrow signed it?'

Bogie snorted. 'How can he sign it? Bloody Airport Boy has done his famous disappearing act! Doesn't even tell his papa where he's going! Well done, *beta*, good to see you youngsters taking an interest in politics!'

Further questioning revealed nothing more than a 'business

trip'. Bogie really had no idea where Heathrow was or when he would return – assuming he was going to return at all. *How could you let him go like that?* I felt like yelling. *You're his father: you're supposed to interfere!*

I called Ravi.

Gone just like that I don't know why he bothered turning up in the first place, Well maybe it's good that he's gone this is beginning to sound like Women on the Verge, *Oh so now I'm on the verge I thought I was Madonna at the last count, Darling you're missing my point which is that when the heroine tries to track down her missing husband she starts unearthing all sorts of unsavoury truths about his past who knows maybe Heathrow's got a secret ex-wife too ooh wait, This is not helping, Sorry sweetheart but we always knew that spell was going to be a long shot, It's not just the spell I'm upset about Ravi it's the way he was about to say something important on the phone but then he didn't even call me back it's like he's forgotten how we used to be, Well thirteen years is a long time for some shallow idiots, But that's just it I never thought that Heathrow, Zarina are you still there? Yes sorry Ravi I have to go Bogie's invited himself to dinner and Mum wants me to buy extra chapattis, OK just don't spike the gazpacho, Oh shut up.*

I did not always acquiesce so easily to these last-minute dashes to Tandoori Junction. Tonight, however, it was a relief to escape the house and ponder the latest, devastating turn of events. Heathrow was gone again.

Could I have made a mistake in my execution of the *wazifa*? I was fairly sure I hadn't. OK, I had been scared in the cemetery, and might have rushed the procedure slightly, but I had checked the ingredients several times, and followed the instructions to the letter.

It just didn't make sense. Twice, Heathrow and I had been interrupted at a critical moment, and now his sudden, mysterious departure from the country: it was almost as though something was physically keeping him away from me. Was it possible that Mum's fervent, daily incantations had placed some sort of powerful energetic barrier around him, impenetrable by either me or my feeble, one-off magic?

And, if that scenario wasn't discouraging enough, worse was going through my mind: for here was the voice of logic asking, in its snide, undermining way, if I had really believed that Heathrow would turn up after all that time and sweep me off into some happy ever after? Someone who hadn't got in touch at any point, although he himself had told me he'd thought about it? Wasn't it likely that the real explanation for his elusiveness was not supernatural but utterly ordinary, and that if not quite a 'shallow idiot' as Ravi had said, he was maybe just another guy who couldn't follow through?

Irritation mounted as I frowned at the pyramid of crisp samosas under Auntie Khan's antibacterially cleaned glass. So, what, was it to be another thirteen years before he graced us with his presence? Well, if that was the case, he could quite simply sod off. Better off without him. If he didn't have time, I didn't have—

People who do that irritating tap-on-the-wrong-shoulder thing should make very sure that you're going to be pleased to see them.

'Got you!' said Asif. Grinning behind that beard (which seemed even blacker and bushier than the last time) and hopping eagerly from foot to foot.

Unbelievable. Was *he* going to turn up every time I was hoping for Heathrow? I gave him a prolonged glare, and turned my back again, trusting this would get rid of him.

'You're right, Zee,' he said meekly, behind me. 'I understand why you might feel that way towards me. I should have said more, the other day at your house. I don't think I realised how much I'd hurt you.'

What? Could it be that he was going to talk about *that*, right here in front of Auntie Khan's son, and customers? And more alarmingly, could it actually be that at his last sentence, tears were threatening to well into my eyes? Whatever Ravi said about me being a woman on the verge (and frankly, who could blame me, with the broken heart I had been carrying around for over a decade), no way was I prepared to be that much of a basket case.

I turned, clenching my fists. '*Look*, Asif—'

'Just hear me out, Zee!' Asif interrupted in an unnaturally loud voice – the voice of a man who was going to deliver his message, or die trying. 'I want you to know that what happened before wasn't because of Suzanne, it was because of you. Because you blew me away. I couldn't go out with you and not be serious, so it was like a knee-jerk reaction—'

'*Not here!*' I hissed, jolting myself into action and dragging him towards the back of the shop. Asif's babble continued unabated.

'I didn't choose Suzanne over you. It was just easier. She was married, we were both only in it for the… Anyway, I left her a week after you and I split up. I wanted to ring you but I knew I owed it to you to get my head sorted first. And I have, Zee, I swear. I know what I want now, and it isn't sleazy affairs with white girls. I want someone from my own culture, who knows where I'm coming from. I want you, Zee! So, what d'you reckon?'

What did I reckon? I opened my mouth but finding only a

vacuum where words should have been, shut it again.

'I'm not saying you should rush into anything, we can take it slow if you want. Look, maybe you could come and watch my band sometime? Don't worry, it's not sex and drugs! Everyone's a committed Muslim, and we only write about serious issues. I know you'd like it because you have quite sophisticated musical tastes. And I want you to see how I've changed.'

Apparently, it was my turn to talk. I sensed, at last, the arrival of words in abundance, but still had time to register that he had managed to make me feel more inadequate with his speech of repentance than when he told me that Suzanne had 'got hooks' in him. *I know what I want now, and it isn't sleazy affairs with white girls. I want someone from my own culture!* Zarina Malik: sensible choice of born-again mullahs on the run from the femmes fatales of their youth.

The sound of rushing water filled my head, and seemed to lift me up. Why was it OK to treat me with so little regard? Was I so secondary, unremarkable and *small*? Now, with his tactless dredging, Asif had helpfully converted the misery I had been feeling all evening into a tidal wave of rage. My adrenalin surged.

'Oh I see! Because of me! Not because of *you*? Not because you were, say, weak and dishonest? Of course! I forced you to cheat on me and then *dump* me the minute you had a prickle of something approaching conscience. Well, as I said at the time, I'm fine! I'm only *embarrassed* that I ever went out with you in the first place!'

Mid-flow, it occurred to me that I was standing in Tandoori Junction bellowing loudly enough to reach the back of the Albert Hall. It didn't bother me.

'You haven't changed! You're just as pretentious and self-obsessed as ever, using some silly band to show off. As if I would be impressed by a bunch of smug, self-congratulating fundies! And as for understanding you or your *culture*, I don't and God forbid I ever do. So don't come to my house, don't follow me around and, once and for all, bugger off and leave me alone!'

'Mind out, guys!' Auntie Khan's younger son, Aftab, swung through the door from the kitchen carrying a large dish of freshly cooked *keema mattar*, and headed behind the counter. As he swept between us, I saw Asif's face behind the juicy mince: he looked shocked, pale, wounded. Good.

'Oh, and the next time you want to apologise,' I added, 'try saying sorry.'

Not such a bad day after all, I thought, as I took my chapattis from Afzal. I had dealt with one nuisance, at least. With or without magic, I still had the power to shape my own destiny, and I wasn't about to allow any man to make me feel miserable for long. Heathrow could turn up or not. See if I cared.

Saturday 8 August 1998

Sufya

ON THE EVENING that H returned from his three-day absence, we found ourselves at the opening night of Ishq, a fashionable club somewhere in Clerkenwell, to which H, as a member of the new category of cool, celebrity British Asians, had been invited. The DJ spun Talvin Singh, Trilok Gurtu and Badmarsh & Shri, mixing hypnotic Indian classical moods with bassy acid-house beats. In previous decades, East–West musical fusions had seemed uncomfortable, even forced, but these new avatars were robust and unconflicted: complex weaves of defiant muscular rhythm rendered breezy and alluring by warm, liquid vocals.

It was the usual Asian underground crowd of twenty- and thirty-somethings: Bollywood lookalikes in backless dresses and blonde-streaked hair – all gilded shoulders and bronzed cheekbones – being goggled at by floppy-haired Clerkenwell musos hungry for the kudos of an Indian girlfriend; Hanif Kureishi-style media boys, busy 'networking', with their goatees, retro glasses and droopy, white female companions; and Asian-gangsta lads, bouncing with beanie hats and afro-attitude. And tonight, along with these usual suspects, was more than the average smattering of what Zarina liked to call 'hijab sirens', all headscarves and opium eyes (these days more likely to have spent the morning having coffee at the ICA than observing purdah in a Banglatown two-up two-down). There also seemed to be veritable cohorts of 'trendy-fundies', slick-bearded Muslim boys in Ted Baker shirts and Converse shoes, who clung in small, all-male groups, pretending not to look at women.

The common cause of this odd mix was that they drew a tenuous identity from the relatively new chic of being, or being involved with, British Asians; and – given that we had all grown up together with the distinct understanding that being Asian, unlike being Afro-Caribbean, was *never* going to be cool – there was a distinct whiff of fear in the atmosphere. Were we really cool now, or would one of us give the game away?

I, too, would have been on edge amidst the studied aloofness of this image-conscious crowd, but it was H's ease of presence that enabled me to settle. With unaffected charm he somehow made each stranger who approached him – from the golden-shouldered wannabes to the insecure goatee-beardies – feel like *they* were the special one. Yet, even while meeting the many needs of those clamouring for celebrity contact, he continued to be a companion to me. It was not his fame that was turning my head, but his response to his fame.

'You know what they say,' Jade had said protectively, that morning – the fourth morning in a row that I had not heard from H, 'a bloke by any other name would smell.' When Jade was really exercised, her humour would drop any intellectual aspirations, and normally I would have to laugh; but that morning, I had barely managed a grimace. All the more surprising then, that H's arrival had had such a soothing effect on me.

For one thing, he had a persuasive reason for his disappearance: he had had to travel to the West Bank at short notice, because Ayub, the Palestinian child-star of *My Uncle's Son*, now thirteen years old, had been detained. The Israeli military wanted to question him after one of Ayub's friends – a fifteen-year old on his football team – blew himself up in a Jerusalem market place, killing three innocent passers-by. For weeks, Ayub's father had tried to visit his son in prison, but had come up against a blank wall of bureaucracy: nobody would tell them where he was being held or when he might be released. Finally, they begged H to come to the West Bank, believing that publicity was their only hope of getting Ayub out of custody. 'If I want to get there fast, I have to use unusual methods,' H explained, 'because the authorities have a ton of red tape at their disposal to cause delays to pesky film-makers. So it was tricky to arrange, and I had to leave very suddenly. I didn't want to get you involved with all that, but it wasn't easy to leave without saying goodbye. I just kept hoping that you knew me well enough to understand that I would have had a good reason.'

Of course I knew him well enough, I realised with a shock of guilt. Had I become so habituated to holding men at an emotional distance that I had simply forgotten to activate my instinctual understanding of H – that deep knowledge that came from our past? Now, as I stood with him at the bar of Ishq, I was ashamed to recall my self-centred misery these last few days, while he had been risking himself to help the helpless.

'Did they let him go?' I asked H, when the tide of fans had momentarily stemmed.

'Who?'

'Ayub. Did the Israelis let him go?'

A shadow crossed H's face. 'Yes, but they gave him a couple of beatings first,' he said. 'And while he was interrogated, they lied to him that his two younger brothers had been killed. Anyone would think they *want* him to turn into a hardened criminal.'

It was difficult to imagine the Ayub I had seen in H's film becoming anything that might be described as a hardened criminal. At the time of filming, he and his Israeli Jewish cousin David were both ten years old and were the best of friends. Both were gentle, cerebral boys who seemed mystified by the conflict which raged in the hearts of their peers. At the memorable climax of *My Uncle's Son*, David had persuaded his somewhat unwilling headteacher to allow the two cousins to present a school assembly about being best friends. 'My cousin Ayub is my best friend,' David had declared to his entirely Jewish school, while brandishing an unappealing-looking jam jar. 'When I had my appendix out, he kept it in this jar, because he said it was a piece of me. Even though it doesn't look very nice.'

H must have noticed my confusion and he lowered his voice to explain further. 'Ayub can't talk about anything other than his friend...the suicide bomber.'

'You're not saying that he...?' I was suddenly disturbed, not just at the implication about Ayub, but also at the chasm between my day-to-day academic struggles and H's professional world, where teenage boys were using their bodies as bombs.

For a moment H seemed to find it difficult to respond. Then he said: 'Palestinians talk about a line inside everyone that can get crossed. I think sometimes it's the ones with gentler temperaments who can turn into the most desperate. You know Ayub hasn't spoken to his cousin David since his mother died last year, because he blames Israel for his mother's death?'

'I didn't know his mother had been killed by an Israeli!'

'She wasn't. It was cancer. But it's a strange place, Palestine. All personal tragedy can be used to fuel the anger that drives the conflict. I mean, elsewhere in the world people do feel angry when something goes wrong in their life – they just have nobody to blame. But in Israel and Palestine, there *is* someone to blame – right next door. So if your wife leaves you because you drink too much, you feel more bitter about the occupation, because you can say that it was living under occupation that made you drink. If you lose your job because you're late, you can be more angry with Israel, because Israeli policies are the reason you can't afford a car to get to work on time. And if you lose your mother to illness, you can say the conflict was the reason why she had such a hard life and wasn't strong enough to fight the disease.'

'I suppose Ayub might have a point,' I ventured, recalling from the film Ayub's diminutive mother, Amira, and the demanding circumstances of her life.

'Not to hate his cousin, he doesn't,' said H firmly. 'I just hope that I've managed to convince him to give David another chance. If he could recover that childhood bond it might just re-anchor him…'

H's eyes met mine and, despite the weight of the topic, both of us were suddenly grinning foolishly. He went on, his tone lighter now: 'Anyway, I tried to say to him that it's where you direct the anger that's important. Let's face it: we're *all* angry—'

'Hey, guys, what do you think of the vibe?' Hairy Asif came out of the throng, giving me a distinctly un-Islamic squeeze, and grasping H's hand in the black-power style. Accompanied by two friends who appeared to be dressed as pirates, Asif clearly wanted to give the impression of being great chums with H, although as far as I knew he had only met him that once at my parents' home a few weeks ago. He slid me aside so that he and his companions could stand next to H. '*Salaam*, man, *salaam*,' he beamed, affecting a smooth cannabis drawl. 'Yeah, it's all good, it's all good. Wanted you to meet my band, we're on later – the Orthodogs. This is Bashi,' Asif indicated the shorter, more chunky of the pirates, who was hopping from foot to foot energetically, a black bandanna tied, Amitabh-style, above his meaty little ears. 'His real name's Bashir, but he's better known as Bashi the Paki!' (Here Asif and Bashi uttered high-pitched hyena chuckles and slapped each other's hands.) 'And this is Jehangir, man.'

Jehangir, tall and cool, with a diamond stud in his ear, offered H a cigarette, which I accepted, and then silently lit one himself, while "Bashi the Paki" yapped excitedly in an exaggerated East End street-speak: 'Yeah, man. *Salaam*. Saw your films, innit? Wha' can I say, man? We need more bruvvers like you, kna' wha' mean?'

'Thanks,' said H. 'So what kind of music do you play?'

'Orthodogs, man!' yelped Bashi. 'We is the new religion, innit: rappin' about troof, man, wha's really 'appenin' in the communi'y – the grassroot bruvvers, kna' wha' mean?'

'It's a mixture of *qawwali*, rap and acid house, wouldn't you say, Jehangir?' interrupted Asif, seeming a little embarrassed at his colleague's raving. Jehangir blew a slow jet of smoke and said nothing.

Bashi flinched, perhaps with the realisation that he had not come across as cool. 'Yeah, man,' he said, less confidently. 'Talkin' the troof about bein' young, Muslim and proud…'

'Looking forward to it. What time are you on?' said H, and

Bashi puffed up again.

'Soon, man. Tennish!'

'Nah, man! Is that the time?' drawled Asif, looking at his watch and gesturing to the others. 'Sorry, would be great to stay and chat, but they'll be wanting us backstage... You know what it's like in the business... Safe, man, safe.'

And with that, the Orthodogs swaggered away, their tails high.

When H asked me to dance, I was unwilling at first. For the last few years – in fact, dating back precisely to the time of my Loss – it was as though my physical self had coldly withdrawn cooperation, and an ice-like rigidity would creep into my limbs if called upon to dance. All the ecstasy-and-acid-driven raves of the last ten years had done nothing to thaw the cold war declared on me by my own body.

But H smiled, placing an arm around my waist to move me closer to him, and once again I felt an unfamiliar sense of safety.

It can only be like this, I thought to myself, as the music wove its spell inside us and around us, easing us closer, with someone who knew you as a child, someone who hasn't forgotten who you used to be, even if you've forgotten it yourself. I found myself taking deep slow breaths, as if I had not breathed for years.

Some time later, the spell was broken by loud shouting into a microphone. It was Bashi the Paki calling on everyone to give it up for the Orthodogs, voice of the new religion tellin' it like it is, innit? And, generous with the glow of our dance together, H and I did as we were requested, applauding as Jehangir started up a hypnotic beat on tabla, accompanied by a simple, but effective, swaying riff on bass guitar from Asif. Bashi was leaping around the stage clapping his hands above his head, shouting '*Bismillah*!' like a battle cry, and drawing whoops from the crowd as they eagerly took up the luscious rhythm of a *qawwali* hand-clap.

'We is growin', bruvvers and sisters! We is GROWIN'!' Bashi yelped into the microphone. 'We is not hidin' it any more! We is wearing our Islamic clothes, man, we is growing our beards mightily, yeah! We is saying: WATCH OUT, MR AND MRS *KAFIR*! THIS. IS. WHO. WE. ARE!'

A huge cheer went up from the crowd. There was no doubt Bashi's exuberance was infectious, but this noisy flag-waving from the beardy brigade was beginning to make me uncomfortable.

'*BIS-MIL-LAH!* BRING-IT-ON!' roared Bashi, now leaping into a semi-squat position and thrusting his pelvis as he threw down the gauntlet to 'Mr and Mrs *Kafir*'. 'Say it with me, bruvvers and sisters: *BIS-MIL-LAH!* BRING-IT-ON!'

Inhibited at first, but encouraged by the enthusiasm of a smattering of obvious Orthodogs followers who were leading the response, the crowd – Muslim and non-Muslim alike – took up the refrain: '*Bis-mil-lah!* Bring-it-on! *Bis-mil-lah!* Bring-it-on!' Bashi's response in turn was to utter a long guttural whoop, turn his backside to the audience and thrust his pelvis even more violently.

Male birds, such as ravens, often compete with one another to attack larger individuals, seemingly deliberately seeking out danger – a behaviour that at first sight is difficult to explain. After all, what's in it for the winner of such a competition, except the likelihood of injury or death? Observers have noticed that males alternate such acts of aggression with gestures of courtship towards females, suggesting that demonstrations of 'bravery' might make male ravens attractive to the opposite sex. And in the singles-bar world of raven relationships – where the feeding crowd changes constantly – a male has only a fleeting moment in which to grab the attention of a passing female onlooker. He needs to demonstrate a stand-out capability for aggression, and he needs to do it right here, right now.

As if aware of my musings, the pumped up Bashi now turned to the audience and singled out one of the golden-shouldered beauties near the front row. 'All right, darling?' he leered and thrusted. 'You like what you're looking at, innit?' The beauty looked slightly uncomfortable at having the attention of the crowd, but all around the stage I could see feminine bangled arms reaching up towards Bashi the Paki's gyrating pelvis.

'Like I was saying earlier, we're *all* angry,' murmured H, as though deep in my thoughts. His eyes were on Bashi.

'You mean that? Every one of us?'

'You don't agree?'

'I hadn't really thought of it in those terms. I suppose we all have the capability to be *aggressive*—'

'The trick,' interrupted H, as though thinking aloud, 'is to know your anger. To *befriend* it. Otherwise it jumps out on you when you least expect it.'

It sounded like psychobabble, and with someone else this would have been the point at which the conversation fizzled out. But H had never said anything which did not turn out to have unexpected layers, so I did not hesitate to give him the benefit of the doubt. Moreover, the control of aggression was emerging as a key issue in my research on the biological evolution of moral codes, so I was curious about anything H might have to say on the subject, even if it was a little peculiar.

'OK. So how do I "befriend" my anger then?'

H thought for a moment. 'Well, this might not be the best place.' He indicated the pumping furore of the Orthodogs, now in the throbbing climax of their first song – clearly entitled '*Bismillah!*

Bring It On!' – and the increasingly excited audience. 'But what I do is I close my eyes and imagine my anger is standing in front of me – I literally try to see it there, like a person, what it looks like, how tall it is…and then I try to hear what it wants to say to me…' He closed his eyes and his voice trailed away.

Despite the heat in the room, I felt a shiver. It was as though H were listening to something – or some*one* – that was actually speaking. Then, his eyes still shut, he smiled warmly…*but not at me*. After a moment, he opened his eyes.

'What did it look like then, your anger?' I couldn't help asking.

'Monstrous, as usual! You don't want to know!' laughed H. 'But he's OK – we're on good terms right now, so don't worry!'

'That's good to know.' I smiled, but I was feeling odd. Suddenly there was a side to H that I had no idea about. It was not the fact that he admitted to having a 'monstrous' anger that bothered me. It was more his mode of operation – his referring to his anger as 'he', and that weird, inward smile.

'Don't be freaked out, Dr Malik,' H smiled, and led me off to dance again.

And out on the dance floor, my edginess dissolved and ebbed away. I let myself fill up with the sensations of my body and his making patterns in space, following the deep lure of the swaying bass. No edges between us, no gaps, no hidden spaces for fear or doubt.

Perhaps a couple of tracks went by without my paying much attention to the lyrics or the antics of the band. But then, in the slight lull after some rapturous cheering from the crowd, came the tinkling ripple of an old piano in a familiar tune, and the sound of Jehangir's surprisingly Sinatra-like voice:

'You must remember this,

A kiss is just a kiss...'

I looked at H, and he was smiling at me. After all, it was the song that marked the moment when Ilse walked back into Rick's life after many years of separation. And wasn't that the love story which had launched H on his mission to change all the bad endings?

'...The fundamental things apply

As time goes by...' crooned Jehangir.

But then, instead of the lines about lovers woo, I love you, there was a deafening crash as Asif set up a thrashing rhythm on electric guitar, and Bashi launched into a violent pogoing up and down the stage, yelling at the top of his voice:

'The fundamental things apply!
The fundamental things apply!
You think you're wearing sexy clothes!
You only look like a ho!
The fundamental things apply!
The fundamental things apply!
You think you're wearing sexy clothes!
You only look like a ho!'

Asif and Jehangir were yelling too now, repeating the refrain while the music built in pitch and fury. Meanwhile, Bashi was stomping around the front edge of the stage with the microphone, pointing his finger into the faces of women within his reach as he shouted over and over a single line: '*You only look like a ho! You only look like a ho!*'

I looked around the room. Some of the hijab sirens were smiling at one another in semi-appalled delight, and a number of the trendy fundie men were punching the air or giving one another high fives, shouting 'Yeh, brother! Tell it like it is!' Parts of the crowd were dancing away, seemingly oblivious to events on stage, but elsewhere people had stopped moving and were watching with incredulity as Bashi pumped himself into even higher stages of aggression, bending now to shout into the face of one woman after another.

'You only look like a ho!'

Some of the golden-shouldered starlets were trying to back away from the stage, but the crowd was too dense for them to escape Bashi's reach.

'Where you going, sister?' Bashi snarled at one. 'Don't like to hear the troof? Where's the rest of that dress? You know you only look like a ho!'

The trendy-fundies were practically baying by now, and Bashi's victim was in tears.

'Keep out of this mob, I'll be back for you,' said a voice in my ear and I turned to see H's upright figure, striding through the crowd towards the stage. Where on earth was he going?

I have never known anyone else that could, or would, have done what H did next. I watched in disbelief as he leapt up onto the stage and stood there, tall and still, causing instant confusion among the Orthodogs. Their voices faltered briefly, but they quickly regained the pack rhythm and went at it with renewed fury. Bashi, who had taken a half step back and dropped his head – a move reminiscent of the submission gesture of a male chimp confronted by his superior in the hierarchy – quickly retuned himself and strode forward, his hand outstretched to give H the black power handshake – a threatened primate, trying to build an alliance.

But H did not extend his hand in return. Instead he just stood and looked at Bashi, unflinching and motionless. Bashi's face twisted in rage and fear, but he did not give up his refrain. Instead, shouting so hard that, even from the back, I could see spit spraying from his mouth, he backed away from H and, in a clear gesture of provocation, leapt into the crowd to grasp the shoulder of another female onlooker, before yelling into her face: '*You only look like a fuckin' ho!*'

A white man, maybe the boyfriend of the woman, tried to punch Bashi in the face, but perhaps drunk, perhaps fearful, ended up producing something more like a slap. Bashi attempted a clumsy return punch which missed its target completely, before leaping back onto the stage, his lip slightly bleeding, and his swagger a little less rhythmic. 'Will fuckin' security get this fucker off my stage, for fuck's sake!' he snarled into his microphone, his eyes popping with helpless rage at the motionless figure of H. But by now Asif had lost the beat on his guitar, and even the unflusterable Jehangir had stopped playing. Feedback screamed in the microphone as Bashi's yelp for assistance hung in the air. The crowd was silent.

Somehow, H had won.

Hesitantly, someone in the audience started to clap, and then someone else joined in. The applause began to gather pace, and then suddenly there rose a deafening roar of delight from the crowd. In a matter of seconds, the testosterone-fuelled aggression in the room had been transmuted into something else entirely. It was as though all that tension – generated by several hundred creatures jostling to belong to a highly-ranked social grouping – that tension, which had been rising to a frenzy under the influence of the Orthodogs, had suddenly been released, had vanished into thin air as if by magic, and now each individual in the room suddenly found that they *did* belong – not to some trendy elite, and no longer to a howling pack on the rampage – but instead to a far more noble collective: *one which had done the right thing.*

As he had done in the past, H had once again transformed 'reality'.

And, as the two of us left the club that night, I realised there was no point in being afraid any more of putting myself at risk, of stepping over an edge. I had crossed over without knowing it, and there was no going back. And we had the beauty of the whole scented summer's night ahead of us.

Friday 14 August 1998

Zarina

HELL HATH NO FURY like a second daughter. This is a truth which only those Persephones condemned to the wintry shadowlands can taste. Some know it from the beginning. Others, consumed by the demands of survival, only discover it many years and many battles later, suddenly asking themselves, *Have I always been this angry?*

As children, whenever we were introduced to our parents' Pakistani friends, they would, after a brief and unpleasant scrutiny, pronounce: '*Achha,* this is Number 1… and this is Number 2!'

'Two's more than one!' I would quip emptily to Sufya, but we both knew what was what. One was the original, the winner, the summit of the mountain. Two only the bad copy, the runner-up, the base camp and, in short, what I amounted to.

And yet, did not the number 2 hold within its multiplicity the possibility of movement unavailable to the static 1? Or, put differently, if 1 soars upwards, might not 2 shimmy sideways? And might not the eclipse created by 1's shining pre-eminence, provide a little cover for 2's transgressions?

Whilst everyone was busy applauding Sufya's glittering progress along the road of parental expectation, I was free to escape along paths less travelled – at least by the Pakistani community. Ballet, the writing of stories and, of course, acting in magical movies were activities I ardently embraced from the age of five upwards, discovering, in their pursuit, not only limitless pleasure but also an incipient sense of myself beyond a single digit identity. Towards these unsuitable pastimes, our parents demonstrated a (pained) tolerance that would probably not have been forthcoming had they not already had one daughter who was doing everything right. (Of course, when she later did everything wrong, they were far too stressed to bother with me.)

Heathrow, of course, always encouraged my artistic projects and, later on, when it seemed that he might have gone for good, they became my main passion. Making a conscious decision to trade failed love for successful drama, I set up the Zarina Malik Theatre Company, and wrote, directed, fundraised and publicised with the focus and energy of someone who has one lifeline left. This time luck was on my side and, drawing on the pastimes I had always loved – dance, writing, film – I hit upon a theatrical language, which quickly earned the company a reputation for 'multimedia with a soul'. And, as recognition for my work grew, I turned my back on my anxious, emotional past and, like a phoenix rising from the ashes, reinvented myself again: I was a pioneering artist/entrepreneur, I told myself, and no one could limit my horizons.

And so, as Heathrow's destabilising now-you-see-me-now-you-don't antics continued, I decided to begin casting for *Taj*. It was a relief to know that I had a new production to throw myself into – one that, having at last attracted a proper level of funding, was expected to consolidate the Zarina Malik Theatre Company's reputation as a fresh new voice with plenty to say.

The Taj Mahal was an intriguing subject. Like many people, I had long been fascinated by its reputation as a 'monument to love'. The story of a young, widowed king who devoted his life – not to mention the resources of his magnificent empire – to a building which, even four hundred years later, commands tears of wonder from the beholder, is the stuff of fairy tale.

However, it was not a fairy tale on the conventional model that I was interested in staging. The question I wanted to explore was whether perfect love, as represented in the story of Shahjehan and Mumtaz, really existed – then or now. Was it an enduring universal truth or, like the Taj, a brilliant man-made construction?

It struck me that, like most official histories, the court diaries had been recorded by men, and while much was written about Mumtaz, her own voice was conspicuously absent. If she had penned her own diary, what would she have said? Would she, an artistic, accomplished woman, really have been completely fulfilled by marriage to someone who spent most of his time dealing with wars around the realm?

Mention of a fictional architect in one of the commentaries on the art and symbolism of the Taj got me excited about the dramatic possibilities of introducing a third character into the love story. What if, through her relationships with two very different men, I could create a voice for Mumtaz – one that would speak of the depth of a woman's soul, her longing to live without compromise? She would love both Shahjehan and Suleman, but neither of them alone could complete her. With that thought, I knew I had the beginnings of a play.

The idea of two contrasting male protagonists had practical advantages too, since it saved me trying to cast a single, perfect hero. Both characters had clear strengths and failings: Shahjehan was commanding, energetic, carnal, the man who could fulfil Mumtaz as a woman and mother, yet not intuit her soul. Suleman was gentle, poetic, cerebral, a mystic who offered Mumtaz an ecstatic meeting of minds, but not a lover's embrace. It should, I thought, be relatively simple to find two interesting actors to fit these parameters, so I was not anticipating too many casting nightmares, particularly as the beauteous Queen Mumtaz was already provided for in the shape of Sabah – a talented actress and friend from Asian youth theatre days, whose straight nose and lustrous hazel eyes sent aunties everywhere into admiring raptures.

But by the second day of auditions for *Taj*, I was beginning to panic. Legendary lovers still needed real actors to bring them to life, and so far reality had failed to yield even a glimmer of anything beyond the most excruciatingly banal and unsatisfactory.

To compound the problem, the company's mission statement pledged to provide interesting roles for Asian actors – who were rarely cast as anything other than shopkeepers. But, as usual, all the good Asian actors were busy doing TV (playing shopkeepers). So, after a brief internal debate at the end of a third fruitless day, I decided that show business was show business, ditched the mission, and rang round the agents to say we were happy to consider anyone of Latin, Mediterranean, or Middle Eastern origin – in fact anyone with dark hair and a tan who, with a bit of make-up and under the right lights could pass for Asian. But despite an increased number of applicants on day three, we still drew a blank (or rather two blanks).

'Well we ought to have known, ladies! If more guys could act like heroes, more guys would actually *be* heroes. How many of those have you met, even one-sided ones? Let alone one-sided ones that can keep a beat!' Ravi, as choreographer for *Taj*, had the invidious task of testing the candidates', so far non-existent, movement skills.

'You cannot make a silk purse out of a sow's ear!' Sabah intoned, with exaggerated theatricality.

It didn't help that our heroine was on the tall side. Sabah's willowy, five foot nine inch person demanded that the two men be at least five foot ten or over, and I had specified this clearly in the casting breakdown that had been sent out. Nevertheless, our patience had been tried by a parade of what Ravi called 'vertically challenged wannabes', who had either failed to be put in the picture by their agents, or thought it was worth a try anyway.

Ravi's frustration was not entirely disinterested. Since the day he saw the draft script, he had been angling for the part of Suleman, believing that his innate gentleness and sensitivity, along with his dramatic, if somewhat feminine, looks would make him perfect for the role. At 5'10" including his hair, he could just about play opposite Sabah if she were barefoot.

Sabah herself was totally against the idea as she had made no bones about telling me: 'He's lovely, Zee, but he's just not sexy enough, is he?'

'He attracts a lot of attention when we go out,' I said. 'He's a bit like an Asian James Dean, don't you think? Lots of people would say he's handsome.'

'Pretty,' she corrected me, 'and he can't play straight like James Dean. There's no way he'll be believable.'

In my heart of hearts, I also felt that, while Ravi was an exceptional choreographer, he was only average as an actor. So, on the basis of all this, I had not said yes to him. On the other hand,

I had not exactly said no either, thinking that it did, after all, to some extent depend who we ended up with for Shahjehan – plus common sense would suggest we keep Ravi in hand, in case we ended up with nobody.

But at lunchtime, after another morning of non-starters, Ravi tabled his request again.

'You know, we do have at least part of a solution here. Have you thought any more about me as a possible Suleman?'

His tone was breezy, but his eyes, as he looked from me to Sabah, betrayed his fragility.

'It's a great idea, Ravi, and you know I'd love you do it,' I lied. 'But I don't think we can make a decision until we see what the options are for Shahjehan.'

Sabah nodded over her sandwich. 'See how all the parts fit together,' she said, with a lame thumbs-up sign.

But my best friend was not giving up. 'Well, at this rate, we're not going to have anyone for either part! You need to start making some decisions. At least if you fix Suleman, you'll have two out of three characters and you can cast Shahjehan around me and Sabah.'

I riffled through the audition notes for that day *1. Mr Bean 2. Can't pass for Asian 3. Good-ish but stoned – will be trouble 4. Can't dance (or act) 5. Not tall enough*, and had to admit that Ravi had a point. Plus he was now looking at me so pleadingly that I couldn't bear it any more.

I took a deep breath. 'OK,' I said, ignoring Sabah's warning kick, 'but *provisionally*. And on the understanding that, if we find a perfect Shahjehan, and the three of you don't match up, *we'll have to rethink it*.'

Ravi didn't wait for me to finish before leaping into my arms. 'Thank you! You won't regret it!' He leant across the table to hug

Sabah. 'Oh, it's going to be so wonderful on tour together.'

Sabah threw me a furious glance. Clearly, despite my attempt at a caveat, for Ravi the deal was done and there would be no circumstances that could justify an about-turn. *Please God,* I prayed, *let this work out. Let me find a Shahjehan who makes it work out* – all the time knowing that the only Shahjehan who could make this work would be someone who was as miscast in his role as my best friend was as Suleman.

And then, in the afternoon, Dan walked in. We had not had his CV in advance – his agent had just sent him along, he explained, and would it be OK if he gave a reading?

So he read (acceptably), and he danced (well), and he looked great with Sabah, and it was obvious to all three of us that he would make a fine Shahjehan.

Unfortunately, it was also obvious to two of us in the room that Ravi did not stand up as a credible love-rival. After a hurried (and unhelpful) conference in the toilets, Sabah disappeared, leaving me alone to broach the subject with him. And, when he refused to accept any of my casting arguments, accused me of betraying our friendship in favour of a complete stranger, said if he couldn't play the part he wouldn't do the choreography either, and finally burst into tears and stormed away, it was obvious to me that he would hate me for ever.

Sufya

I HAD GONE TO MY parents' home that evening to try to talk science with Dad, hoping he could help me find a less meandering path through my research. But on arriving at the house I found no such discussion was possible because of an event of terrifying familial significance: Dad had taped *Horizon* over *Chaudhvin Ka Chand*. Unlike Zarina who, in the intervening years since the film first appalled our childhood trio, had inexplicably capitulated to Mum's view that it was a masterpiece of romance, I had never been taken in by the movie's veiled shenanigans. But even I knew instantly that Dad had made an unthinkable error and would pay dearly for it. Indeed, he had already started.

'She won't talk to me, *beta*,' he said helplessly as he opened the front door. 'I don't understand… we have seen that film so many times. And when I explained this to her, she went and locked the bedroom door and now she won't come out even for her favourite

Tandoori Junction aloo pakoras.'

From upstairs came the slamming of a door as Mum announced her emergence from her room. 'Is that Zarina?' she moaned faintly from the upstairs landing. 'Sufya? My head is aching terribly. Bring chai upstairs. I cannot bear to look at your papa. Calls himself a scientist, but can't use his eyes. *Hai Allah…*' she continued in a weak voice just loud enough for Dad to hear. 'What did I do to get stuck with this man who doesn't give a damn for me…' Her voice faded as she disappeared back into the bedroom, still ranting, and banged the door behind her.

'I'll make her some tea,' I said to Dad, who looked stricken. 'You take it easy. She'll calm down, she always does.'

'OK, *beta*. And sorry that I can't talk monkeys with you this evening – there is an emergency at BestCo and I'm having to go back to the office for a meeting. I don't want to leave your mummy like this but she will be OK with you, *hai na, beta*? Try to make her have pakoras.' Dad shook his head in genuine bemusement. 'I just don't understand why this film was so important. Did you hear about bombs at the American embassies – explosions in Kenya and Tanzania? Some new terrorist mastermind is raising his moustache at Clinton. As you would say, the big monkeys have their fingers on the big triggers. All this is happening in the world, so why should your mother get so upset about this old film she has seen a thousand times? *I just don't understand.*'

Of course Dad did not understand. After all, he did not understand the first thing about Mum. Over thirty-five years, he had slowly deduced through painful trial and error some of the things she liked – such as deep-fried, spicy snacks – and often resorted to such material offerings to pacify her, but he himself did not share the same tastes or idiosyncrasies. And though he loved her very tenderly, he had utterly failed in all their years together to *understand* even one of the things that made Mum tick, trying instead to bring her closer to him with the only method at his disposal: rationality.

And Mum, in response, had become more impulsive, unpredictable and eccentric as the years had gone by. The more Dad tried to reason away her notions, the more she would reach for ever more extreme ideas, constantly trying to provoke him with bizarre acts of superstition and witchcraft. (Dad, of course, still could not see the message she was sending him, deciding instead to smile indulgently at her unpredictability and retreat to his study.) It was an all-out and seemingly never-ending escalation of oppositional qualities on both sides. I felt irritated with both of them. What were they doing together anyway?

And yet, Dad would sometimes tell Zarina and me how, back in Lahore before they were married, Mum was famed as the beauty of the local district and how he had secretly wished that he could attract her attention, but had never thought it possible. And he would tell us about the day when a message came to his parents via a mutual acquaintance, that Mum's family might look favourably upon it if a *rishta* came from his home. And when he spoke about that day, recalling the soaring joy that brimmed over in his heart upon hearing this news, his normally unemotional voice would fill with an astonished gratitude, as though he could still hardly believe the enormity of the fortune that had been granted him.

'On that day, I learned that some of the most important things in life are beyond science, *beta*,' Dad would murmur, wonderingly. But it may well have been that he had never seen the point of saying such a thing to Mum.

I sighed as I made the tea and warmed pakoras, dreading the

emotional torrent that I knew awaited me when I went upstairs. Was true understanding between two people ever possible, I wondered, thinking back to the events at Ishq? After that wonderful evening, H and I had wandered out into the night exhilarated with our triumph – the triumph, after all, of love – and I confess that my body was longing for the natural progression of our new closeness. I was convinced that we must both be of the same intention when H shyly offered to take me home. Yet on the doorstep of my flat, he had kissed me rather quickly and shuffled away, leaving me utterly taken aback and filled with self-doubt. *Just what was it that was going on between us anyway? Could I have read the situation so wrongly?*

'How long does it take to make tea?' groaned Mum from her prone position on the bed when I entered the room. 'And not even hot! Zarina knows how to make my tea, but nobody else in this family gives a damn…'

I stifled my irritation at the old themes. Since my Loss, Mum would never reproach me directly for past crimes but, whenever she was upset, she would mutter well-worn phrases which – though indirect – worked like black magic to conjure paralysing guilt in me. 'Zarina knows how to make my tea!' instantly told the whole horror story: me leaving home to do 'whatever I wanted' in uncaring dereliction of my duty… Mum facing censure and isolation from her 'friends' for my behaviour… Zarina staying in the family home for years after her own graduation, paying off the bottomless deficit in daughterly duty left by me. Yes, I had hurt and let down Mum beyond measure, and I had left my little sister to make it up to her. And in so doing, I had bound them together as eternal allies against me.

'Do you want me to make another?' I asked, determinedly

pressing the genie back into the bottle.

'Leave it! Just pass me the pakoras. Where is your papa? Gone out enjoying himself while I am suffering? *Ya Allah!* How did this happen to me?'

'Mum, we'll get you another copy of the movie, don't worry,' I tried to soothe. 'It was an accident. Dad didn't mean it.'

'Mean it, *kya*?' fumed Mum. 'You think I care about a new copy! *Main kitni akeli hoon!*'

'You're *not* alone, Mum...' I said, my own tears suddenly welling up. 'You feel like Dad doesn't understand you, but he does try...and he does...*care*.'

'All that man cares about is bacteria! Who would have thought that I would marry such a creature! *Kya kismet nikli!*'

H appeared in my head. What did *he* care about? *Why* had he left me on the doorstep? I put the thought away. Something else occurred to me.

'Mum,' I ventured. 'What if that angry feeling you have were a person? Can you imagine what it would look like?'

'Like a woman on fire!' returned Mum without hesitation. 'Burning on her husband's pyre, like a Hindu widow!' She closed her eyes.

As a child, I had learned to stifle the anxiety that Mum's melodramas evoked in me, but as I watched her now, apparently picturing in her mind's eye the 'woman on fire' that personified her anger, I was shaken from my usual immunity to her emotional contagion. There was something alarming about the way in which she lay back on the pillows, her chin lifted as though she were braced against some unseen hand gripping the back of her neck, a film of perspiration on her upper lip. It was, I realised with a slight shiver, almost as though the heat of the invisible pyre was too close for comfort.

'How I hate her terrible clinging smell!' she murmured now, turning her head away suddenly as though to escape the image. 'How I wish she would become fire and smoke and be gone, but she is still flesh, burning flesh! Why doesn't she close her eyes?'

By now I was horrified and had to make an effort to steady my voice: 'And … if she could speak to you, what would she say?'

'She would not speak, she would *scream*!'

'What would she scream?'

'She would scream: *Ye kya kiya tum ne?* What is this you have done to me? This wasn't what I asked for! What I prayed for! *This is not the one!*'

I was struggling to understand Mum. Her voice seemed to be dragging up from deep inside her, and her words were slurred. What did she mean, 'This is not the one!'?

'What's going on?' said Zarina opening the bedroom door and walking in.

Mum's eyes opened with a start, and I saw there were tears in them. She looked from Zarina to me in panic.

'*What's going on?*' repeated Zarina, much less casually.

Mum's eyes pleaded with me. 'Dad taped over *Chaudhvin Ka Chand*, and Mum's upset,' I said flatly.

'What?' Zarina understood immediately the consequences of this news, and rushed over to give Mum a hug. 'How *could* he? What is *wrong* with him?'

'Don't talk about your papa like that!' sniffed Mum from inside Zarina's arms, but she sounded a little pleased. 'Anyway, it's good you are home now. Later, I need some help with a *wazifa* for Auntie Mehbooba's new conservatory! She has had such an awful time with these builders.'

'Of course I'll help,' said Zarina, cuddling Mum as though she were a small child.

'I'll make some more tea,' I mumbled, and left them to the warmth of their exclusive embrace.

⁂

In the 1980s, some of the earliest MRI scans confirmed that the parts of the human brain which activate when an individual expresses aggression are those which, in evolutionary terms, are the most ancient. These are the parts of the brain which our species shares with far earlier life forms such as reptiles.

Aggression being arguably the primary survival skill, and our bodies having emerged from the primordial sludge only because at every stage we must have been pre-eminently better at it than all our fellow beings, I had begun to speculate for the purposes of my research on whether it might be useful to consider each member of our species as the literal embodiment of aggression. Clearly, though, alongside our honing of our capacity for dominating other creatures, we had also evolved as social animals, naturally co-existing in communities. How was that possible? Did it not imply that our species' entire social – and 'moral' – code might have emerged as a means of managing a profoundly aggressive nature?

Later that night, I found myself transcribing the conversation I had had with Mum in the bedroom, and reading it over and over:

Me: What if that angry feeling you have were a person? Can you imagine what it would look like?

Mum: Like a woman on fire! Burning on her husband's funeral pyre, like a Hindu widow. How I hate her terrible, clinging smell! How I wish she would become fire and smoke and be gone, but *she is still flesh, burning flesh! Why doesn't she close her eyes?*

Me: And if she could speak to you, what would she say?

Mum: She would not speak, she would *scream*!

Me: What would she scream?

Mum: She would scream: *Ye kya kiya tum ne?* What is this you have done to me? This wasn't what I asked for! What I prayed for! *This isn't the one!*

Saturday 15 August 1998

Zarina

'OK, FABIO, THANKS very much!' I said, aware that I was speaking unduly loudly, in order not to sound flustered. 'Quite a demanding piece…'

'Yeah,' Fabio slumped into the chair opposite and took a long drink from his two-litre Volvic bottle, 'you gotta give it everything.'

He had certainly done that. His interpretation of 'Friends, Romans, countrymen' had been a bewildering combination of unintelligible muttering and full throttle roaring – two gears he had spent the allocated two minutes shifting violently and randomly between, before eventually falling heavily at Sabah's feet, making her scrape back her chair in alarm. (*The Godfather meets Godzilla*, I had scribbled next to his name.)

'So, you've had a chance to look through a few scenes from the play.' I gestured towards the papers which were supplied to each candidate on arrival, and which, for some reason, were now blackened and dog-eared. Had Fabio *worried* them?

'Yeah. It's a great script I could really get stuck into this.'

Sabah gulped.

'Great! Right! Let's have a look at Act 3, Scene 10,' I continued with energy, 'which is the clash between Shahjehan and Suleman. The ghost of Mumtaz has visited both men, to persuade them to stop building the Taj. She accuses them of imprisoning her in a cage of stone, instead of allowing her spirit to be free. Shahjehan is heartbroken that Mumtaz appears to be rejecting his love, but when he finds out that Suleman has spoken with her too, he suspects the Sufi of some treachery and summons him to account. Sabah will read Shahjehan.'

Fabio grinned and wiped his mouth. 'Wicked.'

Sabah slowly sat up straighter, and fixed Fabio with an accusing look, every inch a Mughal emperor. Even though it was the hundredth time I'd seen her effect one of these economical transformations, I couldn't help smiling. She was brilliant.

'*You, conniving dervish, have poisoned the spirit of our Queen against us. What onçe she delighted in, now sickens her. You have deceived her with false philosophies and artful words. Else would she never take pleasure in the companionship of a slave!*'

'*The spirit does not answer the bidding of man,*' Fabio slurred, in Godfather mode again. '*When my lady appears to me, it is because the words of this humble diskipull—*'

'Disciple!' I interjected.

'Oh yeah, wicked...*it is because the words of this humble disciple gladden her soul. His Majesty must fear no betrayal – for our companionship is truly essence without form. Love that is burdened with the base metal of desire cannot transcend death.*'

'*Wretched monk, do you presume to speak of love?*' Sabah

thundered. *'You, who know nothing of the joys we have shared with our Queen! Who can understand the essence that does not rejoice in the form? Desire, a base metal? All creation, all reality, is desire made manifest! But you have no reality, Suleman – you who can count neither blissful nights of union, nor children.'*

'I am content. This humble servant was not worthy of Her living Majesty. Though we did rejoice in the sharing of verse I never offended her favour with an ignoble claim. Through separation I strengthened the purity of my devotion. But now she is flesh no longer. And I beg the King of the World not to lay false claim to the realm of the spirit. To you her earthly body, TO ME HER UNENDING SOUL!'

My heart leaped six inches in my chest as I realised that Godzilla was back. Before I could utter a syllable, Fabio had seized Sabah by the shoulders, hauled her up and, immobilising her slender frame with one hairy forearm, he shrieked, *'ONLY THE TRUE LOVER GLIMPSES THE BELOVED BEHIND THE VEIL!'*

Sabah whimpered, as I jumped to my feet and waved my script in the air: 'OK, that's enough! Hey, *Fabio! Cut!'*

Fabio looked from me to the trembling Sabah and let go. 'Sorry, darlin', yeah?' He grinned sheepishly. 'Got a bit passionate there.'

As Fabio departed, wiping sweat from his face with a Charlton FC towel he apparently carried with him for the purpose, Sabah took a deep breath, said 'Coffee,' and shot out of the room.

Six o'clock. There was no one left to see.

So much for last-minute miracles: served us right for organising another day of auditions when we knew that we had already scraped the bottom of the barrel. Frankly, if we hadn't had the space booked and Sabah wasn't depending on me to show positive leadership, I'd have cancelled the whole thing – especially after I'd spent most of the night awake, replaying the awful scene with Ravi in my head.

You know what I think? The only reason you're so set on some big hunk playing Suleman is because, for you, Suleman's the real hero – the heroine's 'soulmate!' It's Heathrow, isn't it? Why don't you just admit it? For you, no one else is going to be right in that part. So don't tell me it's not personal.

I had been counting on the play to provide an escape from my personal life. But, if Ravi was right, all I had done was bring my personal life to the play – and I had ended up losing my best friend. Heathrow might have blasted in and out, but the shockwaves were still spreading: how many more holes were yet to open around me?

Sabah now reappeared, balancing a huge piece of chocolate cake on top of two coffee mugs.

'You OK?'

I looked at the frothy cappuccino she handed me, and contemplated drowning myself in it.

Sabah sighed. 'You know, it had to happen sooner or later. If it hadn't been you, it would have been another director.'

'Yes, but I'm his best friend. He was counting on me to have faith in him. Especially with all that stuff he's been going through about coming out. Pass me that cake.'

'So now what?'

'Well, we've got our Shahjehan, at least. I spoke to Dan last night and he accepted. And the two of you look great together. So we just keep looking for a Suleman.'

'Sounds good… Can I have some of that cake?'

'*Lovers, when you set your course with faith…*'

The words were spoken from the doorway…or had they, perhaps, simply stolen across the air? It was a familiar voice, the tone passionate yet controlled. I put my fork down slowly.

'*Lovers, when you set your course with faith…*'

Heathrow, speaking more insistently now, was walking into the room. In his hand was the sheaf of audition papers, but his eyes were fixed on me.

'Er…' Sabah was frantically riffling through her script to find the right page, but I knew the scene by heart – *Flashback: Suleman in the rose garden, calls to Queen Mumtaz through the wall of the hareem.* Before I could stop myself, I had spoken her line.

'Your barque will guide the stars.'

'When the moth parts the air with devoted wings…' Heathrow now offered.

'Does not the candle bend towards it?'

I could feel the Queen's excitement beneath every rejoinder. The Sufi had come to share poetry with her once more – each of them, though never having laid eyes on the other, hungering for the intimacy of their secret communion through verse.

Heathrow reached the centre of the room and stopped. *'In the presence of the Beloved, all emptiness is filled, and every meeting is a journey's end.'*

But today Mumtaz would dare more: *'When shall it be so with us? Must we remain entombed in allegory?'*

I felt the brittleness in my delivery – the words laced with bitterness and frustration. But Heathrow did not flinch.

'To receive a friend one must step into the courtyard,' he said.

It was a proposition, as I had been explaining all day, to a succession of baffled actors. And when Heathrow said the line with the quiet intensity I had briefly seen on the night of his return, I felt certain he was speaking through the script to me.

This was magic, but whose? And if I spoke, would I break the spell?

'Then let there be no wall between us,' I breathed at last, coming

out from behind the table, as the Queen entered the rose garden.

'And no more words,' Heathrow returned softly. He took a step towards me.

Sabah clapped loudly. 'Wonderful! Fabulous!'

'Sorry,' Heathrow said, with some embarrassment, as if he had only just realised she was in the room. 'I'm afraid I'm barging in… I picked up the pages outside.'

'Oh – this is Heathrow,' I said, attempting to pull myself together. 'Not an actor… You're not, are you?'

A thought was forming. Could this, after all, be the effect of the *wazifa*? Could magic be working in mysterious ways to bring him to me? It wouldn't be so far-fetched for Heathrow to act in my play – we had done it all the time as children.

Heathrow shook his head. 'I wish I was, after reading that. The architect who's also a Sufi poet! How did you come up with him?'

Was he joking? After the way he had read the scene?

'Well, you introduced us all to Rumi, of course – which is where I learned that Sufis use the language of lovers to talk about the soul's relationship with God.' Somehow I was managing to sound in control.

Heathrow smiled. 'But by making the poetry into the voice of Suleman you've reversed the metaphor. The soul yearning for the infinite becomes a man reaching for a woman. Brilliant!'

What were we doing, chit-chatting about my artistic vision? Had we not, a second ago, been speaking the words of our hearts? My ears buzzed in confusion. If he hadn't come to audition, what was he doing here?

Sabah, who had been listening, open-mouthed, to Heathrow's analysis, now waved her script. 'Except you didn't get to the end… *Mumtaz emerges into the garden,'* she read rapidly. *'Now give me your hand, my Pilgrim. (They join hands and come together, a long look, then Suleman wrenches himself away): Forgive me my lady—'*

'*—I am sworn to a different path,'* Heathrow finished. 'So he... leaves?'

What was the strange look that crossed his face as he stared down at the page in his hand? Realisation? Regret?

'It's just a draft,' I found myself saying. 'It could all change. In fact...'

'Hi, Zee, any luck today? Hi, Sabah.' Sufya was standing in the doorway, a little out of breath. She looked at Heathrow, and automatically lifted a hand to smooth her hair. 'Hi, H.'

And just like that, I understood. I looked at Heathrow and realised what that expression had been. Guilt.

'So, are you ready?' Sufya turned to me impatiently. 'We've only got an hour to find Mum a birthday present before the shops close – don't tell me you forgot, Zee?'

'Sorry... I must have.'

I got out of the door ahead of them, leaving Heathrow holding the script. Sabah hurried after me, still entranced. '*Is he going out with your sister?*' she whispered.

'Apparently.'

'*Day-amn!*' Sabah said, in her best Texan. 'Looks like she got her hero, even if we ain't got ours!'

Sunday 16 August 1998

Sufya

DOG-OWNERS TESTIFY that they can tell when their pet has broken a house rule, even if they themselves have not witnessed a transgression, because the dog skulks around, *acting ashamed.* Many non-human primates, too, show signs of 'feeling bad' if they cross boundaries laid down by the group.

This characteristic, however, applies only to social animals where the ability to follow rules can have a direct effect on community survival. In order to hunt effectively as a pack, dogs must strictly observe group rules, and dog society has a powerful hierarchy to punish transgressors. In such species, natural selection will favour individuals with a talent for prioritising social rules. Even more favoured might be an individual who has 'internalised' the rules – who 'feels bad' about rule-breaking even if none of his peers know about the crime – perhaps the origins of what we, in our own species, call a 'conscience'. Such an animal will 'feel bad' about breaking even a rule which is in direct conflict with its own individual interests.

For the first year of our 'relationship' at Oxford, I refused to have sex with Steve. It was not that anyone had ever sat me down and told me that sex outside marriage would be a crime, or a sin, or was not allowed. Apart from the terse command of '*No boyfriend–girlfriend!*' uttered perhaps a handful of times when we were too young to care about its meaning, it was completely beyond Mum to mention such unutterables as sex and virginity to her daughters, and certainly Dad would never have considered it anything to do with him, if indeed he considered it at all. It was not even that my personal religious beliefs made it a matter of conscience. (In fact, after a couple of years of sudden and fervent Islam in my early teens, I had descended gradually, and painfully, into agnosticism, at first modifying my 'beliefs' in the rationalist way that Dad had, to reconcile them with his scientific training, but finally discarding them altogether as I became convinced that certain passages in the Quran – and, for that matter, in the books of all major world religions – simply could not, with the best will in the world, be interpreted as anything but anti-female.)

No, it was not down to religion, but rather to the fact that by some mysterious osmosis from my home environment – and despite myriad contradictory messages from my British education and white friends – I had successfully *internalised* the notion that I must not have sex outside marriage. Of course I understood that if my parents found out they would be deeply disappointed, but – more than that – it *felt* wrong. Considering the strength of my desire for Steve, and the biological imperatives of my late teens, plus the environment of pleasurable laissez-faire that, despite the new threat of HIV, guided our peers, this inner sensation of 'wrong' was quite a testament to my skills as a profoundly social animal – one that could put group rules above her own biological interests. The Expectations, by their very unspoken-ness, their *unspeakability*, were far more powerful than if they had been overtly stated and externally enforced. They had infiltrated my psyche by stealth and reinvented themselves as my own.

Instead of intercourse with Steve, there was endless unsatiating kissing, all the more maddened and maddening for its despair of leading anywhere. There were also considerable amounts of fully or partially clothed writhing on student bedspreads, (but never *under* the covers). Night after night and morning after morning, we would drive ourselves into a nerve-frayed frenzy of longing, without release or hope of release. During holidays we would not see each other, because my family could not know about us, and our enforced separation was all the more agonised and heightened because our physical need for each other was not met during term-time. Afterwards, I had wondered if our feelings for each other would have lasted half as long had we been able to discharge our lust in a more natural way.

Why Steve went along with it all, I still couldn't fathom. Perhaps with the inexperience of youth and the relative intercultural innocence of an impoverished boyhood in Northern Ireland, he didn't realise how abnormal it was. Perhaps he really was in love with me in some unusually abstract way, and clung to some hope, despite what I had told him, of us marrying and living happy ever after. Or perhaps he simply believed I would give in to his not inconsiderable charms eventually. Whatever it was that made him stay with me for that first year, the strangled nature of our relationship gradually began to take a toll on him.

From the light-hearted boy he was when I first caught sight of him holding forth in the college bar, making every one laugh with his left-field Belfast humour, he became quieter, more serious and more insular. As time went by, he stopped wanting to go out with other friends, preferring to spend time alone with me, and wanting me around all the time, even when he was studying. I began to feel a little stifled by the intense coupledom, and, sensing this, he became watchful and sensitive. He imagined that I was interested in other men, and I had to spend hours reassuring him. I was hurting him by pulling away, he would tell me, and I, young and flattered by the drama, would curb my impulse to escape, instead flinging myself – the tragic beloved – on the dagger of our doomed twosome. There would be more agonised writhing on the bedspread, tears, confessions and forgiveness. It was awful, but compelling.

Late in her first term at Cambridge, I went to visit Zarina. When I had been at home the previous Easter, I had said nothing to her about Steve, not wanting to put her in the position of having to lie to our parents. Over the summer, I had told the family I had to study for a fictional dissertation and that I was not coming home at all. It had been hard to keep such a secret from my sister, when for so long we had told each other everything, and I knew she must be perplexed at how distant I must have seemed. But there was nothing I could do – I felt estranged from the innocence of my previous life at home, when we – conflicted as our generation of British Muslim children were doomed to be – were at least still on the same side of the fissure between 'our culture' and the rest of society. For me now, my parents had somehow – without their knowledge – transmuted from the benign annoyances they had been in our childhood into sinister enemies of my adult happiness and freedom, and, close as we had been, I was not sure that Zarina would understand any of this.

But I had only been hanging out in her new bedsit for half an hour before, unable to help myself (and perhaps assuming that having escaped the family home and well into university life, Zarina would be experiencing some similar dilemma), I found myself spilling the whole tragic yarn – how much Steve loved me, how much I loved him, how it had gone on for a year, how painful it was, what a relief it was to finally tell her.

She listened with fitting attention for such revelations but, while she seemed sympathetic, I noticed she did not quite give the response I had hoped for. The old Zarina would have been goggle-eyed at the drama and captivated by the very idea of thwarted love. Breathlessly and helplessly, she would have been *on my side*.

But as I came to the end of my confession, and heard my tale with the newness of my little sister's ears, it suddenly seemed to me that I sounded a little *fraudulent*. And, instead of whole-hearted support, did I detect a little *contempt* in her hastily lowered eyes? Was it me, or was it she, that was no longer communicating with our former honesty?

It turned out that I had been right to worry. As Michaelmas Term ended, I left my parents a hurried answerphone message to say I was staying an extra two weeks in Oxford to attend an optional specialist course. Then, for over a week, I didn't ring home at all, unless it was a time when I knew nobody would be home, so that I could leave a dutiful message on the machine without having to answer questions.

But ten days into the Christmas holiday, Steve and I were wrapped up in a blanket together on the window-seat of my college room, soaking up some pale December sunshine, when there was a knock on the door. 'Come in!' he had called out, laughingly extricating himself from one of our endless kissing sessions. The door opened and Mum came in, closely followed by Dad.

'Get packed!' Mum had ordered, and overcome with shame and guilt I had done as I was told. After rather bravely introducing himself to a stony silence from Mum and a brief nod from Dad, Steve looked at me for help, and receiving none, said he would 'leave you to it, then'. I did not say goodbye to him before I was taken home for the rest of the holidays.

⁂

'It's a classic case of *Homo sapiens* getting in the way,' said Jade authoritatively when I wondered aloud whether elsewhere in the animal kingdom any male could be found who would successfully attract a potential sexual partner only to abandon her before the act. 'Top Monkey must be chomping at the bit.'

'Well, I hope so,' I said glumly, thinking that she and I had perhaps had a little too much wine. 'Maybe he's just old-fashioned or romantic about these things. Or maybe,' my heart sank a little, 'he's got some religious objection. After all, he *was* brought up like me – a kind of a Muslim – I just don't know what he thinks about all that.'

It wasn't possible that H, now in his mid-thirties, with all his travels and exposure to the world, still subscribed to the no-sex-outside-marriage group rule, I was sure. But then why had he shuffled away from my doorstep again last night after we'd been shopping with Zarina for Mum's birthday present? (The two of us had stopped for dinner in Clapham, talking all the while with the ease of our familiar communication, and then, once again, he had offered to take me home.) Could it be that, years later, he retained some sediment of the internalised guilt about sex that had run so deep in me for so long? Perhaps that would explain the precipitousness of his disastrous secret marriage to the Iranian girl. But how did this square with the independence of mind that I had always felt was his central character?

'It doesn't really matter what *Homo sapiens* thinks,' said Jade emphatically. 'It's his *feelings* that are the most likely problem.'

'By which I suppose you mean he doesn't really want me?'

'Not at all. Of course he wants you, and more to the point Top Monkey wants you. It's just good old *Homo sapiens* performance anxiety that's getting in the way – he's terrified he won't satisfy you. But don't worry, all you have to do is wait. The male hormones will just build up until they overcome the fear. Top Monkey will take over. And that is what I call an inevitable law of nature.'

I laughed at Jade's analysis, but, while she was often right about such matters, I found it hard to imagine that H, who had walked onto stage in front of several hundred people and used nothing but his silent presence to soothe a hysterical mob – H who had spoken of 'a good relationship' with his 'monstrous' anger – would be somehow at the mercy of an emotion so flimsy and vain as Jade's 'performance anxiety'. Our feelings for one another seemed so natural, and H had seemed to recognise and manage all my fearful moments so perfectly. Was it possible that he had fearful moments of his own, moments he could not manage perfectly?

Last night, I had dreamed about the bin again. The metal pedal bin, with the yellow plastic liner, and the medical stickers on the lid. I did not know if this bin was something I had actually seen in the operating theatre – after all, at the time I had opted for the general anaesthetic – or whether it had in fact been subsequently invented by my subconscious. As usual in the nightmare, I pleaded with them not to put her in there, but they did not seem to hear me.

I woke up and lay in the dark, trying to calm my breathing. I wondered what exactly H knew about my Loss. I had not yet found the moment to ask him, and it was unlikely that Uncle Bogie would have felt able to talk about anything so indelicate as my damn bloody abortion, even though he had been there that night twelve years ago when I had screamed the truth at my shocked, assembled family, shattering once and for all those beloved Expectations.

Strange how things turn out, I thought. What if I had just slept with Steve throughout that second year at Oxford? Wouldn't I have just got it out of my system like all the other sisters and brothers were doing with their secret *gora* partners, and then, having 'had my fun', proceeded innocently with an arranged marriage? If I'd allowed myself that invisible transgression, would I then have felt the need to confide in Zarina, and would she in turn have felt it necessary to go and blab to our parents? Would Mum have gone bananas, or threatened suicide? Would I then have terminated our relationship so ruthlessly, driving Steve to take that razor to his wrists, so that, afterwards, in the drama of the moment, overcome with guilt and the desire for some healing closeness, I had ended up having that fateful one-off sex with him anyway?

And if none of that had happened, and I had not suffered my Loss alone for so long before I finally told them, would Mum and Dad have ever given up trying to get me to fulfil the Expectations, and faced instead the ugly censure of their friends and relatives? And would Zarina have become so bitter if she had not perceived me to have 'ruined her chances', and sentenced her to a life of trying to make it up to our parents?

It was as though by keeping my own *Homo sapiens* in charge, by denying myself the natural expression of my Top Monkey desires, I had unleashed a torrent of monkey demons – wild, destructive forces that had spread into the lives of my family, my lover, my community and beyond.

And yet, I wondered guiltily, if events had been different, would I still have been available when H returned from his travels to be with me? After all, now that the two of us were together, did not all that had gone before have that unscientific quality of 'meant-to-be'?

Zarina

DAD WAS REALLY unbelievable. One would think, after the *Chaudhvin Ka Chand* incident, that he would have gone out of his way to get Mum a lovely present for her birthday, without being reminded. Yet, here he was, asking what I was doing with wrapping paper and Sellotape.

'Dad, *please* tell me you haven't forgotten!' I was still raw from the events of yesterday and in no mood for his blithering.

'I've been so busy at work: some people are saying they have got food poisoning from BestCo pork, and we've all been firefighting…' Dad looked at me helplessly, his eyes begging me to give him a clue.

'Oh for God's sake, Mum's birthday! Your wife's birthday! Remember?' Why did he do this stuff all the time? His forgetfulness was neither harmless nor endearing as far as Mum was concerned: it was insensitive and hurtful.

'Zarina, *beta*!' Dad wailed in dismay. 'I wrote it on a Post-it note!

I was determined not to forget this year! Where can it have gone?'

'I don't know, Dad. But maybe you should stop worrying about that, and go and buy something. You've still got half an hour before everyone comes.'

Dad blundered out the door, still lamenting his mistake, and despairing of finding anything at such short notice. I shook my head and continued wrapping the turquoise pashmina – Mum's favourite colour. Sufya and I had found it in the first shop we went into, which was a relief because I didn't feel like hanging around with her and Heathrow all evening. The two of them were ridiculous, doing their best to act like nothing was going on, she discussing jewellery and handbags with me as if he wasn't there, and he pretending to look at sequinned shoes.

Sufya gave me her half of the money, and I went to pay. Behind the assistant's enormous backcomb I could see them both by the door – impatient to get on with their date, probably. There had been, scarcely an hour earlier, a brief moment of dazzling, rainbow-shimmering perfection. *To receive a friend you must step into the courtyard*... But he had not come to see me: he had come to meet her. There was nothing for it but to go home.

'I'll leave you two alone,' I said pointedly, as soon as we came out of the shop.

'You don't have to,' Sufya said with affected lightness, a glassy, dishonest look in her eyes. Heathrow mumbled something deprecating and incomprehensible. I stared at them: what a pair of shuffling idiots – neither of them would meet my eye.

'Right. Bye,' I said, and went to get the bus.

At least Heathrow wasn't expected at today's festivities – I couldn't have faced him. I finished wrapping, and took a last look round the living room. Picking up Dad's newspaper and specs,

I glimpsed my reflection in the showcase (which housed our graduation photos and a model of the Taj Mahal) and grimaced. I hated looking at myself in shalwar kameez, a garment which, in my view, only suited the well-rounded and voluptuous. I still fitted into the one we had made for Eid (under protest) when I was sixteen, and it hung around me like a slithery pillowcase on a long-haired scarecrow, my bony wrists sticking out of the ends.

The alternative, however, was wearing the à la mode ensemble Ayesha had brought back, one for me, one for Sufya, from her last trip to Pakistan: 'You both look *so* much better when you wear your *own* clothes! *Hai na,* Auntie Ji?' *Your own.* A term bandied about by Pakistanis – your own clothes, your own language, your own people – when they really meant *their own.* It was a tacit agreement dating back years that Sufya and I would respond to such makeover attempts by digging out our old shalwar kameezes to look doubly ludicrous at the next family event – a brief which the polished glass of the showcase told me I had more than fulfilled today.

But a moment later the doorbell rang, and Sufya was revealed in the porch wearing her jeans. Of course. What had I expected, after last night's treachery?

'It's in here,' she muttered irritably, indicating the stuffed rucksack she held under her arm. 'I was too embarrassed to wear it on the way. Let me in!' I stood aside and she shot upstairs. 'Hurry up!' I called after her.

Next to arrive was Uncle Bogie, who bawled, '*Assalam-u-alaikum, beta! Wah!* You look like a proper Pakistani girl! Give this to your mummy!' and handed me a heavy brown cardboard box. He strode into the living room and switched the TV on to the cricket, while I went upstairs, shaking the box dubiously. In the old days, Bogie used to turn up with extravagant gifts of Italian shirts and French perfume. Nowadays it was more likely to be tapes of the latest Quran translation.

Of course plenty of wayward Pakistani men rediscovered religion in their middle age. But in Bogie's case, the transformation had been characteristically dramatic. A decade earlier he had been in Italy visiting friends from the old movie days, and embarked on a torrid affair with a young starlet, who, alas, as it turned out, was only using him for his contacts in the industry. Within a month, this inamorata announced that she was leaving him for a buck-toothed assistant cameraman, driving our uncle, on a starry Neapolitan night, to put a loaded gun to his chest with only the Holy Book in between. 'If God wants me to live, he will let me live!' he had shouted as he pulled the trigger. The bullet lodged itself in the body of the Quran, and a split second later, Bogie was reborn as the bane of our lives.

Mum was in her room, putting the finishing touches to her make-up. As I watched her purse her lips and apply her favourite Avon Berry Spice, I was overcome with nostalgia. How many times had I stood there as a little girl, watching her get ready, touching the organzas and chenilles of her kameezes, sniffing her perfume, and dreaming of growing up and inheriting her famous beauty. (A legacy which had not materialised.) I caught her eye in the mirror, and smiled.

'What are you wearing?' She turned around in alarm. 'And what is that?'

'Uncle said to give it to you.' I passed it to her. 'Watch out, it's a bit heavy.'

Mum sat at the dressing table, resting the box on her lap. She brushed a hand across it, then looked up at me.

'Well, go on then!' I urged, sitting down next to her. 'It's only going to be a bumper box of headscarves or something.'

Mum frowned. Then she opened the box. 'Oh!' she breathed softly, bringing her hands to her cheeks. I peered over to get a look: a DVD of *Chaudhvin Ka Chand* with a little satin rosette taped to it, rested on a silver machine which, on closer inspection, turned out to be a DVD player.

'Great!' I said. 'We need one of these. Now Dad can't tape over it. Good old Uncle Bogie!' Mum said nothing. She was turning the DVD over in her hands, looking at the beautiful photographs of Waheeda Rahman and Guru Dutt.

'Firdaus?' Dad's voice came from outside. He tapped tentatively on the door.

'Quick, put this away!' Mum said. 'So expensive. Your papa might feel bad.'

'Serves him right,' I protested.

But Mum had already slid the box under the bed and was calling '*Haan*, Ahmed, come in!'

Dad entered shyly, holding a box of Ambala sweets and a tomato plant from Woolworths. He smiled at me and winked, mightily pleased with himself.

'Oh! So many gifts!' exclaimed Mum, lifting her cheek as he bent to kiss her.

'Happy birthday, *meri jaan*,' Dad said tenderly, 'and many happy returns of the day!'

I tiptoed out, a little misty-eyed, and closed the door quietly behind me. From downstairs I heard bellowing jokes and tinkling laughter above the cricket commentary, and gathered that Ayesha and Habib had arrived, and were being entertained by Bogie.

I found Sufya in my room. She was kneeling on the floor, hunting in her bag for something. I decided a direct approach would be best.

'So what's the story with you and Heathrow?'

Sufya paused without looking up, then continued rummaging.

'No story, really... We went out a few times. Don't think it's going anywhere.'

'Is that why you didn't tell me?'

Sufya relinquished the fruitless search and looked up exasperatedly. 'There was nothing to tell, Zee, OK? We used to be close so I didn't want to just write him off but...well, we were children then, weren't we?'

She got up and turned towards the mirror, trying to smooth her hair, while I absorbed this. She seemed serious about not being interested. And it was true that, for Sufya, who seemed to drift off-handedly from one liaison to the next, 'going out a few times' with someone wouldn't merit any big announcements. I was cautiously relieved: it didn't sound as though the relationship had got very far, and maybe it had just been a half-hearted capitulation to parental bullying. I now revisited their behaviour yesterday in a more optimistic light: actually they hadn't seemed like a couple madly in love. There was nothing like the chemistry between him and me, which was unmistakable.

In a slightly better mood, I gestured at Sufya's bare legs which were protruding un-Islamically beneath the blue kameez. 'Interesting look.'

'Bloody shalwar's got a massive tear in it,' she said. 'Sorry, but I'm going to have to wear my jeans underneath. Which will amuse you, because I'll be a replica of Habib.'

I looked at her reflection. The incongruous teenage kameez was stretched to bursting point across her bosom, revealing a typically sensible sports bra between the gilded buttons. Despite my annoyance with her, I felt a bubble of laughter rising into my throat.

'You wish!' I giggled, pointing at the mirror. 'God, Suf, we both look horrific!' Sufya looked, and began to snigger as well. She pulled a grotesque face and curtsied, and we both fell about, shrieking with laughter until Mum's voice called from downstairs, 'What is this haa-haa, hee-hee? Guests are waiting here! Come down!'

I stifled a yelp. 'Ssssh!' Sufya said. 'Shut up and help me get ready!' Still snorting quietly, I picked up her jeans from the floor and straightened them out. But as I handed them to her, my eyes locked suddenly onto the object she was holding in her hand: my hairbrush.

My heart stood still. 'W-what are you doing?'

'Brushing my hair, moron, what's it look like?'

I stared at the hairbrush. As if in slow motion, I saw it move back and forth, back and forth through Sufya's hair.

'B-but that's my hairbrush!' I brought out loudly, stupidly.

'I know, sorry, I can't find—'

I cut her off: 'Have you used it before?'

'I don't know. I suppose so. Look, we haven't got time, can you—'

But with a shriek I had leapt at her and wrenched the hairbrush from her hand. I peered at it and saw a strand of her hair nestling between the bristles – the bristles from which I had carefully extracted the contents for the *wazifa*, just a couple of weeks ago. I screamed again at full volume, hurled the hairbrush across the room and collapsed against the wall, covering my head with my arms. *I had buried Heathrow's picture with Sufya's hair!*

'Fucking hell, Zee!' Sufya ducked to avoid the flying brush, one hand nursing the wrist I had twisted in my headlong assault. 'What is it? What's wrong?'

Why, why, *why* was she always in my way? I had remained hopeful, through years of disappointment. I had explored all avenues – even NAZ Marriage Bureau – with an open mind. In the end, I had even done a spell to circumnavigate the obstacles to my happiness. But *she* had got into the spell and now *she* was going out with Heathrow! Because she could never let me have anything of my own, not even a hairbrush. How could I hope to stake my own claim? There would never be a single patch of ground that she hadn't already peed on, a single pie that she hadn't already got her fingers into. I clutched my ribs and groaned.

By this time, Mum and Ayesha were in the room. The conversation rattled back and forth above my head:

'*Hai, hai*, what is this? Sufya, what is going on? Zarina, get up!'

'I d-don't know… I used her hairbrush… Zee, what's wrong?'

'*Hai, hai!* All of this screaming and shouting over a hairbrush?'

'She always takes *my things*!'

'*Hai!* She's your sister, she hasn't got fleas! Sufya, why do you use her things? You're not a beggar! Zarina, stop crying!'

'Leave it, Mum! Ayesha, don't just stand there, get some water!'

'*Haan haan*, water! Just a minute! Don't worry, Zarina, me and my sisters used to fight all the time over clothes and jewellery…'

A beat.

'*Chalo*, Sufya, everyone is downstairs. Zarina, wash your face and come down when you feel better, OK, *beti*?'

Silence.

I stayed in my room all afternoon.

Sufya

ME: [ENTERING ZARINA'S bedroom with a cup of tea] Are you OK?

Z : [her eyes are red] Thanks, I suppose so.

Me: I'm sorry about your hairbrush.

Z: It's OK.

Me: [sitting on bed next to her] It doesn't seem like it's OK…

Z: [silence]

Me: Everyone's worried about you.

Z: [pushing the teacup away] Actually, they're appalled.

Me: So, would it help if I got you a new hairbrush and promised never to use it?

Z: No! That's not the point, Suf, and you know it! It's not about the bloody hairbrush!

Me: What is it about then?

Z: [angrily] Obviously, it's about you just getting whatever you want, and me never getting bloody anything.

Me: So, what have I got that you want?

Z: Nothing. Let's just drop the subject.

Me: Don't you think it might help to talk about it?

Z: Since when do *we* talk about things, Suf? Let's face it, you don't want to hear what I have to say, and I don't want to say it. Neither of us needs to go there, so just drop it.

Me: [after a pause]: So if your anger were a person, can you imagine what it would look like?

Z: Oh please, what's this? Spare me the amateur psychoanalysis.

Me: Come on, Zee, I'm trying to help.

Z: Don't think you could handle it, Suf. She's *monstrous*. [Faint smile.] You look shocked.

Me: So. If she could speak, this monster, what would she say?

Z: [closing her eyes and suddenly drawing herself up straighter] She would say, enough is enough. I'm going to do something about it, and I don't care what anyone thinks. I'm not taking it any more. [She smiles, a strange inward smile.]

Me: What is it she's not taking any more?

Z: Having her bloody life decided for her by someone else's whims...only ever getting someone else's leftovers...feeling like a secondary character in someone else's fairy tale...

Me: And by someone else, you mean me?

Z: [opening her reddened eyes and looking at me defiantly] I told you you wouldn't want to hear it.

Me: [taking a deep breath and stifling the urge to yell at her] So... what's she going to do about it?

Z: [looking away] Doesn't matter.

Me: [after a pause] I still don't know what the hairbrush had to do with any of this.

Z: [shrugs] Doesn't matter.

Zarina

AFZAL SAID THAT HIS mother was upstairs in the flat, so I made my way through the lunchtime crowd, up the narrow steps in the storeroom, and into the familiar sitting room where satin throws embroidered with mirror-work were draped over the divans. On the low coffee table was one of those plates with sections holding pistachios, sultanas and pine nuts in their shells, and the faint scent of cardamom hung in the air.

Auntie Khan, kneeling on a green velveteen prayer mat, was just finishing her *namaaz* with a round of prayer beads, so I sat on one of the divans and waited. As I listened to the *tasbih* clicking smoothly through her practised fingers, accompanied by the rhythmic whisper of her prayers – '*Rabbana alayka Tawakalna, wa ilayka Anabna, wa ilaykal Maseer*' (our Lord in you we put our trust, and to you do we turn in repentance, and to you is the eventual destiny) – a feeling of peace began to take hold of me, and I closed my eyes.

It was like yesterday: I could see myself, Sufya and Heathrow sitting in a row on the floor, concentrating on the chapters of the Quran which rested on cushions in front of us. It was here that we had come after Heathrow's signature *Maulvi Madness* had led to the furious exit of the eponymous Maulvi, declaring that we were thoroughly disrespectful and unteachable.

Mum found that nothing she could say would convince Maulvi to set foot in our house again, and that Dad who, like us, didn't see why it was so important for us to 'finish' the Quran in Arabic, wasn't doing much to back her up. At last she suggested we go to Auntie Khan instead, but on pain of death if we upset her in any way.

As if we would want to. Auntie Khan was the epitome of kindness and the soul of diplomacy. She wore the garb of the dignified, elderly matriarch – simple shalwar kameez, and a snow-white *dupatta* draped over neatly parted silver hair – but I always felt she understood more about the conflicted heart of the British Asian child than such a traditional exterior might suggest. Accordingly, she taught us to read the Quran in Arabic, but quietly, without exaggeration or sanctimony. She taught us respect by example, and one glance into those penetrating blue eyes magnified by black-rimmed spectacles told you loud and clear that you did not mess.

Now she got up from the prayer mat and hugged me. She felt so fragile. I was suddenly ashamed that, apart from occasional encounters in the shop, I had not been to visit her once in all these years.

'Zarina, *beti*, how are you? How is Sufya? And Heathrow? And Mummy, Daddy?'

'*Assalam-u-alaikum*, Auntie! Fine, thank you, everyone's fine. How are you?'

'Allah is merciful.' Auntie Khan motioned me to sit down again, then took a seat opposite me, folded her hands serenely and waited for me to speak, while I hesitated, not sure how to begin.

It had occurred to me as I lay on my bedroom floor, the afternoon of Mum's birthday, that the discovery of Sufya depositing her hairs in my brush – even though it had come as a violent and utterly unsuspected ambush – offered new and important intelligence. I was now convinced that, despite the initial lack of evidence, the *wazifa* had had an effect – albeit on the fortunes of the wrong sister. I recalled my earlier feeling that some supernatural force was keeping Heathrow from me: I myself might have bound him with Sufya's hair. It was a mistake that had to be corrected – for everyone's sake.

I looked up to see Auntie Khan's eyes fixed on me. '*Kya baat hai*, Zarina?' she asked kindly. 'What's the matter? You look burdened.'

'I need your help, Auntie,' I said, and told her the story I had concocted. A friend of mine had used a *wazifa* to put a love spell on a man she did not really want. Previously the man and I had had some feelings for each other, but now he was hopelessly bound to a woman who did not care for him.

If Auntie Khan suspected I was not being entirely honest, she did not say so. She merely nodded thoughtfully, and when I had finished, she said, 'Quranic *ayats* are not to be taken lightly. This girl has been very irresponsible with that poor man.'

'She knows that now. I was wondering, Auntie, whether you could give me a *wazifa* – a stronger one – to release him, and put things back the way they were?'

Auntie Khan frowned. 'What makes you think I have such a thing? There are certain *wazifas*, yes, blessed by the *pirs*, but they are for everyday troubles, overcoming griefs—'

'Yes, I think Mum has some books,' I said, trying to sound uninformed though my eyes still ached from last night's secret – and fruitless – ransacking of Mum's sizeable library. 'She says there are *wazifas* available for everything.'

Auntie Khan, however, would not be led. 'And even then,' she continued firmly, 'they are only prayers, to be used on the understanding that the outcome is for Allah's wisdom to decide. To do such magic as you suggest – and I know there are people who do it – is not right, Zarina. It is not Islamic, and it can be dangerous. Is it better for us to pray with a pure heart for what is best for us, or to use unsanctioned practices to play God ourselves? Now tell me exactly, what kind of *wazifa* did your friend do?'

I gave a brief summary of the spell, the hair, the photo, the burial in the cemetery. Auntie Khan was silent, her face serious. Finally she said quietly, 'That *wazifa* must be dug up and burned.'

'Yes, Auntie, I'll tell her, but shouldn't she do something to restore him to—'

'Your friend must never do such a thing again. And if you want to help, Zarina, pray for this man. I will pray for him too. God willing, he will find peace.'

Auntie Khan got to her feet. Clearly, the meeting was over. At the top of the stairs, she smoothed my hair, kissed me kindly on the forehead and turned away.

Downstairs in Tandoori Junction, all eyes were glued to the TV, and I was momentarily distracted from my troubles because Dad's interview was on. With thirty-two people across the country now ill after eating BestCo pork – eleven of them elderly and in a critical condition – questions had been raised in the press about whether the supermarket chain might be failing to meet government standards. Sales of meat products had taken a tumble, and the 'firefighting' that Dad had mentioned, had suddenly extended to him being sent out to bat for BestCo on *London Today*.

The BestCo bigwigs had no doubt calculated that the scholarly appearance of their senior food scientist would be just the ticket to allay consumer fears – and it was proving a shrewd supposition.

'Are you saying that the people making these claims are lying?' demanded the young female reporter.

'Not at all,' Dad said courteously. 'I am just explaining the detailed checks, which would have made such an oversight impossible. The tests I have just described to you are part of a rigorous protocol put in place by my department, which exceeds legal requirements for meat testing.'

I stood proudly amongst the viewers in Tandoori Junction who, since being on TV is every Asian's dream, were thoroughly impressed.

'So what would you say, Dr Malik, to those consumers who are voting with their wallets, and boycotting BestCo?'

'There is no danger in consuming BestCo's meat products, it is absolutely safe to do so,' said Dad.

'The pork too?'

'The pork too, of course.'

'Would you feed it to your family?'

'Without hesitation,' said Dad, and then added something else, which was drowned out by the reporter who was rattling off, 'Thank you. Unfortunately we have to end it there. So that's the message from Dr Ahmed Malik of BestCo food safety: BestCo meat is safe to eat. Sarah Wilson, *London Today*.'

For a moment, there was a shocked silence among the Tandoori Junction crowd. Then, as one, they turned and stared at me accusingly.

'He said he *would*, not he *does*!' I looked indignantly from one to the other. 'He was speaking *theoretically*... Oh, never mind!' As I left the shop, one old banshee said loudly, 'Poor Firdaus! She is such a God-fearing woman!'

'Piss off, Auntie Pigface,' I muttered under my breath, tugging the door sharply behind me.

'Hello, Zarina,' a lilting voice drawled insolently. 'Causing a scandal?'

Auntie Khan's prodigal niece, Goldie, was leaning against the shopfront, chewing. As always (though she must have been pushing forty by now), she was dressed like a Bollywood heroine, today resplendent in a red, flouncy, flamenco-style skirt with matching boned top and hoop earrings.

Goldie was probably the only 'girl' in the community who was even more trouble than us. She had arrived suddenly when we were in our teens, amidst whispers that she had been divorced for insulting her in-laws. Her parents had apparently refused to take her back, saying she had tortured them enough, and they couldn't have her in the house any more, so her elderly aunt, out of the goodness of her heart, had got lumbered with her.

If Auntie Khan had entertained any notions of stilling Goldie's unruly spirit through her trademark kindness and encouragement, she was soon disappointed. Goldie continued rude and selfish, refusing to participate in any way in Auntie Khan's home-life. She never cleaned up after herself or made her own tea – she certainly never helped in the shop or with the Quran lessons. Instead, the sound of Hindi film music and Goldie's thumping feet echoed at all hours from the flat above Tandoori Junction as she diligently practised the latest numbers.

At other times, she was to be found lounging around the

neighbourhood in her flamboyant outfits, eyeing boys and sensually eating the pakoras to which she helped herself in fistfuls from the shop. Once, Auntie Khan managed to get her married into a simple grocer's family from Tooting who were delighted with her, and promised to treat her like a princess. But within a couple of months, the grocer was left with a broken heart, and Goldie was back, going about her old ways, and threatening Auntie Khan with suicide if she ever tried to marry her off again.

With such rebellious credentials, Goldie might have earned a grudging respect from me and Sufya, had we been a bit older, and she less spiteful. As it was, we dreaded running into her after Quran lessons, to be pinched, chewing-gummed or have our physical inadequacies ruthlessly broadcast to the other students. 'Hello, schoolgirlies,' she would drawl, nimbly brushing a beautifully manicured hand across our hairy, adolescent knees, and bursting into peals of laughter. 'God, don't you *wax*?'

Now, having briefly looked me up and down (thankfully I was wearing jeans), she shrugged gracefully and enquired, 'Want to do a deal?'

'No thanks.' I turned to go.

'I heard what you asked *Maasiji*,' she said with a cunning smile. 'Tch, tch, tch, got ourselves in trouble, have we?'

Bloody hell, how did she manage to spy on me? I turned back. 'So?'

'So-oo,' Goldie spat her chewing gum onto the pavement, 'I have a proposition for you.'

'Not interested,' I said.

'No?' Goldie was undeterred. She sauntered towards me swinging her hips. 'Not even if I can fix it for the pumpkin to be Cinderella?' She threw her head back, and laughed delightedly. (She really ought to have auditioned for the movies. She would have been good.)

'It's OK,' she said, taking my chin in her red talons and pouting soothingly at me as if I were a five-year-old. 'I want to help you. We bad girls have to stick together, *na*? Now, I have a contact in Banglatown, and I can get you…' she paused and then, glancing quickly round whispered, 'a pukka sizzling love spell!'

I hesitated. 'Does it work?'

'Hundred per cent, *yaar*! Forget your old lady's *wazifas* – this is proper Indian *jadoo*!' Goldie patted my cheek. 'You'll get your guy, my little woolly. And all I need from you is a phone number.'

'Uh-huh. Whose?' *Better not be Heathrow.*

'*Whose*?' Goldie mocked. 'That lovely boy, of course, with the goofy eyes – the one you were talking to inside the other day… Qashif? Arif?'

'ASIF?' I stared. 'What on earth do you want with him?'

'Tch tch, baby, don't ask about grown-up things! I'll get you the spell, you just give me the number. Deal?'

And so, despite Auntie Khan's refusal, and through the most unlikely of accomplices, I procured the necessary *wazifa*, and got rid of Asif in one fell swoop. This time, it seemed luck was on my side.

Sufya

SHE HAD ALWAYS been such a shy little girl, hiding herself from new people from the start – behind our parents' legs, behind curtains, behind me. She was terrified of cameras, and would cry when people tried to photograph her, yet she was irresistibly drawn to dressing up, nursing fierce longings for items of my doted-upon first daughter wardrobe: a pink gauzy dress with a matching rose-garland headdress, a white Russian-collared fake fur cape with matching hat – these were the stuff of dreams to the toddler Zarina, but were destined only to come to her after having been thoroughly worn out and discarded by me. By the time Zarina finally donned these treasures, not only were they well past their luminous best, but the audience – our parents and their friends who had gasped and clapped at my every move – had long since gone away.

And yet Zarina and I had been comrades – sharing our room, our dreams and our secrets throughout our early years. When H came to live nearby our world became complete, and – convinced that what divided us was insignificant compared to what united us – I had never thought much about the million pieces of ice that were lodging one by one in Zarina's heart.

Now, I considered talking to H about the way Zarina had described her anger against me. I wondered what he would say about it. Had he been aware, when we were growing up, of that hairline fracture – or was it already something deeper? – between Zarina and me? When we two sisters had fallen out as children, it was often H who somehow found a neat way of bringing us back together. Perhaps he had always seen the threat to us. Perhaps, now that he was back, he could fix it as he had done before.

He was on the phone when he answered the door of his Camberwell flat. Barefoot, and dressed in dark Chinos and a navy T-shirt, he wrinkled his eyes and gave a heavy shrug to convey both apology and the fact that the conversation was a difficult one which could not be interrupted. 'That doesn't sound good. Not good at all…' H stood aside to let me go up the stairs ahead of him. He raised his voice as though to make himself heard over a bad line. 'Listen, I'm going to find a way to help you, but please try to calm down… Is there anyone else with you? Where's your brother?'

The flat was on the first floor of a Georgian terrace conversion, and the stairs came up into a beautiful white-painted open-plan living room and kitchen, with a dark wood floor. H did not have much furniture, but I recognised instantly, from countless long-ago visits to Uncle Bogie's place, the embroidered ottoman-style sofa. Amongst Bogie's eccentric clutter and clashing tastes, it had seemed little more than a piece of junk, but, in the sparse elegance of this room, the ottoman, placed slightly away from the wall and facing an expansive white-framed window (beyond which could be glimpsed the shimmer of summer treetops), reappeared as a piece of art.

H, still on the phone, indicated that I should sit, and lifted an open hand to convey that he would be five minutes. 'OK, here's what we'll do – I have a good friend who's a lawyer, and he's based not far from you.' His tone was authoritative yet gentle, and I felt a sudden touch of pride. 'I'm going to call him now and he will meet you. Can you think of a place where you could talk safely?' He disappeared into a room to the left of the kitchen area. I watched the door swing to behind him, and wondered idly if it was his study, or his bedroom.

The window was slightly open and, overlaid on the vibration of H's voice from the next room, came a hint of summer evening birdsong and a note of vanilla scent from what I now observed to be a flourishing magnolia tree in the front garden. I breathed in the quietness, and surprised myself with a sudden thought of how it might be if I lived here too, how relaxing it might be to hear that voice in the next room while I worked on my research, how very *natural* that might be...

I interrupted myself from this uncharacteristic reverie. The fact that H was detained on the phone gave me the opportunity to take in the detail of the environment he had chosen for himself. On one wall hung a large, modern, flat-screen television – evidence of H's passion for his work – but over it, he had draped an ornate, oriental cloth embroidered with birds and flowers in turquoise and yellow. Next to the TV was the framed, and famed, shot of Bogie in Brat Pack-style finery with Claudia Cardinale on his arm, which my parents also displayed in their living room. On the floor beneath stood a few piles of books and DVDs, clearly waiting for a home, but placed with a certain care, so that a relationship between the pure geometry of the items and the irregularity of their arrangement was somehow revealed. Had H done that deliberately, I wondered, knowing, as I did, how busy he had been since he moved in? It struck me, in contrast, as slightly shameful how little care I had put into the Brixton flat, even though I had lived there for years.

Behind the ottoman, on the white wall, were hung two large black and white framed photographic prints. The first was a wide-shot of an arid, rock-strewn hilltop on which, at some distance, H could be seen standing with a film cameraman and a camera on a tripod. H was pointing towards the horizon, and the other man was following his gaze. The pale shalwar kameez-type suit and the dark Pathani-style waistcoat that H wore were being buffeted by the desert wind, and the same wind had swept his dark hair up and back. Even from this distance I could see from the deliberate planting of his feet and his upright posture an absorption and focus that made me smile in recognition.

The second picture was a close-up print of H with two small dark-eyed boys, who I instantly recognised as Ayub and David from *My Uncle's Son*. H was standing facing the camera, shown from the waist up, in a pale short-sleeved shirt, and the two children, in shorts and T-shirts, had their arms clasped around his neck. Ayub was draped over one of H's shoulders and David over the other, their faces beaming, their bare feet dangling. No father and sons could have appeared so delighted by each other's antics.

'Every time I sat down in a chair, those two would clamber onto me,' said H, suddenly behind me. 'Then they would yell at me until I stood up. I had to pretend to be a giant, carrying them off for my dinner. Must have done it a thousand times.'

'They pretty much had you wrapped round their little fingers, then.'

'In fact, I was the main beneficiary in that relationship. The two of them shared their own world – much better than the one around them – and they let me into it. Honorary ten-year-old.'

'One plus one plus one…?'

'That's right. They *were* like us!' H grinned. Then: 'I'm glad you're here.'

'I like your place.'

'Well, I just moved in, and there's still a lot I'd like to do. But it's good. I like the space and the light, and – well – I'm pleased *you* like it.'

Standing there with him in his apartment, in the space arranged by that director who – famously – had not lost his child's eye, I experienced a peculiar sensation, something I could only describe as a kind of *interior crumbling*. Suddenly my face grew hot and I could not look at H. I had no way of hiding from him.

'So where's this film I'm invited to see, then?' I blurted, into what seemed like a bottomless silence.

'Yes, the film!' said H. 'Not that that's the only reason I wanted you to come, but we should get it over with, right?'

He had been away for two days – working on something which he had seemed unwilling to discuss – and we had not met since he had abandoned me on my doorstep that night before Mum's birthday. And despite the confusion – even turmoil – in which he had left me on that occasion, all my fears were once again laid to rest when, on his return, he called and invited me to come to his place to see his new film which, he told me, he had not yet shown to anyone. 'It's something very close to my heart, I suppose,' he had said, a little shyly, on the phone, 'and it's still work in progress, but I wanted you to be the first person to see it.'

Once again I had found myself feeling silly for indulging ill-founded fears and suspicions when H was so honest and consistent. And as for the unconsummated nature of our attraction, I felt certain now that that was the unspoken possibility that lay behind the invitation to visit him at home.

'But you mentioned when we spoke on the phone that there was something you wanted to talk to me about,' said H, as I sat down on the sofa and he removed the cloth from the viewing screen. 'What was it?'

At that moment, I decided not to say anything about Zarina. As children, the three of us had never spoken to one another about our internecine tensions. When he had healed our sibling rifts in the past, I had not asked him to do it – he had simply seen the problem and responded. There would be something unfair to Zarina, I decided, something against the rules of our three-way friendship, if I entered into confidences with him about her. After all, that friendship held in it so many of the memories of our sisterly closeness, so much of the treasure of our best selves. Not much in my life felt sacred any more, but the memory of that friendship always would.

Besides which, I did not want to ruin the moment.

⁂

A child, perhaps four years old, squats on rough ground by a wheelbarrow. An impatient wind tugs at his lilac short-sleeved shirt and ruffles the rounded integrity of his dark head, but he remains immersed, a small embodiment of intention. With two diminutive hands he lifts a pale object from the wheelbarrow, and places it carefully into the dust at his feet. Then he strokes it with the tip of a forefinger. The gentleness of his handling makes the viewer wonder if the object is perhaps a baby bird found fallen from the nest. Then, again using both hands, the infant lifts another object from the barrow and lays it close to the first. He places it so gently that the action makes no sound. Once more, he soothes the object with a tiny fingertip. The camera comes close to the rounded cheek, dark lashes aligned with intent downward gaze, the question mark of the small, full mouth. The boy is murmuring to himself – indiscernible words, spoken in the calming up-and-down tones a mother might use for a bedtime story – half story, half lullaby. Arabic? He lifts a third object from the barrow. The camera reveals that the object is in fact a jagged fragment of white ceramic tile. Slowly, the boy places it on the ground next to the two other pieces. He nestles its edges close to its neighbour's – of course it does not fit exactly – and then draws his forefinger gently across the uneven rift between them, still burbling softly to himself – or to the tile pieces? – as though inviting the fragments to close the gap, to merge, to heal like skin. Then he reaches for another piece.

A wide shot reveals the backdrop to this tender ritual. The boy crouches tiny beside a dusty road which snakes around a rock-strewn valley. Olive trees sprinkle the terraced slopes above the road, and in the distant elbow of the hill, small flat concrete houses can be seen. The boy is on the side of the road which drops down. Behind him rises a giant heap of concrete rubble festooned with all colours of fabrics leaping in the wind. Here and there strangely masticated household objects – a crushed orange pail, a plastic suitcase with a bite out of it, the spokes of a munched umbrella – flail among the dereliction. On the other side of the wheelbarrow looms the visceral underside of what seems to be an uprooted olive tree. The boy, even more diminutive from this perspective, yet no less concentrated in his head-down purpose, continues his assembling of shattered tile. Behind him, his home and garden seem to have chewed themselves up.

A small fingertip coaxes a crack to close. Shattered fragments nestled close. A sing-song incantation.

And then, in the wide-shot, something bizarre. The dust around the pile of rubble begins to rise. At first it is barely discernible, a shadow only. But then it grows and gathers in density, darkening into a rising mass that balloons like the hem of some vast robe filled by the wind, before suddenly, with a soundless rasp, being sucked into the pile of rubble as though the shattered house has taken a great gasping lungful of breath.

Gently and precisely, another piece of white ceramic is laid beside its wounded comrades by two small hands. The round head in its absorption does not lift as a deep rumble begins to come from the rubble.

And now, in the wide-shot, a bulldozer has appeared and seems to be battering itself against the demolished house. And as the child whispers his lullaby, it seems that stone by stone, with an agonised retch that becomes a groan and then a roar, the house is picking itself up and putting itself back together.

The child continues to work. A huge flat slab of concrete is lifted by the bulldozer and seems to clamber on top of the four walls which have now emerged, pitted and cracked. The roof is sucked down onto the structure, sealing itself with a hefty sigh. The bulldozer continues to lurch unevenly at the resurrecting building, and cracks in walls and windows suddenly close and smooth away. The bulldozer goes to work on the tree, and the tree returns to standing.

In the final shot of the film, the small boy slowly stands up, turns and runs into his home. The door closes behind him and the shot freezes. A caption appears:

> *This film has been constructed with footage from the demolition of a house in the West Bank this year. Elyas was four years old when the Israeli Defence Forces demolished the house. Elyas' father, a school teacher, had been accused of a terrorist offence. His family were given 15 minutes to leave the house before it was destroyed. Elyas' father was later found to be innocent, but an Israeli settlement has now expanded onto this site, so the family cannot return to their land. They remain homeless.*

H pressed the button on the DVD remote and the screen went blank.

'Still just reversing the action, I'm afraid!' said H, as I drew breath. 'This piece is going to go at the end of a longer documentary about house demolitions... Are you OK, Suf? You look a little pale.'

'It's so...effective.'

A wide smile broke across H's face. 'I'm relieved!' he said. 'I couldn't work out if I had crossed a line. What I didn't want is to pretend there's some fairy-tale ending to the story.'

'That little boy, Elyas, how did you get him to do that?'

'That was the beautiful part,' smiled H. 'I didn't. He started to do it spontaneously that same afternoon after the bulldozers left. Once I saw what he was up to, I got the idea to reverse the footage of the demolition and make it look like he was magically rebuilding the house.'

H paused, his eyes becoming shadowy. 'I know this family very well – my fixer in the West Bank is Elyas's grandfather. He's one of my closest friends.'

'And the Israelis had no good reason for bulldozing their home?'

'When I first went to Palestine, I didn't believe it either. But now, I've filmed so much injustice there that I sometimes think I should destroy my archives.'

'Destroy them! Why? Isn't it important that people should see what's happening?'

H spoke slowly: 'It's the kind of material that – if you let it – would destroy what you might call…faith.'

I knew H was not referring to religious faith. After *My Uncle's Son* won the Palme d'Or, a profile piece had appeared in *The Guardian* asking if H was the lone voice of healing for the Middle East. *The young Muslim film-maker who's making Israeli cinema-goers weep* was the sub-headline. *In this director's hands, the camera becomes the eye of the child…* wrote the reviewer, clearly much affected, *unable to see the world as divisible into an Us and a Them.*

'I don't want it to change me, Suf,' H said as if in answer to my thoughts. 'I have to stop myself from falling into…certain traps. Simplifying too much, or not listening. Sometimes I have to force myself to open up and listen even when I don't want to hear another word of their miserable justifications, because otherwise…well otherwise the anger takes over, and then you're lost.'

Through a determined exercise of his will, H's 'faith' had not been destroyed: he was still trying to listen, to speak to 'them', still trying to change the bad endings. Somehow, while I had let go, H had held fast and true to his younger self, to the promise we had once made to ourselves, and this remained his quest and his meaning. Looking at him now, brimming with passion and sincerity as he spoke of the challenges he had faced to covertly film the house demolition, I felt a flood of agonising recognition; a cloudburst pouring into a void so thirsting, so immense, so painful and encompassing that – wandering in it for years as I had been – I had lost the memory of any other way to be. Suddenly, I could not understand how I had allowed him to stay away so long.

Zarina

AT 9.30 P.M., UNDER COVER of nightfall, and dressed in stage blacks, I arrived outside Heathrow's flat. Luckily, I had only had to wait a few days for the new moon required by Goldie's spell.

I paused outside the garden gate to check out the territory. It was a Georgian house with steps up to the front door. First floor, Uncle Bogie had said in answer to my casual enquiries. The curtains were drawn and although a glow of lamplight was visible in one room, no shadows passed in front of it. I surmised that he was still away and, in accordance with the hundred and one Bogie Rules of Household Security, had left a lamp on a timer to deter intruders. The downstairs apartment, I had been informed, was unoccupied, which suited Heathrow because he could work undisturbed.

I had hoped to arrive a little earlier but this had proved impossible with the hell that had broken loose at home in the wake of Dad's apparent pork-condoning comments on national TV. In vain did he protest that he had also said, 'But my family doesn't eat pork because we are Muslims,' which had been drowned out by the interviewer's closing comments. Mum considered us thoroughly disgraced within the community – where our ratings had steadily been falling since the days of Sufya's and my Oxbridge glory – and worse (though only slightly), in the eyes of God. She had not emerged from her room for two days, citing serious spiritual damage, and even now would barely utter a word to Dad.

Bogie had shaken his head reproachfully, and said, 'For God's sake, Ahmed, you had them on the run! You should have told them: whosoever eats the filthy pig will reap what he sows!' Tonight, he had brought round a book detailing the scientific bases for doctrines prescribed in the Quran, and regaled me and Mum with a chapter on how abattoirs required special procedures for the slaughter of pigs because pork did indeed contain greater numbers of harmful bacteria than other meats. Thankfully, I didn't have to listen to all of it before they let me escape.

To receive a friend, one must step into the courtyard…

Luckily the gate was not rusty and I entered the garden quietly. I chose a spot underneath the magnolia tree whose branches spread like a fragrant canopy over the small square lawn, almost touching Heathrow's windows at the top. From my BestCo plastic bag, I took out three large packets of kidney beans. The spell had said any kind of sprouting legume, and since I knew symbolism was important in such matters, I had chosen beans – in homage to the 'hill of beans' in *Casablanca*.

I carefully poured out the beans to make a wall, about five centimetres high and half a metre long on the ground. Then I added two other walls so I had a triangle big enough to sit in. This took a good ten minutes to get right, and by the time I had finished, my legs were so stiff from crouching that I had to smother a groan as I stood up.

I referred to the next part of Goldie's step-by-step notes:

2. Sit in the triangle.

Careful not to jog the beans, I took up a cross-legged position and glanced quickly round me. The street was quiet. A tall, unkempt hedge rustling gently behind me shielded me from the view of any stray passers-by. The voluptuous magnolia blooms shimmered secretively in the darkness, and gave off a musky scent. I seemed to be in an enchanted garden, full of seduction and promise.

3. Recite the A'udhu billah 3 times.

Despite my elaborate preparations and the inviting romance of the garden, I felt myself baulk slightly at the idea of chanting amongst the vegetation like a possessed gnome. However, I had learned from experience the consequences of imperfect execution, and was determined that this time there would be no skimping or rushing. Every aspect of the *wazifa* would be performed carefully and ceremoniously. Taking a deep breath then, I sat up straighter and intoned clearly, three times, the words which preface prayer: *A'udho billahi mina al Shaytan al Rajim. I seek refuge in Allah from Satan, the outcast.*

I finished with a dramatic flourish, turning my face upwards. Although the moon was still too new to be visible, I could have sworn I saw a sliver of white light flash once, like a knife in the dark.

4. Close your eyes and begin the zikr: Ya Ilm, Ay Tilism/ Ya Himia, Ay Simia.

The practice of *zikr* involved, as I knew, the manifold repetition of a certain word or words to generate a nexus of spiritual energy. Such words were vessels of ancient lore, and the art of combining them to make powerful magical formulae had been developed over centuries by sorcerers and seekers of truth, and handed down in secret. Here was a chant comprising four words. Three were unfamiliar to me, perhaps Arabic or Farsi? The first, I knew: *ilm*, meaning "knowledge" – of things belonging both to this world and to others. It boded well for the efficacy of Goldie's spell.

I checked the correct sequence one last time and closed my eyes. The first stage was not to speak the *zikr* aloud, but to say it internally, building up the power of the words: *Ya Ilm, Ay Tilism!/ Ya Himia, Ay Simia!*

Quickly I found the rhythm, allowing the *zikr* to ebb and flow in time with my breathing: '*Ya Ilm, Ay Tilism!/ Ya Himia, Ay Simia!…*'

As the incantation gathered power, I seemed no longer to be producing the words. Instead they were unfolding behind my eyelids, etched in the blackness, as if by a fiery torch.

'*Ya Ilm, Ay Tilism!/ Ya Himia, Ay Simia!*' All of a sudden it seemed to me that there were voices around me taking up the chant. My heart thudded in my chest – something extraordinary was happening – but still I didn't open my eyes, determined not to break the momentum. The chorus of voices grew in volume until it seemed to echo round the huge dome of the sky. I was a tiny point in the centre of a vast swirl of noise. Involuntarily, I began to sway my upper body in a circle, hearing my own voice now joining the celestial chant: '*Ya Ilm, Ay Tilism!/ Ya Himia, Ay Simia!*'

My eyes now opened of their own accord, and the glowing words I had seen in my imagination were actually outside me, hurrying past on the air. As the chant accelerated, they stretched into taut bands, whizzing blindingly round me like Saturn's rings. Deeper and deeper my body dipped and swayed, my hair coming undone and whipping my face as I went. I felt my arms unfurl and open upwards and outwards.

'Ya Ilm, Ay Tilim!' The racing words ripped the breath from my chest, igniting memories in their wake. The lights on the river, Heathrow's laughter as he helped me to my feet, Auntie Khan, *Such things are not to be taken lightly,* Heathrow kissing me, the photograph of the two of us disappearing into the hard ground, Heathrow coming towards me, murmuring words of love…

There was a sharp burst of what sounded like gunfire, a scorching heat on my face, and black spots crowded into my vision. Then, as they cleared, I saw a flaming body lying in the undergrowth a few feet away, a man in a white tuxedo and slicked-back hair who, I now realised, was not dead, but in the process of rolling over, apparently unperturbed by the ribbons of fire curling around him. As dread took hold, I recalled Mum's stories of the apparitions that a lonely traveller passing at night through an Indian forest might encounter – the many cunning forms they would take to deceive him. And even before he turned his head towards me, I knew exactly what I was looking at – and it was not Humphrey Bogart as Rick. *Remember, beta, we are beings of dust, the blessed angels are beings of light, but the ones who are beings of fire are called djinns!*

For a split second I thought I had been kicked in the ribs, then realised it was only my glands gushing adrenalin. My ears sang, my skin bristled and I could smell my own fear. *Please God make it go away!* My brain turned over at blinding speed and flashed up Mum's admonitions on what the traveller must do: *avert your eyes from the evil spirit, keep walking and recite the ayat-ul-kursi until you leave the dark place!*

Yes, yes, the *ayat-ul-kursi*! I hunted frantically for the prayer, but the *ayat-ul-kursi* is complicated at the best of times, and the words would not be found. OK, any prayer! '*Bismillah…*' I tried to say –

in the name of God – but God's name evaporated on my parched tongue, and my mouth moved soundlessly like a suffocating fish. As for averting my eyes, or walking away, it was out of the question. As the burning Bogart-djinn stared at me through the endless black holes of its eyes, I could feel the pull of the powerful magic that bound me within the triangle, and knew for deadly certain that I was trapped.

Sufya

H MOVED A STRAND of hair from the side of my face, tidying it behind my ear. 'It means a lot to me that that story moved you, Suf,' he said, tenderly. 'It…*helps* me.'

His fingertip brushed my cheek, and it seemed that a match was struck and flared in my blood. My eyelids dropped. There was a softening, a blurring, a brush of warm breath, of lips, of hands. Something inwards toppled and slid even as my body felt suddenly lifted, weightless.

And I realised with relief that we had reached at last the point where nothing would keep us apart – not my family's expectations, my rationalist escapes, nor my fearful heart – not H's unpredictable absences, nor his putative performance anxiety. Call it destiny, call it fantasy, call it Top Monkey. Call it: *love*.

Zarina

'"THE PROBLEMS OF THREE *little people don't amount to a hill of beans...*"' I shrank back in the triangle as the Bogart-djinn nudged some straggling kidney beans back into line with a fiery boot-toe, causing a spatter of self-detonations. 'But you and me, kid, we know different, don't we? When they get on that plane with somebody else... Well, you may as well be dead after that.'

The glittering eyes met mine for a moment. He gave a grimace of a smile, drew back his foot, and took a cigarette from the inside pocket of his jacket, lighting it with his own finger.

'Please—'

'Ever think, kid, you should accept the role you've been given?' he interrupted, his hard, dry voice accentuated by a constant low crackle. The flames clung densely around him in the night's blackness, throwing a red glow onto his scarred lip. 'Your uncle said that to me once – he was a straight-up guy, one of the good ones. Course, all he ever got for it was a walk-on part in somebody else's movie. That ring any bells for you?'

As he spoke, the hiss of fire became a piercing, high-pitched whistle, and my eyes – though barely open against the stinging heat – were drawn to his chest where the left breast pocket of his tuxedo seemed to be ripping away. As I watched, the skin beneath began to tear and blister, as though gouged by an invisible, searing claw. Sizzling chunks of pink, bleeding matter were falling from the wound, pieces of rib charring and snapping away until his chest was nothing but a raw, jagged hole, tongues of flame licking at its edges. Imprisoned within the triangle, I tried to cry out, but the fire snatched the air from my lungs. My body shook like a dry skeleton, and I could feel terrified tears turning to salt on my burning cheeks.

'Made that myself,' the Bogart-djinn remarked, looking down with satisfaction. 'Old Rick literally ate his heart out! I think you know something about that too, kid. Or should I call you Number 2?' His mirthless chuckle gave way to an appalling coughing fit – a sharp, staccato rattle like stones raining down from an explosion, accompanied by a ghastly staggering and flailing. Then he doubled over, gaped and deposited a rank mix of blackened blood and rotting flesh on the ground. God in heaven, what was going on? How I regretted trusting Goldie and her promise of a 'strong *wazifa*!' How I cowered and quivered in the face of this sarcastic, self-cannibalising monster!

Reading my mind (of course), the Bogart-djinn suddenly zigzagged his upper body closer, flames snaking round his head. 'You find me disgusting, kid?'

I shook my head, and tried to lean away, but fires were smouldering all around me now as he hissed and spat words into my face: 'Course, pain ain't your thing, is it, Number 2? You hate it – don't even want to see it. You're tough, you fight for what you want, and the uglier it gets, the more you like it! Well, I'm going to give you your prize: you've earned it. You'll get your precious Heathrow. But this ain't some fairground ride, it's a one-way ticket on a non-stop train. Either one of you tries to get off, you won't be seeing each other again, not in this life. Understand, kid? Double-cross and die!'

Up until that point, I had feared only my destruction. Now, as his words burned holes in my barely conscious brain, I realised with horror why the djinn was there, and the nature of the pact I had unthinkingly solicited by invoking him. I registered a slight slackening in the force binding me and, summoning all my strength, kicked down part of the triangle wall, staggered to my feet and shouted, 'No!… Stop!'

But the djinn's contours were already disappearing – crumbling and caving into flames. 'You heard me: double-cross and die!' he rasped. A sardonic grin twisted his mouth before it too dissolved in a shower of sparks. 'Here's looking at you, kid!'

'Stop!' I shouted again. 'Wait!' I lurched towards the fire, but was flung back as it shot upwards in an enormous spiral. Whistling, screaming, the white-hot column hurtled towards the sky as though sucked up into a cavernous vacuum – then there was a deafening blast, dark thunderclouds gushed and pooled across my vision, and I passed out, as blazing branches rained down around.

Sufya

THERE WAS A SUDDEN explosion followed by a rasp of air that sounded like a giant boiler igniting. As I turned towards the sound, I saw a six-foot-high wall of flame approach before expiring just inches from our deliciously entwined bodies on the ottoman. Recalling the feeling of lightning in my body which H had induced at my parents' home a few weeks ago, I briefly wondered if this fire was another psycho-physiological phenomenon elicited by the extraordinary energy between the two of us. Was it some mind-manifestation of the proverbial *flames of passion*?

'It's the tree outside!' gasped H, shielding my body with his. 'It's been struck by lightning!'

He was right – forced in by a fierce wind, great tongues of flame were shooting into the room from the open window. We scrambled behind the sofa to put more distance between us and the source of the flames, and crouched together, gasping for breath. By now the curtains were burning, and the Persian carpet too, the air filling with acrid smoke. The roar of the flames was deafening and there was something bizarre about the continuous wind that funnelled the flames in our direction, as though from a huge and ghastly blowtorch.

'I've never seen anything like it!' murmured H, as we peered from our hideaway, clutching items of recently removed clothing over our noses and mouths. 'We've got to get to the stairs...' He took my hand and for a moment we hesitated, surveying the claw-like fingers of flame that were clutching into the space that separated us from escape. But the heat and smoke in the room were already intense, and we both knew there was no choice. The wind seemed to draw breath for a second, and we saw our chance, leaping into the sudden gap between the flames.

But before we could reach the top of the stairs, a monstrous gust of wind ripped a burning curtain from the window and hurtled it across the room, a mighty cloak of fire descending upon our defenceless bodies like a flaming banshee.

In that moment, when the dark burning closed around the two of us, when I realised that, weakened by smoke and heat, we did not have the strength to repel it from its target, and I felt the searing heat of it drawing around me like a thick burning skin, H's hand grasped mine, and I found myself uttering a silent prayer with all the fervour of my once-scientist heart: let there be some resurrection, some haunting, *some future life*. Let this death not be the end of the story of H and me, so long promised and so newly begun.

The flames went out as suddenly as they had started, and – spluttering – I peeled the sodden but still smouldering curtain from my head to find that H was doing the same, and that we were surrounded by firemen with extinguishers.

Wednesday 9 September 1998

Zarina

BRUISED, BATTERED AND terrified, I had skulked in the house for two weeks, not daring to go out, and jumping every time the doorbell rang, certain it would be the police wanting to question me as to my whereabouts on the night of the conflagration. I had heaved myself up and escaped back home when the blaring of fire engines a few streets away roused me from unconsciousness, but it was possible that I had been spotted by a neighbour or passer-by. Someone had called the fire brigade – perhaps that person had also seen me making a getaway?

When Bogie said that Heathrow had actually been home at the time of the fire, I rushed into the bathroom and was violently sick. Despite his assurances that Heathrow was unhurt ('A miracle, by the grace of God!') my guilt and horror knew no bounds. Intending to bring about our union, I had almost brought about his death!

Not to mention the Bogart-djinn: in the cold light of day, of course, he seemed nothing short of the most fantastic delusion, and I prayed fervently that I had imagined him in the trance-like state induced by the chanting. Couldn't it be that I had witnessed nothing more untoward than what everybody else accepted as the explanation for the strange events of that night: in the storm that had suddenly blown up, the magnolia tree outside Heathrow's apartment had been struck by lightning, and the fire had spread to the building?

Mum, when I casually questioned her about how one might go about conjuring a djinn, said she had never seen a formula for it, nor known anyone who had done it, and it would take years of sustained, spiritual practice to develop the necessary mastery.

'*Hai Allah!* Imagine what would happen if people could get such knowledge over the counter – how many djinns and *balaas* would you be finding on the street?'

'Instead of at the community centre, enjoying tea and samosas, you mean?' Dad enquired, wandering through the kitchen in search of his glasses.

'Tch, tch, shame on you, Ahmed!' Mum called after him, though she chuckled into the washing up for several minutes afterwards.

Despite Mum's comforting words, my hackles still rose when I remembered the Bogart-djinn – his crackling voice, the burning hole where his heart had been. I alone had been in the garden, and what I had seen had seemed very real indeed.

I wanted to call Goldie and give her hell, but quickly realised that this would be folly. She might well have heard about the fire on the Tandoori Junction grapevine, and if I let on that I had caused it, I could just imagine her satisfaction at having something to use against me. How much she knew about the actual working of the *wazifa* I had no idea, but she might have already put two and two together in that criminal mind of hers. No, the best policy would be to lie low, and if Goldie herself asked me about the 'pukka sizzling love spell', to say that I had taken Auntie Khan's words to heart and decided against it.

After a few days, the situation began to look less dire. I was relieved to hear that Heathrow had gone away filming again, leaving the insurance company to sort out the mess. He had not called out of the blue after the fire, or sent me a love letter, or acted in any way that might lead me to believe that the forces of darkness had granted my wishes on their dreadful terms and for this, again, I was grateful. It looked as though I might have got off with a scare and a warning, and this time I was determined to learn my lesson: no more *wazifas* – they were nothing but trouble. I reflected that if I hadn't panicked the day of the hairbrush incident, I needn't have got involved with Goldie and her terrible spell anyway. Sufya had told me herself that her relationship with Heathrow had been a non-starter. Now, I decided, I would stop meddling and give him a chance to come to me of his own accord.

It seemed to be a time of reckoning all round. In recent days even President Clinton had showed genuine contrition, and apologised for his relationship with Monica Lewinsky. His aides were quick to applaud this as an act of courage – praise that was not completely unjustified, I thought. After all, politically motivated or not, wasn't this the right – and possibly hardest – thing to do? He had made a mistake and he asked for forgiveness.

I too breathed a little prayer of repentance for any role I might have played in the fire, hoped that it would all end there, and welcomed a return to normality (or as close to it as life in our house ever got.) After the last round of *Taj* auditions, I had decided to hold off casting for a few weeks, when more actors might be back from the Edinburgh Festival. And while I hung around at home, helping Mum make chutney and recovering from my ordeal, I pondered on the unresolved problem of my play without a hero.

If, as Ravi had said, I had started out believing Suleman to be the 'real hero' of the play, I was now beginning to think more about Shahjehan: he might not be a poet, but there was a lot to be said for a man who took action without waiting to be asked. And, in that case, Dan, I now realised, would not do: the role needed more inspiration. On the other hand, he was a reasonably good actor, and it would be a shame to lose him altogether. It therefore made sense, while we searched for a stronger Shahjehan, to try him out in the role of Suleman.

So, feeling quite pleased with this creative development, I rang him up.

Hi Dan it's Zarina how are you, Hey boss very well very well enjoying the script you'll be pleased to hear I've learned most of my lines, Already wow, Yeah I'm really getting into it I wasn't sure about Shajehan at first I thought he might be a bit too Arnie action-hero but actually there's a lot more to him isn't there and it isn't every day you get the chance to play an emperor, Well actually that's what I was ringing about, Oh yes, Yes I was wondering whether you would consider having a look at Suleman, I thought I was playing Shahjehan, Well to be honest Dan so did I but you know how it is with casting it's really difficult to set things in stone until you have all the actors and since Suleman is still open I thought it would be worth getting you to try it so we can work out where you might best be placed and what you would enjoy most, Well that's nice of you but I'm enjoying Shahjehan and anyway like I said I've already learned most of it, Sure sure but you might like Suleman even more and it is the bigger part of course, I'm not that shallow, No I'm not suggesting for a minute that you are but well to be frank Dan it would really help me if I could keep my options open for now and if you could try Suleman for me, Right, Is that OK, Well you're the boss I'll just unlearn all of Shahjehan and try to get into a completely different character, That's great Dan I really appreciate it, Right, So maybe you could have a look at it and we could get together in a few weeks for a reading, Fine, Take care and I'll be in touch, Bye, Yes bye for now Dan.

I put the receiver down, sweating slightly, and pulled a face at the phone. Despite all the charm he had laid on in the audition, Dan had been surprisingly difficult to persuade. Never mind, I had got my way for now. And he would come round if it turned out to be an inspired decision. Nevertheless, I knew it was risky to rile Dan, when he was the only hero I had.

Sufya

THAT WEDNESDAY afternoon, I had taken an extra shift in the lab looking after Darwin, who had been somewhat deprived of company over the summer holidays. It was rather comforting to note the constancy of my chimpanzee admirer, as I had been missing H, who had been away filming for two whole weeks now. This time there had at least been phone contact, but our brief and intermittent conversations did not bridge the emptiness created by his physical absence.

That morning, Richard had called out of the blue to announce that he was in London for a conference and did I fancy another book consultation, or failing that, did I fancy having dinner with him for old times' sake? His call felt fortuitous because at long last I felt there was some progress in my work. So, after I had shared a long, smelly embrace with Darwin, I became immersed in my writing, for once with some excitement.

The semen of the male fruit-fly contains a toxin that, when he has recently mated with a female, will destroy the sperm of any other male that tries to impregnate her – an immense advantage over his competitors' genes. Irrelevant to the successful male is the fact that, over time, the build-up of toxins in the female will poison her: as long as his offspring have hopped off into the world, he need not concern himself with what happens to their mother. In an ingenious experiment, researchers at the University of California prevented females from evolving while letting the males compete against each other. After forty generations, the males which were thriving were those with the strongest toxins in their semen. Females who mated with them had a shortened life expectancy.

Then the researchers carried out another test. Preventing the poisonous males from evolving, they let the females compete with each other. And this time, after forty generations, the females which were thriving had developed methods of detoxifying the male offerings, and had evolved away the shortened life expectancy.

Of course, fruit flies are not the only species in which the sexes are engaged in a covert and deadly genetic arms race, as I was discovering in my trawl of the literature. Across the animal kingdom, heterosexual males were secretly evolving mechanisms to procreate not at their own expense, but at the expense of their chosen mates, and our own species was not exempt.

Consider the placenta, which is a strange organ, not really part of the female, determinedly diverting – as it does – blood vessels and nutrients from her body to feed the growing foetus.

The growth of the placenta is accelerated by certain foetal genes derived from the father, while women have developed genes to counteract ferocious placental growth – coming as it does at the expense of their own bodies.

In the worst cases, where the paternally derived genes are allowed to force the pace of placental growth unmoderated by the maternal anti-growth genes, the woman can develop a virulent form of cancer called choriocarcinoma.

And this battle to control the pace of foetal development continues throughout the pregnancy and beyond, in one form or another. For instance, certain paternally derived genes make babies into more active breast-feeders, once again leading to accelerated growth of the offspring at the price of the mother's physical resources.

I began to feel the shape of my work developing. What was important for males to survive and reproduce was not the same as what was important for females to survive and reproduce – in fact the two were sometimes directly opposed. And if our moral codes were a product of evolution – a mechanism for survival – was it not then likely that there might be two different moral codes: one evolved by males and one evolved by females? And therefore, might the problem between men and women be that *each gender inhabits its own moral universe, sometimes in direct opposition to the moral universe of the other?*

The controversial possibilities of my thesis excited me. I was not sure that anyone had set out to investigate a question framed in quite this way. When, at our last meeting, I had mooted my idea to Richard, he – old-school in his behaviourist approach, as well as in his good-old sixties feminist ideas of gender equality –

had dismissed it. But, now that I had more evidence, and after his impromptu phone call – Zarina, of course, would have interpreted the timing of his phone call as a *sign* that my research was on the right track – I found myself relishing the idea of discussing the theory again with him. After all, I reasoned, if I could find the answers to Professor Richard Stone's criticisms, I would certainly become able to defend my arguments against lesser *Homo sapiens*.

Darwin was pretending his arm was stuck between the bars again, and, feeling charitable, I ambled over to his enclosure to indulge him with a cuddle, when an unexpected visitor burst into the lab.

Me: What are *you* doing here?

Asif: [marching up to me] You think you're so clever, don't you? You and your smart-ass film-maker boyfriend with your so-called liberated lifestyle! Do you realise that, because of your antics at our gig, we lost two bookings?

Me: If you've offended your audience, how is that our fault? And I don't appreciate your coming to my workplace to yell at me…

Asif: That's your problem, isn't it? Yours and your stuck-up sister's! You think you're so damn special! You think you're better than ordinary decent Muslim women, don't you? I mean, when was the last time you went to the masjid?

Me: As far as I know – thanks to people like you – our local mosque doesn't admit women nowadays. And it's no business of yours whether I go or not. Even the most elementary study of Islam would tell you that a person's relationship with God is solely between that person and God, and no concern of other people – least of all bigots at the local mosque!

Asif: Exactly my point! Women like you go around thinking whatever you like, doing whatever you like, without any regard for our culture or traditions! And then you give lectures about 'the most elementary study of Islam'! Well, I've got news for you, sister. Islam isn't 'a study'! It's a *force*, it's a *power* and it's a *community*! I'm part of that community and it's about time you and your sister decided whether you are in or out! You both just think you're so special...

Me: But what gives you that idea? What if we don't live by your so-called 'rules' not because we feel 'special' but because we just don't *agree* with them? I mean, aren't we *allowed* to disagree with your interpretation?

Asif: [more uncertain] Well, within reason, there's room for debate yes...but...well I used to think like you before my mum died, and then I went to Pakistan, and there, with the grace of Allah, I sorted my head out. And I realised you just can't pick and choose what you believe and what you don't believe. The world's not like that any more! You need to decide whose side you're on! I mean look at what Clinton's doing bombing innocent Muslims in Sudan and Afghanistan to divert attention from his adultery! Look at Israel celebrating fifty years of murdering Palestinians and bulldozing their homes!

Me: You're very angry about the world situation.

Asif: Too right, I am, sister! It's an ugly place, and people like you can't shut their eyes forever!

Me: So if your anger were a person, what would it look like?

Asif: [suspiciously] What's this – some kind of bourgeois parlour game?

Me: No. I'm just trying to understand. Just close your eyes and see what comes into your head. Don't think about it.

Asif: [hesitating, then closing his eyes as the narcissism of the exercise wins him over] If you really want to know, the first thing that comes into my head is my mum's body being lowered into a grave in Pakistan!

Me: That's what you see when you think about your anger?

Asif: [opening his eyes] And you know why that is, sister? Because even after thirty-five years of living in this country, *my mum didn't want to be buried here*. She didn't feel like this was her home. It didn't matter that I live here – her only son – she still chose to be buried thousands of miles away! That's how unwelcome this country made her feel!

Me: [after a pause] I'm sorry.

Asif: [suddenly furious again] *Sorry?* Don't fucking patronise me! You don't need to feel *sorry* for me! Feel sorry for Muslim children in Palestine! Muslim children in Bosnia! Muslim children in Kosovo! And it's about time you and your stuck-up sister woke up to what's happening to our people, because you can't be part of the club if you don't obey the rules! That's just how it goes!

Me: [having to shout, because – not only have I lost patience – but Darwin, who has been growling softly since Asif's entrance is now screeching and rattling the bars of his enclosure] It's not a *club*, Asif, and that's your biggest mistake! For you, it's got nothing to do with Islam and everything to do with being part of some yobbish boys' gang!

Asif: *Owwwwww! Ge' 'im off me!*

Me: [trying to prise Darwin's fingers from Asif's beard. Unfortunately, I wrench a tuft of Asif's hair instead.] Darwin! Let go!

Asif: Wha' the 'uck! Oowww!

Me: Sorry! Darwin! Let him go! [I run for my bag and dig out my make-up mirror, but Darwin isn't interested. I try to offer myself for embrace, but to no avail. Asif is screaming in pain, while

Darwin screeches maniacally.] There's nothing for it – you're going to have to kiss him.

Asif: *WHA'*?

Me: Do it! *Kiss him on the lips!* It's the only thing he'll understand!

[Asif looks utterly wretched but kisses Darwin, who immediately lets go and grins.]

Asif: [clutching his torn beard and furiously wiping his mouth] That animal should be *put down*! It's a *pervert*! You and your sister and that ape better watch your step! [He backs away and then runs from the lab.]

⁂

After Asif had left the lab I briefly wondered about kissing Darwin myself, but decided not to set a precedent. And when Richard wandered in a few minutes later, I ended up talking very little about my new research findings but instead spent two hours with him at the British Museum coffee shop discussing Asif and the rising popularity of reactionary orthodoxies among young British Muslims.

Richard, with his liberal Jewish background, seemed a little too amused by the story of the routing of the Orthodogs, and by what he called 'Darwin's attack on fundamentalism', but if – as Asif had said – I had to choose whose side I was on, I was certainly not on Asif's.

'So these Orthodogs...' said Richard, thoughtfully, 'are they part of some organisation? I mean, what do you think he meant by telling you to "watch your step"?'

'Why do you ask?'

'Well, for instance, there's an organisation that was going

around London campuses throwing acid in the faces of unveiled Muslim girls, wasn't there? They had a couple of cases of it at North London after the Rushdie affair – my friend David who's Head of Politics over there knew one of the girls that was attacked.'

'Oh God, Asif wouldn't be part of anything like that!' I said. 'He just wants the thrill of being part of some pack. I suspect that's what these groups are to a lot of British Asian boys – a way to feel scary instead of scared. I don't think many of them would ever actually *do* anything about it.'

'But so much of his agenda seems to be about women, doesn't it?' probed Richard.

'I don't know,' I said, feeling a little defensive upon hearing – even from my learned friend – the stereotypical observations about Islam, (which side *was* I on?). 'You can't ignore the political context. I mean, I don't think they would be like that if it wasn't for what's going on in the world…'

'Hmmm. You're probably right. So, what you're saying is: the males are angry about the political situation, and that means the females get it in the neck.'

'It's not as simple as that, Richard,' I laughed. But a small part of me was wondering if maybe it *was* as simple as that. Or worse still, was it the other way around – rather than the political situation creating dangerous male–female dynamics, were male–female dynamics creating a dangerous political situation? Wasn't that entirely possible, given my suspicion that the male moral sense – as it was manifesting to drive these moralistic young Muslims – was in some part an evolutionary product of their war with females?

'Maybe it's simpler still,' Richard smiled. 'If these young men were allowed to have sexual relationships, d'you think there would be so many of them stirred up by the problems of far-away peoples?'

'It would be a bit grim if all our idealistic or altruistic behaviour could be drained away by having more sex, wouldn't it?' Once again, I was surprised to find myself defending my extremist brothers against the assumptions which seemed to me to underlie Richard's humour. Given that my own views were likely to be closer to his than to theirs, why was I bothering?

'Works for bonobos.'

Later that evening, I dropped in unannounced at Mum and Dad's, hoping that the aftershocks from the Dad-would-feed-pork-to-the-family episode might finally have died away. I had not told them about my near-death experience at H's flat, because I did not wish to allow Mum any satisfaction that my relationship with H had progressed. Bracing myself for what I might find, and what I would have to hide, my heart sank as the door to my former family home was opened by perfect cousin Ayesha.

'Sufya!' she lilted, affecting great warmth as she embraced me. '*Khalaji*, it's Sufya!'

'Where have you been gallivanting for so long?' grumbled Mum as I went into the living room. 'Why did you not come before? You know what your donkey of a papa did?'

'Sorry, Mum. I've just been very busy with work. I did leave messages. How's the cold?'

Mum muttered something about how outrageous it was that nowadays people thought that machine messages were how you should respond when the whole family had been humiliated on *London Today*. After enjoying my discomfiture for a while, Ayesha skilfully diverted Mum back to the subject of her famous recipe for *masala* fish. I tried to appear interested, but could muster little enthusiasm for the discussion of spice-grinding methods. Neither of them seemed to mind when I mumbled something about an email I had to send and switched on Dad's computer.

Notwithstanding stereotypes, the conversation with Richard had caused me to ponder further on the motivations of the Orthodogs. Recalling the anti-female aggression of Bashi the Paki at Ishq, I could not help wondering to what extent Richard was right about the real target of these militant young Muslims. If they were so upset by the world situation, why did they focus so much of their energy on controlling women? Might their behaviour provide further insights – relevant, if not scientific – into my investigations of the origins of moral values?

As soon as I dialled onto the internet, I discovered that the media-savvy Orthodogs had their own website: Orthodogs-tellinitlikeitis.co.uk. On the home page, under *Find out more about what Orthodogs believe*, was a link to 'Brothers in Islam'. This organisation, it turned out, was formerly known as 'Brotherhood of Islam (UK)' – and a quick cuttings search ascertained that this was in fact the very same group which had achieved notoriety in the late eighties for allegedly scarring the faces of unveiled females on university campuses, although nothing had ever been proven. The Brothers in Islam website itself gave very little information on what people like the Orthodogs might believe, contenting itself with a couple of italicised quotes, one from the Quran – *Allah changes not what is in a people until they change what is in themselves* – and the other from the organisation's leader, Usman Khailvi: *When Allah's work is to be done, the Brothers will rise to do it.*

Scrolling down the webpage I came across a small black and white photograph accompanied by the words: *For further information about Worldwide Islamic Jihad, contact Tariq Anwar at 0181 681 0024*. I reached for my mobile in amazement. It was the same Tariq Anwar who had been at Oxford with me, where I had at first treated him with extreme suspicion – coming as we both did from the same 'community' in South London. 'I think my mum knows your mum,' Tariq had mentioned, neutrally, when we had first met, and that was enough for me to avoid him like the plague, until – two full years later – we had accidentally been thrown together one night in the college bar after a few drinks apiece. It was only then that Tariq confessed that he had been avoiding me too, and suddenly we were comrades in arms.

'My mum's desperate to get me married off,' he had complained, some months later when we bumped into each other in Broad Street and stopped for a coffee. 'I can't get her off my back!' By then, I was deeply embroiled in the drama of my star-crossed romance with Steve, and heartily sympathised. 'What we both really need,' I found myself thinking aloud, 'is to find someone our parents would approve of, who's in exactly the same situation. Once the parents were all off the case, we could just get a divorce and get on with our lives…'

My voice trailed off as I realised what I had accidentally suggested, and I looked up to catch Tariq looking at me, significantly. 'I've been thinking the exact same thing,' he said.

There was a heartbeat of silence. 'Of course, what we *really* need is a *proper* drink!' I laughed and waved to the waiter, pretending we both knew it had never been a serious suggestion. Handsome and eligible as Tariq was, the idea of even a *fake* arranged marriage turned my stomach. Neither of us ever mentioned it again.

When he graduated, Tariq had gone on to become a prominent civil rights lawyer, nowadays mentioned in the papers in conjunction with the high-profile racism cases of the day. Rumour had it that he was a key contender for a Labour seat in the next election, so it seemed highly improbable to me that he would knowingly be the spokesperson for an organisation with the unsavoury associations of Brothers in Islam.

'*Sufya Malik!*' came Tariq's deceptively relaxed drawl at the end of the line. I could picture him swinging back in his executive chair, smiling his long-lashed, Omar Sharif smile. 'Long time no hear!'

After the usual pleasantries, I asked him straight out. 'Tariq, do you know anything about an organisation called Brothers in Islam?'

'Yes, actually. I'm doing a little work for them – helping out with public relations. They're a proper grassroots organisation, but you know our people – they just don't know how to present themselves. I've been trying to…well, give something back to the community.'

'But, aren't these the same people that did all that acid-throwing a few years ago?'

'Sufya! Sufya! Sufya!' I could sense Tariq shaking his head and smiling at the end of the phone with the air of someone fully steeped in the machinations of realpolitik, talking to an endearing novice. 'You should know better than to believe everything you read. That's what I mean about the need for PR assistance.'

'You mean that was made up?' I asked, feeling suddenly foolish and not a little guilty.

'Come on, Sufya.'

'Oh, I see.'

'You should get involved with the community yourself, then you wouldn't fall into these media traps.'

'Tariq, your name's on the website with a line about worldwide Islamic jihad!'

'No! Is that still up there?' Tariq laughed. 'I told Mo to take it down months ago. That's his attempt at joking with me. Geek humour, what can I say: give the guy a break?'

'OK,' I agreed. 'Well, shall I come to the next meeting with you, then? You know, to find out what it's all about?'

'Er, maybe not a good idea. It's…er…well…it's *brothers only*, this one.'

'Oh. I see.' *Brothers only*. The words did not sound like those of the secular socialist Tariq I used to know. *What was happening to everyone?*

'When are we going to have coffee, anyway?'

I agreed to call Tariq soon to get together, and hung up feeling irritated. Everyone, it seemed, wanted to know which side I was on. Even I was beginning to wonder whether I ought to be taking up a position instead of treating it all as part of an intellectual inquiry. And yet, was it possible to show any loyalty to a 'community' where even educated, liberal males like Tariq excluded me without batting an eyelid?

'What meeting are you going to? Anyone I know?' enquired Ayesha, who had been talking to Mum but clearly eavesdropping on me.

Ayesha had heard about the Brothers in Islam, and even knew one or two of them. 'If you're interested, you should talk to Asif, you know,' she purred. 'He's involved with that bunch.'

'Well I know someone who's involved with them too, but it turns out they don't allow women at the meetings, anyway!' I grumbled.

'Outrageous!' pouted Ayesha, lifting a kitten-paw in mock-horror. 'But those beardies aren't your scene, are they?'

'I thought I'd look into it… You know, find out what all the fuss is about.'

'Well,' said Ayesha, archly. 'If you really want to do it, I can get us in.'

Friday 25 September 1998

Zarina

THE GRASS ON Wimbledon Common was scorched and yellow after the long summer. I glanced at Heathrow, who was squinting up at the wooden signpost through his glasses. 'Windmill! Half a mile. This way.' We started to walk again slowly.

'You're very quiet,' he said. 'You OK?'

'No,' I replied, and continued toiling up the hill.

'Zarina…' Heathrow stepped in front of me, 'don't be like that.'

'Why not? I don't see why you have to leave. What's wrong with it here?' *What's wrong with me?*

'Nothing's wrong with it here,' he said, trying to disguise his impatience.

'Then don't go!'

His face was drawn as he looked at me, but he said nothing. Feeling a sob shake my chest, I turned away and sat down on the grass. Heathrow sat down next to me and put his arm around my shoulder. In the distance Queensmere Pond glinted between the trees.

'Zarina, this summer with you has been…the best.'

'You're just saying that!' I let the tears roll down.

He shook his head. 'No, listen, the best! If it hadn't been for you, I wouldn't have stuck around this long. And of course I'm going to miss you, but I have to go. It's what I've always planned, you know that. I can't help it, I'm a damn bloody gipsy boy, remember?'

'But you don't have to be,' I insisted. 'You can be happy here! Doesn't this summer prove that? You've got everything: family, people who love you—'

'God, it's all so simple for you, isn't it?' He withdrew his arm. 'I'm not you, Zarina. You know where you come from, who you are! Where do I come from? Bloody Terminal 3, Long Haul! And honestly, how can you be sure you all love me when there's a whole side of me, a whole past no one knows anything about?'

There was a short silence, while I plucked loud tufts of grass and Heathrow ran his hands through his hair. Then he said quietly, 'My first day in school, I couldn't speak much English, and every time I opened my mouth a stream of some other language came out. I remember I couldn't make the teacher understand. She probably would have preferred it if I'd just shut up, but I didn't. So in the end she decided to pretend I wasn't there. I ended up wetting myself because the stupid woman couldn't figure out I needed the toilet!'

Instinctively I reached out my hand, then thought better of it. For all our closeness, Heathrow rarely volunteered any information on those early experiences. 'Heathrow, that's… I don't know what to say.'

'I know,' he said with a short laugh. 'Funny, I can't even bring up a single word of that language now…except sometimes when I'm dreaming maybe. But I remember that feeling of being invisible, of not being able to make anyone understand. And when I think that there are people who feel like that every day of their lives, it makes me crazy. Look, Zarina, maybe I'll never find out where I came from, I realise that. But I can't just get a job in London, and live some sort of fake life where I never try to make a difference and never try to change things. You understand that, don't you?'

I couldn't deny it. Aged nine, he had wanted to change all the bad endings. When he saw awful things on the news he would be moody for hours. We had always known he would go off into the big wide world as soon as he could.

'So,' I managed reluctantly, 'Tehran then.'

'Well, it's a good place to start. My Farsi is pretty good now, and I've applied for a project at Kiarostami's institute – film-making with bereaved children. Remember what Magical Movies meant to us?' I could see the shadows that had hung around him dissolving as he spoke – he was in his element again. 'I can't give them their innocence back, but I can help show them that they can make something worthwhile and all their own, no matter how small and insignificant they feel.'

I looked at him and sighed. 'OK, you can go.'

Heathrow pulled me into a hug. 'Thank you, that's very magnanimous! Anyway, you'll be going to Cambridge soon. You won't be around either.'

'Just don't forget me, OK?' I said, tightening my arms around him.

Heathrow looked at me questioningly for a moment. Then he leaned forward and kissed me…

I really had to stop going over all this old stuff. I was only torturing myself. I crushed the memory forcefully and turned over in bed.

That wazifa must be dug up...

Suddenly I was sitting bolt upright, Auntie Khan's words echoing round my brain.

That wazifa must be dug up and burned!

'Yes, yes,' I muttered, leaping out of bed and dragging on my jeans. 'Dug up, yes. Dug up and burned! Shit! How could I forget?'

In the dead of night, it only took me twenty minutes to get to West Norwood. As I parked, I glanced at the luminous clock on the dashboard: 2.30 a.m. Then I switched off the engine and the lights. In the darkness, the cemetery was a mass of black, jutting stones and undefined shadowy places. The crescent moon was hidden behind cloud. I was gripped by the memory of the other night in Heathrow's garden and the terrible appearance of the djinn, and, for a second, I had to put my head on the steering wheel and hold on tight, till my thumping heart began to slow again. Then, exhaling slowly, I took the torch from the glove compartment and got out of the car. *Never again. This is absolutely the last time!*

Once inside it wasn't too bad, I told myself. No owls hooting, no scudding clouds or breaking twigs, just the sound of my breathing as I made my way through the graves, and the dancing beam of the torch which I pointed down as much as possible to avoid attracting attention. *Look for the angel...a bit further...*

I found her without too much trouble. There she was, hands clasped in eternal prayer, wings spread out protectively watching over the sleeper laid to rest beneath.

I swept my torch over the ground. It was uniformly dry and leaf-strewn, no patch of disturbed earth, which might give me a clue as to where the spell lay buried. The trowel I had abandoned on my last visit was nowhere to be seen either. With a sinking feeling, I realised this could take longer than I had thought.

Half an hour later, I flung away the twig with which I had been scraping at the soil. Where was it? I should have found it by now! All around the grave were little holes and piles of dry earth but no sign of the *wazifa*, or the photo with the hair wrapped around it – it was as if the ground had digested them.

Suddenly, out of the corner of my eye, I saw something move behind the gravestone and, looking up, I beheld the silhouette of a tall man a few feet away. Motionless, he appeared to be watching me.

For a second my heart stood still and my knees turned to water. Then I heard my own scream echo freakishly round the cemetery. I scrambled to my feet, grabbed my torch and trained the light on his face. He winced and shrank away as the shaking beam hit him. Then, slowly straightening up, he peered at me, shading his eyes with one hand. 'It's me!'

'*Heathrow?* What are you doing here?'

'Sorry. I didn't mean to scare you.' His voice sounded strange, unsteady. 'I couldn't sleep. I was out walking…' He trailed off.

'Are you OK?' I put the torch down on the gravestone, and Heathrow took a step forward into the light. His face was pale and there were beads of sweat on his forehead. He tried to smile. 'Zarina…'

'Heathrow, what's wrong?' I was frightened by his demeanour. For what seemed like an eternity we stood rooted, staring at one another, he with a sort of anguished plea, me with mounting terror. At last, I whispered, 'Heathrow, please…'

At this, a flame ignited in his eyes and his body quivered tautly into life. He half turned as if he planned to walk away, then suddenly he took two rapid strides towards me and, despite the involuntary shriek that escaped me, pulled me into his arms.

'Zarina!' he groaned, pressing his face into my hair and almost crushing me in his embrace. 'Zarina…'

Hesitantly, I put my arms up around his neck and curled my fingers around the ends of his hair. A shuddering sigh passed from his body to mine. 'Forgive me, Zarina,' he whispered. 'I made a mistake.'

Sufya

IT TOOK SOME EFFORT to struggle into the burkah and by the time I had it on, I was sweaty and irritated. But I had to admit to a new-found respect for Ayesha. She had pressed me a couple of times with her offer to get me into the men-only meeting, and eventually I had abandoned my usual cousin-avoidance policy. Perhaps this was Ayesha's attempt at ending hostilities, and I, under the benign influence of being in love, decided to give her the benefit of the doubt. Besides, I was curious to know what she had in mind.

Ayesha, for her part, seemed pleased when I accepted her offer, but would not reveal the detailed plan. Instead – on the night of the meeting – she turned up at my flat brandishing full-length black burkahs. Although it was not clear to me exactly how being veiled was going to get us into a men-only meeting, she seemed to have no doubts. 'Trust me, *yaar*, I know what makes these people tick,' she lilted, as she stood in front of my bedroom mirror and slipped on her own burkah with a wriggle of her slender hips.

'Ayesha, why are you helping me?' I had asked her when she arrived, wondering at the absence of my cousin's usual languor and sneer.

'Can't stand those fundies telling us where we can and can't go!' she had returned, zestily. 'Now, where is your bedroom, please?'

It turned out, to my amazement, that Ayesha had been actively involved in the women's movement in her college days in Karachi, campaigning against the gradual disenfranchisement of women that had begun in the 1980s with the rise of fundamentalism. According to her, a burkah was a tried and tested way of getting into places where you weren't wanted. 'We used to do it all the time – elementary Trojan horse tactics!' she explained, as she turned to look at me through the little mesh that covered her eyes.

This was the fullest burkah you could get without being mummified and it was unnerving to see Ayesha suddenly thus transformed. After all, when we were growing up and the burkah was hardly seen in London, Zarina and I had secretly felt superior to those who occasionally passed us, listlessly pushing their pushchairs or tugging a couple of silent toddlers by the hand. To us as children, such women had seemed to be rendered faceless, shapeless and voiceless, without feature or personality, without dignity or will.

But, as we grew up, the burkahs had changed in their symbolism – mutating from the brand of the oppressed to the banner of those defiantly proclaiming their religion against a hostile world – and we, the condemners, had become the condemned. It was no longer possible to walk past a burkah in the street without a slight shiver at the sense – real or imagined? – of cold appraisal that seemed to emanate from those hidden eyes. *Who are you trying to impress?*

came the scornful question – real or imagined? – from silent, hidden lips. *How far will you go to be one of them?*

If it was a jolt to see Ayesha metamorphosed into the voice of my inner-interrogator-on-behalf-of-the-Muslim-community, it was even more alarming to see Richard taking on the same form. I realised now why Ayesha had laughed so heartily when I had called her to ask if she could get Richard into the meeting too.

'I'm really not sure about this, Richard,' I told the burkah-clad professor, who was gleefully twirling in front of my bedroom mirror.

'Oh, *I* am,' came Richard's voice incongruously from behind the veil. 'I'm not missing this for the world!'

'Ayesha?' I pleaded with my cousin's shapeless form to help me.

'Women and Jews, what's the difference, *yaar*?' chanted Ayesha's burkah, to my dismay; after all, Richard was at the very least a senior colleague, and we did not joke about his Jewishness.

'Yes! I read somewhere that Muslims are the new Jews!' rejoined Richard's burkah with enthusiasm. I tried to reason with the two of them, arguing that Richard could surely gain entry to any men-only meeting without recourse to dressing as a woman, but Richard, backed up by Ayesha, seemed to think that the entertainment value of smuggling in a Jew in a veil far outweighed any other concerns.

'Oh come on, Sufya! They're hardly going to ask me to undress, are they?' chuckled Richard, who I now realised had probably consumed a few glasses of wine prior to his arrival.

'It will be even better if they do,' added Ayesha, supportively.

Of course, later on, Tariq would tell me that I had been naive and disrespectful to allow any of it to happen. But at that moment, it was almost as though by hiding our bodies and faces, we had become unexpectedly powerful, and it has to be said that it was somewhat intoxicating. And so it was that we set off to the Brothers in Islam meeting as though it were all some kind of a big joke.

And – just for a short while – I managed to forget about the dull ache in my chest which was due to the fact that once again I had not heard from H for some time. The significant event which had taken place in his Camberwell flat had been followed for several days by an appropriately higher level of communication and closeness. But now, he had been away for three weeks and, for the past seven days, his mobile had, without prior mention or warning, been switched off.

Zarina

Slipping slowly through the hourglass, the sands of time occasionally cast out a golden nugget. A glittering moment of experience whose dazzling intensity equals ten lifetimes of dull splendour. A shining thread of connectedness, born in eternity, and spinning effortlessly beyond death. That long night in the cemetery with Heathrow was just such a glimpse of immortality.

From the second our bodies met in that homecoming embrace of longing assuaged and forgiveness freely given, it was as if a divine fire fused us together. Joined by a kiss, sucking the bitterness from each other's hearts and filling our mouths with sweetness, we fell among the graves.

At first, our desire, stretched taut from its unspoken childhood roots, paid no heed to delicacy but catapulted towards fulfilment. A stone grazed my elbow sharply as he pushed me down. He winced as I bit into his shoulder and dragged him onto me.

Later, I shook and cried at his tenderness. 'Did you ever think of me while you were away?'

'Even when I wanted to forget.'

Above us, the clouds slipped away and the shining moon glided slowly through the ripe autumn night as, again and again, my true lover and I rose up to receive one another.

❖

I half woke at dawn, feeling the pale heat of early sunshine warming my stiffened limbs. For a second I wondered where I was. Then I made out the words,

OH FOR A TOUCH OF THE VANISHED HAND
AND A SOUND OF THE VOICE THAT IS STILL

graven in disconsolate italics onto a weathered plinth just next to my head. Above it a stone cross rose towards the sky, wreathed sumptuously around by a carved vine with a profusion of five-pointed leaves and wheel-shaped blossoms – passion flowers. At the top of the shaft, a dove captured for eternity in downward flight was illuminated by the same shaft of slanting sunlight that fell on my skin. As I squinted up at this poignant tribute, I sensed Heathrow watching me, and rolled onto my back to find him resting on one elbow, and looking as if he might have been awake for a while. His eyes were soft and dark, the wild light of the previous night now smouldering peacefully.

'You look like a goddess in that golden glow,' he said, slowly tracing a finger along my collarbone. 'We should have done this years ago.'

'Remind me why we didn't?'

Heathrow grinned. 'Other than the *no girlfriend–boyfriend* rule?

We came close that summer though, didn't we? It slightly took me by surprise.' His eyes became thoughtful as he looked back. 'When we were kids it was adventurous and exciting for sure. But then you turned into someone who could seriously distract me from my plans. I felt we were reaching a point where we wouldn't be able to see past each other and, being brutally honest, I didn't want you – anyone – to have that much power over me. What I failed to realise was what I would lose when I cut you off… how far I'd drift. I didn't know until last night.'

I closed my eyes and felt sunlight dancing on the lids. Could I really be resting like a satiated honey bee on an ear of lavender, listening to my beloved speak these words of tender regret? Here at last was the reunion I had been imagining since the day of his return, and a sense of everything returning to its rightful place. Now the worry over what magic I had or had not done shrank and shrivelled into mere superstition, for the old recognition between Heathrow and me shone bright and real as the climbing sun itself, leaving no shadow where a djinn might enter.

As we too rose to wander hand in hand among the graves, the glory of the autumn day lay like a blessing on the cemetery. Translucent yellow leaves were dropping like fragile medallions from the trees that grew abundantly among the densely clustered headstones, and floating slowly down to land amongst grassy tufts, or scatter across the winding, mossy paths. Branches heavy with glowing amber berries bent gracefully towards the earth. The air was thin with the breathless silence of the season which sensed Persephone's imminent departure for the underworld. But still the ornate statuary – pensive angels, shrouded urns, heroic crosses – many blackened with age, some now leaning at odd angles, bore witness to God's promise of the Life Eternal as, below the tussocked ground, the dead, their peaceful charges, slumbered on. We picked our way among them, pointing out inscriptions to one another.

To Live In The Hearts Of Those We Love Is Not To Die

or *Until The Day Break And The Shadows Flee Away*

or simply, *At Rest*.

In between, Heathrow asked me about the last thirteen years, hungry for details of what he had missed, so I filled him in – focusing mainly on the artistic development and skimming over the embarrassing boyfriends. I had grown accustomed to regarding my life as some sort of stunted compromise that I pursued in the absence of him. But Heathrow, as on the day of his return, appeared genuinely impressed by my theatrical achievements, declaring them the natural and perfect path for me and, as it became clear that his eager and attentive interest was not feigned, it began to seem to me too that, despite those years of dereliction, perhaps because of them, I had, in fact, ended up somewhere better than the fairy tale I had imagined for myself. Like a sparrow who has tumbled hopelessly from its nest, I suddenly felt something shift in my relationship to the ground. In the space of an instant, I stopped falling and sensed my capacity for flight.

'But your work has genuinely made a difference,' I now said, eager to give back, and to show him I was no longer the resentful child of thirteen years ago. '*My Uncle's Son* was a rewriting of the Isaac and Ishmael story: you showed the world how two cousins born on opposite sides have changed the bad ending! That's what got you all those nominations.'

Heathrow pulled me closer as we walked. Hopeful though it was, he said, the story of *My Uncle's Son* was only one of childhood relationship. It would need nurturing and developing if Ayub and David were to have any real prospect of deviating from the paths already mapped out for them. 'An age-old blood feud is a tough narrative to counter. That's why the follow-up documentary is the best thing to come out of that award. My job now is to keep reflecting back to those children who they truly are. Because every time the camera holds up a faithful image of them, every time it records a different story from the one they're hearing all around them, it gives them another chance.'

I found myself recalling a moment from the film in which Ayub, sitting on his bed wearing a faded Spiderman baseball cap, was describing Israeli shelling. 'The *boom boom* is scary, but it's better to hear it,' the subtitles translated, as he spoke softly, his delicate blue-black eyebrows knitting into a worried frown. 'When it goes quiet, *then* you have to worry. That means it's going to land close by, and you must lie down as fast as you can… *Hit the deck!*' he suddenly yelled in English, and flung himself face down on the concrete floor, lying motionless as the camera panned along the length of his body. Then he looked over his shoulder and pushed up his cap, grinning from ear to ear. 'Like that. *Inshallah*, I will be safe and it will only hit one of Masood's goats!'

We walked on for a moment, our feet leaving silent prints in the lush grass. I glanced at Heathrow, who I could see was still thinking about Ayub and David. Then I said softly, 'What about the story we were told? You, me and…'

'Sufya?'

I nodded as we came to a standstill where a giant shadowy yew brooded over a sober collection of unadorned rectangular headstones. 'That she's the one you should be with. Did you start believing it too?'

I hadn't intended to bring it up – the last thing I wanted was to tarnish our hard-won happiness with mention of my sister –

but the way it didn't seem to be playing on *his* mind bothered me. Now, as Sufya slipped between us, I realised the sun had gone in, and my body, registering for the first time the effects of last night's abandon, and a lack of food, was beginning to tremble.

Heathrow, meanwhile, seemed half-ashamed, half-irritated. At last, meeting my gaze, he drew his fingertips across his forehead and said slowly: 'You need to understand, it's been years since I risked feeling anything. In Israel, expediency dictates that you keep a sensible distance from your emotions, because if you're not careful, they can get you killed. But after Leili's father asked me why I had married her if I had intended to treat her with so little regard, I was disgusted with myself...and what I'd deliberately become. I came back hoping to find the integrity I – we all – had as children.' He shrugged. 'I suppose I couldn't switch mode straight away. Sufya – when we were kids, she was usually the one who kept things on track, wasn't she? Always questioning, trying to make sense of it all with her scientific mind... I suppose I thought it would be...*safer*.'

I stared at him. 'Right,' I said. 'Of course. Much less embarrassing than falling for the family lunatic.' I lurched out of the trees towards the nearest path, tears of furious despair blurring my vision. It had been so perfect, and now...to discover that this was what he thought of me – the reason he had been avoiding me all these years!

There was a crunching of leaves, and he was in front of me, blocking my way. 'It's *me* who's become a lunatic!' he shouted. 'Safe? I've been going off the rails! I came here last night like a crazy man with a pack of wolves behind him!'

'Because you can't accept who you are!' I yelled back, beside myself. 'You want Ayub to stay true to himself, but what about *you*? You can't even admit what you want, because it might conflict with some idealised version of yourself that you have in your head. You *use* people to prove to yourself that version is real – Leili, Sufya, whoever! You've always been ashamed to be the abandoned boy with a hole inside. But I don't see you like that, Heathrow! I may be silly and irrational, but I *know* you – I believe in us, the experience of you and me! It's so obvious – why can't you trust it?'

There was a pause. I pressed my tears into my sleeve, and glared at Heathrow to discover him looking at me with quiet passion. 'Last night I ran out of stories,' he said. 'I knew I couldn't go on. I was face to face with that abandoned boy you mentioned. God only knows what instinct brought me to this cemetery! And when I saw you, it felt like stepping on a landmine. I was expecting to be blown apart when I touched you but instead…I found peace. All this time…and the truth turns out to be that I'm joined by my entrails to the girl I left by the windmill, the one who is *always* demanding surrender, daring me to feel and—'

But with a leap I was upon him, my limbs were around him, and my laughter flew into the silent, golden trees as Heathrow squeezed me in his arms. 'I never forgot you, Zarina. I *do* trust this, and I'm sorry it took me so long, I'm sorry about Sufya and…I'll fix it, for all of us. Don't worry.'

'Just don't be afraid!' I clasped his face and looked into his eyes. 'Promise, Heathrow?'

'OK,' he said. 'I won't.'

Sufya

ON OUR ARRIVAL AT THE community centre in Whitechapel Road, the two bearded bouncers had dismissed us with a brusque and unapologetic 'no ladies'. But Ayesha, true to her promise, got us in. '*Bismillah al Rahman al Raheem!*' she had begun in a bell-like voice, clearly audible to the queue of men behind us, and had then launched into a stream of impressive Arabic. The bouncers had seemed dismayed, but convention required them to listen as Ayesha first recited and then translated: '…which, as you will know, brothers, is from the *hadith* – Muwatta of Imam Malik, to be precise: "*Do not stop the maid servants of Allah from going to the mosques of Allah.*"'

'It's the rule, innit,' said one of the bouncers, uncertainly. 'No ladies, that's the rule!'

'Anyway, this isn't a mosque,' said the other, triumphantly.

The queue was beginning to build up behind us, but Ayesha

showed no sign of caring. '"*The believing men and women,*"' she said portentously, '"*are helpers of each other. They collaborate to promote all that is beneficial and discourage all that is evil. Those are the people to whom Allah would grant mercy.*" Al-Taubah 9:71. Brothers, are you going to disobey the holy book and the holy prophet, *alayhi Salatu wa Salaam*?'

The first bouncer looked at the other, who lowered his eyes, perhaps hoping that ignoring Ayesha would make her go away.

'Let 'em in,' said a voice from the line behind us. Someone else grunted in agreement.

'She has a point, I suppose…' the first bouncer said, with a hunted look.

His colleague shrugged helplessly. 'OK,' he said. 'I'm not supposed to let you in, but as long as you stay behind the curtain at the back!'

By now, my attitude to my cousin was undergoing a considerable overhaul. Who would have guessed that behind the bitchy-socialite perfection there lurked such a subversive?

As we passed through the doors, I did not dare look behind me to see the bouncers' reaction to Richard's falsetto '*assalam-u-alaikum!*' Following Ayesha's lead, I dived behind the heavy green velvet drapes suspended from a ceiling rail at the back of the hall. Perhaps, I surmised, community halls regularly used by Muslims were nowadays equipped as a matter of course with such facilities. Right now, I was grateful for somewhere to hide.

Together with my overexcited co-conspirators, I peered round the edge of the curtain. In front of us was row upon row of backs of heads from a whole spectrum of ethnic backgrounds, all of them male. Many were in white *topis*, a few wore Arab *keffiyeh*; some were grey-haired and dressed in shalwar kameez, but most were younger, in tracksuits and even business suits.

On the platform at the front of the hall stood a tall young man in a well-cut, dark-grey suit holding a microphone. He was fair-skinned, perhaps mixed race, and wore fashionable, retro-style glasses. His beard was neatly shaved into a trendy goatee.

'Brothers! This week the so-called leader of the free world gave us all a bit of an insight…' the speaker announced, pausing with the wry smile of a stand-up comedian, and prompting chuckles from the audience. 'The Grand Jury asks him what's meant by "sexual relations", and what does he say? The President of the United States doesn't know!'

There were guffaws of laughter from the assembly.

'And isn't it reassuring to discover that while Monica Lewinsky was performing a *non-sexual* act on him, Bill Clinton was taking phone calls about matters of state?'

There was more laughter.

'Explains something about US foreign policy, doesn't it?'

There was no doubt that Usman Khailvi was a talented orator. Once he had the audience laughing, he briefly closed his eyes and raised his hand with a gentle, paternal smile. The assembly fell silent, effortlessly transitioned from raucous to respectful. '*Bismillah al Rahman al Raheem,*' murmured Khailvi with quiet humility, invoking the help of the divine for the speech he was about to give. 'We ask Allah to bless our meeting here today, and to help us to make the right decisions for ourselves and the great Muslim community of which we are a part…'

His voice was grave and thoughtful, his bearing upright and dignified. He had something of the look of a young Trevor McDonald. The speech that followed took in a wide terrain, from the brutal crushing of Chechnyan rebels to the efforts of Israeli extremists to derail the peace process in Palestine. He emphasised the need to act, the sin of standing by and watching these crimes take place, the requirement on each individual to exercise democratic rights of protest. He did not read from notes, but quoted regularly in Arabic from the Quran, and at these moments closed his eyes in reverence. There was no shouting or encouragement to throw acid in the faces of unveiled women. It all sounded like perfectly reasonable political discourse, from an intelligent and devout young Muslim. There seemed little material for my inquiry into the root causes of fundamentalist anger. Perhaps, I thought, Tariq was right and I had fallen too quickly for the propaganda of the noxious British press.

When Usman Khailvi came to the end of his rousing address the audience cheered and clapped, and another suited young man, also with a goatee beard, perhaps modelled on that of his leader, leapt onto the stage and announced Brother Usman would now be happy to take questions from the floor.

A hand shot up from the front of the hall and someone asked whether Brother Usman did not think that direct action was called for, that the Quran sanctioned violence when in self-defence, and that, as Muslims were under attack worldwide, was it not time for the Brothers in Islam to unite with those who were giving their lives overseas against the enemies of the *ummah*?

There was a wave of 'hear hear!' and '*bismillah!*' as the questioner finished speaking, and near the back of the room a small pack of young men grunted gorilla-style. Usman Khailvi smiled and lowered his eyes. The hall fell silent. When the speaker raised his head, he looked grave. 'How can I stand between any brother and his conscience?' he asked, humbly. 'Our faith requires that we ask only Allah for guidance. That is what I do, and I can only offer this to you for an answer.'

'Allah says fight the enemies of Islam!' shouted one of the young men, thrusting a fist into the air and causing the gorilla chant to break out once more among his comrades.

At that moment there was a loud altercation at the back of the hall. The doors burst open and a column of about twenty police officers in riot helmets jogged into the hall holding up their batons, followed by the dishevelled bouncers who were still shouting, 'You can't go in there!'

'I'm sorry, gentlemen,' said one of the policemen, nervously. 'A young male has been attacked on a bus not far from here, and we have reason to believe this was on grounds of his Jewish persuasion. Nobody may leave. We will need to search everyone. Lads, take up positions!'

The crowd muttered angrily, and people began to rise to their feet as police officers spread quickly out around the perimeter of the audience. To my horror, I saw one of the policemen striding towards our curtain. 'Sarge, there's the females in here,' he said with pink-lipped importance as he sharply pulled aside the curtain, to reveal Ayesha, Richard and me cowering in our burkahs.

'What are *they* doing in here?' shouted one of the hyped-up young men, though it was not altogether clear whether he was referring to us or the police. Either way, it was not a welcoming shout, and was reinforced by a growing rumble of anger from others in the hall.

'Everyone remain calm,' said Usman Khailvi into the microphone from the platform. 'Nobody here has done anything wrong, there is nothing to fear.' Then he added, 'This is just the police going about their normal business of harassing innocent Muslims. We don't need to react. Let them have their fun.'

'We are *not*, I repeat, *not*, here to harass anyone,' said the nervous sergeant, his top lip sweating slightly. 'In fact, we have a female police officer with us to search the ladies, because we respect your customs. Suzy? Perhaps if you could do the honours, we can allow these ladies to leave first…'

All eyes were on Suzy, the red-cheeked WPC who was advancing towards us. I thought of running for the door, but there was no point, she was already upon us. I felt like I was going to faint.

Of course, Suzy chose to search Richard first. And as her hands moved down his body, I saw her eyes widen in surprise and alarm. In slow motion, I watched her head turn towards the sergeant and her lips part. 'Sarge!' she said, her voice echoing with crushing inevitability around the entire hall: 'This one's a *male*!'

There was a heartbeat of silence and then all hell broke loose. Three PCs jumped on Richard, and dragged his burkah off him, confirming to the angry crowd that he was – in fact – a male.

'*They're Mossad spies!*' yelled someone, and a pumped-up young man leapt from the crowd to tug violently on my burkah, causing me to lose my balance. As I fell to the ground, hitting my head hard against the back wall, I was aware from the shouts around me that scuffles had broken out in various parts of the hall – perhaps as the police tried to prevent others from rushing at us, the alleged Mossad infiltrators, or perhaps because some members of the audience had decided they were simply not going to be searched. I heard Ayesha cry out too, and then the burkah was tugged from under me, up and over my head, to reveal a row of surprised, male police officers.

'This one *is* a woman!' one yelled in alarm.

'So is this one!' yelled another.

'Sergeant, do you have a warrant to search these people?' came a voice on the microphone. I lifted my head from the floor to see who was speaking. It was Tariq who now stood beside Usman Khailvi on the platform. He spoke calmly and coldly. 'Because if not, you had better leave. Particularly as you have just allowed male officers to publicly assault and undress at least two Muslim women.'

It was probably Tariq that got me, Richard and Ayesha outside afterwards, but I did not see the meeting break up because at that point the blow to my head had its delayed effect, and I briefly lost consciousness.

'Sorry, Tariq,' I said when I found myself sitting in the passenger seat of my car with him next to me. Ayesha and Richard were quiet in the back seat, like a couple of bad children after a telling-off.

'Too fucking right, Sufya,' said Tariq. 'Is this all some kind of a *game* to you?' He did not wait for a reply but got out of the car and slammed the door before he marched away.

I felt dreadful that night as Richard dropped Ayesha off and – after I refused his offer of a lift to A & E – drove me home in silence. The pain in my head was matched only by waves of self-pity as I wondered where H was when I needed to be held and told that I was not a naive over-intellectual fool, that I was not a traitor to my community, and that it really did not matter whose side I was on.

Perhaps it was some kind of an effort to forget these painful feelings, or a simple child-like longing for comfort and consolation, or perhaps it was a rush of anger against the man who had sought a new intimacy only to become utterly unavailable. Perhaps it was a combination of all these things – but whatever it was, it was an unforgivable lapse of judgement that caused me, when we pulled up outside my flat, and he suddenly leant towards me with unmistakable intent, to return the rather too lingering kiss of my former PhD supervisor.

⁂

Tariq: I appreciate the apology, and the brunch too, and you look pretty good considering the mess you got yourself into last night, but I still don't get it.

Me: [glumly] Me neither. I thought I might find a fresh angle on my book. I just didn't realise…

Tariq: But that's just what I don't get – *why* didn't you realise? I mean everyone's thinking about Islam these days – establishment included. It's the hot topic, *so why aren't you*?

Me: I… I don't know. I think I should just stick to animals. They're far more civilised.

Tariq: See, this is where I get pissed off again, Sufya: there's enough bad press about Muslims without us joining in as well!

Me: I wasn't singling out Muslims!

Tariq: Look, it was OK when we were young, right? We could pretend it didn't matter then. We were just Pakis, harmless Pakis. But things have changed. I go into those meetings with the Home Secretary and all the excellent liberals that advise the big man. To them we're book-burners, wife-abusers, terrorists – that's how they see us. Most of them don't count me on their team even though I'm sitting right in the middle of them.

Me: But I can't be on a team with all the fundies.

Tariq: They won't have you in the Paki-bashers or the Islamophobes.

Me: I don't think it's as stark as that.

Tariq: You have to face facts. You know the reason that I agreed to marry someone my parents chose for me? Because one day the penny just dropped: doesn't matter how much we try to be one of them, we're never going to get a look-in. We'll always be outsiders.

Me: [after a pause] Are you still angry with me?

Tariq: No, not with you. Just angry in general when I get onto this subject.

Me: So if your anger were a person, what would he or she look like?

Tariq: Like my great-great-grandfather, Jamshed Shah Bahadur. He was a sepoy during the Indian mutiny. They say he went wild with a bayonet and cut down four British officers. They had to put seven bullets into him to stop him.

Me: And what would he be saying?

Tariq: [fiercely] He'd be saying: *We were in their own army and look what they did to us. How can you trust them? Give them hell!*

Me: Is that what you want then – to give them hell?

Tariq: [leaning back and winking one long-lashed lid at me] Well it's either that or find out what's happened to those Bloody Marys we ordered!

Me: [laughing] So are you in trouble with the Brothers because you know me?

Tariq: Not really. I *did* have to tell them you were stalking me, though. Any chance you might be? No, I didn't think so. Bit of a shame.

Saturday 26 September 1998

Zarina

DAZED AND EUPHORIC, I finally drifted home at about three o'clock in the afternoon. Dreamily, I put my key into the lock – only to feel the door wrenched open from the inside. Scarcely had I gasped in surprise than I gasped again in horror. For standing in the doorway, hair on end like an avenging angel, and wearing an expression of unabated fury stood none other than Sufya.

'You *should* be scared!' she snapped. 'Where on earth have you been all day? Mum tried calling everywhere. It's a madhouse here!'

Mumbling something about a script workshop, I ducked into the hallway, where a strange assortment of sounds brought me up short. From the living room came the fervent sing-song of a bevy of women reciting the Quran, Mum leading the prayers in a voice cracked with anxiety. Meanwhile from upstairs came a loud thumping and Dad's pleading voice: '*Yaar,* please come out, you need to see a doctor!' And what was just about recognisable as Bogie shouting and groaning from behind the bathroom door: 'Leave me alone, Ahmed! I don't want doctors!... My God will save me from this uncleanness!' His words were cut off by an appalling, booming retching.

'What the...?' I turned back to Sufya, who was standing on the porch looking up and down the street for the source of the wailing sirens which now filled the neighbourhood. Sure enough, seconds later an ambulance pulled up sharply, and paramedics were rushing past me and up the stairs. 'This way, love?'

'Yes, straight ahead!' Sufya, following close behind, paused to peel off the rubber gloves she was wearing, and shove them along with a bottle of antibacterial spray into my arms.

'The kitchen needs sorting out,' she said. And glancing over her shoulder a few steps further up, 'Well, go on!'

Avoiding the living room, I stumbled into the kitchen where pots, pans, utensils, and Mum's entire crockery collection, including her Royal Doulton cherry blossom wedding service, were piled in the sink and arrayed over the worktops, everything coated in a layer of lemon-scented cleaning fluid. Walls, windows and doors were also smeared with white suds. In the middle of the slippery floor, like a prisoner in the dock, stood a lone bucket on a sheet of newspaper. Cautious inspection revealed that it held a Tupperware container, a plate and a fork soaking in what smelled like maximum-strength chlorine bleach.

I squirted the spray vaguely into the air. Then I set it down on the worktop and went upstairs to find out what the hell was going on.

The lead paramedic, a burly Australian with a blond moustache, was now rapping on the bathroom door. 'Sir?' he called. 'Sir! Can you hear me? Are you all right?'

'Leave me alone, infidels!' Bogie groaned. 'My God is testing me! Aaaarggghhh! *Ya Allah!*' He vomited deafeningly.

'Fuck's sake,' muttered Sufya, folding her arms.

White-faced, Dad stood to one side with the second paramedic, a fresh-faced young woman with a glossy brown ponytail, who was scribbling busily in a notebook. 'Is there anything he's eaten that could have brought this on?'

'P-p-pork!' Dad's voice was barely audible through his shaking lips. 'He ate some p-p-pork…with some chilli pickle, but I don't think it was the p-p-pickle!'

'Raaarrrrgggghhhh, *Ya Allah!*' The bathroom door shook, and we all winced.

'Could the pork have been off?' asked the ponytail girl, with forced calm.

Dad closed his eyes. For a second, he did not respond. Then: 'It is possible,' he whispered.

The lead paramedic now looked at Dad. 'Hang on a minute! Aren't you that food scientist from the news?' Dad did not seem to hear.

'Sir!' urged the paramedic. 'Talk to me! Where did that pork come from?'

Dad opened his eyes. 'BestCo,' he said. 'From one of our processing plants. I was doing a spot check and I found a van full of it in the loading dock. The driver said it was for dumping.'

We were all gathered around him now, for the moment leaving Bogie to gag and gargle alone.

'I-I looked at the quality control sheets and I could see the full batch of tests had not been performed. I wasn't happy the protocol had been relaxed without my authority, so I took a sample of the pork home in my lunchbox. I was going to perform some tests…for my own satisfaction.'

'And your friend ate it by mistake?'

Dad looked round the circle, his face stricken. 'A terrible mistake! I p-put it at the back of the fridge. I was going to test it this morning. But Bogie came round after early prayers and fried it for his breakfast while I was in the shower – he must have thought it was...' He trailed off, staring into space.

'Chicken!' Bogie wailed from inside, as Dad uttered an inarticulate sound and clutched at Sufya's shoulder.

'Whoever asked for that pork to be dumped knew it was contaminated,' he said faintly.

'Right!' The Australian barged back to the bathroom where it had gone ominously quiet. 'Can you hear me in there, mate? Give me a shout if you can... Hey, Tone!' he called down the stairs to a third paramedic who was waiting on the front path. Tone stuck his head through the open front door. 'Tell 'em we've got severe food poisoning, possibly dodgy supermarket pork! And get the stretcher up here!' Tone nodded and dashed back to the ambulance.

'We need to get you to hospital, mate!' The paramedic put his ear to the bathroom door. 'Mate? Can you open up for me?'

'*Yaar*, this is some very dangerous bacteria!' Dad, pulling himself together, joined in. 'Don't be a fool!'

'No!' yelled Bogie defiantly (thankfully still conscious). 'This is not bacteria! This is a punishment from God for eating the flesh of an unclean animal! Let me take my punishment! My God will do the best for me! If he wills me to live, then I shall live!'

By now, Tone was standing at the foot of the stairs with the stretcher. 'They're ready for us. What's the situation?'

'Won't come out, mate. Some kind of Jehovah's Witness. I reckon we call the fire brigade and break it down!'

'OK, that's it!' said Sufya. 'Mind out the way!' And grabbing the metal stick that was kept on the upstairs landing to open the loft hatch, she marched over to the bathroom door and gave it an almighty *THWACK*, denting the wood and sending chips of gloss paint flying.

'Listen to me, Uncle! You've got Mum, Dad and everybody out here worried sick because you've ingested some life-threatening toxins! Don't make it worse than it already is! Who knows if God cares but I'm pretty sure that H does – if anyone ever knew where the hell he was! So for *his* sake, I'm not going to let you die in that bathroom!'

WHACK! This time she made a jagged vertical crack in the door.

'I mean it, Uncle! Open the door before I *smash it to pieces*!'

She was raising the stick for another attack when suddenly there was the sound of the key turning in the lock.

Instinctively we all took a step back as the door opened and Bogie appeared, looking truly dreadful. His face was drawn and yellow, and veins stood out tortuously on his forehead. His whole body trembled and he leaned heavily against the door frame, gasping from the effort to stay upright.

The Australian and the ponytail girl rushed to support him. 'Easy there, mate! Good on you.'

Mum and the aunties were huddled together in the hallway downstairs. '*Hai, Allah!*' they murmured, when they saw Bogie's condition. 'Allah have mercy!'

As he collapsed onto the stretcher, Mum hurried tearfully forward, and tied a little black cloth pouch around his neck. 'We have made you a health-giving *tawiz*! Don't be afraid, *bhai*! Ahmed and I are coming with you!'

Eyes rolling, Bogie pressed the amulet to his lips, raising his other hand in a theatrical gesture as the paramedics rushed him down the front path, Mum and Dad hot on their heels. There was a brief business of getting into vehicles and shutting doors, then they were all gone in a blaze of lights and sirens.

'*Achha*, children, *Khuda-hafiz!* God protect you! Take care, *hain*?' The aunties drifted out and dispersed, still shaking their heads.

Sufya and I were left on the doorstep.

'Well, you got him out,' I ventured at last. 'I suppose he'll be all right now.'

She turned to me suddenly. 'Do you have any idea where H is?'

I managed a minimal headshake.

'Right,' she said after a moment. 'I'm out of here. I'll call later. You'd better use some of that antibacterial in the bathroom.'

I watched her drive away, then shut the front door slowly and leaned against it. I was shocked, exhausted and, frankly, embarrassed at the way we all carried on, and the exhibition we had made of ourselves in front of those paramedics.

And suddenly, instead of being worried about Bogie's wellbeing, I was flooded with resentment – resentment at how, between them, my family effortlessly hijacked my every happiness – no matter how brief or hard-won – with some ridiculous hullabaloo. Scarcely had I felt the warmth of my spotlight before they were all careering blindly into it like a gigantic pantomime horse, and butting me unceremoniously into the pit.

And how come *I'm out of here* was always Sufya's line? I should be the one getting out of here: I should run screaming down the street, fling myself in Heathrow's arms and never come back. I rang him but, getting only his answerphone, hung up. It occurred to me he might have heard by now and be on his way to the hospital. Besides, I knew full well that more hell would only break loose if I did not get upstairs and scrape up Bogie's vomit.

Thursday 1 October 1998

Sufya

THE DOOR OPENED and there stood Zarina in her pyjamas. She had been crying, and there was something helpless in her gaze. Spontaneously, I put my arms around her, sensing that, for once, my little sister would accept comfort from me. Even horrors like Uncle Bogie's grave illness, it seemed, could have positive effects.

Yesterday there had been more family drama when Dad had been dragged from his vigil at Bogie's bedside to speak at a press conference hastily organised by BestCo in response to the spiralling food scare. Though there had been no new cases of poisoning allegedly linked to BestCo pork, two eight-year-olds were still fighting for their lives in a Leeds hospital, while a score of elderly people also remained in a critical condition around the country. The papers were full of it, with wild speculation comparing the potential problem with last year's BSE crisis. At the press conference, in the presence of reporters from around the world,

Dad had read a prepared statement to the effect that there was as yet no conclusive evidence that *any* of the cases were directly linked to BestCo pork, that he had personally ordered an extra level of testing on all products as a precaution only, and that the meat was certainly safe for consumption.

But Dad had appeared strained and lacking in conviction as he delivered the statement, and the journalists, sensing weakness, had responded with increasingly aggressive questioning. Only a few minutes into the session an ITN reporter had leapt to his feet with a direct – and personal – accusation: 'Dr Malik, isn't it a fact that you are a Moslem and that your religion forbids you to eat pork? Why then did you tell us you would feed BestCo pork to your family?' The BestCo Head of Publicity had had to close the press conference as other journalists began to clamour: 'Why don't you want to answer that, Dr Malik?' and 'Why should we believe anything you say, Dr Malik?' The incident had been shown on numerous TV channels the previous evening, and I had heard it again on the car radio as I drove to our family home this morning.

Zarina returned my hug, and for a brief moment it seemed that the dark genie that lived between us was no longer there. I felt her body hiccup with a noiseless sob, and my own tears welled up. But we swallowed our respective grief and she stepped away suddenly, dropping her eyes. Something in her stance told me that the genie had returned.

'He's much worse today,' she murmured. 'Mum and Dad went ahead with Ayesha.'

'I've been trying to reach H but he's been out of phone contact for a couple of days,' I said. 'I hate to think he has no idea what's happening.'

'Oh, he's back, actually,' said Zarina, lightly. She turned and headed towards the kitchen. 'I saw him at the hospital yesterday.'

The carpet seemed to jump under my feet. 'He's back?'

'Yes, thank goodness! Did you manage to pick up that saffron?'

Steadying myself with effort, I did not reply. In a slightly softer voice, Zarina called from the kitchen: 'He told me he's been meaning to call you…'

Somehow, I got myself to the kitchen door to see her running over to the stove to turn down the heat under a saucepan of milk which had been just about to boil over. Hardly aware of what I was doing I handed her the small packet she had asked me to bring, and watched as she swiftly tore it open and poured the entire contents into the hot milk, causing it to turn a deep swirling red, and releasing a pungent odour. She grabbed a wooden spoon and began to stir the mixture energetically, reaching for Mum's cardamom jar at the same time. 'Anyway, I thought the thing with you and H wasn't going anywhere last time we spoke?'

'Zee, what are you doing? They'll be wondering why we're not at the hospital.'

'It's for a *wazifa* that Mum wanted us to do for Bogie before we leave. We have to pray over it.'

It was only now that I noticed that the framed photo of Bogie with Claudia Cardinale had been taken from the living room wall and placed on the kitchen table, along with two long red candles and Mum's velvet-bound Quran. Irritation leapt up in me. 'Zee, you know perfectly well, I don't do that stuff. It's ridiculous – I don't believe in it!'

'You don't believe in it so it's ridiculous?' Zarina grabbed a hand whisk and began to beat the hot red liquid in the pan into a foam.

'It's ridiculous so I don't believe in it! No reasonable person could consider it even remotely likely to work…'

'Does it have to be as cut and dried as that?' Despite my rising irritation I noticed that my sister was, unusually, maintaining an even tone. 'Maybe it just helps people to feel like they can do something – anything – rather than just sit there and be a victim...'

'Who could be more of a victim than someone who resorts to such a ludicrous belief-system!' I snapped. 'We're just wasting time here. We should leave.'

Zarina switched off the heat under the pan and for a moment paused her bustle of preparations. She turned to me. 'Supposing it's not the system but the *belief* that's the important part? Don't you agree that faith can make things happen?'

I stared at my sister. 'You know, it wouldn't harm you occasionally to make use of that Cambridge education. Don't worry, you'll still be the favourite daughter.'

'Why don't you just answer the question?' Zarina insisted. 'It would just take us a few minutes to do this *wazifa*, and if Mum believes it can help Bogie, well maybe we could just add our belief to hers and...who knows? Where's the science to prove that it *won't* work? Does scientific method have anything to say about what really matters? About human needs and relationships? Does it have anything to say about *love?*' The last word lingered on her lips. *Always so dramatic.* I was sick of her.

'I haven't got time for this, Zee! While you concoct your absurd potions I'm going to the hospital to say goodbye to our dying uncle!'

Zarina shouted after me as I headed for the front door. 'Well, guess what, scientific method has just washed its hands of Uncle Bogie! And so, apparently, have we, since you won't lift a finger! Why didn't you just leave him in the bathroom?'

The bell rang just as I opened the door, and I was confronted with Habib, waving his car keys. 'Your mum sent me to get you both,' he said, importantly. 'They think your uncle hasn't much time left.'

'It's OK, I'll take my own car – you can take Zarina!' I muttered, as I brushed past him.

⁂

Comedic and irritating though Bogie was at times, he was flawlessly authentic, and his presence in our lives enabled us to breathe the scent of what it might be to live without our second-generation confusion. Despite the scorn that Zarina and I had always poured on him, in our hearts we grudgingly held him in a kind of awe, because he was one of the few people we knew who was shamelessly, ridiculously and wondrously *himself*. But for H, Uncle Bogie was, of course, much more than all this – he was the one who had rescued him as a helpless, abandoned infant at Terminal 3, the man who had consistently loved him in his hapless, booming, big-hearted way – not only his father, but his only relative in the world. By the time I arrived at the hospital, I had forgiven H for not calling me on his return. Of course his priority had been to be at his father's bedside.

Uncle Bogie lay in the intensive care room under a tangled undergrowth of tubes, his vast frame shrunk to one impossibly frail. His eyes were closed and under the oxygen mask an irregular breath groaned in his throat. Mum was sitting by the bed, holding his hand, weeping softly as she whispered prayer after prayer. Holding Mum's other hand was Dad, who was the only one who looked up as I entered the room. His expression did not change as his eyes met mine. He looked like he was about to burst. Behind them stood Ayesha, her head covered over with a *dupatta*, her mascara smudged on her cheeks, a rosary passing silently through her fingers.

And there, on the other side of the bed, stood the tall, straight-backed figure of H, eyes closed and head bowed. His arms were by his sides and I saw that his hands were clenched. My heart leapt into my throat and seemed to get lodged there.

I walked quietly to his side and gently brushed my fingers over his closed fist so that he would know I was there. His eyes flickered open and he turned his head slightly to look at me. The agony in his glance went right through me and I suddenly wanted to do something, anything, to take away his suffering. I tried to put my arm around him, but he looked away again and closed his eyes. '*Don't,* Sufya,' he whispered. '*Don't touch me.*'

I drew my hand away and stood there. There was only an inch between us but his words had turned it into the span of the infinite universe. The bleep of the heart monitor, the buzz of the air-conditioning and the rasp of Uncle Bogie's breathing were the only sounds in the room, along with Mum's tearful whispers. Was this his grief speaking, I wondered, or something else? Could he be angry that I had not been at the hospital yesterday as Zarina had, or, worse, could he somehow have found out about that stupid, oh so stupid, kiss with Richard? I dismissed the thoughts, furious with myself for such self-absorption: what H was enduring at this moment had nothing to do with me.

Uncle Bogie's breathing became more laboured. Mum opened her eyes in alarm, and then closed them tighter than ever. She began to pray more audibly, her words punctuated by half-stifled sobs.

'Should I go and get someone?' I mouthed to Dad, the only person whose eyes were not closed.

Dad shrugged helplessly. 'They said there's nothing else they can do.'

There was a knock at the door and Zarina entered. She walked straight to Mum and handed her a small thermos. I watched as Mum took the flask and, with a tearful smile, kissed the hand that had brought it. Then, opening it quietly, she smiled lovingly at me too – no doubt thinking I had helped prepare the magical milkshake within – before carefully pouring a few warm red drops onto Uncle Bogie's inner wrist, now murmuring her prayers with a softer, calmer tone.

Habib ambled into the room, a cold drink can in hand, noticeably less stricken than everyone else.

Uncle Bogie's breathing and Mum's prayers wove the seconds into a long and painful thread by which we were all suspended.

I remembered Bogie's famed suicide attempt in which a copy of the Quran had saved his life. 'I said to my God, if you want me to live, then save me. Otherwise I am damn bloody *gone*!' he had told us so often, defiantly lifting his Hollywood jaw. Only Uncle Bogie lived life like this, somewhere on the edge of reality and movieland, somewhere you could fire a gun at your heart and have the bullet stopped by the Word of God.

It was against the rules of cinema that such a person be saved from a bullet only to be ignobly dispatched by a rotten sandwich. But it was not a movie we were watching now, it was the well-charted action of salmonella on the human body: destiny decided by science, not by the laws of story, not by wishful thinking, not by faith, however devout.

Then suddenly, Uncle Bogie started to gag under the oxygen mask. Mum, and Ayesha opened their eyes in alarm. I looked at H but he seemed unable to move, his face shadowed. 'That's it!' I cried. 'I'm going to get someone! Uncle…' I put my lips close to his ear, '*hold on! Please!* I'll get someone to help you!'

As I ran for the door, I could hear – above the sound of praying and sobbing – the terrible flat tone of the heart monitor, and, though I did not look at him, I could sense H still standing motionless and rigid, as though impaled on that needle-sharp frequency.

Zarina

I WASN'T AT ALL SURE I could watch Uncle Bogie die; and the thought of what would happen to Heathrow if he did was like a red button in my brain – I couldn't go anywhere near it. So, even after Sufya abandoned me, I refused to give up. I got into Habib's Datsun with a thermos containing the blood-coloured milk, stuck the candles in his cup-holders, spread Mum's Quran on my lap, and prayed for a miracle all the way to the hospital.

It was obvious, as Ayesha opened the door to Uncle Bogie's room, that Habib had not exaggerated the gravity of the situation. Barely conscious now, his skin taut, grey and papery, Uncle Bogie had clearly taken a turn for the worse this morning. Mum and Dad sat in their usual chairs to one side of his bed; Heathrow, wearing the same clothes as yesterday, stood on the other, holding Bogie's skeletal hand and stroking his flattened, greying mane. He looked up as I tiptoed to the bed and delivered the precious thermos to Mum: his eyes were wide, and his jaw worked briefly like a struggling butterfly. Then he turned back to his father.

Behind him, Sufya loitered miserably. Uncle Bogie's illness had, of course, delayed any conversation between her and Heathrow – we had both taken it as read that it should wait. But seeing her earlier, so obviously not indifferent to the relationship – in fact, cracking up – and now, hovering there, suspended... I bit my lip and looked away.

The warm, red milk was trickling from Uncle Bogie's wrist and soaking into the white bedspread, as Mum let it fall drop by drop. Was it wishful thinking, or was his breathing sounding slightly less ragged?

Silently I took up the prayer being whispered by Mum, and echoed by Ayesha: *A'udhu bi'izzatil-Lahi wa Qudratihi min Sharri ma Ajidu wa 'Uhadhir. I seek refuge with Allah and with His Power from the evil that afflicts me and that which I apprehend.*

Sending myself deep inside the words, I allowed my eyelids to slide shut.

And then, from the heart monitor, that awful alarm...

As Heathrow looked wildly round for help, Mum and Dad leapt to their feet, and I stumbled in the direction of the door, only to be overtaken by Sufya who ran shrieking into the corridor. Filled with dread, I now turned back towards Uncle Bogie and beheld him looking strangely young, or rather, not young – ageless. His breath was still, and with the strain now wiped from it, his face resembled a sculpture. A sculpture with large, living eyes which, as I watched, slowly swivelled towards his right shoulder, as though someone were standing there – and contemplated that someone with an expression of grim humour.

Mum gasped and seized Uncle Bogie's face between her hands,

forcing him to turn his head towards her. *'Aankhen band karo!* Close your eyes!' she said firmly, 'Don't look at him – no, don't! If you don't look at him he won't take you!'

Bogie struggled briefly to extricate his head, then gazed at Mum for a full second, his eyes holding hers with a look of complete clarity and recognition…then his breath escaped in a peaceful sigh…his eyelids fluttered…and were closed.

Immediately, the room was filled with medics shouting instructions and herding us all outside. Only Heathrow remained, pinned against the wall, arms crossed tightly over his chest. Clustered around the porthole in the door, we could hear the blasts of electricity surging through Bogie's lifeless body, which arched and flailed gruesomely.

Dad groaned, Mum prayed loudly on jerking breaths, Ayesha shuddered and reached for Habib, Sufya placed a hand over her mouth. Kicking myself for allowing them to evict me, instead of slipping to Heathrow's side, I could only watch through the glass as the doctors, pounding Bogie's undignified corpse, tampered vainly with the dense fabric of death.

Then, just as suddenly as it had exploded, all activity within the room ceased. The medics stood for a moment with heads bowed. Slowly they took off their gloves. The doctor in charge murmured something about time of death. Somebody else flicked a switch and the endless mocking siren fell silent.

The doctor came out of the room and stood before us as the other medics and nurses shuffled away down the corridor, murmuring condolences. He looked at Mum sympathetically. Her prayers trailed off and she stared back at him, her face a tragic question mark.

'I'm so sorry,' he said. 'Perhaps you'd like to spend some time with him—'

But Mum had already torn back into the room and thrown herself over Bogie's body.

'*Nahin!*' she screamed. '*Yeh kabhi nahin ho sakta!* This cannot be! *Maine tum se kaha tha, dekhna mat!* Why did you look when I told you not to?' And she shook the body so violently that Bogie's teeth rattled.

Rushing in after her, we all quailed at the scene. Sufya gave our father a shove as I simultaneously appealed, 'Dad!'

'Come on, Firdaus, *jaan*. It's too late.' He approached the bed and gently drew her away. 'He's in the care of Allah now.'

As they left Uncle Bogie's side, a sense of desolation began to descend in the room, like a thick and penetrating dampness. Battling against it in search of God knew what words of comfort, I turned towards Heathrow – just in time to see him fall forward, away from his wall. I threw up a hand to steady him, but he shot past me towards the bed, eyes blazing, as though he too were about to launch a demented attack on the corpse. Ayesha let out a squeal.

I think we all saw it together. As Heathrow sent the now disconnected monitor crashing to the floor, Bogie *suddenly sat bolt upright!* One smooth movement like Frankenstein's monster. Except there was nothing monstrous about his expression: it was Uncle Bogie's famous look to camera, moving seamlessly from surprise, to confusion, to a broad smile.

'By God!' he murmured in wonder as he settled back into the arms of his son, who now smiled radiantly at me over his head. 'By God, another great comeback!'

Friday 9 October 1998

Sufya

H OPENED THE DOOR and, as I walked past him without a word, I registered the expression of alarm that crossed his face. He followed me up the stairs and from his silence alone I confirmed his feelings towards me. After weeks of non-communication, I had expected nothing else. But that did not matter now.

Apart from the absence of curtains, he had had all the fire damage repaired. Thus for him had the drama and significance of that night been erased. Outside the window, the glossy leaves that remained on the charred magnolia gleamed in the autumnal sunshine. In the haven of his white-painted living room, where a few weeks ago I had allowed myself that momentary daydream of a life with him, I turned to face H. I felt serene.

'I'm sorry. I was going to call you.'

'That's not why I'm here. I'm pregnant.'

A multitude of phantoms first whitened then darkened H's

features.

'I-I'm confused...did we actually...?' His eyes strayed to the ottoman posed beside us.

'I know. I didn't think we had either. But we must have been closer than we thought...'

H continued to stare at the sofa. Distractedly, he ran a hand through his hair.

I took a deep breath. 'H, forget it. You don't have to say anything. You've been avoiding me ever since and it's obvious that this relationship is going nowhere. So – as far as I'm concerned – you're off the hook. But I need to tell you that I'm going to keep this baby. I think you know enough about my history to understand why. You can be part of its life or not, but I've made my decision.'

It was a simple speech and now that I had made it, the plan was to leave. But H looked up, and something in his expression held me. His eyes were hollowed by a cavernous, receding darkness. Despite all that had happened, I wanted to reach out to him – to offer comfort – but I held back, frightened by the emptiness in him.

'It must be a shock.'

At this, he seemed launched into movement, taking a powerful stride towards me. My heart leapt inside my rib cage with a violence that almost propelled me into his arms, just as I saw him ricochet away again. He crossed the room and stood with his back to me, the straight line of his shoulders set hard. 'You don't have to be kind!' he muttered.

'Look, we can talk later,' I said, briskly. 'You'll need time to let it sink in.' I did not glance back as I headed down the stairs and out into the street. As his front door closed behind me, my breath shortened and my legs were suddenly leaden. Though I had thought myself prepared for the bad news I knew was coming, inured to his indifference or worse, I had not been ready at all. A hundred yards down the street I could walk no further and had to lean on a nearby gatepost, a feeling of almost unbearable pressure in my chest.

Then suddenly he was there, his arms around me.

'You can't do it, H!' I choked, pulling away from him. 'You've always felt it was your job to fix things, but whatever you feel for me is just what it is. You can't find a universal solution this time. But if you could only work out what it is that really matters to you, and trust it, then you might know what to do. I know what I want, and nobody, not even you, seems to come into the equation. This time, I won't – I can't – abandon my baby.'

His eyes were a storm of emotion as he grasped my shoulders, holding me in front of him as though to ensure that his words could most directly and deeply strike their target. 'Sufya, please understand. If there's one decision that will determine my whole life, this is it. From this point on, everything else becomes theoretical. I rejected your kindness a minute ago – now I'm asking for it. You know enough about *my* history to recognise that this isn't a choice for me either. Just like you, I cannot abandon this baby. And I will not abandon you.'

Friday 16 October 1998

Zarina

NOTHING WORSE THAN *actors making a meal out of a love scene that's not even a love scene!* But this had been going on for the last two pages and, as we reached the end of it, they were well into it, emoting away – indulgence, indulgence, indulgence!

'*I am your true friend, your true lover,*' averred Dan, fixing Sabah with a look of manly sincerity to which she meltingly responded, '*For our communion is spirit, not matter.*'

Dan smiled gently and played with a lock of her hair. What was with the gratuitous gestures? This was a reading!

I glanced at Kevin, a 'mate' of Dan's from drama school, who had come along to be considered as a possible Shahjehan. Dan had described him over the phone as the most gifted actor in the year, omitting to mention that he looked nothing like a Mughal emperor. With slightly deep-set blue eyes, wavy amber hair, and neatly attired in stonewashed jeans and a charcoal V-neck sweater, he was leaning forward in his chair, watching the others intently.

Sabah now took a step towards Dan with the uplifted face of the courageous heroine declaring her love: '*I am your true friend, your true lover...*'

'*For we meet not on earth, but in the ether!*' Dan's expansive arm movement took in the grotty surroundings of the duty manager's office, to which we had been relegated after a mix-up with the booking.

And then, for God's sake, they actually kissed! (Which showed how little they had understood the text.) A last lingering look, a final holding of the moment, and they turned to face me expectantly with the cleansed, post-coital expressions of actors who have just accessed profound truth in their performance and will now receive the embrace of the moved-to-tears director.

I regarded them for a moment in silence. Then I tossed the script onto the floor next to my chair, and said, 'Well, that doesn't work, does it? Sorry, Dan, it was worth a try, but we were right first time, you'd better stick with Shahjehan.'

Sabah, crestfallen, looked up at Dan – who picked up her cue and promptly stepped into the role of male protector.

'It's interesting you say that, Zarina,' he began in his best voice, 'because I felt – in fact, I think we *both* felt...' (the corroboration-seeking look to Sabah, the eager nod back) 'that it *did* work. We really *found* something there. Didn't we?'

Sabah nodded again. 'It worked for me. I mean, I know we'd refine it and everything in rehearsal, but it feels right, Zee.'

'Not to me it doesn't. And I'm afraid it's not about refining it. It's much more fundamental than that...Trust me, OK?'

Sabah looked resentful but said nothing. Not so Dan.

'Just a minute!' He raised his hand with the air of a man who is called upon to draw a line. 'Can we hold on, just a minute? It's a little difficult to know what you're trying to achieve here. I mean, I was originally cast as Shahjehan, then asked to read Suleman, and now you're saying you want me to go back to Shahjehan!'

'That's right,' I said shortly, and since he continued to eyeball me, 'Look, there's no need to be upset, Dan. If you recall, I said it would be useful for me if you could try Suleman, which you have, and I'm grateful, but the exercise has just confirmed that my first instinct was correct.'

'But that was a really good reading!' Dan burst out angrily. 'I mean, am I allowed to know what was wrong with it?' Sabah shrugged agreement and looked at me challengingly. (So she was ganging up with him – despite the fact that she had known me for years and had only met Dan twice!)

'OK,' I said. 'OK, Dan, since you ask, your interpretation is too simplistic. You're playing Suleman too straight. He's not Mr sensitive, sincere I-really-understand-you-the-way-Shahjehan-never-will! Which is what you just gave us, isn't it?'

Dan looked half-furious, half-confused, so I sailed on, 'Anyone can just play the top of the text, but you need to get underneath it. Suleman is basically a very damaged, powerless man who uses his liaison with Mumtaz to augment his fragile sense of himself! And all this talk about their connection being outside the bounds of the everyday and therefore somehow superior, is deeply suspect. The fact is, during Mumtaz's lifetime, Suleman is not *capable* of following through with her, and it rather suits him that she's now a ghost!'

'It's interesting, isn't it?' a pleasant voice with a light Glaswegian accent volunteered.

Everyone turned to see Kevin thoughtfully holding up a pencil.

'Sorry... I hope I'm not speaking out of turn,' he added, 'but I was reading the end last night, and I was asking myself why Suleman doesn't stand up more to Shahjehan when he threatens to cut his hands off. I mean, he's got nothing to lose, right? And I got the feeling that maybe this guy would *prefer* to have his hands cut off – and have an excuse for copping out – rather than going after the woman he truly loves, which would be much more terrifying.'

I looked at Sabah and Dan. 'Exactly,' I said flatly.

They appeared to have got the point now. She glanced at me sheepishly, as Dan nodded slowly and scratched his head.

'Yeah, I did sort of play it on the level,' he said eventually, 'but, erm, I didn't get what you're both saying about Suleman from the text.' He leafed uncertainly through his script, trying to work out how he could have missed what had only recently become clear to me, its author, whilst apparently being perfectly obvious to Kevin.

In what now seemed like the dim, distant past, Ravi had accused me of believing Suleman to be the real hero of the play. Well, not any more. The fundamental weakness of Suleman's position had hit home for me – right around the time Heathrow and Sufya had suddenly announced their engagement. There was no explanation for such unexpected news: the family had not asked for one, being bowled over with joy, and I, despite leaving numerous messages for Heathrow, had been given none. I had even turned up at his door, but of course, he wasn't home, having, according to my sister, gone abroad again. Then Dan had called, saying he had got to grips with Suleman, sorry for his abruptness last time, and weren't we supposed to be meeting this week?

More to distract myself from going crazy, I returned to the question of Suleman and saw, of course, that whatever reason a man might try to give for rejecting his soulmate, fear was what it all came down to – hadn't Heathrow told me as much in the cemetery? I had just failed to comprehend the depth and tyranny of it. He had promised to love me fully at last, but now something had made him retreat again, and he couldn't or wouldn't tell me what it was… When I considered Suleman from that perspective, Dan really wasn't right for the part. It needed someone less straight: someone more deceptive.

'I agree, the subtext wasn't totally clear,' I conceded to Dan. 'But, assuming you're happy to play Shahjehan again, I've revised the big confrontation between the two men, and I think you'll like it.'

I passed a copy to Dan, then looked at Kevin still sitting politely in the corner, and hesitated – he had, after all, been hoping for the role I had just given back to his friend. 'This is the scene you mentioned, Kevin, where Suleman justifies to the furious Shahjehan why he's been speaking with the ghost of the Empress…'

'I'd be happy to read Suleman, if it helps,' he said immediately, getting to his feet and holding out a hand for the pages.

'…I have done no wrong. When the spirit of my departed lady visits me, it is because the words of this humble disciple delight her soul. His Majesty must fear no betrayal for our companionship is truly essence without form. While the Queen lived too, I loved her purely, years of separation only strengthening my devotion.'

'A fine philosophy for a dissembling monk!' Dan returned (perhaps mollified by the number of new lines he had been given.) *'You did not reach for her, Suleman, because you feared your own unworthiness! You were not equal to the fierce brightness that was our Queen. You did with reason tremble that your paltry verses would cease to amuse ere long!'*

'Let it be so, for your contentment. But accept, O Majesty, that I did never challenge your claim, and do not you now challenge mine.

To you her beating heart, to me her unending spirit. Your wrath shall have no power over me. Cut out my tongue, cut off my hands, my soul shall still fly to greet my lady!'

'So, the demon hastens to become a martyr? Behold his eagerness to place the dagger in my hand! No! I decree that you shall make your own destiny this time, Suleman – yours and mine! Come: prove that you are worthy of Her Majesty's immortal soul!'

Following the stage directions, Dan threw down an imaginary dagger. *'Take up the knife, Suleman, and slay me. For as I live, I swear that I will not leave to you even the ghost of the ghost of my Queen. Take up the dagger, I say! Strike me down for the sake of your beloved!'*

The script now directed Kevin, as Suleman, to falter, but instead I saw him scramble for the imaginary dagger, turn towards Dan, and place a hand squarely on his shoulder. Dan, surprised but obviously deciding to go with it, knelt down slowly, never taking his eyes off his adversary. He drew a quick breath, but did not flinch as Kevin held the dagger to his throat.

As Kevin now gazed out over Dan's head, eyes full of fire and determination, I had a sudden flash of Heathrow in the cemetery, framed by the golden trees: *I'll fix it – for all of us*... But, looking again, I beheld the would-be hero, Suleman, slackening his arm and slipping to the floor in a soundless agony of defeat and self-loathing.

'Thus does the coward steal the words of dervishes,' Dan rattled off, getting to his feet energetically, his earlier disgruntlement forgotten. 'Nice moment, mate – I thought you were about to rewrite history then!' He clapped Kevin on the shoulder.

'Told you this guy was good, didn't I, boss?... Oh, you fucker! You've made her cry!'

Sufya

AGAIN, THE METAL BIN with the yellow stickers.

'Another bad dream?' asked Jade sympathetically when I went into the kitchen at 2 a.m. She was sitting in candlelight with her new boyfriend, Ralph, a gaunt, long-haired musician and – like most single males these days – part-time DJ. The smoke-filled air smelt comfortingly of marijuana. I decided to minimise my interruption of Jade's evening. I would make a cup of tea and head back to bed.

'It's silly,' I admitted, as I filled the kettle, maintaining a light tone of voice for Ralph's benefit, 'but I was hoping that the dreams might stop now...'

'You mean now that you're getting married?' asked Jade.

'Yes, I suppose so. That *is* ridiculous, isn't it?'

'Not surprising, Dr Malik,' Jade smiled. 'Even Oxford science graduates can't help believing in the magic of happy ever after. Just another example of the power of the Cinderella myth. We're all done for, thanks to that pathetic cow.'

As usual, Jade was right on the nerve. When I had accepted H's proposal, it was the first time in years that I had taken an action which felt spontaneous and wholesome. Then H had suggested that we should be married as soon as possible and – thrilled by the recklessness of the idea – I had agreed to set a date only a few weeks away. As I surrendered to a long-ago toppled idol – the possibility of happiness through marriage – I had found myself lifted by a wave of emotion so surprisingly strong that it seemed it might really carry me, despite all my accumulated heaviness, across my own river Jordan into some promised land. Had the fairy tales been true all along with their covenant of a happy ever after to wash away all suffering? I marvelled at the immensity of the relief. I had not known that I wanted so much to believe.

'You'd think that as we invented her, she'd be easier to dispatch,' Jade was saying. 'There ought to be some way of… *exorcising* her.'

'Oh come on,' said Ralph suddenly – in a surprisingly posh and sulky voice – looking up from the spliff he'd been rolling since giving me a cool nod in response to my hello. 'Aren't you being rather cynical? I mean, the Cinderella story couldn't have lasted this long if it wasn't pukka kosher.'

'You see?' Jade exclaimed to me. 'Blokes love the idea of Cinderella – it works for them, and it's not because they believe in happy ever after, is it? He's only said that because he knows it makes me trust him, and increases his chances of a shag, haven't you, gorgeous?' She kissed Ralph's unappealing pout with a laugh, seeming not to notice his irritation.

'Maybe Ralph's right though. I mean, what if Cinders isn't just a social invention to control the female libido? Supposing the reason she has such an effect on us is that she comes from somewhere deep in a *female* moral universe? Maybe she's not even a *recent* invention – maybe happy ever after is what every female chimpanzee dreams of too!'

'*Wow!*' snorted Ralph. 'Better leave you two to it – one of you will be bobbiting me next.'

'It wasn't a criticism of men,' I tried to clarify, worried that I had contributed to freaking out Jade's latest boyfriend (much as I already did not like him). 'I was just saying that perhaps women can only blame ourselves for our illusions…'

'Whatever! Not guilty! Spare me!' smirked Ralph, clasping his hands over his groin, his spliff dangling from his lip.

I decided to exit before I made things worse. But just as I had gathered together tea and biscuits to take to bed there was a sudden loud banging at the front door.

'God! Who's that? It's 2 a.m.!' said Jade, sweeping the joint-making equipment into her *paan* box and snatching the spliff from Ralph's surprised lips. 'Is it your fiancé kicking down the door?'

'If only,' I answered as we headed down the hall. But I knew it would not be H. 'Why don't we delay the gratification?' he had responded gently, when I had told him how tired and sick I had been feeling in the first weeks of pregnancy. 'We can wait till after the wedding before you move into my place. By which time you'll be feeling stronger.' 'Well, I suppose it's not that long…' I had begun, taken by surprise. 'That's settled then!' H had said. 'We have to make sure you're well-rested for the wedding.' A part of me had wanted to protest that – embracing the presiding spirit of recklessness – I ought to move in right away. But I had had to agree that, exhausted as I was, I could not face the disruption at the moment, and as for sleeping together, I could not imagine doing anything but sleeping anyway. On one point though, I had insisted.

We were not going to tell anyone in the family about the pregnancy. Not until the first trimester was over. 'Not even Zarina?' H had asked. 'Least of all Zee,' I had replied.

'Sufya! Sufya! Are you all right, beta jaan?' boomed an unmistakable voice from beyond the front door.

'Isn't that your uncle?' asked Jade.

I nodded and almost hung my head at what I knew must now happen. For, whatever ridiculous dramatic imperative had brought Uncle Bogie to my doorstep at 2 a.m., I could not very well leave him out there in the cold, recovering as he was from his illness. And if there was anything more painful than the reality of spending time with Bogie, it could only be the embarrassment of watching him interact with my non-Asian friends. Such occurrences had been traumatic enough in the past, but now – I recalled with a jolt – he was to be my father-in-law, and that would make it a million times worse.

'By God, *beta jaan*, I was going to break it down!' roared Uncle Bogie, barging into the flat, his hair flying wildly about his agitated features. He halted to stare suspiciously at Ralph. 'And who is *this?*' he demanded, his finger close to Ralph's nose.

'This is Ralph, who is a…friend…of Jade's.' As always, I was struggling – in the face of Bogie's inexorable momentum – to recall that it was *he* who owed *us* an explanation, and not the other way around.

'Don't worry, Uncle,' laughed Jade, who seemed to enter into the subcontinental custom of calling elders Uncle and Auntie with far more ease than I or Zarina. 'Ralph's not a threat to your son's honour!'

'OK,' said Bogie, gruffly, but continued to stare suspiciously at Ralph, who, though retaining a smirk, was becoming somewhat shifty and rodent-like under the shameless scrutiny of the bigger man.

'Uncle, it's two a.m. Are you OK?' I ventured at last.

'I had a damn awful dream about you, *beta*, and by God I just put on my *jutas* and came.' Sure enough, in evidence under my Uncle's leather jacket were silk paisley pyjamas and Gucci slippers.

'Well that's very kind of you, but I'm fine, really,' I murmured with a slight shiver. I recalled my own nightmare and decided I did not wish to know what dream could have troubled Bogie to such an extent. Perhaps now, his fears allayed, he would go home to bed.

But far from departing, Uncle Bogie began to stride around the flat, opening cupboards and looking under furniture, all the while muttering in Arabic under his breath. 'Damn bloody djinns…!' he mumbled in response to my questioning stare, and then added as though I would understand completely: 'We have to take it seriously now we have a wedding coming up.'

After a few minutes he emerged from my bedroom and headed towards the kitchen, passing Jade, Ralph and me, still standing foolishly by the front door. 'All clear!' he said jovially. 'So are you going to offer your uncle a damn bloody hot cup of tea, or not?'

Over tea, far from explaining himself, he chose to lecture a bemused Jade and Ralph about the dangers to the soul of sex outside marriage. Then, to me, once I had fully turned to abject humiliated stone, 'Sufya *beta*, you should teach your friends. Otherwise, how will they learn?'

But, as he left, he put his hand to my cheek in a kind, fatherly way, and said: '*Beta*, I'm very glad that good-for-nothing Terminal 3-wallah is doing as he is told for once. It is as it should be.'

Sunday 8 November 1998

Zarina

'THE BRIDE WEEPS *as she ascends the doli.*

Goodbye, sweet friends of childhood...'

The same aunties who had assembled like a Greek chorus to bewail the poisoning of Uncle Bogie were now, barely three weeks later, seated in a circle droning out wedding songs in a tuneless cacophony, like a flock of colourful, oily-haired crows.

Mehndi... For the older women of our community, even the word was redolent with a fragrance as intoxicating as that of the aromatic henna which it described. This was a fragrance that wafted of girlish dreams, the tearful farewell to the parental home and the promise of a new life with an unknown beloved. (Of course, their grumpy, unappealing husbands were all known to me, and that the aunties remained so starry-eyed after thirty years of married life was frightening testament to the efficacy of cultural brainwashing.)

The actual ceremony of a *mehndi* – so named because

traditionally it was an occasion when the bride's friends would gather to decorate her hands and body with henna in preparation for her wedding – was therefore guaranteed to bring hordes of middle-aged bacchantes crawling out of the woodwork. Screeching out the old songs and thumping sweatily round the circle in an attempt at *bhangra*, they would regale each other once again with their romantic reminiscences and upbraid the younger women for not entering into their raucous revelry.

Sufya's *mehndi* was no exception. Mum, knowing that the engagement of her daughter to a famous film director would grant her, if not a complete return to ascendancy in the community, at least a solid four-star rating and one in the eye to those who had said our fall from grace was irreparable, had taken care to invite any auntie within a ten-mile radius, and was delighted at the strong turnout.

The bride's 'friends', on the other hand, were meagrely represented by me, Ayesha, Goldie and Jade – who was the only one enjoying herself: flushed and enthusiastic, in her black eyeliner and parrot-green shalwar kameez, she was smiling and nodding at the overexcited throng. Accompanying her today was her three-year-old godson, Krishna, also clapping along happily to the deafening, rhythmless thud which Auntie Tasnim was pounding out on the *dholak* with an ice-cream scoop.

The remaining three of us were stationed silently against the wall. Why Goldie was sulking I didn't know, but Ayesha's subdued demeanour was certainly caused by Habib and his lack of interest in having a baby, which I had found her tearfully confiding to Mum in the kitchen last week: '*Ma'shallah*, Sufya is settling down, I just thought Bibbles and I should be planning our future too: we have been married three years already. But he said he wasn't ready for children now – or possibly ever!' (Poor Bibbles – it seemed my sister's wedding was almost as much a thorn in his side as it was in mine.)

I glanced at Sufya: more beautiful than ever in a pale pink *lahnga choli* – the traditional long skirt and blouse – she was wedged between Mum and massive Auntie Mehbooba. Apart from refusing any and every item of food or drink thrust in her direction, and, of course, all exhortations to get up and dance, she was just about managing to tolerate and even feign pleasure at the whole ritual, despite the life-threatening sway of bodies inches from her nose.

Again, the breath-stopping twist of pain, then the floating sense of unreality. *Am I really sitting here, bearing it?* Again, the rapid scanning of my options, all leading to the same conclusion: to sit here a bit longer, bearing it, waiting for a moment to get my sister alone.

I hadn't thought it would come to this. I had been shattered, of course, by what Heathrow had done, the way he had done it, and his (continuing) avoidance of all contact with me. But even as I grieved, squirmed and hated him for his faithlessness, my gut told me he would be back; that his actions were being dictated by an overload of panic and relief in the aftermath of his father's brush with death.

I couldn't have predicted that the stress would produce a freak-out of this scale. But I had been with him during those days at Bogie's bedside, witnessing how, beneath the unwavering self-control, he was waging a silent and bitter war with the spectre of Terminal 3. Somewhere, deep within his cellular memory, a vestigial trace of hopelessness had reactivated itself and was grappling for dominance; threatening to arrest the fierce progress of his life, and leave him frozen like a climber on a mountainside. Though it tested me almost beyond the limits of my own endurance that he should have reverted to the idea of Sufya as a safety rope, I also knew that, given time, he would recover...and I would forgive him.

But time was exactly what we didn't have. The wedding had been set, with unseemly haste, for the end of November – only a few weeks away (the family perhaps also sensing that the bridegroom might have second thoughts if they didn't hurry up). The best option would have been to engineer some sort of delay, but with Mum now galloping blinkered and foamy towards the finish line, and determinedly not-asking-any-questions-about-anything, I had to be careful what I said. If I spooked her with even a casual note of caution, she would only berate me for inauspicious utterances, and redouble her efforts.

Coming clean to her about my relationship with Heathrow, and asking for her help might be counterproductive. It wasn't that I feared the shock and horror that would reverberate through the family – more the opposite. Such was the mythical status of a marriage between him and my sister, so imminent now its realisation, that they would definitely sacrifice me rather than jeopardise the wedding. I would be the fall-guy and reap the blame for bringing about a lapse on the part of the bridegroom – which nevertheless would be deemed of little material significance other than as a stark warning not to let me anywhere near him until after the wedding (and probably never again).

No, the only party for whom my confession would constitute sufficient reason to halt the proceedings was Sufya. So, loath as I was to have it out with her in some horrible scene – which after all was supposed to have been Heathrow's job – I would tell her. In fairness to everybody, she ought to know the truth and, in the end, she would be grateful for my honesty.

But opportunities to speak to Sufya were in short supply, occupied as she was with all her bridal business. Any time I managed to catch her on the phone, she would be 'rushing in' or 'flying out'; why didn't I come with her, Mum and Ayesha to Tooting tomorrow, she would suggest, and we could talk then – offers which were of no use to me and I would find various excuses for. I turned up at her lab, but she was in a meeting. I knocked on her door at midnight, but only managed to disturb Jade who sleepily told me that my sister was out with Heathrow: they were trying to spend as much time together as possible before the wedding. It was nice to see me, she yawned, how was I anyway?

The evening of the *mehndi*, I was in my room, seething with frustration and impatience. Tonight, at least, would be my chance – too late to save face in the community, but still in time to make a difference. The doorbell rang, and I heard my sister's voice in the hallway: perfect – half an hour early! And scarcely had I leapt off the bed than Sufya was already in the room, wearing a hunted expression, and waving a collection of brand new, unopened cosmetics at me. She sank onto the little white chair in front of the dressing table. 'Help me,' she said.

Look, Suf, Heathrow and I were together barely a week before he proposed to you. He loves me! Impossible to be so brutal, wielding a fluffy brush: as usual she had taken me by surprise. It didn't matter – I would work up to it. Opening her foundation, I began dabbing it onto her submissively upturned face, and asked her if she didn't think things were moving a little too fast between her and Heathrow.

'Definitely,' she said. 'But let's face it, when it comes to me and commitment, a snail's pace would be too fast.'

'But I didn't think you were even together any more,' I persisted, putting down foundation and searching among her purchases for blusher.

But when I looked up, her eyes were fixed on me. 'He came back,' she said. 'There was a moment when I thought he couldn't handle the closeness, but he came back, and I forgave him. That's what you do when you know they're the one. Everybody's allowed one freak-out, don't you think?'

Staring speechlessly at my sister in the dressing table mirror, I saw both our faces reflected back. For the first time – and contrary to years of accumulated testimony from all and sundry – I suddenly realised how similar we looked. The same hair, styled differently, the same skin with a shade's variance in tone, the same challenging expression! We were like two halves of the same sentence; two notes in a chord; two—

No, I thought forcefully, we are *not* the same. We are not the same to *him*. 'Look, Suf—'

'*Hai, hai,* still gossiping!' Mum interrupted, entering backwards through the door with Sufya's freshly pressed outfit draped across her arms. '*Chalo,* get changed quickly! Zarina, go downstairs. Auntie Naz has brought the *mehndi*. She says she will only give it to the sister of the bride.'

Fine, I thought, stamping down the stairs on shaking legs towards grinning Auntie Naz, I needed to take a breath anyway. I would tell Sufya later – before the evening was out. *He came back*, indeed! Would she still be so smug when she found out where he had been? I would sit through the evening's celebrations, and wait for the moment to play my trump card – hoping, despite our disturbing conversation just now, that it would still *be* a trump card, and that the fact of Heathrow's having slept with her sister would prove more of a stumbling block to Sufya than it had to me…

Returning to the present, and the seemingly interminable progress of the *mehndi,* I saw that Mehbooba had now replaced Tasnim at the *dholak*, and the group had moved on from traditional songs to popular Bollywood numbers. Next to me, Goldie, who was looking unusually respectable this evening in an understated brown silk outfit and simple pinned-up hair, gave a loud sniff. What was up with her anyway?

'Let's go into the kitchen,' I whispered. 'We should get the *mehndi* ready.' Goldie nodded and we picked our way through the dancing aunties, who were rotating unsteadily to the Sufi-inspired classic, '*Mera Piya Ghar Aya*', ('My Beloved Has Come Home'). Catching Sufya's alarmed don't-leave-me-here look on the way out, I mouthed '*mehndi*' and held up my hand, '*five minutes.*'

In the kitchen Goldie turned her back and buried her face in a tea towel. Ignoring her, I opened the boxes of Brides' Favourite Henna provided by Auntie Naz, and poured the finely ground green powder into a large bowl. Uncertain how much water to add to achieve the right consistency, I filled a glass, sloshed a bit in and prodded the mixture with a wooden spoon.

In the living room, I could hear Mum beginning a rendition of an old favourite, which she was always cajoled to perform on such occasions:

The moon's tender gaze, the peacock in the rain

Say my beloved has come…

The *mehndi* was forming gritty lumps beneath my haphazard stirring. I didn't care, as long as we could get it onto the guests and get them out of the house.

The restless winds are mad with lo-ove…

Mum lilted away romantically as the aunties *ooh*ed and *aah*ed.

'Give it to me, girlie, it's not a bloody mud-pie!' sniffed Goldie suddenly at my ear.

I handed over the bowl, folding my arms as she expertly added water and mixed it first into a dark green sludge, then into a smooth, reddish-brown paste. As she worked, she dabbed her eyes constantly with the end of her *dupatta*.

'So,' I said eventually, since she showed no sign of drying up. 'Do you want to tell me what's wrong?'

'Feel sick!' Goldie snapped, in a thick voice. She pushed the bowl away sharply, and burst into loud tears.

'Your bloody, goggly-eyed boyfriend!' she sobbed furiously. 'Come on, *yaar*, don't tell me you're such a baby you don't get my drift? I'm pregnant, Miss Zee-Zee-Top!'

'ASIF?' I was aghast. Then suddenly suspicious: 'Are you sure, Goldie? Telling the truth isn't exactly your strong point.'

'Like you're such a goody two-shoes yourself!' Goldie retorted swiftly.

'I may have done some things I'm not particularly proud of,' I began indignantly, 'but—'

'It's not a lie, OK, baby-*jaan*?' Goldie broke in wearily, apparently deciding for once against having a fight. 'I used that phone number, we got together, everything was hunky-dory, OK? But when I told him about his little beardy baby he freaked out, and stopped calling me, *bahan chaud, saala!* If I get hold of him, I'll cut him into tiny pieces and sell his kebabs in the shop!' But scarcely had she uttered this blood-curdling threat than her tears welled up afresh. She grabbed the *mehndi* bowl and stirred the contents forcefully, hiccupping and shuddering as she did so.

'What's going on?' Sufya, half-irritated, half-insecure, was hovering in the doorway. Goldie, startled, dropped the bowl on the floor where it smashed loudly, splattering globules of henna paste over our feet. Sufya stared at the mess.

'Goldie's boyfriend's being an arse!' I said crudely, to break the shocked silence. 'First he seduced her and now he's become a speck on the horizon, the spineless user!'

'Oh,' Sufya said. 'Poor thing.'

What was it that told me? Was it that she had brushed her belly for the merest second? Was it that I suddenly remembered she had touched neither food nor drink since her arrival? Or was it just that everyone around me seemed to be talking about getting pregnant?

I crouched down to gather the broken pieces of bowl. 'Goldie's really upset,' I said slowly. 'Why don't you take her outside for a cigarette?'

'Sorry,' Sufya replied, without missing a beat. 'I've given up. Don't let Mum see that mess – she'll say it's at least forty years' bad luck.'

Too late – bad luck was already among us.

Auntie Khan appeared in the kitchen looking for her niece, and when the latter refused to rejoin the party, decided to take her home. Goldie cried openly as she left. Then a fracas broke out in the living room when some of the aunties, in an attempt to dispel the gloom, got the *dholak* going again and tried to get Sufya to dance. She refused, Mum told her off, Sufya exploded back, and it was all over. By the time I managed to get the last of the *mehndi* off the floor, nearly all the guests had already dispersed, leaving half-emptied plates and glasses around the carpet. Only Jade's cherubic three-year-old godson remained seated, beating out a dirge on the abandoned *dholak*, and caterwauling delightedly, 'Aiiii…yeeeeee… ooooohhh…'

As I stood transfixed, Jade muttered, 'Excuse me,' swept him up, extracted the ice-cream scoop from his chubby hand and, since Sufya could just be seen disappearing down the front path, it fell to her friend to embrace our mother, telling her not to worry, things were always tense before a wedding.

Wednesday 18 November 1998

Sufya

WITH ALL THE preparations for the wedding, I had been forced to put my research on hold even though, after many months of floundering, it had been going rather well. The decision was made more difficult by Richard, who – despite saying he accepted my long apology, and despite agreeing that the kiss had been 'nice but just one of those things' – had been quite cold with me ever since. 'I'm not sure further delays will be helpful,' he said, when I discussed postponement. 'But it's *your* project – you must know the situation better than I.' He clearly had nothing to add, and I dared not broach the subject again.

Meanwhile, H had made it clear that, as far as the wedding was concerned, he wanted what I wanted and then it had been assumed by everyone that I wanted whatever Mum wanted. And it was true to say that to some extent I *did*. After all that had passed before, it was a surprising relief to allow her to score her long pursued goal:

a full-on Muslim wedding for one of her daughters. But, though I wanted to please her, I had underestimated the outlandishness of Mum's requirements for the fullest scoring of this goal, and we argued over seemingly every detail, most of all about the number and variety of allegedly essential occult rituals. Mum cried when I refused to visit a saintly *pir* for blessing, took to her bed until I agreed to utter lengthy prayers into the dead of every night and threatened not to eat if I did not douse myself with potions in the mornings. Certain foods were prohibited, others were mandatory. I must not look over my left shoulder, I must leave my shoes parallel when I took them off, and God knows what else.

I wished Zarina was more involved. In the back of my mind was the hope that if the wedding was a way of meeting Mum's long-disappointed expectations, it might also have the effect of enabling Zarina to drop some of her charges against me. And I knew too that her grim humour would have been a welcome antidote to the mind-boggling shallowness of constant wedding chatter with Mum and Ayesha. But Zarina, it seemed, was having a difficult time with her production, and was rarely available.

And in the few moments of reflection that I stole while driving from one wedding project to another, I did not for a single second allow my mind to rest on the secret that was at once the greatest solace and the greatest terror I had ever imagined. Instead my heart thudded in my chest at the direction my life had taken. How was it that suddenly I – the outcast, the failure, the bitter disappointment – was planning a wedding of a scale and religiosity that would be the envy of 'the community', marrying my childhood sweetheart and making all my parents' dreams come true?

I was not familiar with the role of good daughter and now, trying to read from the script, I felt uneasy. It crossed my mind that, unnoticed in the general hubbub, the real me might have been suffocated by the bride-to-be. Who was I before I became *this*?

In the course of hunting through my wardrobe for some item, I came across a pocketful of crumpled fliers that I had picked up that night at Ishq with H, among them a leaflet that caught my eye. In a faint and slightly traumatised typeface, it said:

Embarrassed to be a MUslim?

It's not easy to be a Muslim these days, is it? If you would like help and support from like-minded people, come to one of our discussion groups.

Why be an EMU all alone?

Underneath the text was a line drawing of a large bird (surely an ostrich rather than an emu) burying its head in sand. Below that, in small curly text, the leaflet announced that it came from the EMU society and gave the venue of weekly meetings: Tooting Library, Wednesdays at 7 p.m.

At first I snorted and crumpled the flier, but later I found myself rummaging in the bin to recover it. I reread it with curiosity. Ever since I could remember, I – and Zarina – had been embarrassed to be Muslims. When we were tiny and forbidden to eat the pork in school lunches, the dinner ladies would serve us last, so that all eyes were on us when our plates were plonked down, the meat unceremoniously substituted with a block of dried-at-the-edges cheese. In response to the inevitable whine of 'Why has she got that, Miss?' from an ill-mannered infant, the tight-lipped dinner lady would reply: 'Because she doesn't eat the same food as us. *Do* you, dear?'

If it was embarrassing to be a Muslim then, it was more so in our teens. When other girls talked of boyfriends and bikinis, I would pretend to be engrossed in my thoughts or a book. And when I, during my devout phase, objected to carrying a Christian hymn book into prayers, the deputy headteacher Mrs Hodge laughed and said perhaps I ought to present an assembly about my religion. 'After all,' she said to me with a sideways smile, 'you know what people think of Islam, don't you? I mean, nudge nudge, wink wink, four wives and all that.'

Though crushed by the weight of the four-wives-and-all-that assumptions, Zarina and I had – out of a pained sense of loyalty – felt that we must try to set the record straight wherever we could. As we grew up, we learned the liberal defence of Islam from our father: that the Quran pronounced pen to be mightier than sword, that Islam gave women the right to own land centuries before the West, that veils and dowries were not part of the quranic text. Most importantly, true Islam placed the individual's relationship with God above all else, shunning intercession by popes, saviours or mullahs – all the gentle arguments of Dad's egalitarian Islam.

Of course, all that was before Islam had come out of the closet dressed in its new fundamentalist clothes. Once books had been burned in the streets, the assumptions about who we were became monstrously large. And, though I wished there were some way of redressing the balance, of explaining that to most Muslims I knew these behaviours were as alien and frightening as they appeared to the wider community, the novel social rupture was too beloved by the media – both right-wing and liberal – and, without conscious decision, I had quietly exited the tumultuous cultural clatter, my embarrassment transmuting into alienation and self-exile.

But, now that my forthcoming Muslim wedding to a Muslim man – complete with an unconventional version of pre-marriage celibacy – had brought me face to face with my historic quest to be a Muslim without really being one, I was suddenly looking twice at the EMUs leaflet. I was intrigued by the touch of humour in it. Perhaps, I wondered, somewhere out there on the other side of the veils and beards, there might be others like me? Might it even be possible finally to find a way of being a Muslim and being *comfortable*? It was not something I felt able to discuss with H: considering that his work placed him on a brutal frontline where the dehumanisation of Muslims had life and death consequences, the problem of my 'embarrassment' in the face of trivial misunderstandings seemed, well, *embarrassing* to relate to him. It was a Wednesday and, on an impulse, I decided to go to an EMU meeting.

I found the musty little discussion group ensconced in one of the bare, box-like rooms available for hire beneath the main library. There were eight people present, sitting cross-legged on the floor, all of them young. Three were women, of whom two were in headscarves. But otherwise the clothes were Western, mostly jeans among both males and females. All the men had beards, but in a trendy Western style. A discussion was already under way, so I seated myself near the door so as not to attract attention.

A woman in a neat navy headscarf was speaking, in high-pitched tones. '…as sister Hema was saying, they point the finger at us because some people are burning books. I mean, I don't agree with it, I wouldn't do that myself. But how come no one says anything to the people who insult Islam for fun? How come we're the ones who are called "ignorant" and "backwards"? Why should we have to feel bad about those book-burnings when Rushdie was the one being offensive? And just so he could get publicity. He should have known better.'

To my slight surprise, the speaker's remarks were greeted with applause from the rest of the group.

'Thank you, sister Rehana,' said a long-haired young man with a gold stud in his eyebrow, clearly the chairperson of the proceedings. 'Those were powerful words.' There was a conscious silence as the young man looked down at his hands interlaced in his lap, as though to contemplate further the wisdom of what had been said. I noticed several others lowered their eyes too, nodding their support and appreciation. I was starting to feel uncomfortable – I had hoped the group would have been bigger so that I could hide in the crowd if I felt out of place. And I had the distinct suspicion that I might be out of place already.

Then the eyebrow-studded one lifted his head and looked straight at me. 'And, we have a new member of the group, today,' he said and fell silent. Everyone turned to look at me, smiling. I felt all the expectations leaping out of their eyes like tentacles. This was the last thing I needed.

'Hello, all,' I said, breezily.

'It's all right,' said Eyebrow Stud, looking sympathetic.

'What is?' I asked him, with a tinge of dread.

'You don't have to say it, if you don't want to.'

'I don't have to say what?'

'I think we all know where you're coming from. You want to say it, but you're feeling...?' He looked at me to complete his sentence, as though talking to a small child.

'...Embarrassed,' he finished, as I looked at him blankly.

'We've all been there, sister,' said another of the brothers as the group nodded in unison.

There was a slight pause while I considered my position. I had certainly not come here to have religious twenty-somethings analyse my feelings. Still, I thought, perhaps I should give them a chance.

'I'm Arif, and I'm embarrassed to be a Muslim,' Eyebrow Stud said slowly and deliberately, and looked at me meaningfully. A bubble of disbelief caused me to splutter, but nobody else laughed. Clearly, I was meant to say something similar.

'I'm sorry to hear that, Arif,' I said, pronouncing his name in the anglicised way that he had done himself – *a-reef*. 'And is it helping you to be here, or is this little set-up not even more embarrassing?'

There were several exclamations of indignation from the group, but only a flicker crossed Arif's smiling face. I wished I had not been so uncontained. It was just that, under the spotlight of a group of Muslims – no matter how conflicted they might turn out to be – I felt under attack, exposed, immature. 'It's OK,' said Arif to the group. 'All feelings are valid here. Especially such difficult feelings.' He turned to me. 'That's a lot to carry around by yourself, sister.'

'I was like you,' said the second woman in a headscarf in a loud, self-assured voice. 'I was embarrassed even to wear my hijab, you know – I can't believe it now, but I was. And coming here has changed me, it really has. I mean, look at me now. I wear it everywhere, even down the pub with my friends. And you'll be the same soon. Don't worry, you've taken the first step, which is coming here.'

'Actually, what worries me,' I found myself replying with some heat, 'is that people can sit around and say we don't need to be embarrassed about book-burnings. We *should* be embarrassed. Just like we should be embarrassed that we think covering our hair or growing a beard is spiritually significant! And we should definitely be embarrassed about believing that you have to put your shoes parallel in case some evil spirit steps into them, or whatever it is, and as for a bride not being allowed to eat eggs before a wedding—'

'Let me stop you there, sister – forgive me, but that's a lot of points for the group to discuss,' interrupted Arif. 'Although I must confess, I haven't heard of the shoe thing, or the egg thing…'

'Me neither,' chimed the women, looking at each other in confusion.

'Nor me,' said one of the beardies. 'Can you quote the relevant *hadith*, sister?'

'Well, whatever,' I stammered, momentarily uncertain as it dawned on me that some of the annoying rituals foisted on me by Mum were nothing to do with Islam as known by the mainstream. 'My point is that I didn't come here to stop being embarrassed about things that *are* embarrassing. Why aren't we talking about putting our own house in order? Why are we trying to go back to a historical time period over a thousand years ago?'

There was a gasp from the group, and I rose to my feet. 'I came here for *support*, not *judgement*!' I heard myself declaring.

And even though I was dimly aware that it may have been me doing the judging, I could no longer stay in the room. I stormed from Tooting Library, to find a traffic warden gleefully ticketing my car.

Zarina

AT FIRST I HAD NO intention of speaking to Asif on Goldie's behalf. On day one she had identified herself clearly as foe rather than friend, and she had stuck to it. She had never missed an opportunity for spite, ridicule and, if she could get you on your own, the odd slap, pinch or lump of chewing gum in the hair, for all of which amusing pastimes I – being the younger and smaller – was easier to target than Sufya. Goldie was also the person who only recently had palmed that dreadful spell off on me, something I was unlikely to forget anytime soon.

But the main reason, of course, was that I didn't need to hear about anyone else's impending motherhood. Though the presence of a baby completely explained Heathrow's recent behaviour, and therefore, on one level, took the sting out of it – it also, unequivocally, spelled the end of my hopes. I knew Heathrow: regardless of how he felt about me, being at the centre of his child's life would trump everything. For the sake of that little being, he would soldier on with Sufya, and make the best of it. If the pregnancy weren't so hush-hush, he would have explained everything, I was certain; he would have asked for my understanding and, eventually, I would have given it. So why not give it now? The only thing missing would be the tearful scene in the middle, one last embrace and the whispered confirmation to each other that what we had had was real.

Let me whisper it to myself then; let it echo around the emptiness inside me: Heathrow had loved me, and would have been with me, were it not for the cunning endgame played by Sufya. The day was lost; the task now to grit my teeth, and find a way to go on into a lustreless future.

One step at a time. What plans I was capable of making now revolved only around getting through the wedding with dignity, and moving out of the family home as soon as possible afterwards. They certainly didn't include championing Goldie, and persuading Asif to stand by his baby too – for that, I had no compassion left.

But Goldie wouldn't give up. She rang me every day, somehow managing to catch me by calling at odd times or withholding her number. She had no one else to talk to, she sobbed, no one to take her side. And, marooned as I was in a house full of festivity, with even play rehearsals not due to start till December (though I lied to Mum about this in order to have a steady excuse to be out), Goldie's despair and loneliness struck a chord with my own. Gradually her phone calls became my only relief – a disembodied voice pouring out the pain I couldn't express. Helplessly enthralled, I would press the receiver to my ear while Mum, who didn't want me associating with 'that girl', glared, and Goldie begged, wept and threatened suicide on the other end. At last, I agreed to help.

Maybe, I thought, as I applied my handbrake with a jerk outside Asif's Tooting flat (for which, Goldie told me, he had traded in his Stoke Newington pad after rediscovering his roots), it would even be good for me to do this: I would speak for all the babies of the world, and prove to myself that I could accept the loss of Heathrow. And, I added, if I could face my situation, why shouldn't Asif have to deal with his mess?

The sound of live music emanated from the basement flat as I got out of the car. This, I deduced with some surprise, must be the band Asif had referred to in Tandoori Junction. At the time of our brief liaison, he had worked in IT solutions, and although I knew he cherished secret dreams of being in a rock band, I had no idea he could actually play anything. But astonishing as it was that Asif could be a bona fide musician, even more astonishing was that, by the sounds of it, this band actually seemed to be quite good.

To the lilting tune of Sonny and Cher's 'I Got You Babe', a velvety male voice grooved:

'They say we don't speak RP
Don't pronounce it like good English should be...
They don't know we've made our own
Mix of street and pukka Punjabi!
Bro-o-thers...(do-do, do-do, do-do)
Si-i-sters...(do-do, do- do, do-do)'

For a minute, distracted by the music, I paused. I wondered what the next verse would be: *so let them say my beard's too long?* But suddenly – just as I was looking for a rhyme – 'I Got You Babe' was abandoned and a frenzied drum rhythm burst forth, with a shrill, excited voice shrieking over the top:

'If it ain't got an innit in it, it ain't in it, innit!'

('Innit!') shouted the backing vocalist enthusiastically. Surely not Asif? Since when had he replaced his pseudo media-speak with East London chat?

After a few repeats of this refrain, the high-pitched voice, backed up by Asif, began to rap:

'Speaking wiv conviction (Innit!) Speaking wiv troof! (Innit!)
Shouting wiv da power of da new Asian yoof! (Innit!)
Speaking wiv passion (Innit!) Burning wiv pride!(Innit!)
Burn dem towers of Babel and all da sinners inside!(Innit!)
Burnin', burnin', burnin'!(Innit!)
Burnin', burnin', burnin'!(Innit!)'

What was this rubbish? I remembered my mission, hurried down the steps, pressed the bell, and heard a loud ring inside the flat: brrrrrrrrrr!

The music broke off abruptly. A pause. A quick murmur of voices. Then rapidly approaching footsteps, and the door was flung open by a short chunky Asian man wearing a bandanna and an unpleasant snarl.

'I'm telling you, Missis Next Door…' he was saying, 'dis is not neighbourly! Oh! Sister!'

No sister of yours. 'Is Asif in?' I said clearly, so that I could be heard inside the flat. The chunky guy looked over his shoulder, then back at me.

'You a fan?' he asked hopefully.

'No,' I replied pleasantly. 'So is he there?'

'It's cool, Bashi,' came Asif's voice from inside. 'Let her in.'

Without taking his eyes off me, 'Bashi' gestured with a jerk of his head that I should follow him inside. If I was slightly nervous, there was no way I was going to show it, so I shut the door behind me and marched after him along the narrow corridor, mentally noting a fire extinguisher which might be useful for hitting someone over the head, should escape prove necessary.

'Hey, Zee, what's up?' Asif said calmly, as I picked my way into the cramped living room and stood amongst the clutter of amps and cables.

A tall dark-skinned man with a diamond ear stud, whom I took to be the owner of the velvet voice, eyed me coolly from the only sofa. Bashi stood behind me in the doorway, arms folded. No one asked me to sit down.

'What's up?' said Asif again, continuing to tune his guitar. 'We're a bit busy.'

I stood up straighter and shook my hair back. 'Can I have a word with you?'

'Yeah, yeah, that's cool. Don't mind the brothers. What's on your mind?'

Apparently, Asif's strategy was to hide behind his mates, and embarrass me into slinking off without saying anything – and it almost worked. But then Bashi sniggered behind me, and I found myself saying loudly, 'It's about Goldie actually. She wants to know what your intentions are, now that you've got her pregnant. She's left you about a hundred messages. Would you like me to play them for you?' I looked at Asif's answering machine, which was sitting on top of the TV, incriminatingly flashing FULL.

Asif turned pale. The tall man raised his eyebrows. Bashi stopped sniggering.

'It...er...isn't working,' Asif said huskily. 'Look, how about a cup of tea? Let's go into the kitchen.'

I allowed him to usher me out of the room. As we passed him Bashi said, 'What's goin' on, man?' Asif ignored him.

'Two sugars please,' said the tall man silkily from the sofa, and pulled out a pack of cigarettes.

'I can't believe you, Zee!' Asif said angrily in the kitchen, as he slammed tea-stained mugs and spoons onto a plastic tray with a photograph of Mecca on it. 'I know you and your sister have made it your mission to have a go at me whenever and wherever possible, but are you actually going to start barging into my house to do it now?'

'Oh, don't tell me you're going to act the victim!' I shot back. 'Do you have any idea what you're putting Goldie through? She's going out of her mind while you're in here with those morons, singing about raping and pillaging!'

'Keep your voice down, for fuck's sake!' Asif hurriedly shut the door, as my volume increased.

'What is this getting women pregnant thing, anyway? *What do you think contraception's for?*'

'Zarina, I swear—' Asif came towards me, his face red with rage.

Shit! Have I gone too far? As he seized my wrists and pinned me against the sink, I thought about the fire extinguisher in the corridor but there was no way to get to it.

Asif leaned over me, eyes bulging. I stared back like a rabbit in bulging headlights. Then he took a deep breath and, releasing his grip slightly, said in the low, firm voice of an orderly calming a hysterical lunatic: 'It wasn't me. I swear.'

I tore my hands away and shoved him. 'Get off me, you ape! That's not what she says!'

'Well, she's lying! For fuck's sake, Zee, after everything I said to you in Tandoori Junction, do you really think I'm interested in girls like Goldie? Or in fucking around? How many times do I have to tell you? I'm a committed Muslim!'

I rubbed my wrists and looked at him cynically. Asif threw up his hands.

'God, I really screwed up with you, didn't I, Zee? As far as you're concerned, I'm now Satan – for ever and ever, amen! And there's nothing I can do or say to change your mind, is there?'

I was firm in my resolve not to believe anything he said, but I couldn't help noticing the note of defeat that had crept into his voice.

'This isn't about you and me, Asif, it's about you and Goldie!'

'There is no "me and Goldie"! I hardly know the girl. Look, she called me once, and I had a coffee with her, but I told her I wasn't interested in anything more – that's the whole story!'

'So you never slept with her?'

'No.'

'And the baby?'

'Well, how the hell do I know? You obviously know her better than I do, but she strikes me as the sort who – look, don't take this the wrong way – I just mean she might have been around the block a few times.'

We were interrupted by Bashi, who shoved open the door and said, 'What's happening with the tea, man?'

Asif made two mugs of tea and put a dish of decrepit sugar lumps on the tray, while I, ignoring Bashi's hostile glances, pondered on what Asif had said and whether, in my debilitated state, I had been too quick to believe Goldie. But she had been so convincing! Then again, wasn't she always? And, slimy and untrustworthy as Asif had been in the past, he had seemed genuinely upset by her accusation. Could I, as he had complained, be predisposed to think ill of him whatever he did? And was I now becoming the aggressor, by habitually punishing him when I was really upset about Heathrow?

'Look, Zee, I have to get back to rehearsal,' Asif was saying, having despatched Bashi back to the living room with the tea. 'But, it's true what I said. I'm sorry about Goldie and all that, but it's not my problem – and you shouldn't make it yours, either.'

We walked silently down the corridor but, as he opened the front door for me, I turned and said, 'I'm sorry if I shouted at you unfairly, OK?'

Asif smiled. 'At least there wasn't any *keema mattar* in the picture this time. And you can shout at me all you like: I deserve it. I'm hoping it means that one day you might forgive me.'

I couldn't say that I did forgive him – my forgiveness was all used up. And it was just as well, because a second later he made me furious again.

'Zee, listen!' he said, running after me as I was opening my car door. 'Erm... I just wanted to warn you: the brothers are...how can I put this? *Not happy* with Sufya.'

'What brothers? And what do you mean, *warn* me?'

'Heathrow gave us a bit of trouble at a concert a while back, and she was with him. I tried to talk to her about it, but she wouldn't listen. And then, apparently, she busted into a religious meeting... Look, she's getting married soon and maybe she'll calm down, but just tell her to keep a low profile, OK? She doesn't want to attract the brothers' attention, believe me.'

I looked at him in disbelief; he was as weak as ever. Obviously, whatever 'brothers' he was talking about had 'got hooks in him', exactly the way he once said Suzanne had.

'And why are you telling me all this, Asif, instead of standing up to those fascists?' I challenged him. 'What's *your* position on it, anyway? Are you in the business of threatening people now? I heard some of your lyrics by the way, and I was wondering – is that beard growing into your brain?'

'God, you sound like your sister now!' Asif went red again. 'Look, you can't just go round, all high and mighty, fucking with people's sensitivities—'

'Shame on you, Asif.' I got into the car and slammed the door. *And thank God I didn't let you off the hook too much.* As I started the engine, he banged his fist on the roof and stormed back to his mates inside the flat.

Tuesday 24 November 1998

Sufya

'Hi, Sufya, this is Eric Havers speaking. I hope you don't mind me calling out of the blue like this?'

Eric Havers! Head of Food Safety at BestCo, Dad's long-time boss, and object of pre-teen crushes from me and Zarina in the days when he would visit our family home, laid-back, urbane and drily witty. I had hardly heard from him since I had had a work placement at BestCo while in the sixth form. It was not long after that that Eric had been promoted to head of department and had appointed Dad his right-hand man, becoming, Dad explained in answer to our enquiries about why he never visited us any more, 'just too busy to socialise'.

'I was wondering how your dad was doing,' said Eric, in the expectant pause that arose after he had offered me his congratulations and said how much he and Helen were looking forward to the wedding. 'I wondered if he seems to you to be under any unusual stress, perhaps because of the wedding or something going on at home?'

'I don't know, Eric,' I said, guardedly, feeling the awkwardness of my position. In fact, Dad had not been himself ever since the poisoned pork episode, seeming unusually heavy and preoccupied. In the midst of the wedding furore I had not found the time to ask what was troubling him. All I knew was that he had been trying to find out how BestCo's safety-testing regimes had been downgraded without his knowledge. 'Why do you ask?'

'Oh well, I don't want to overplay it, of course, and I wouldn't have called if we weren't family friends and so on, but he just seems to have been acting a little…how shall I put it, *out of character* recently. I don't want to use the word, really, but a little *paranoid* even. I've tried to talk to him about it, as a friend, you know, but he's not the talking type, is he? I wondered if you could shed any light on it…'

'I don't think I can, Eric, I'm sorry. I've been so busy recently.'

'Yes, I understand. Well, don't worry. I'm sure I'm just imagining it, and it will all blow over. Probably just fatherly concern about his beloved girl getting hitched, eh?'

When I got Eric off the phone, I called Dad and told him what Eric had said. Dad was shocked. 'I don't know what he's doing,' he muttered. 'Why is he calling you like that, trying to make me look like I'm losing my marbles?'

'Maybe he's just concerned, Dad. After all, you've been under a lot of pressure…'

'He's *in* it, Sufya, like the rest of them. He's not on my side.'

'Dad, what's going on? Are you in trouble of some sort?' I said, anxiety jumping up in me, accompanied by guilt that – once Bogie had recovered and the story had disappeared from the papers – I had hardly thought about the poisoned pork scandal and its potential consequences for Dad.

'He told me he didn't know why the testing regimes had been relaxed, and that he would investigate,' Dad said, 'but instead of doing that, he's trying to make me look bad. Maybe I should have gone to the police, but I have always considered him a friend, as well as a colleague. I never thought he would put me in this position...'

'Don't worry, Dad,' I said, feeling slightly helpless at hearing him sound so lost and confused. 'I'm sure it will be OK. Shall I come over and we can talk about it?'

'No, no, *beta*.' Dad's voice changed to his usual reassuring tones. 'You have better things to think about. After the big day, we will talk. Now your cousin Ayesha is here and she wants a word with you...'

And then Ayesha came on the phone to recount how she had narrowly prevented Bogie and Mum from segregating Wandsworth Town Hall into male and female sections. 'I told them, *yaar*, Sufya will scream blue murder if you try some purdah-style *baqwaas* with her. She is not the type...'

I thanked Ayesha for her intervention, breathed a sigh of gratitude that my cousin had turned out to be my unlikely ally in the wedding wars, and allowed myself to forget Dad's problems for now, resolving to talk to him directly the wedding was over.

❋

Across the animal kingdom, the practice of mate-guarding is widespread: the male does not let his female out of sight, especially when she is in heat. In a classic 1933 text, ornithologist Edmund Selous described the exertions of the male blackbird to keep an eye on his beloved:

'The male bird follows her all about, hopping where she hops, prying where she pries, and seeming to make a point of doing all she does except actually collect material for the nest... Then, the one laden, the other empty-billed, they both fly back in just the same way...for the cock is as busy in escorting and observing the hen as she is in collecting material for building the nest.'

Among some species of dunnock, the male is so hot on the heels of his mate, hopping to meet her everywhere she turns, that the female sometimes struggles to gather enough food. Male spiders are often attracted by a female's pheromones which waft downwind from her web, so, after mating with her, the male destroys the female's web to ruin her chances with other males. In insects like the water strider, the guarding males save themselves energy by permanently mounting the females, who are then forced to carry their husbands on their backs – a perfect vantage point for the jealous guys of the water strider world.

In some cases, mate-guarding has unpleasant side-effects for the males, too. Among numerous species of bee, for example, the lower abdomen of the male explodes after mating, part of it sticking to the female and providing a kind of posthumous mate-guarding.

Of course, there would be little need for any of this if males were not so inclined to seek copulations with one another's partners. But recent advances in DNA technology, allowing scientists to test the paternity of offspring, demonstrate that across the animal world, sexual monogamy (as distinct from social monogamy) is almost non-existent. Among mammals, the situation is particularly extreme, with only around a dozen reliably pair-bonded animals out of over 4,000 mammal species.

Current thinking among evolutionary biologists is that males seek copulations with more than one female in order to maximise their chances of passing on their genes. Yet, from the bees to the birds to the hoary marmots, males find themselves confronted with the same dilemma: how can they chase other females while at the same time keeping an eye on their own mate?

The veiling of women could be interpreted as a very handy solution to this dilemma, avoiding all the unpleasantness of exploding abdomens. Once veiled, a female becomes – essentially – self-guarding.

So, I wondered, only days away from my fairy-tale wedding, from which moral universe did the notion of monogamy – the ethic of fidelity to which H and I were committing – originate? Did it come from the male moral universe, where nudge-nudge-wink-wink copulation with as many females as possible was a top priority – in which case the institution of marriage simply amounted to another form of mate-guarding?

Or did the imperative for fidelity evolve in an arguably female moral universe, in which the demands of child-rearing – childhood being a particularly drawn-out affair in our species – made it critical to keep a male around? (Of course, the distinction is not a pure one: males too have a stake in seeing that their offspring make it to adulthood, as all their hard work – copulating with numbers of females – would otherwise go to waste.)

One thing was for sure, monogamy was a much clearer concept for the flatworm *Diplozoon paradoxum*, a fish parasite which meets its life partner as a virgin larva, whereupon the two creatures literally fuse halfway down their bodies. They remain thus joined till they reach sexual maturity and beyond, to be put asunder finally by nothing less than death.

At any rate, mate-guarding did not seem to be an issue for H, who had suddenly put his arms around me and announced that he would be away for the entire week before the wedding.

'At least this time you warned me before disappearing,' I muttered into his shoulder, trying not to sound like a nagging wife. H's absences, I reasoned, were something I would have to get used to, and, in being free himself, he made me free too, and wasn't this the basis for a healthy partnership? A *Homo sapiens* partnership, disentangled from any murky, Top Monkeyish, mate-guarding roots?

'I wouldn't go, if I didn't have to,' murmured H, his cheek close to mine. 'And even when I'm gone, I'm still with you…my flatworm soul fused to yours at the core…' He placed his hand softly on my belly, and our foreheads touched as my gaze turned down.

'I wish we could fuse *properly*…' I whispered, breathing him in.

'We will! And once joined, only death can come between those flatworms – isn't that the way it goes?'

He seemed so calm and so certain – so free of doubt and fear – that it was contagious. I closed my eyes and rested in the deep, humming connection between us. Not for the first time, I felt the strange urge to whisper gratitude for the existence of a universal order in which another individual could have this effect on me.

And so I said goodbye to H, aching with the chill of yet another separation, but warmed by the prospect of meeting again on our wedding day with the promise of glorious and endless future fusion.

Zarina

FORGIVE ME, ZARINA, I made a mistake…

The night before the wedding, I dreamed of him again: his breath on my ear, his hands in my hair, the smile in his eyes as he kissed me over and over. And as the sun rose in its inevitable way, I awoke, black misery flooding into my mouth at the sickening realisation which, try as I might, I could not make into a comfort: today it would be over.

I pulled down the *Wedding Schedule!!* that Ayesha had printed out with elaborate colour coding, and helpfully Sellotaped to the mirror. In royal blue, it gushed: *6.31 a.m. Heathrow touches down at…Heathrow!!!!!* So he was up there somewhere, right now, winging his way to his bride.

I got up and went about the business of showering and dressing, in order to comply with *7.00 a.m. Zarina up and ready (well in advance of Bride)* – the bit in brackets coded purple to signify a diktat by Mum. Finishing my make-up, I looked at my reflection: face still yellow from recent trials, despite the fake blush, heart beating dully beneath the heavily embroidered fuchsia blouse, hand resting on the pearl choker. I was reminded of those Hindu widows who, wearing their finest jewels and silks, choose martyrdom on the funeral pyres of their dead husbands, believing that as their bodies burn, their souls will be united with their beloved in the next life and forever. Except I had no husband, dead or alive. So less a Hindu widow, and more an Iphigenia, perhaps – slaughtered against her will to bring fair winds for the wedding ship…

But apparently one sacrificial goat wasn't enough, and Mum, enlisting the services of Auntie Tahira's husband and his van, had managed to procure the real thing from Horns 'n' Hooves – a supplier of quality livestock she had discovered by surreptitiously scanning the classified section of *Country Living* in BestCo's magazine aisle.

'Baaa!' it bleated balefully at me when, at midday precisely, I opened the door.

'Are you sure it's going to…cooperate?' I said, looking at it doubtfully. The goat, hooves squarely planted on the front porch, head lowered menacingly, glared back like Long John Silver through one of the black patches on its flea-bitten fur.

'Don't worry, don't worry!' Auntie Tahira's husband said, wiping sweat off his bald head with a hankie and bracing himself with one foot on the step, as the angry goat strained against the rope. 'I think your mother just selected a vigorous breed!'

'Ah, Nasim *bhai!*' Mum, no doubt hearing the bleating and scuffling, hurried downstairs from Sufya's room, and clapped her hands. 'Perfect timing! Now we can pacify any *balaas* with a sacrifice! Allah be praised!' (As if any self-respecting evil spirit would be pacified by that hideous creature.) 'Ahmed… Ahmed!'

Dad opened his study door slowly and came out, wearing a look of dread which, unfortunately, eye contact with the furious goat did nothing to diminish.

'Firdaus, *jaan*,' he said, attempting a firm tone, although everybody present, including him, knew he had no chance, 'I already told you, I want nothing to do with shedding the blood of some poor, innocent animal—'

'Baaaaaaaaaa!' bellowed the goat, baring its teeth. Dad blanched.

'I suppose you want bad luck to fall on your daughter's head instead?' Mum said, for at least the tenth time since she had put *Ritual Sacrifice of Goat* on Dad's last-minute to-do list. 'For God's sake, Ahmed, stop complaining! Nasim *bhai* has got the goat for you now! All you have to do is kill it! I've already put newspapers down under the pear tree!' And she hauled the evil-looking goat over the doorstep with a swift jerk, and handed the leash to Dad.

'Ask Bogie *bhai* to say a prayer!' she called, as Dad skidded after the goat, who, spotting the garden through the open back door, was now heading full-tilt down the corridor towards the fresh green grass.

'The poor boy's a scapegoat, by God!' thundered Bogie, erupting out of the living room as Mum disappeared back upstairs. 'Nothing but a bloody scapegoat for those bastard trigger-happy troops! He was probably just protesting when those *haraamzaade* shot him – and now they're calling him a terrorist to cover it up!'

He was referring, of course, to the shooting of a British man in Hebron, news of which had beamed into our living room on the breakfast news. 'They won't name him! And do you know why? Because he's just some poor, pacifist bloody scapegoat, by God!'

'There's no justice, is there, Uncle?' I shrugged, feeling a certain schadenfreude in the way my family were, on this most joyously anticipated day, seizing any and every opportunity to behave even more extremely like themselves.

'*Haan, haan, beta jaan!*' Bogie seemed surprised that I had thought he required any response. 'You go and enjoy getting your sister ready, with the other girls! *Chalo!*' He patted my head affectionately and went back to the living room, apparently oblivious to Dad, who could be glimpsed chasing the goat round the garden.

Upstairs, I found Sufya, seated in front of the full-length mirror that had been carried from the landing into her room. She looked breathtaking in her deep red *gharara* – the blouse, beneath which no baby bump was yet visible, of plain satin, the wide trousers embellished with alternate panels of crushed velvet. Rekha, Specialist in Bridal Styles, stood behind her deftly twisting up fronds of short hair and fastening them with sequinned pins, supervised by an audience of Mum, Jade and Ayesha.

'More hairspray!' Mum said. 'It needs to be hard, so she can put the *dupatta* on her head.'

'I told you, I'm not putting the *dupatta* on my head, Mum!' Sufya said with studied patience. 'And I don't want hard hair!'

'Maybe you should just soften the front,' Jade offered, pulling a few strands loose over Sufya's forehead.

'Beautiful!' cooed Ayesha. 'But what about a hairpiece, Rekha? She needs more height if she's wearing the *dupatta* on the shoulder – lots of brides are doing it now, *Khalajaan*, it's very fashionable!'

Fortunately, Rekha seemed inured to such interference and calmly carried on, pausing only to survey her handiwork now and then, and smile at Sufya in the mirror.

Sufya herself looked flushed and anxious. She caught my eye, as

I hovered behind the others.

'Please tell me that was not the goat arriving,' she said.

''Fraid so,' I confirmed. 'The goat is officially in the house.'

'In the garden!' snapped Mum. 'And you girls should be grateful to Uncle Nasim for getting it here at all! At least someone is worried about your welfare, even if your father is not!'

'Baa,' floated up through the window. 'Baaaaaaaaaaaaaaa!'

'It's so helpless!' Sufya persisted. 'I can't bear it! Can't you do something, Zee?'

'*Khubberdaar*! Don't you dare!' said Mum, folding her arms.

'To be honest, it's not that helpless. It looks as if it can take care of itself,' I said. 'Actually, you might want to interview it about its relationship with its anger – it's probably got something interesting to say.'

'I know what it would say!' Sufya glared at Mum in the mirror. 'That it's about to be needlessly slaughtered for the sake of one person's superstition!'

'And we're about to be prosecuted,' Jade added. 'Did you check Horns 'n' Hooves' terms of sale, Auntie?'

'You girls concentrate on getting ready!' scolded Mum, going red under her powder. 'The car will be here in half an hour.'

Half an hour. The words struck me with the force of an enormous, swinging pendulum.

Half an hour, and we would be on our way. We would take Sufya to marry Heathrow…

'Firdaus *bhabi*!' Uncle Bogie shouted from downstairs. 'Mrs Tasnim is on the phone: she says the *mithai* is ready but her car is not starting, and Bismillah Taxi is fully booked. Do you want me to go?'

'No!' Mum said, rushing out onto the landing in alarm. 'You're supposed to be leading the *baraat*. The father cannot be missing from the bridegroom's procession! *Hai! Hai!* Tasnim is so unreliable!'

'We need the sweets to greet the *baraat*.' I brushed past her. 'Unless we all want to stand there empty-handed when Heathrow arrives. *I'll* go.'

God bless Auntie Tasnim and her unreliability! I exited the house at a run, thankful on this day for the smallest of mercies. The guillotine still awaited but at least I had been spared the humiliation of the tumbrel – in this case the triumphal progress to Wandsworth Town Hall in Sufya's garlanded Rolls Royce.

Sufya

When I had discovered on the morning of my wedding that nothing less than a goat sacrifice was imminent, I could think of no other course of action but to pretend the whole thing was not happening. Otherwise Mum and I might have had the worst argument of our turbulent history. Besides, I felt somewhat safe in the knowledge that Zarina's support for Mum's superstitious practices would not extend this far, and that therefore, between them, Dad and Zarina would somehow sort it out.

It was only on my arrival at Wandsworth Town Hall – nuptial venue of the daughters of all Mum's friends in years gone by, this was the natural location for Mum to serve up the cold dish of her revenge – that I realised the scale of the error I had made in leaving so much of the organisation in the hands of Mum and Ayesha.

Though I had known that Mum was going to invite as many 'community' as were willing to have their noses rubbed in it in exchange for a few plates of free biryani and some *shaami* kebabs (and since I detested most of these people, I had simply given her mine and H's list of friends and left her to it), I had not considered the kind of ill-conceived cocktail that might result. Now, as I surveyed the reception hall for the first time, I bitterly regretted this lapse.

A single glance at the ethnic distribution around the hall revealed that the presence of alcohol had already segregated the guests roughly along the lines of Muslims versus non-Muslims (the latter group including *unacceptable* Muslims). On one side of the hall, cold-shouldering any insensitive waiters who wandered in their direction with trays of champagne, were veritable droves of suburban aunties in shiny Technicolor clothing, with equally shiny, heavily made-up faces, and dilapidated husbands in tow. Some of the more benign ones, like Mehbooba and Tasnim, were familiar, but most of them I simply did not recognise, and they did not recognise me either. Without the usual systems (men this way, women that way, bride and groom on the stage, etc) the aunties and uncles were noticeably uncomfortable. They stood with their grown-up sons and daughters in awkward family huddles, fanning themselves with feigned disinterest, while surreptitiously squinting at the other guests.

Their grown-up sons and daughters did not look happy either. Most of these had been married off long before, and must have enjoyed the idea of alleged high-achievers like Zarina and me being left on the shelf. Some of the girls we had played with as kids were now wearing hijab – despite the fact that their parents were not – and were surveying the mixed-sex mêlée with a hint of contempt. I even recognised a couple of the men who had been pointed out to me at Asian gatherings by matchmaking aunties – only to be summarily rejected, of course – in days when people thought ours was a 'normal' Muslim family.

Most of the beribboned and besuited younger children – the products of my contemporaries' marital successes – were already charging up and down the stairs, hanging from the fittings and clambering over furniture, arousing the barely disguised anger of the town hall security staff.

Meanwhile, on the other side of the hall, I observed a few colleagues from the magazine, together with Jade and some suit-types who – when I spotted Eric and Helen Havers among them – I concluded must be Dad's BestCo friends. Also on the 'non-Muslim' side were some fashionably dressed arty types from various ethnic groups – clearly H's friends from the world of film, including a couple of big name directors. One of these, I noticed, had already been cornered by Habib, and I could tell by his rigid smile that Bibbles must be trying to sell one of his Muslims-have-kinky-sex-too documentary ideas.

Perhaps because they were vastly outnumbered by the Muslim contingent, or maybe just as disoriented by the lack of structure at this particular wedding, the non-Muslim section of guests – although on the surface of it more sophisticated and metropolitan – appeared no more at ease than their more colourful but sulky counterparts on the other side of the hall. Many were knocking back the champagne at a rate which betrayed their discomfort.

'Right, come with me, Sufya, and don't be rude! I'm going to show those *balaas* what's what before the *baraat* arrives!' Mum tried to drag me towards the aunties, but I quickly armed myself with a passing glass of champagne and hurried away as though I had just spotted a long-lost friend. Mum, judging that it would anyway be easier to lord it over her erstwhile friends if she did not have the alcohol-glugging bride in tow, had to be satisfied with taking Ayesha with her on her long-awaited lap of honour.

Mimicking (as far as was possible in south-west London) the traditional arrival of the groom on horseback in the bride's village, Mum and Ayesha had of course arranged that the groom and his party would arrive an hour after the bridal party. Now, as Ayesha disappeared into the fray with Mum, I suddenly felt lost. Traditionally, I should have been hiding away behind the scenes somewhere with my female entourage until the *baraat* arrived, but I had vetoed this old-fashioned notion, and the consequence was that I was suddenly a bride entering her wedding without any announcement, without any particular plan of action, and worst of all, without a groom.

In that moment, I longed for Zarina, who had still not arrived with the *mithai*. Among all these people who found comfort in their crowd, in their rituals, in their tradition, Zarina and I belonged only to each other – she would have known instantly how I would feel on being confronted with this throng. But Zarina was not there.

'*Beta jaan!*' beamed Uncle Bogie, appearing out of nowhere. For once I was relieved to see him. 'You are looking very smart! Now there is someone you have to meet. *Bismillah*!' He took my arm and led me across the room towards the door.

So the *baraat* had arrived! My heart gave a leap. *At last*, I thought, *I can't be here another minute without him*. Mum would be furious, though, that we had not all been outside to greet the groom's party with the traditional cheers and sweet-giving.

But the person Uncle Bogie ushered through the door to meet me was not H and, as we came face to face, I saw that he was as horrified to see me as I was to see him.

'You remember *Maulanaji*? From Streatham Mosque?' boomed

Bogie, joyously. 'He has come specially to do your *nikaah, beta*!'

As I said hello, I noticed that Maulvi was actually shaking in his shoes (which – I couldn't help fixating on the detail – were those peculiar square-toed rubber shoes which featured in *Maulvi Madness* – were they the same pair twenty-five years later? Or could there possibly exist some bizarre and long-established shoe shop which supplied this odd footwear year after year without going out of business?). I attempted a smile. But Maulvi only stared back at me, flicking a lizard-like tongue nervously over his lips.

'Excuse me, I er…have to…er…go,' I murmured, and, dragging Uncle Bogie to one side, I whispered, 'Where is he, Uncle?'

'Oh, damn bloody Airport Boy! Air traffic controller strike in the brain as usual!' grinned Bogie, unperturbed. 'Calls up yesterday saying I should come here without him, and he will arrive later. When you are his wife you can give him damn bloody hell about it! *Beta jaan*, what is the matter? Oh sorry! I should have mentioned this before! Now you are upset…'

The sudden concern in Bogie's expression was too much. I turned away, muttering about having to do something, and headed for the ladies' toilet. There, at last, I found Zarina, grappling with a large coat-rack on wheels.

'Will you call H's mobile? Bogie's arrived but he's not with him!' I pleaded, noticing through my rising tears that Zarina, in her beautiful pink and silver dress, was somewhat pale.

'OK,' said Zarina, turning paler still. 'I just need to get this thing to the lobby, and then I'll try the payphone there.' And she disappeared with the coat-rack.

I took a few deep breaths and swallowed the offending tears. *Of course he would come. I knew him, didn't I? My childhood friend. Of course he would come.*

I still did not know what strange instinct had drawn me to take that second pregnancy test. I had not had any symptoms that might have given rise to suspicion. In fact I was still experiencing a quite classic version of morning sickness. Still, I took the test, and then immediately had to run to the chemist to buy a third, fourth and fifth testing kit.

I sat against my bedroom wall with the phone in my hand until I knew he had landed in Israel and then I dialled H and told him the result. He had only been away for a few hours but, in that time, I had become a hollowness in which I could feel the subtle tremor in his voice like a wail in a cave. *But he had reassured me, hadn't he?* He had shown strength that I knew came directly from his feeling for me. The wedding was only days away and the bad ending would become a new beginning. That's what he had said and without those words I would have been who knows where.

Back in the hall I was in time to witness the arrival of Richard, hand in hand with Darwin, who was sporting a fetching pink bow-tie to supplement his customary lab coat. A momentary hush descended as the guests realised there was a large chimpanzee among them, and all eyes turned to see Darwin's long arms encircle me.

'Well at least someone will marry her if the damn bloody groom doesn't turn up on time!' Bogie exclaimed from the far side of the hall, and – across party lines – the guests dissolved in laughter. Some of the tension in the room was gone at last. And for my part, I was very grateful for the sincerity of Darwin's embrace, and to see Richard smiling warmly at me after weeks of coldness.

'I'm so glad you came – *both* of you,' I said, squeezing Richard's hand (we both sensed it was not worth the risk of a hug in front of an uncaged Darwin). 'Have you forgiven me, then?'

'Nothing to forgive,' said Richard good-naturedly. 'You look wonderful, by the way.'

With the ice broken among my guests, and a thaw in a precious friendship, I suddenly felt myself relax. For just that moment, I experienced a hint of the glow a bride might expect to feel on her wedding day.

'I know you're busy,' said Jade, arriving breathless by my side, 'but who is that bloke over there? The one with the gorgeous long hair. You have to introduce me!'

The bloke she was referring to, I saw, was Asif, tucking into the first kebabs that had been laid out on the long tables by Aunty Khan's sons, who had begun to serve the food. 'What's *he* doing here?' I found myself asking aloud.

'Sorry, *yaar*,' Ayesha drawled sheepishly from behind me. 'I already had sent the invitation when you banned him. Doesn't matter, you don't have to talk to him.'

'*I'll* talk to him,' Jade said, dreamily.

Oh well, I thought. Now there are two non-human primates at this wedding. But I had no energy for worrying about Asif's presence. It was the *absence* of H that now scraped like a giant claw in the gut, threatened to tear open an emptiness that could have swallowed us both, *would* – if released – obliterate bride, groom and all expectant guests, to leave only a gaping crater in the earth where Wandsworth Town Hall now stood. *Where could he be?*

Zarina

One of my favourite plays was the Spanish tragedy, *Blood Wedding*, in which the cold, young Moon satisfies its craving for warm blood by lighting the path of Death towards the lovers. So I could sort of see the thinking behind the idea that the ritual sacrifice of an animal would divert the attention of blood-lusting spirits away from the newly-weds.

Nevertheless, it seemed to me that, when Mum yanked that particular goat over the doorstep, she might just have invited in the very *balaa* we were supposed to be warding off. And when I bumped into Dad in the drive, bundling it – still very much alive – into the back of his Audi and saying he would find someone to 'deal with it' at the local mosque, and meet us at Wandsworth Town Hall, I had an uneasy feeling that the evil creature would now not be got rid of so easily.

The chaos that greeted me at Auntie Tasnim's house was

the first sign of its malign influence. Far from being 'ready', the *mithai* was only just coming off the cooker and was cooling in large baking trays on the kitchen table, waiting to be cut into pieces and decorated. Auntie Tasnim, though clearly delighted to see me, was still in her dressing gown, wearing a tea towel over her rollers. '*Hai, hai*, the *burfi* is starting to stick!' she exclaimed, slamming down a tray of steaming halva and rushing over to the hob to stir a boiling mixture of condensed milk and almonds which was burbling volcanically over the edges of a huge aluminium stockpot. It was only with difficulty that I persuaded her to write off the *burfi* and go and get changed, while I hurriedly scattered crushed pistachios and silver leaf over the trays and carried them to the car, hoping they would cool down on the way. At last, we set out for Wandsworth Town Hall – with steam misting up the windscreen, and Auntie Tasnim squealing at me to go slower – and arrived half an hour late for the *baraat* (a mess-up which, again, I rather welcomed because it meant I was spared the ordeal of welcoming Heathrow on the steps).

But the mischief did not end there. Having handed the *mithai* to Tasnim and her waiting 'helpers', I was met in the car park by a conspiratorial Dad with a familiar pleading look in his eye...

'What do you mean "gone"?' I almost shouted.

'Ssshh!' Dad warned, grinning cheerfully at Auntie Sultana's husband, who was enjoying a sneaky cigarette within earshot.

'Gone where?'

'It's OK, *beta*, it can't have gone far, it's here somewhere, you just have to help me locate it, before your mother finds out.'

'You mean you brought it *here*?' Picturing the many varieties of havoc that could be wrought upon the festivities by a rampaging goat, I spread my hands in disbelief.

'What else could I do, *beta*, I had no choice! I had to be back here in time for your mother and Sufya!'

Dad and the goat had apparently had a fruitless trip to the mosque, where they were informed by one of the younger *maulvis* that, unfortunately, ritual bloodletting in the car park contravened the terms of Wandsworth Council's lease, which permitted standard acts of worship/religious study only. However, they might try Auntie Khan's sons who, the *maulvi* said, had organised the carrying out of such *qazas* for other families in the past. So Dad had driven over to Tandoori Junction only to be told by Afzal's teenage daughter that Auntie Khan and both her sons had already left for Wandsworth Town Hall with the wedding food.

So, hoping that if he could have a quiet word with Afzal, everything might yet be sorted out before lunch was served, Dad had brought the goat with him, sneaked it in through an open fire exit, and hidden it in the pre-school toilets at the back of the building which, as it was a weekend, nobody should be using.

'But when Afzal and I went to get it, it had disappeared,' Dad finished, bewildered. 'Someone must have let it out – there was no way it could have opened the door on its own!'

Knowing that goat, I wasn't so sure. 'Great. Thanks, Dad, as if I didn't have enough to do!' I grumbled, as Dad squeezed my hand gratefully and went back to father-of-the-bride duties.

Fortunately (or unfortunately), hunting down the goat did not prove as difficult as I had imagined. About five minutes later, I went to put Auntie Ismat's mackintosh in the cloakroom, and found the beast nestled up against Ayesha's cashmere shawl. I could see its red eyes glowing accusingly from between the coats. Before it could utter one of its ominous bleats, I darted outside, shut the door and propped a chair under the handle.

The moment had come. To find Dad, I would have to enter the wedding hall and face Heathrow for the first time since I had left him asleep in his flat, the morning after Bogie's miraculous recovery. Taking a deep breath, I pushed open the doors and spotted Dad with Mum at the far end, *salaaming* the seated aunties and embracing the standing uncles. In between, a sea of faces turned to look at me: scores of the moustachioed tweedle-dums once advertised to me and Sufya as suitable life-partners, now somewhat middle-aged and eager to show off their diminutive, fair-skinned Pakistani wives and appallingly spoilt, frilly offspring. With my best Number-Two-but-Still-Gracious smile, I straightened my shoulders and sailed up the length of the hall, avoiding catching anyone's eye – especially avoiding looking up at the stage where Heathrow and Sufya would, according to custom, be seated on display – and touched Dad lightly on the shoulder.

'It's in the cloakroom!' I hissed. 'Get Afzal, and sort it out before anyone tries to go in there!'

'Too late.' Dad gestured at Afzal who had just begun moving down the first table, serving *shaami* kebabs. 'It will have to stay there a little longer. Can you arrange somewhere else for coats? People are still arriving.'

I nodded and escaped thankfully – but scarcely had I entered the ladies' powder room, where I had been told by a friendly German girl in the box office that I would find some free-standing coat rails, than Sufya rustled in.

'Thank God!' she said. Her face was white, and she was scrunching the embroidered end of her *dupatta* in a tense fist. 'H isn't here yet.'

'What? Why?'

Tears welled up in her eyes. 'Bogie came without him. There's a payphone in the lobby. Can you call his mobile and find out what's going on?'

'His flight's probably late, that's all.' I didn't think I was the best person to be chivvying him along, but Sufya, of course, was looking at me like I was her only hope. 'OK,' I said, at last. 'Wait there.'

I dropped a pound into the payphone, and after staring for a moment at the flashing display, dialled the number. My heart leaped as it started to ring. What on earth was I going to say? But of course, he wouldn't answer it. He was probably on his way and he wouldn't bring his mobile to his wedding, would he?

But on the sixth ring, just as I was expected the call to divert to the familiar message, *Hi, this is Heathrow, sorry I'm not here…* someone picked up.

'Hello?' said a man's voice, sounding a long way away. Then a sort of rushing noise down the line.

'Heathrow? Is that you?… Hello?'

There were a couple of clicks and then another man spoke, in a slightly American English.

'What is your name please?'

'It's Zarina,' I said. 'Where's Heathrow? This is Heathrow's phone, isn't it?'

'What is your location, ma'am?'

'Who are you?' I said, getting slightly annoyed. 'Where's Heathrow?'

Beeeeep! The line went dead. *Insert coins* said the message on the display.

I emptied my purse into the slot, and redialled. Straight onto divert: *Hi, this is Heathrow…* I disconnected and immediately called again: *Hi, this is…* Now I was really concerned. Something was wrong. Who was that man? I pressed the phone to my forehead.

Oh, where are you? I wished I *could* speak to him now. Once more, I dialled the number, willing it to ring, willing him to materialise at the other end, but again only his voice, warm and cheerful, *Hi, this is Heathrow, sorry I'm not here, but leave a message and I'll get back to you.*

'Heathrow,' I said, 'it's me – Zarina. Please call and tell us where you are. We're all at the wedding waiting… I'm not sure what's going on… Anyway, if you get this message, everyone's expecting you – Sufya's expecting you. Just call, OK?'

I looked up to see Ayesha hurrying towards me. 'Sufya wants you,' she said. 'She's going to do her vows.'

⁂

Inside the green room, Maulvi sat down cross-legged in front of Sufya, as in days of old when he used to teach us the Quran. Mum lowered herself onto the floor next to the bride, and signalled me and Ayesha to do the same. Aunties Tasnim and Mehbooba, as independent witnesses, sat on the other side.

Maulvi madness must have been in the air again. To have half the couple take the vows when no one knew where the other half was? And with that evil goat still slap bang in the middle of everything?

'Shouldn't we wait for Heathrow to arrive?' I said again.

Maulvi held up a long-suffering hand, and shook his head with slow pomposity. 'Separately, separately,' he repeated, as if addressing himself to an imbecile. 'In Islam, man and woman, separately.'

'I know it's separately,' I said irritably. 'But he ought to be in the building, at least! Am I the only one who thinks that phone conversation was *weird*?'

'Wrong number!' Mum snapped. 'Bogie *bhai* says he is on his way. If you can't be happy, be quiet!'

'Auntie Khan's already serving the food,' Sufya said miserably. 'People were hungry.'

'And the vows are not public, anyway,' Ayesha consoled, 'so there's no point in asking them to wait.'

'*Bismillah al Rahman al Rahim!*' intoned Maulvi. '*A'udhu billahi…*'

And so, floating above the proceedings like a dead fish in a tank, I watched my sister get married to Heathrow. Of course, she didn't understand the Arabic of the *nikaah* and kept complaining that she didn't know what she was agreeing to. But Maulvi, no doubt recalling how we used to feign incomprehension just to annoy him, ignored her and carried on. And when he asked her if the marriage was acceptable to her, she replied, '*Qubool hai*.' I accept.

In the presence of the witnesses, he asked her three times, and three times she accepted.

⁂

Opposite me, Asif was doing his best to pretend he didn't like Jade draping herself drunkenly all over him, and trying to feed him morsels of kebab. He shrugged at me apologetically and rolled his eyes. As if I cared. Numb as I was, it was like watching some surreal puppet show.

As Jade laughingly managed to push the kebab into Asif's mouth, another hand thrust a samosa abruptly in his face – a hand that I now saw was attached to Auntie Khan wearing an expression of stern accusation. She bent down and muttered something in his ear… Asif choked violently on the kebab and as Auntie

Khan moved on, Jade solicitously thumped him on the back and massaged his shoulders. 'So tense, poor love!'

Might this have anything to do with Goldie, and had Asif in fact lied to me after all? I wondered dully. Goldie would have been able to confront him herself had she been here, but her parents had removed her from Auntie Khan's care (though none of it had been *her* fault), and sent her to stay with relatives in Coventry. Well, that wasn't my problem either. As the hall resounded with the convivial hubbub of people warming up from the delicious food, I gave my mind over to the worry that had been snapping at my heels all day – ever since the wretched goat with its jagged black patches had revived the memory of a djinn with dark holes in its body.

How strange that the spectre I had long ago dismissed as a figment of superstitious imagination, the genie I had thought stripped of its power to intimidate and control, should now – as though it had only been waiting for a signal – suddenly burst forth, uncorked, potent, ten times as real as anything going on around me, and more terrifying than ever!

This ain't some fairground ride, it's a one-way ticket on a non-stop train. Either one of you tries to get off, you won't be seeing each other again, not in this life. Understand, kid? Double-cross and die!

When I dismissed that vile, mocking Bogart-djinn as a hallucination, was it possible that I committed a terrible error? *Not in this life… Double-cross and die!* Those had been his words. As I recalled them, I could feel once again the sting of sparks on my face, the tug against my scalp as my hair stood up on end, brittle in the heat of his fire. I made a grab for my water glass and knocked it over. Where was Heathrow? Who was that man who had answered his phone?

'Eat something, Zarina *beti* – you have been looking after others all day,' Auntie Khan was now saying kindly, putting a plate of biryani in front of me. I couldn't respond. I wanted to fling myself on her bosom and whimper from fear and guilt. Why hadn't I listened to her when she had tried to warn me against the use of magic!

Uncle Bogie, emerging from a hurried consultation with our parents, was striding towards the DJ and asking for a microphone. The DJ relinquished control without a fight – no one was interested in the cool underground vibe he was putting out anyway. He handed a mic to Bogie (not that the latter ever had any need of extra amplification) and sat down to tuck into a plate of kebabs that was waiting on top of the speaker. As the hall grew quiet, I fixed my eyes on Uncle Bogie, and prayed with my whole heart that he had an explanation.

It started off OK. Bogie told a few jokes – was he filling time because he knew Heathrow was on his way, or because he hoped that he was? He cracked the usual one about long-haul delays, then changed tone and spoke with touching affection of how he had waited for this moment since Heathrow and Sufya were small children, how he was proud of them both and how this was the happiest day of his life. Many in the hall knew of his recent illness, and his words were greeted with a spontaneous burst of extended applause. 'Ssshhh!' I hissed vainly at those around me, in agony to discover what he would say next.

'And now,' Bogie began, 'I would like to make a few observations about marriage.'

'*Christ!*' I muttered. I glanced at Sufya. Standing with Mum and Dad by the stage, she had gone rigid. I saw her nudge Dad and whisper something urgent to him, but he just smiled reassuringly and took her hand. *Mistake.*

'Marriage is sacred in Islam,' Uncle Bogie continued sententiously. 'The Prophet, Peace Be Upon Him, said it is the Islamic duty of every man and every woman to get married, by God!'

Had he forgotten, or was it irrelevant, that he himself had never married? I wondered suddenly. I saw Sufya again say something to Dad. Dad smiled and put a finger to his lips.

'Why? Because it is accepting God's command to live in the fullness of existence, *subhanallah!* Islam is not like Christianity or Buddhism. It does not praise the virtues of a single life! What is the single life?' Bogie looked slowly and pointedly at Jade and one or two other white people. 'Let me tell you, my friends. It is only a failure, by God. Barren and unrighteous.' He seemed suddenly emotional.

The silence in the hall was now absolute. There was the odd wail from a baby, hurriedly shushed by its mother. Jade had undraped herself from Asif and was looking down at the tablecloth, her cheeks slightly pink. Dad's boss, Eric Havers, took a sip of champagne and raised his eyebrows expressively at his wife, Helen. Ayesha placed her hand over Habib's, while he stared coolly out of the window.

'Woman is Adam's rib!' My heart sank as Bogie fired his next salvo. What was this all for? He didn't know where Heathrow was, obviously. 'Without man, woman does not exist!'

Several people shifted in their seats, others cleared their throats. One or two aunties turned pointedly to one another and resumed the conversations they had interrupted moments before. Uncle Bogie, eyes uplifted to heaven, remained oblivious to all of this, and to the fact that Dad, hustled forward by Sufya, was at last approaching from auditorium right.

Beginning to enumerate the qualities of the virtuous woman, he got as far as '*Obedience! Chastity!*' before he was ambushed. As Dad gently took the microphone and returned it to the DJ, I saw Sufya seize Bogie's arm and frogmarch him down the length of the hall, disappearing with him into the lobby. There came the sound of her voice raised… Bogie remonstrating… Two loud slams as the huge wooden doors of Wandsworth Town Hall were pushed shut…and then my sister came back in, grabbing somebody's glass of wine on the way, and downing it in one. Her eyes searched the tables and finding me, clearly signalled, *Why the fuck are you just sitting there?*

I rose woodenly to my feet. *Please God, just let him be alive.* As the din of excited gossip grew in the hall, and my sister's wedding slid inexorably into chaos, I could truthfully say that of all the times I had waited for Heathrow – all the times I had longed for him to come – this was when I would most have welcomed his appearance.

From the corner of my eye, I could see Mum blocking the path of Auntie Khan who was about to circulate with the dessert. She was saying something heatedly, to which Auntie Khan, her hands full with plates of steaming sweet rice, was shrugging apologetically, and gesturing at the clock.

Afzal, wiping his hands on his apron, was now being led by Dad towards the exit behind the stage. I surmised that, at last, the goat's number was up.

Yes, I thought, with a sudden rush of fury. *Kill it! Kill it, then maybe this bad luck will go away.* It was all I could do to stop myself running after them and killing it myself.

Sufya

EVERYONE KEPT TELLING ME not to worry, and to *have fun, it's your wedding day*, but, all around me, my wedding day was disintegrating into a farce. Mum was practically hysterical and in the midst of a furious row with Aunty Khan's younger son about who had told them to bring out the food when 'the boy' wasn't even here. Uncle Bogie had had to be put outside after his attempt to commandeer the DJ's microphone to deliver a long sermon on Islamic womanhood. Jade, instead of attending to best-friend duties, seemed to be cuddling up with Asif in the corner. Habib had drunk too much and vomited over Helen Havers. Ayesha was practically in tears trying to clean him up, and calm Mum down. Dad kept running in and out of the hall like a madman. Against my better judgement I had uttered my promises to an absent groom, and, in the process, had practically come to blows with the infuriating, lip-licking Maulvi.

Of course, in the light of this performance, the jealous sons and daughters of 'the community' were hardly troubling to disguise their sniggers as they gobbled up fistfuls of kebabs.

Meanwhile, one by one, H's guests introduced themselves to me, acting like they had never heard of me. 'We've known each other since we were kids,' I found myself saying over and over again, only eliciting doubtful smiles – particularly from the women – in return. But even as I repeated the mantra to the tide of strangers, I felt more painfully the claw in my gut. Yes, we had known each other when we were children, *but did we know each other now?* Yes, I trusted the H of our childhood with everything that was precious to me – and I had trusted the one who had promised he would not abandon me, the H who, only a few days ago, during that phone conversation, had put aside his own disappointment and stopped me from being submerged – but was this the same H who now was keeping me waiting without a thread of explanation on our wedding day?

At last the possibility that he would not come at all arose in me like a dark djinn escaping from a long-sealed vessel. *I don't believe in you*, I whispered to the spectre, *I don't believe in fate*. But whether or not this was a phantom of my own mind, I knew it would not be dispelled so easily. It was as though it had come to my wedding for a purpose.

And then – as though in slow motion at the bottom of a dark and roaring ocean – it began.

First, the din of drumming on the outer doors which I had closed so firmly behind Uncle Bogie. Then, the crash as the doors burst open and the police rushed in, guns raised. The screams as mothers and fathers clutched their children and dived for the floor, the splintering of glass and crockery and the cries of alarm, an officer shouting, 'Nobody move! Nobody move! You're all under arrest!'

Darwin's blood-curdling screech as he leapt into the air, feet first, towards the heads of the advancing police marksmen, the sway of the rifle barrels as they turned like grass in the wind to point up at him, the brief spatter of gunfire and the sigh and thud as Darwin hit the floor. And even as his all-too-human blood began to rise from the holes in his body like water from a lawn-sprinkler, the sudden clattering of hooves, as, out of nowhere, a demonic red-eyed goat galloped forth, scuttering between the legs of the startled marksmen and out of the door into the dusk beyond. Mum under a table somewhere sobbing at Dad, 'You should have killed it! *Ya Allah!* Now we are all cursed!'

Then, the silence, in which it seemed that I was the only person left standing, facing an army of police and smoking guns.

And finally, Uncle Bogie pushing through the police and staggering towards me, his hair flying and tears pouring down his face, wailing in a voice slurred with agony: 'He is dead, Sufya! He is dead! They shot him in Israel this morning! They are saying my boy was a terrorist!'

Zarina screaming.

End of Book One

Acknowledgements

Our thanks to Maryam Mafi and Azima Melita Kolin and to Harper Collins Publishing Ltd for their very kind permission to quote from *Rumi Hidden Music*; to Professor Frans de Waal and to Professor Karen Strier for kindly allowing references to original primatological research; to Warner Bros for permission to quote from the movie, *Casablanca*; to Warner Chappell Music and Round Hill Carlin for permission to quote from *As Time Goes By* by Herman Hupfeld.

Special thanks to Susan Smith at MBA and Cathryn Summerhayes at Curtis Brown, who separately believed in the novel; to Scott Pack for his invaluable advice and support; to the talented and generous collaborators who turned our manuscript into a book – Nell Wood, Liz Hatherell, Clio Mitchell, Mia Baines, Angie Brew; to the Arts Council of England who supported an early draft with a Time to Write grant; to the late, incomparable Becky Swift at TLC who supported the commissioning of a script report, and the brilliant Anna South for the thoughtful and transformative insights in that report; to the amazing Angie and Joseph Brew, whose highly original film experiments were the inspiration for Heathrow's early efforts.

Our gratitude also to the many friends and colleagues who have generously read, critiqued and championed the book: Hilary S. Carty, Professor Maggie Humm, Claire Dale, Joseph Sissens, Celia de Wolff, Kathlene Collins, Michele Carlisle, Diran Adebayo, Yasmin Hossain, Neelim Sultan, Pat Foster, Graham Jameson, Claire Brown, Isobel Williams, Jo Spencely, Sarah Evans Cartwright, Monty Ravenscroft, Haroun Hameed. Their insights have been invaluable in shaping its final form, and any flaws that may remain are entirely our fault. Also to Sean Egan, Dorothee Muller, and Inam Siddiqui for giving us the benefit of their respective expertise on legal and translation matters; Dr Michael Tilby, Rachel & Ken Hollings, Mira Kaushik and Trevor Phillips who have kindly shared advice and contacts.

Heartfelt thanks to Stef Penney, Yasmin Alibhai-Brown, Boyd Tonkin, Viv Groskop, Wayne McGregor, Jamie Lloyd for generously giving time to read and support the book.

Last, but definitely not least, our love and thanks to our families who have supported and encouraged us on this long journey: Raj, Sinan, Haroun, Raif, Omar, Shazi, Farzeen, Afshan.

Printed in Great Britain
by Amazon

58411814R00201